I0769875

"THE INSTRUMENTS OF FATE"

BOOK ONE

THE DESTINED ROAD

J.M. Testa

The Destined Road

J.M. Testa

© 2025 J.M. Testa

Published by: Expatiatus Magical Arts

Edited by: Lisa Messinger

Cover Artwork: Jess Testa

ISBN-13: 978 8 9907468 0 0

Printed in USA

Jen
Ben
Karen

Êadura üv

"I want to be a healer, and love all
things that grow and are not barren."

- J.R.R. Tolkien, The Lord of the Rings

Illustration by Jeannette Testa

Contents

PART I: THE CALM

Chapter 1: Middling's Plight 14

Chapter 2: The Elven Plot 63

Chapter 3: A Ride of Warning 93

Chapter 4: Thrindūl 119

Chapter 5: Navigating the Truth 144

Chapter 6: Battle on the Midlands 174

Chapter 7: Uniting Vostheloren 210

PART II: BEFORE THE STORM

Chapter 8: Fated Company 244

Chapter 9: Cornering Darkness 279

Chapter 10: The Passage of Aūraèlon . . . 316

Chapter 11: The Black Isle 342

Chapter 12: The Onus of Time 385

Chapter 13: Torn Asunder 425

APPENDIX

Characters in Order of Appearance/Mention 441

Locations by Realm 451

Locations Mentioned (not on map) 454

Items 455

Elven Phrases 455

Dwarven Phrases 457

Drawn Map of The Black Isle:

   Athœvab Entrance 459

Biddance of the Naovïlrūn 460

Song of the Èlavïl 462

N
W
E
S
Kâr Boldhir
Dholdron-lier
Northgulch
The Mistvale
Dawnshire
Westvein
Eltåh
Middling
Grey
Northern Run
North Drÿs
Calumet
Terrishire
Waterlate
Gleddurat
South Drÿs
Besanrault Ocean
Orollon
Clerlūn
Torrerìn
Narnim
Yeacralas
Enbron Woods
Oülle
Müren
Màdiz
Gilèdo
Versard Bay
Marez
Logrosca
Tarravedra

VOSTHELOREN

Northkeep
Stoneheim Grove
Whitewater
Oburim
Cannet
Besland's Creek
Calm Rill
Pass
Wild
Mountains
Rothetara Lake
Oldfjord
rest
Badaruel Isle
Irrihead
Brierhil
Thrindūl
Minithon
Shallows
Marshlands of Drys
Haverlow Woods
Leriacūl Sea
Ynifjord
Frondynn
Aurilon Peaks
Broken Pass
Remeirath Gorge
Broekk
Highlands
Avïria
The Black Isle
Desolation Steppes
Leonan Point

PART ONE
The Calm

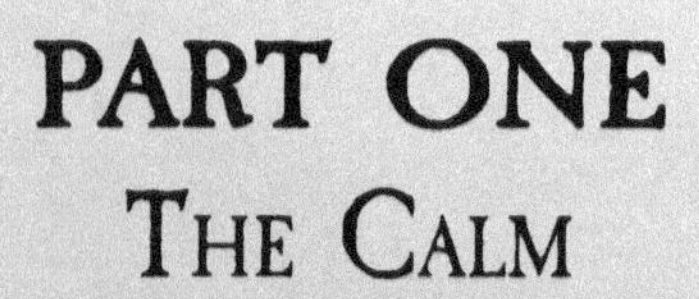

Photo by John Towner on Unsplash

1
Middling's Plight

It was the day of Marez's annual autumnal celebration, Marival, to commemorate the prosperous spring and summer and bring offerings for a comfortable winter. The corner band was tucked up against the eastern wall, nearest the stone fireplace that was hardly ever used — the body heat alone in the establishment lent the hearth to dust. Upon the creeping of night, The Siren's Whistle became the beacon of the southern coastal realm, and the atmosphere was always lively.

Tagwen took a long breath — inhaling the savory aromas of roast lamb, herbs, and vegetables. Her dark eyes were shadowed by her cloak's hood as they watched the barman shuffle back into the kitchens. She wrapped her hands around the mug of brew she had been served and pulled her sleeves down to cover more of her pale arms. Though nervous, she smiled on hearing the celebrations taking place around her.

Breccan, her captain, was also present, as was customary. Tagwen admired her doughty nature as she made small talk with the locals sitting nearby — the resonance of her laughter carrying throughout the establishment.

"Made this one just for you, m'ladies! I'm glad you could show." Mercher Preece beamed as he returned and laid steaming bowls of soup in front of Tagwen and Breccan. He was a large man, amply built, bald atop his head, but with a thick black mustache that framed his mouth.

"Gosh, I've missed this, Mercher. Your cawl is legendary. Thank you so much." Tagwen smiled at the gentle giant, his mannerisms jolly and light despite the tiredness in his eyes. This was arguably the busiest night for the chef and barman — save for Seas Day in spring.

Breccan tied her curled ginger hair behind her head before taking up a spoon. She moaned with delight as she took the first scalding bite of the lamb soup and washed the heat down with a swig of ale. She then stretched and cracked her neck, preparing for the next bite, drawing eyes from the regulars at the corner of the bar.

"Even in my prime I wouldn't dare challenge you to a duel, m'lady Breccan," said one of them.

"Face it, mate," Mercher interjected, "ya'd not challenge anyone even in yer prime. I'd heard the stories, a softie at heart ya always were."

"In all fairness, I am always afraid of challenging Breccan to a duel. So, you're not alone there," Tagwen said to the old sailor, who smiled shyly in response and directed Mercher's attention to his empty stein.

"Says the daughter of the Lion who practices fighting blind. My dear boy Callon told me about your trainings. Your father, seas rest his soul, may have been a great swordsman, but it's near-magic in your hands, m'lady," complimented the sailor's companion.

"Quiet now, no drawing attention to 'er, Hellig," Mercher warned.

Tagwen bowed gently in thanks to the chef as she pulled her slipping cloak hood forward and continued to enjoy the hearty meal and music. Behind her, below the revelry, she overheard three fishermen talking amongst themselves.

"Saw three gulls and a crow aboard the bow of the *King*… dark times, I reckon," a dry voice said. "Splittin' o' the seas and the like," he continued. "Gates teh the edge of the world just waitin' teh swallow us whole."

"Not sayin' I believe in all that," another, deeper voice responded, "but sher's been a weird time since the king died. Fish seem'd scared o'nets all'a'sudd'n, an' it's not pick'd up."

"Tellin' ya I'd seen it b'fore. Them birds prowlin' the *King* just 'fore Arlon died — can't be no different now," the first voice recalled.

"That's King Braithe to you! And nonsense! You both been predictin' the comin' of the end long as I've 'ad 'air on my chest. Next, you'll be tellin' meh the *elves* are still about!" a third voice yowled with laughter. "King was alive near three months aft yer prediction, Blàr," he mocked.

Tagwen huffed a small laugh. *The elves. That's amusing.*

"An what d'you know 'bout the workin's o' the unknown, Shìm?" Blàr sneered.

"Mor'dn you, I'll wager!" Shìm retorted.

Tagwen heard the shuffle of seats as if they were about to

square off and quickly turned around. "Gentlemen! This is too fine a night to be spent squabbling, no?"

Neither man took their eye off the other until the middle one noticed Tagwen, stood, and elbowed the side of the man standing to his right.

"Oh, shove off, Pàl!" Blàr howled. He then noticed Pàl's gaze and turned to Tagwen, eyes wide and breath choked. "Yer Majesty!" he exclaimed, moving to kneel, but Tagwen gestured for him to remain standing.

Then the man she assumed to be Shìm slowly turned around to meet her gaze and bowed his head.

"We're terribly sorry, Yer Majesty. Hadn't known yeh was here," Pàl apologized.

Tagwen noticed the tavern had gone dead quiet as everyone stared at her. She touched the top of her head in realization that her hood had fallen, then fumbled for the nearest stool to stand upon it. "Dear people of Marez, and all of the Yeacralan Realm, I am so honored to join you on this day of celebration — for our families, our kingdom, and for our seas. Please do not let my presence trouble your spirits this evening."

"Here, here!" Breccan cheered from the bar.

Tagwen smiled and leaned over so Breccan could hand her a pint. She lifted it in the air, and everyone nervously followed her lead. "The sea gives, the sea takes, but with her—" Tagwen bellowed, and the room answered disjointedly:

"We are never alone!"

A beat of awkward silence passed before Tagwen held her stein in the air again. "Next round's on me!" she announced, finally eliciting applause and hoots from all.

She stepped down and merriment returned to the room.

"Gentlemen," she bowed to the three fishermen, "I can assure you, I will protect our people, no matter what comes. Gulls and all." She nodded at Blàr, who stood about a head below hers. A faint smile lit up his aged face as his cheeks reddened.

"Thank yeh, m'lady," Shìm said. "Happy Marival."

Tagwen bowed and returned to her seat at the bar, where Breccan was chuckling.

"And what's got you so tittered?" Tagwen probed.

"Can't take you anywhere unseen. Makes my job ever so exciting," Breccan said as she polished off her ale.

Tagwen smiled slyly as her gaze drifted.

"Oh, I've seen that look before," Mercher noted, polishing a glass. "What's got yer current swirlin'?"

Tagwen blinked for a moment and tapped her spoon on her bowl a couple of times before she looked at Mercher. She then leaned over the bar so she wouldn't be overheard. "Is there something wrong with the catch? I haven't been made aware of anything," she whispered.

"No, no, dear lady. Just usual slowin' for winter. Ya know how it is. Men count by fish and if they're one short a haul they see it as a sign. Think nothin' of it. I'd let ya know," he reassured and set his hand gently on hers. "Yer doin' just fine, m'lady, and anyone who's got a problem with ya will have to go through me first," he smiled.

"And me," Breccan added. "They'd have to go through me too… and," she paused to flex her solidly-muscled arm on the bar, "I'd like to see 'em try."

"Are ya sure ya weren't born out of a storm, Kenefick?" Mercher joked and reached across the bar to hug both women, who both reciprocated.

"May the guidance of the sea follow ya both where ya tread — and should anyone give ya any trouble, I'm here," he proclaimed.

"Happy Marival, Mercher," Tagwen gushed.

The festivities went long into the eve and Tagwen and Breccan caught the parade as it passed. The procession of music, dancers, and citizens would head through the entirety of the city and down to Versard Bay — where those paying homage to the sea would toss flowers, herbs, or other verdure into the waters as an offering of thanks for all the sea had provided the past season. Tagwen preferred to wait until the crowds dispersed so she could have a moment of silence. She would pick wildflowers or fallen flora on the way down to the bay: one for her late mother, one for her brother Elnan (who decided to no longer show), one for herself, and now she would add one for her father.

Before she and Breccan set off, they helped Mercher tidy up as the crowds dwindled. Suddenly, she was tapped on the shoulder. She turned and saw Blàr meekly standing in front of her.

"I'd lost my wife, Eubha, nearly just as the king died. She was my every'thin'." He began to tear up.

"I am so sorry for your loss, Sir Blàr," Tagwen said.

"Ye can call me Morys, Yer Majesty — never been much of a 'sirs'." He bowed and wiped his face. "Anyhows. This all teh say," he pulled something out of his pocket, "she gave this teh me at our weddin', an' it's kept me safe all these years. I think you'll need it 'fore the end." He extended his open palm to reveal a corded necklace with what looked to be a half clamshell on the end.

"She claimed it's a scale from the giant sea drake 'er great, great, great-grandfather or so encountered on a voyage once at the beginnin' of a bygone age. Not sure I ever believed those legends, but for 'er sakes, I pretended I did. May it serve yeh as well as it's done me," Morys said as he laid it in her open hands.

"Sir… Morys, I can't take this — it's clearly very dear to you," Tagwen protested.

The gentleman wrapped his calloused, dark hands around hers. "I know she'd be 'appy knowin' it went to protect King Braithe's daughter, since we never 'ad the fortune of having our own. Be careful out there, lass. I might be an old sea-coot, but I've learned teh listen teh the seas, an' there's an eerie sound on 'er winds."

With that he stepped away, bowed as far down as his back would allow, and joined his companions, who waited for him at the door.

Breccan walked up behind her and asked, "What was that about?"

Tagwen looked down at the necklace in her hand — the cordage was worn with age and re-knotted along the strand. The shell, though timeworn, was a shimmering deep blue-black; the likes of which could not be from any mollusk in the area, and it was peculiarly shaped, though Tagwen could not discern whether that was due to age or its natural composition. She did not believe the myths, but was touched by the token nonetheless.

"A scale of Bludrynd if you can believe it," she responded, straining to keep the smirk from her face. The tales of the drake that haunts the waters of the world piqued her interest when she was a girl, but coming upon her twenty-ninth year, she placed no stock in the stories of old.

Sad there are still those who fear the seas, Tagwen thought somberly.

"Ahh… fascinating." Breccan snorted. "You ready to go, then? Mercher said he's got this taken care of if we want to head to the bay."

"Yeah," Tagwen nodded, as she tucked the trinket into her pocket, "let's go."

With hearty goodbyes, the two set out on their walk to the shore. They would pick up various plants that seemed to have fallen in the streets after the parade, in hopes of not wasting a good offering. Breccan would grab three: one for her own late mother, one for herself, and one for Lucas Kenefick, the monk she considered a father — and whose last name she had claimed for her own.

As they walked through the streets of Marez, Tagwen stopped and extended her well wishes and offered handshakes to passersby. She had seen her father do that often and wanted to continue the practice. Though it came with more than one uneasy eye, she tried to not let that deter her. Breathing in the frigid oceanic air calmed her nerves as she and Breccan turned down each alley instinctively. She brushed her hands along the rock walls as they made their way through, counting the stones like she did in her youth — Tagwen felt as if she had memorized each one.

Market awnings in the lower town flapped in the breeze, but all else was still. Vendors turned in early during holidays such as this so that they might be able to partake in the celebrations. Though she missed the general hum of the city, Tagwen loved these moments of peace.

Approaching the bay, under the glow of the moon, they could see the sea decorated in gifts. The ships in the harbor were draped in garlands that the children of the local schools had made from grasses, dandelions, and dried fruits just for the occasion. There were torches still burning, posted in the sands, their flames dancing in the winds as if they were part of the celebration.

Tagwen and Breccan walked the longest dock and sat at its end for a moment of silence for both the sea and each other. Tagwen looked longingly at the horizon, its edges darkened by an endless storm far off in the distance.

"They don't look at me like they used to," she said quietly.

"Of course, they don't," Breccan agreed. "You're their queen now."

"Do you think they see me as the next Olwenna?"

"No… no," Breccan shook her head. "Some can fall to

superstition, sure, but no one can truly look at you and think of The Usurper. Plus, you're not even related."

"How do you know they don't think it? They get quiet and so proper with me. They seemed so much more at ease when — when I wasn't queen," Tagwen bemoaned, looking at Breccan.

"Tagwen, no royal in their right mind, sneaks into a local tavern to hang out amongst the people," Breccan laughed. "And then buys the whole bar drinks!" She put her hand on Tagwen's shoulder as the young queen chuckled through her tears. "It's just different now, is all. Give 'em time. You've had the crown for less than a year. And hey, one of them even gave you a gift! For what it's worth, I suppose."

Tagwen nodded, and after a moment asked, "Do you remember the first Marival we snuck out for? We were barely… what, fifteen?"

"Thirteen," Breccan smiled. "I distinctly remember getting caught on this very dock."

Tagwen snickered and looked back out to the vista. "Every time I look out there, I remember what you told me that night."

Breccan cleared her throat. "'If the sea meant for the whole world to be darkened, the sun would never climb over the shadow'. Have my mum to thank for that one."

A solemn silence passed and Tagwen looked over to her captain. "Thank you for sneaking out with me one last time."

Breccan nodded with a gentle smile and stood. "Shall we?" she asked, extending her hand to her queen.

Tagwen nodded and Breccan helped her to stand, and the two made their way back to the keep.

***

Dawn came as it always had, but the sun's rising through clouded skies felt triumphant to Tagwen this day. Her handmaiden, Renlyn Bethel, entered her room to find her already awake and partly dressed.

"Good morning m'lady. I surely hope I am not tardy," Renlyn said. Her warm blonde hair was tied neatly in a braided crown and her soft gray eyes sparkled in the peeking sunlight.

"Nonsense, Renlyn. Have you brought breakfast?" Tagwen asked, motioning to the tray Renlyn was carrying.

"Of course, m'lady." Renlyn curtseyed and set the tray on the table nearest the door and began setting up.

"I hope you've remembered to bring a plate for yourself," Tagwen said.

"Only because you insist, Your Grace. You are far too generous to me, given my position." Her fair face flushed at her queen's remark.

"Again, nonsense. I enjoy your company and I know the kitchen has made fresh rye and the last blackberry preserves of the season — your favorites, are they not?"

Renlyn bowed her head with a grin. "You honor me, Your Grace."

The two young women enjoyed a light breakfast and pleasant conversation. As Renlyn then helped Tagwen with the remainder of her suiting and wrapped her hair in her signature bun, a rapping was heard at the door.

"Your Majesty!" a voice called.

"You may enter!" Tagwen called back. Her hand gripped the hilt of her sword.

A guardsman entered and bowed. Tagwen released her hand from the blade.

"Apologies for the abrupt entry, Your Majesty, but the messenger from Middling's brought a missive for you," explained the guardsman as he handed Tagwen the letter.

"From Middling, are you certain?" she asked.

The guard nodded, and Tagwen wondered why the messenger would not meet with her, himself.

"Is he still here?" Tagwen asked.

"Probably just barely on his way out, Your Majesty," the guard replied.

"Take me to him," she ordered, tucking the letter into the satchel upon her weapons' belt.

She followed the soldier to the foyer, where she saw a familiar face nearing the castle's exit — Gòrdan MacCaibe of the Dawnshire township in Middling. Tagwen recognized his kind brown eyes and neatly cut blonde-graying hair as she stepped through the main hall's door. He had been a messenger of King Dùghlan's court for over two decades now, and Tagwen could recall seeing him report to her father's court when she was a child. He had not shown since last delivering the request of Tagwen's hand in marriage from the Prince of Middling, Jaelan, and that was four years ago.

"Master MacCaibe!" she called.

Gòrdan stalled his exit and turned in her direction. "Queen

Braithe," he bowed. "I am sorry to have not said 'hello', but I figured your guardsman would be fine enough to hand you the note. Is something wrong?" He was a stoutly-built man, for being in his early fifties; stocky around the edges, but his jaw was sharp under a well-trimmed yellow beard.

Tagwen let out a breath from rushing to meet him. "It has just been quite some time since I've last seen you. How are you? How are Mairi and Artur?" she asked. Her heart ached a little; she wanted to ask if his husband had been found, but she regretted that his name was long lost to her.

Gòrdan smiled and chuckled in relief. "Fine, fine, we are well. Quite wonderful of you to remember them, Your Majesty."

He must still be gone, she lamented. She then thought herself foolish; the man had been missing for nearly a decade — far too long a time.

He bowed again. "Forgive me, Queen Braithe, but I must ask to take my leave. I am behind on this route already, I fear," he regretted.

Tagwen blinked a moment, slightly confused as to the rush. She had not met with Gòrdan in this new post; Middling had not had any contact with her since becoming queen.

Her hand rummaged for the letter, and held it up. "Any idea what this is all about? Must not be gravely important, but I fear it's another request from his royal highness…" she paused, and looked at the messenger. "It's not… is it?" she asked, worriedly.

Gòrdan shook his head. "I believe that ship has sailed as it were." He nodded his head toward the note. "Prince Jaelan made mention it was for recognition of your new queenship. Seems rather late, but perhaps what with the approaching anniversary of dear King Arlon's… passing, he's finally decided to present his acknowledgements formally."

Tagwen stared at the envelope as she held it in both hands and rubbed a thumb along the blood-red wax seal — it was poorly pressed.

Belated acknowledgment that my father is gone. Lovely.

She beheld the messenger once more. "Well, thank you, Master MacCaibe."

He looked uneasy for a moment as he adjusted the tote strapped across his person. "I understand if you'd rather discard it, dear lady, but he seemed surprisingly genuine in his request to deliver it to you."

Tagwen nodded, unconvinced. "I appreciate you telling me. Do not mistake my lack of enthusiasm for disdain towards his highness," she cautioned.

"Had not crossed my mind, Your Grace." He bowed once again. "Thank you for coming to meet me, but I must insist on requesting my leave now, Queen Braithe."

"Are you sure you cannot shelter here for the evening? Take some rest? Provisions? I'd be delighted to host you for dinner," Tagwen offered.

Gòrdan shook his head. "I am afraid I must be going. My sincerest apologies, Your Majesty."

Tagwen recalled then his origins from Dawnshire; his emphasis of the "j" in her formality was a trademark for the region. He was one of the most agreeable from Middling in her opinion, right alongside the king's daughter, Mòrrea, and her dear late mother, Brìghde.

She smiled warmly at him; she did not want to impede his work. "I shall not keep you any further, then. Go, and be well, friend. Give my regards to your children, and the Dùghlans as well, will you?" she asked.

He bowed, "Of course. Pleasant day, Your Majesty."

Tagwen guessed it would be a grueling journey back (a forgiving projection), given the start of rain as he left, which would likely pick up for the next three days, at least. Gòrdan trudged through the corridor. The shuffle of his worn and patched boots echoed in the hall until he was gone — headed North to return home. The trip from Westvein, Middling's capitol, was a week's ride in fair weather, permitting there had been no rain to cause the great river to flood onto the Road.

Traveling along the Western coast by boat would have been faster, but the kingdom in Middling, like all others, had resisted the temptations of the water. However, the first king of the Southern Realm had seen the ocean's potential, despite the dangers its waters posed, which led to Yeacralas' navy and trading prowess. The Marezian Navy, therefore, boasted the most fearsome sailors and ships in the known world — much to the woe of the Rogues of the Black Isle.

Tagwen shuffled to the banquet room in the eastern part of the main corridor. There she sat at the fir table's head gazing out the window a moment; the skies were cloudier and trickles of rain had already begun to form upon the panes.

A waft of sweet, aromatic air brushed past Tagwen as a

servant of the house carried tea from the parlor directly behind her. He did not notice Tagwen in the large high-backed chair, and she was grateful for the moment alone.

Setting the note upon the table, she leaned back disheartened, and looked at the portrait of her father upon the western wall.

I miss you, papa.

Arlon's stoic face stared; his dark eyes beheld none of their former kindness. Tagwen hated that painting. It felt nothing like him.

Taking a deep breath, she placed her hands upon the table and lazily fumbled the letter open; it was not dated — it had been written hurriedly; the ink hazy:

King Roìbert Dùghlan requests your presence in haste upon receiving this call to make for Westvein at all cost - with mind that the fate of the human kingdoms is dependent upon your actions.

Tagwen's brows furrowed as she moved to the edge of her seat. She squinted her eyes in an attempt to focus, reciting the words upon the page aloud.

"The fate of the *human* kingdoms? What?" she muttered under her breath.

Breccan came waltzing into the hall where Tagwen was frantically re-reading the note.

"What ya got there?" Breccan asked.

Tagwen shook her head. "I do not know, I—" She thumbed

the clearly once-soaked parchment in her hands.

"Something wrong?"

Tagwen stood and paced as she silently read the muddied script over and over, the echoes of each iteration seeming to overlap.

"Tagwen?"

"What do you make of this?" she asked as she thrust the letter toward Breccan.

Breccan scanned the note, stopped, and looked at Tagwen with a brow raised. "As you well know, I've never understood him. He's an old man who rambles at anyone about anything. It's probably not near as dramatic as he's making it sound."

"Fair," Tagwen paused, "Now what if I told you Gòrdan explained that this was a letter from Jaelan who described it as a 'recognition of my queenship'?"

"Why would Gòrdan do that?"

Tagwen folded her arms across her chest, strumming the rings of her mail in contemplation. She regarded Breccan sternly. "I do not know. What reason would he have to mislead the letter's purpose?"

Was that why he was in a hurry? Why wouldn't he deliver something of this magnitude directly to me?

Tagwen's thoughts continually buzzed with questions of the like. She knew Gòrdan reasonably well, he was a friend of her house, and there was amiable relations among the two kingdoms as far as she was aware.

Does Jaelan think Gòrdan untrustworthy? Why would Jaelan be writing a note on behalf of his father?

"Maybe Jaelan lied to him," Breccan answered, garnering Tagwen's attention.

Tagwen dropped her hands and walked toward one of the doorways that lead into the main hall. She looked around and saw Castle Guard Tarragona entering from the southern doors.

"Tarragona!" she called.

Brisking to a trot, the guardsman approached and bowed, "Your Majesty. How may I help you?"

"See if the messenger of Middling has cleared the city, bring him to me if he is still here," she ordered.

"Shall I gather a party to pursue him if he is not found within our walls?" Tarragona asked.

Tagwen bit at the insides of her cheek for a moment. She thought of his insistence that he leave, that perhaps he knew *something*, but she could not imagine his visit was malicious.

Was he scared of something?

"No," she replied, hesitantly.

Tarragona bowed once more, and Tagwen saluted (a closed right fist across her chest) to dismiss him and walked back into the banquet room, closing the door. Breccan was sitting in her former seat.

"Maybe at last he's finally gotten some sense and decided to disband the monarchy. At least one can dream," Breccan offered as she waved the letter in the air like a small pennant. A grin crept across the captain's light, freckled face and scarred lip — an unfortunate reminder of her stint in the Black Isle, much to Tagwen's regret.

"Well, regardless of our collective misgivings about this

request, and Dùghlan's disposition, if I can't get Gòrdan to explain, I will not leave such a call unanswered. I want you to begin assembling a company."

Breccan counted on her fingers. "I estimate perhaps ten additional men? We shouldn't overindulge in our presence there. It is *Middling*, after all."

"Do you think that's enough? If this proves to be as… harrowing as he's claiming?"

Breccan scoffed before taking a moment to weigh the question in her mind. She sat straighter, calculating. After a minute, she nodded. "Yeah, honestly, it would require a fair-sized regiment to go against us, and taking too many without knowing what we're up against might make us too slow to be of any use."

"Has the *Latona* been cleared for sail yet? A sloop should be enough for this."

The door opened and Princess Rhona, Tagwen's younger sister, was standing in the doorway. "Apologies, don't mind me."

"I shall take my leave and inquire, my queen," Breccan said before handing over the letter and departing.

"I'll await your findings," Tagwen said with a nod.

Breccan bowed and turned to exit, and bowed again to Rhona as she passed.

"Why does she still do that?" Rhona's tightly curled auburn hair covered her raised eyebrow. "She's been in this family longer than I have."

"It's a mix of things, I think — some training and other times to simply vex me. Is there something you need?"

"No, not particularly. I heard Gòrdan was here earlier and

wanted to find out what that was all about."

"Come look at this." Tagwen unfurled the curled paper and handed it to her sister, whose seafoam-blue eyes scanned it and looked up in confusion. She was the only one of the three siblings to look like their mother, in fact, nearly her twin — a trait Tagwen adored.

"This is… strange. What are you going to do about it?"

"Well, this is the first call the men of these lands have sent since I became queen. It warrants my presence. Even if it proves to be but the crazed ramblings of an aging man whose only purpose has long been to simply occupy land. But—"

"But what?"

Tagwen stopped and shook her head. She could not bring herself to explain given all the uncertainty. "There's just much to prepare for."

"When would you leave?"

"Earliest would be tomorrow. I asked Breccan to find out if the *Latona* is ready yet."

"You're going by sea? The sky for miles is dark and questionable at best. The water is likely no different. Even sailing for just a couple of days is treacherous — especially in autumn."

Tagwen grimaced, pinching the bridge of her nose, and paused for a moment before turning her gaze back to her sister. "If *Latona* is not ready, I guess we'll make by land. No sense in sailing anything else. Though I would much prefer to not take the Road," Tagwen frowned.

"I know you," Rhona said. "You're just like father — a fish out of water. Please, do consider what I've said."

Like Arlon, Tagwen had begun learning to sail before she could speak proper words. She'd even spent most of her youth on expeditions in and around the Besanrault Ocean's coast with her father. She sighed. "As much as I miss sailing, I wouldn't risk the lives of our men or the ships. You know that."

Rhona nodded. "I'm only making sure," she smiled. "It has been a time since you've been on the water, but you've been doing well here, and I'm sure there will be chance in future for you to set upon the seas again."

Tagwen returned her smile, remembering the days of sailing her own small craft around the bay and dreaming about voyages around the world.

A knock upon the door frame pulled her from her thoughts; Tarragona was alone in the threshold.

"Gone then?" Tagwen asked.

"Afraid so, Your Majesty," he replied.

Tagwen nodded and gestured that he was dismissed, catching Rhona's knitted brow in her periphery.

"Wanted to give Gòrdan some provisions for the road. I felt bad he left empty-handed," she lied.

Rhona frowned. "Wish I got to say 'hello'. Was he in a rush because of this?" she asked, holding up the curling page.

Wish I knew, Tagwen pondered, but simply shrugged.

"Worry not about this, okay?" she implored, taking back the letter. "For now I simply need to see what my options are. *Latona* would be sufficient for near coastal waters — even in storms."

Rhona opened her mouth as she readied to protest, but

Tagwen clarified, "*but*... only if the repairs are completed. Breccan seems to think keeping numbers light makes us most effective, and I trust her instinct. So, I would not challenge the sea by sailing anything larger."

Relief eased Rhona's shoulders. "Thank you," she breathed.

A moment later, Breccan returned with news that the *Latona* was not fit to be taken under sail. Tagwen groaned with deep disappointment and made ready for what was sure to be a taxing journey.

***

It had been a day since the letter first came — a day spent assembling the traveling party, prepping the wagons, and packing for a hopeful estimate of a week's crossing. The earth seemed to take pity on the Yeacralans, as the initial cast of rain had eased. Renlyn twisted the queen's long brunette hair into a tight bun, adjusted her chest plate, and sheathed her longsword, Mercy, to finish Tagwen's prep just as the door swung open.

The shout of "Gwennie!" and the patter of little feet did not startle her, as she was accustomed to her niece barging into any room.

"Nani!" Tagwen exclaimed as she swooped her niece off the floor and into her arms, sitting the little girl on her hip. Rhona leaned against the doorframe catching her breath from attempting to avert her daughter's intrusion.

"Enania, we talked about this," she huffed.

"Oh, now you know I don't mind, do I, Nani?"

"Nope!" Her toothy-gapped grin spanned the whole of her face and was framed by golden waves of hair — a trait of her father's, Seathan Caimbeul, a Horseman of Logrosca.

Rhona rolled her eyes at her sister. "Don't say I didn't try," she warned.

"Gwennie, where you going?" the little girl asked.

Tagwen's jaw tightened, and she looked to Renlyn to indicate she was dismissed.

Renlyn bowed and left the room.

"Tagwen has to make sure some people are safe, baby," her mother answered.

"I'm going to be back as soon as I can, I promise."

Enania looked down and stroked the lion crest on Tagwen's armor. Rhona may have been the child's mother but there was no replacing the love that Enania held for her aunt.

"How long do you think you'll be?" Rhona asked, shifting her gaze between the two.

Tagwen paused for a moment before she took a big breath and covered Enania in kisses, to a much-delighted squeal, tossed the girl up in the air and caught her, and gave her one more big forehead kiss before she handed her over to her mother.

"Gwennie is going to come back as soon as she can, okay?" Tagwen said, trying to sound reassuring to her beloved little shadow.

"Okay." The child's striking green eyes traced the lines on her little thumbs — that color also her father's.

"Honey, why don't you see if Mairead is ready for your lessons today?" Rhona suggested. Mairead Ghuinne had been the teacher for all three of the Braithe children and was now tending to Enania — the first and only grandchild.

"Okay," replied Enania, distracted by this request, and eagerly leaving the room.

"I estimate to be gone about a month. There is no telling how long we'll be needed, though," Tagwen said.

"What if something more serious is going on? How will I know?" As she fidgeted with her hands, Rhona's tender gaze fell on the image of her sister; Tagwen was tall, gallant, capable.

"I'll have a message sent to Kâr Boldihr. Adrelghard is sure to get it by the time I would be headed back. I'll invite him down and let him know that if he gets here before me, to seek us in Westvein and ask for support from the dwarves. I know not what we are set to face, but the sky has cleared a bit and I think maybe there is a chance the earth is on our side in recompense for the sea being closed to us."

Before Rhona could respond, Tagwen took her into an embrace.

"You and Enania stay here and stay safe, regardless of what happens, understood?"

"Tagwen, you know—"

"That's an order."

Rhona tightened the hug before pushing back, and polished Tagwen's chest plate with her sleeve.

"Go then, and may the lands be kind and the Road forgiving — and may the guidance of the sea follow you where you tread."

To lighten the mood, Tagwen nudged Rhona's shoulder. "Wanna sneak up on Elnan like we used to? I mean to tell him of this journey, and he could use the laugh," she snickered.

"As fun as that sounds, I should probably check that Enania actually is on her way to lessons," Rhona said with some regret.

"When did you become the grown up one?" Tagwen teased.

"The moment I knew I could beat you at doing so. Must be difficult to not be good at everything," Rhona smirked.

Tagwen scoffed and hugged her sister once more before sending her on her way. Then, mustering her strength to meet with her brother, she collected her things and crept to her wardrobe. She had not dared take the King's suite, instead remaining in the corridor where she'd grown up next to her siblings' rooms.

The wardrobe was a tall fir construction stained with a deep maroon; the color of the Marezian vestments. Creaking open the large doubled doors and brushing aside the collection of coats, Tagwen spotted the latch on the back panel. She had found this tunneled entrance in her perusal of old castle documents when she was a girl and thought herself quite ingenious for having discovered it — only to find out that Elnan had already known of its existence.

Through nightmares and sleepless nights, Tagwen would unhook this very latch to seek comfort from her older brother, whom she would often wake. Without fail, he would stir, they would rekindle the dying fireplace, and he would talk her through her frights. It had been many years since the latch had last been used.

This is silly. Just go talk to him, she thought. *No, no it'll be funny — he hasn't laughed in a while,* she convinced herself.

Twisting the handle, Tagwen gently slid the false wall open, revealing the interior of Elnan's wardrobe on the other side. Careful to avoid making too much noise, she crept through the threshold and slowly opened the doors that led to the room.

"I could hear you coming from your own room. Brass has a way of clanking, you know," Elnan said, sitting in his wheeled chair at the closest end of the center table but facing away from the armoire.

With a sigh, Tagwen clattered through the remainder of the hideaway and into his room, sliding the false wall closed.

"You could have pretended not to hear anything," she suggested.

Elnan chuckled, turning his chair to face her. "For where do you head that warrants suiting?" he asked.

Rustling through her effects, she procured the letter from Middling and handed it to him.

Elnan scanned its contents. "Is this legitimate?" he asked.

Tagwen swallowed nervously. "MacCaibe brought it here, so I'm inclined to believe its origins at the very least," she said.

Still scanning the note, he asked, "Did Gòrdan know anything about this?"

"He did not seem to, but it would not be unreasonable to assume this sort of information is safer if known by fewer," she replied, trying to convince herself.

Elnan looked up at her. "You're taking the Road then?"

Tagwen nodded.

"You seem uncertain," observed Elnan.

Tagwen rubbed and twisted her hands about themselves.

"This is my first opportunity to show the kingdoms I am capable of this post. But I have not crossed the Road in years, nor been in Middling since father—" she stopped.

Elnan reached for her hand. "The moment you swore the oath of our true kings and forefathers was the very same that proved your leadership to the realm. Father would be proud," he reassured her.

Tagwen took a breath and gazed at her brother. She recalled then the surprise attack at Leonan Point — the assignment that would render Elnan disabled. She cringed at the thought. It had been the first expedition she had taken as Lieutenant under her brother's command.

After years of training, and covertly insisting her father's captain let her take the sailor's test, Arlon would relent in allowing her position — impressed with her strength and tenacity.

The Braithes' post had been ambushed by the Rogues of the Black Isle. Amidst the encounter, Elnan was caught by a dagger to the spine as he moved to shield Tagwen from what would surely have been a fatal blow. He had landed in her arms almost lifeless, but Tagwen managed to remove him from the fray — saving his life.

He had developed a cautious optimism since then, but still insisted on relinquishing his right to rule to Tagwen, though the people would largely have preferred Elnan's ascension to the throne.

"Who is to accompany you?" he asked.

Blinking to return herself to the present, Tagwen answered,

"Uhm — Captain Kenefick and ten men of her discretion. I know Sergeants Catach and Matharnach are in attendance."

Elnan nodded. "They've served this kingdom impressively. Seems you'll be well guarded. But do be careful, Tagwen. Sometimes the land does not favor those who were born for the seas."

Tagwen bent down and hugged her brother, who returned the affection.

"I will be home as soon as I am able. Take care until then," she said.

Elnan smiled and returned the letter. His wavy dark hair and blue eyes were a perfect mix of their parents'. "I will be here," he said with a nod.

Tagwen turned to leave, but Elnan called out to her before she exited the chamber.

"Oh! And do say 'hello' to Prince Jaelan for me," he teased.

An audible groan and rolling of her eyes made Elnan chuckle.

"Reckon I could hand him a note or something if you've got it out of that diary of yours," Tagwen responded with a grin.

Elnan laughed heartily. "Fair play, skiff."

Tagwen smiled and moved to the door. "I'll see you soon, schooner," she said.

Elnan smiled and waved goodbye.

Closing the doors behind her, she pressed a hand to them in a wish of goodwill for him, and with a heavy sigh, collected her pack and headed out to meet Breccan and the rest of her men.

"We're clear to head out, Your Majesty." Breccan held out her hands to collect Tagwen's belongings to pack onto Seasaìdh, a grand mare whose jet-black coat and mane blended into shadows when she ran. She had been gifted to Tagwen by her dear friend, Adrelghard Tugrom, the liaison for the dwarves of the Dholdron'lièr Mountains in the far North. Tagwen stroked Seasaìdh's face and held it in her hands as they touched foreheads. She silently recited in her mind the prayer of her people, knowing somehow the beast could hear her:

Go in haste and with honor.
Follow bravely the sights you have set ahead
and may the guidance of the sea
follow you where you tread.

The party was met by the rolling hills of the Northern Yeacralan region just inland of the bay. Formerly lush and green, the landscape now exhibited the beginnings of dormancy in this early autumn. The morning was glittered in mist and dew, the weather was cool, and the skies were blanketed in soft heather clouds. The first day of their journey came calmly and Tagwen was relieved to think that Gòrdan had been greeted with an easy start to his crossing as well. By the evening, the group finally reached the small town of Oülle.

Through the misty darkness, the regiment approached the town gate and Breccan knocked upon the watchman's door.

After a few silent moments, a rustling was heard, and the peephole slid open to reveal an aged pair of dark eyes — lively despite their many years.

"Marezian soldiers? What purpose have yeh to enter Oülle at this hour?" the watchman demanded of Breccan.

Breccan pulled her honey-blonde steed, Arofel, to the side — revealing Tagwen to the watchman.

The watchman's eyes went wide as the screen was quickly shut. He ran, lantern in hand, to open the gate. A stout old gentleman clad in simple clothes and a coat to stave off the chill stood before them.

"Yer majesty! It's an honor to have yeh grace us with yer presence. Please do come in. Do yeh plan to stay or are yeh making yer way through to the Road?" he asked.

Tagwen smiled and bowed her head graciously at the nightman. "We seek lodging for the evening, and perhaps a meal, should the kitchens still be available. We intend to depart from here at first light to continue along our present heading," she explained.

The man nodded. "What brings yeh out of the beauty of the coast, m'lady?" he inquired.

"What was your name again, kindly gentleman?" Tagwen asked.

Blushing under the lamplight, the man straightened his posture. "Tom Bivins, Oülle Gate Master, at yer service," he beamed.

Tagwen bowed her head to him. "Master Bivins, would you be able to tell me of your inn's availability to host myself and my men?"

Tom looked out toward the small town where the inn was

located. "Few have made their way through the good 'ole Breezy Thicket. Should be ready for yeh, yer majesty. Sure, not like the accommodations of Marez, but we hopes to serve yeh well," he said with pride.

"Wonderful. I am certain that your offerings are perfectly suitable. Sea's blessings, Master Bivins," she replied with a smile.

The watchman bowed dutifully and ushered the regiment into the town.

Townsfolk who were still about at the odd hour stopped and stared as the cavalry passed by them. Tagwen nodded and smiled at them but elicited only the occasional bow. Others turned their gaze away or quickly moved indoors. Tagwen knew this town had a scarred history with Olwenna Glas' reign — and subsequently her even more tyrannical son, Reese Glas-Bowen. They were wary of another queen who was not intended for the throne.

Tagwen looked ahead to the inn — keeping the onlookers in her periphery.

They approached the lodging and those on horseback dismounted.

"Ruiseal, Hellig, see that the horses are tended and stabled. The rest of you make your way inside and don't embarrass me, yeah?" Breccan instructed.

"Yes, Captain," they responded in unison.

Breccan saluted to dismiss them and then escorted Tagwen inside — remaining close and watchful.

Stepping through the front door, Tagwen was met with a

familiar, sudden, and awkward silence. Patrons sitting at the bar and various tables paused to take in the group's arrival. A serving girl had just come out of the kitchen with a basket of breads, and upon seeing Tagwen, dropped the basket to the floor. Tagwen instinctively bent down and assisted her as she began gathering the rogue loaves.

"T-terribly s-sorry, yer m-majesty," the waitress stammered.

Gathering the last loaf and handing it to the girl, Tagwen smiled reassuringly. "It is quite alright."

The girl curtseyed awkwardly, almost dropping the basket again before scuttling back into the kitchen.

Amidst the continued silence, Tagwen made her way to the bar table and addressed the man she determined to be the barman. "Good evening. Are you the person I should speak with about food and lodging for myself and my men?" she asked.

"Ahem, yes, Your Majesty… hm… I am Torcadall Pablan, owner of this here Breezy Thicket. I-uhm… how long will you be with us?" he sputtered as he took in the rest of the company.

"For just the evening, Sir Pablan. Any accommodation you can spare would be most welcome — there are a dozen of us in total," Tagwen said.

Torcadall nodded to her and her unit. He turned, snapping his fingers at a server who was gawking at the party. "Show these fine soldiers some beds, and kick MacCaull out of the room for the Queen," he ordered.

"That will not be necessary, sir," Tagwen interjected. "A simple boarding will be sufficient."

At this, Torcadall and many others seemed to relax — some

even resumed their evening.

Torcadall smiled. "Good to see the familiar graciousness of your father in my establishment once again, m'lady. You and your men are welcome here. Please," he gestured to the taproom. "Make yourselves comfortable and I'll have the kitchens fix you up a proper meal," he offered.

"Many thanks," Tagwen replied, claiming a seat nearest the fireplace. Breccan joined her, stretching and yawning. Tagwen rubbed her hands, warming them in front of the fire.

The sounds of the bar resumed, and a soft lute began to play.

"You sure we can't head back home after this? Maybe we can even take a vacation and visit Gilèdo — or Logrosca is closer to here, I suppose. Either way, Middling is probably fine," Breccan joked.

"Careful what you say. We may still be in Yeacralas, but this town has citizens from across the land," Tagwen warned.

Breccan leaned over the cracked, off-balance round table. Her mail raked across its surface. "If anyone here knew anything, it would be the talk of the town. I'm sure of it," she whispered.

Tagwen contemplated the thought for a moment. "Even so," she said, "I would hate to jeopardize this excursion on account of not hearing anyone gossip about the matter."

Breccan sighed and leaned back in the equally off-kilter wooden chair, wrapping her hands behind her head. "True," she agreed, blowing a loose curl of gingered hair off her face.

Tagwen gazed about the inn — a modest two-floored construction, a sizable fireplace, center bar. It was not unlike The Siren's Whistle except for its lack of familial comfort. She glanced around and caught the eyes of random patrons. Most quickly turned away — except for one gentleman in a corner.

He stared at Tagwen under the shadow of a cloak hood. His dress did not signify any particular region, nor was anything of his person terribly distinct, but he beheld Tagwen strangely.

Tagwen attempted a slight smile (with no discernible change from the man) before turning to accept the dinner and mead being served at her table.

"Thank you kindly," she said to the waitress, who curtseyed in response.

When she glanced back at the man's table, he was gone.

"Som'thin wrong?" Breccan asked, taking in a mouthful of boiled potato.

Tagwen shook her head. "I'm sure it's nothing," she replied. *One day I hope they're less afraid of me,* she wished.

The boiled potato and vegetable array of carrot and leek left much to be desired, but the leg of roasted hen was palatable. They ate in companionable silence, grateful for the warm meal.

The mead was arguably the crown jewel of the evening. Tagwen sipped it whilst Breccan had already gotten herself another pint.

A few at a time, Tagwen's men made the rounds to bid the queen a pleasant evening before retiring to their lodging — until finally it was only Breccan and Tagwen left.

The pub crowd had picked up, and few seemed to notice Tagwen's presence, much to her relief. All the while, Breccan was making jovial conversation with other patrons, who kept supplying her with complimentary drinks.

Tagwen was enjoying this vague moment of normalcy, but could hardly keep her eyes open, and tapped Breccan on the arm.

"Time to head up, milady?" Breccan hiccupped.

Tagwen nodded as she stifled a yawn.

Breccan stood to help her up, nearly tripping over a leg of the creaky stool. They both chuckled as she caught herself and gave an overly dramatic bow to Tagwen.

"Time to put you to bed," Tagwen snickered as she steadied Breccan.

"No — you. I'm the captain here," Breccan giggled.

"Mhmm."

They wormed their way through the crowd, clambered up the stairs, and found Sergeant Matharnach posted outside a door. Sìne held a perfect stance as the two women approached. Her light brown hair was uniformly tied behind her head, and her pale skin and blue eyes warmed in the sconce-light that glowed across from her.

"Evening, Your Majesty," Sìne greeted.

Breccan saluted her, "Matharnach."

Tagwen smiled as she regarded the knight. "This room open, sergeant?" she asked.

"Indeed, Commander. The MacLeòirs have claimed a cot, but there's one reserved for you and the Captain. I'll be your watch for the night," she answered.

"Thank you much, Sìne. Pleasant evening," Tagwen said.

Sìne bowed and opened the door for them.

Tagwen helped Breccan into bed and removed her boots and gloves. The captain fell almost immediately asleep. Tagwen shook her head and moved to nestle on the other side. Passing the window peering into the town, she caught sight of a lantern flicker. Squinting to see through the dirtied glass, she saw two cloaked figures. She could not make out either face until the smaller of the two gestured toward the inn. It was the same peculiar man from earlier.

After pointing, he turned back and received a small pouch from the other. They both then went their separate ways. Tagwen breathed a sigh of relief as they moved away from The Breezy Thicket.

Satisfied with their departure, she began to get ready for bed. She thought for a moment about waking Breccan to help her out of her mail.

The captain snored loudly in answer.

Setting her suit upon the floor, Tagwen snuck into bed — the linens scratchy against her skin. The revelry of the bar below and the snoring choir in the room left little chance that she would sleep tonight.

At dawn, Tagwen stirred and briskly readied herself before waking Breccan, the MacLeòirs, and asking Sergeant Matharnach to wake the others. As she waited, Tagwen made her way downstairs and greeted a lovely woman tending the bar.

"By the Besanrault!" the woman exclaimed upon seeing Tagwen. "Tom really wasn't pullin' meh leg. What can I do fer yeh, Yer Majesty?" she asked.

She wore a woolen scarf draped over her gray hair and wrapped around her neck. The bagginess of her eyes told a tale of long years beset by toil, but the sweetness in them reminded Tagwen of her own late grandmother, Enania Llewelyn.

"I am here to pay the charges for myself and my men — have you the total?" she asked the woman.

"Yes! Let me see here," the woman replied as she shuffled through a disorderly stack of papers. Finding the right one, she held it close to her dazzling blue eyes and squinted harshly, accentuating the lines carved into her dark copper face. She looked at Tagwen and smiled. "Seems the tab's been counted fer, yer majesty," she said.

"By whom?" Tagwen frowned.

The woman peered at the ledger once more, shaking her head. "Don't reckon a name's been left, m'lady," she replied. "A gift from the seas, eh?" she chuckled, her laugh lines growing deeper.

"Indeed," Tagwen muttered. "Well, thank you, ma'am. And a thanks to the gifter, should they ever make themselves known."

"Quite a dear — just like your mother," the woman complimented.

Tagwen smiled, "It's not often I have the pleasure of being compared to her. People usually see my father."

"Well, meh sister told me much about 'er — bein' yers and yer siblins' teacher all those years. Loved Lady Ròsach teh pieces she did — bless the Lady's rest," she said.

Surprised, Tagwen tilted her head slightly. "You're Muireall? Muireall Ghuinne — Mairead's sister?"

The woman nodded happily. "It's Muireall Bivins now or been so for nearly twenty years I suppose!" she laughed.

"Goodness, it has been a while since I've seen the old crone or meh boy Eachann — long time since either 'ave stopped by. Do give 'er meh love once yeh get back, will yeh?"

Tagwen bowed her head. "Of course. I will even insist she take some time off to see you," she promised.

Muireall clasped her hands with joy. "Ah! What a dear y'are. Many blessings to yeh. Oh, what's that old sea prayer?" She scrunched her face in thought before snapping her aged fingers. "May the guidance of the sea follow yer treads," she beamed.

Tagwen did not have the heart to correct her, but instead bowed graciously before taking her leave. By then, her men and a seemingly well-rested Breccan had made it downstairs and were awaiting food and further orders.

The cooks would not be available for some hours, so Muireall brought bread, cheese, and mead out for the Marezian regiment, refusing to take any steel in payment, despite Tagwen's insistence. The group ate and drank contentedly until it was time to leave.

"Ya'll be careful now!" Muireall called out as they bid her thanks and farewell.

Though still early morn, the town of Oülle was stirring as market vendors and farmers readied for the day.

After gathering their stabled wagons and four-legged companions, the group made a peaceful exit out the northern gate to reach the proper start to the Road.

The Road was established in the late Second Age to create safe passage across the Vostheloren continent and serve as territorial boundaries between the three kingdoms of men. It began at the Northernmost region of Oburim, forked in the center of the continent to reach Middling, and then down into Oülle. The connection to Marez had been interrupted during the Bloodless War between the kings of Middling and Yeacralas nearly a hundred years ago and was never recommissioned.

Oülle was the last occupied town in the Yeacralan region before entering the Greyrest — a land owned by none, as it sat between the surrounding kingdoms of men and the forested lands of Brierhïl to the East. Beyond the hamlet, shadowing a patch of the Road, were the Enbron Woods. The forest stood between the company and the Outrider outpost that served as a halfway point to the ruins of Clerlūn.

Upon their approach, Breccan spotted something at the mouth of the woodland. "Hold!" she commanded, raising her right fist to stop the procession.

"What is it, Captain?" Tagwen asked.

"It appears to be a horse, but I can't discern a rider. It seems to be staring at something on the ground."

"Proceed with caution! Weapons at the ready!" Tagwen's order straightened the backs of her men and they advanced forward in formation.

Their approach didn't spook the horse. In fact, it hardly even looked at them, and they soon understood why. The sight before them was ghastly — a mangled body tied to a large evergreen tree. It was hardly discernible, as animals had clearly taken their fill and its eyes were being pecked out by corvids that the horse continually attempted to shoo.

"Search the area," Breccan commanded, seeing that Tagwen had become fixated on the sight before her.

Tagwen dismounted Seasaìdh and walked up to the pale white horse who had stayed loyally by the side of the one she assumed had been its rider. It turned to Tagwen and nudged its nose into her chest, looking defeated.

"There, there. You've done well, my friend." Tagwen rubbed the horse's face before she took his reins over to Seasaìdh and tied them together.

"What in the dark depths happened here?" Breccan asked while kneeling by the body.

"Certainly nothing good, but I do think someone wanted this to be found. That would be the only explanation for why they left them here and left their horse unscathed."

Sending a message to someone, certainly.

Tagwen traced the weapon marks in the purplish, thin, scaly bark of the tree. Holes where there had once been arrows were now deep-red calloused wounds, though this mess was not the work of Outriders — they had more respect than to leave a corpse on display. However, a strange carving was etched into the wood above the corpse's head — a crescent moon above a cordate leaf. The image bore no recognition to Tagwen.

The rope used to tie the body was also unusual. Patches of the twine appeared to be smeared with soot, but there was no sign of fire in the vicinity. Tagwen's eyes finally permitted themselves to fully take in the image of the body, and her gaze moved to the well-worn leather boots. Though caked with mud and splatters of blood, she recognized the patchwork sewn onto the shoes — it was Gòrdan.

Tagwen's eyes widened, and her mouth fell open as she gasped, "No!"

Breccan, undisturbed by the outburst, turned to her queen. "Well, that confirms my assessment. I'm afraid it is him."

Confusion flushed Tagwen for a moment as her eyes flickered between the carving and his body.

Who would want him dead and sign the kill no less?

"This is weird though, right?" Breccan poked at the carving, rubbing the crimson sap between her fingers and off on her trousers.

"I truly never figured Gòrdan to be strange in any way, but this — I have no idea what he has gotten himself into," Tagwen said.

"Well, whatever it was, he's not exactly getting himself out of it." Breccan cringed.

Tagwen grabbed a flask from her pack and knelt in front of Gòrdan's body. She dug a hole by his feet and poured some of the liquid from the waterskin inside. After filling the small hole with water, she covered it with fresh dirt then bowed her head and murmured, "May the guidance of the sea bring you to rest—"

"Commander, we found something," a soldier interrupted unintentionally as he walked up behind Tagwen and Breccan paying their respects.

The young man, no more than twenty years old, went pale when he witnessed the scene up close and quickly handed Tagwen a tattered sheepskin tote before he turned away to hurl.

"I'm deeply sorry, Your Majesty. I've just never—"

"He has been cared for now. Find your peace," Tagwen patted him on the shoulder and sent him back to the rest of the company.

"What's in the sack?" Breccan asked while she continued to survey their surroundings.

Tagwen opened the bag she recognized to be Gòrdan's and found a mishmash of papers. Most looked to be nothing of note except for one letter that appeared to be attached to the back of another.

"Knife," she said.

Breccan took her knife out of its sheath and handed it over.

Tagwen gently cut at the adhesive that seemed to be keeping the notes together until they were separated. She read aloud:

I am writing of the Elven Plot on record, should my demise prove untimely. They have taken to ruining our lands and our crops. They have decimated a patch of farmland bordering the Greyrest and I'm sure this is only the beginning. Our allies will abound, and we will descend on them like wolves. The elves will not win.

Roìbert Dùghlan

Breccan crossed her arms. "He's truly mad. If they are even around, elves have never left the Brierhïl, let alone waged an unprovoked attack. It's unheard of," she scoffed.

"Regardless, why is Gòrdan seemingly in the middle of all of this?" Tagwen reread the letter silently to assign it any logic.

There had been no reports of this kind of behavior anywhere and it would be in violation of the long-standing agreement that elves and men never interact. Tagwen herself had never seen an elf.

"Your Majesty, the vicinity has been cleared. There's not a soul in sight," Sergeant Catach reported.

"Thank you, sergeant," Tagwen said uneasily. "Form up to continue to the outpost."

Lachlann bowed before rejoining his men and the traveling party continued warily. Night fell by the time they reached Oakbreak Stand, where they would make camp. Oakbreak was one of the smaller steads of the Outriders and was sheltered on the outlet border of Enbron Woods. The forest was not the largest found on the continent, but it was dense with evergreen conifers, regardless of the season, which was why the Outriders were partial toward it. The agreement between the kingdoms of men and the band of nomadic rangers stated that each could share the locations as safe resting places, but Tagwen did not feel safe. It seemed as if there wasn't a single creature for miles, which unnerved her. The air was still, and the land quiet.

"I implore you to sleep, Your Majesty." The young soldier who had found Gòrdan's pack earlier had approached Tagwen, who was sitting, observing the campfire.

"I am afraid I cannot, but I appreciate your concern, soldier," she replied, her gaze unwavering.

"Did you know them? The corpse-er man, I mean." The soldier's voice trembled as he spoke.

"Would that matter?" Tagwen turned to face him.

"I... I would imagine so, ma'am."

"Eldropp, is it?"

"Yes, Your Majesty. Eldropp, Queensman Thesden Eldropp." The young man stood at attention.

"Thesden, we should not care whether we know those upon whom injustice has been inflicted, but rather seek to root out injustice everywhere, even if its victims are strangers to us. That being said," she paused, frowning, "I did know him. Gòrdan MacCaibe was a good man. I grieve for his children."

Mairi and Artur, now completely fatherless.

The evening passed and the group made for Clerlūn at first light. Impenetrable fog blanketed the Road, and the silence of their surroundings engulfed them. Luckily, the desolate village of Clerlūn had not been flooded, but they did not regain a clear view of the path until they reached the Lunennete Bridge at the marshes of Drÿs. The spandrel-arched stone bridge offered a secure crossing and the traveling party ventured across without incident. It would be another day until they reached the Road's fork in the Greyrest, and much to their dismay, the rain had begun to move in from the Mistvale — the encircling mountain range of the West. They would see neither person nor creature for days, until they made their way into the first town of Middling, Eltah. Tagwen noted that the scorched farmland mentioned in the hidden note was nowhere to be seen — the entire region looked to be untouched and unkempt.

Dawnshire was only an hour out of their present heading, and Tagwen made the determination to visit Gòrdan's children

to inform them of their father's passing. It was the wealthiest of
the Middling hamlets, which is to say that they were afforded
the luxury of a cobbled road. Most of the homes were small, one
room constructions, despite accommodating sometimes three
generations of families at a time.

Tagwen had never been to the MacCaibe household, but
was directed easily enough by a silent pointing finger from a
surly-looking farmer. The house was dark, the door closed,
and Tagwen could not see or hear anyone, but there was a
faint smoke plume emanating from the chimney. The company
stood surrounding the home silently. A snort or stamp of a
hoof occasionally broke the quiet as Tagwen dismounted and
approached the weather-beaten timber door with Breccan behind.

"You sure you want to do this?" Breccan asked.

"If not us, who will tell them?" Tagwen frowned. Her fist
was a hair's breadth away from knocking when the door creaked
open. "Hello?" she called out. "Mairi? Artur?" Tagwen's throat
began to tighten as she did not hear any response. The patter in
her chest called her hand to her blade as she rushed inside.

Breccan followed her queen's stride, causing the rest of the
company to follow her lead in unison.

Within the home, Tagwen investigated with sword ready,
but all else was silent. She walked around the central hearth,
its embers dulling as the fire was dying out. Scent of burnt
cabbage and scorched game filled the room, and Tagwen saw the
remnants of a soup charred at the bottom of the pot suspended
above the pit.

Maybe a day, day and a half, no more, she thought as she

inhaled.

"Mairi? Artur?" Tagwen called again, pacing delicately throughout the home. Creaking planks beneath her feet and those of her company were her only answer. She saw the children's straw beds unmade, cabinets and dresser drawers opened, and random articles of clothing strewn about the floor, but the house was well-maintained otherwise.

"I think they left in a hurry," Breccan said.

There were no signs of a fight, and for that Tagwen was relieved, but not knowing where the children were made her anxious. "Check out back, look for any sign of them," she commanded over her shoulder, not quite meeting the gaze of her men.

Breccan approached Tagwen's side. "Where do you think they'd run to?" she asked.

Tagwen shook her head as she sheathed her sword. "Maybe they have family elsewhere, but that they felt a need to run concerns me. They might already know about their father, though how, I haven't a clue." She walked toward one of the small beds, removed the leathered glove from her left hand, and reached for the crumpled blanket upon the cot — cold.

"They've been gone for at least a day," she finally said aloud.

Breccan nodded. "Smart kids to leave the fire going just enough; makes ya think someone's home at least. Doubt anyone's noticed them leave."

Scanning the empty bed made Tagwen's heart ache; imagining ones so young needing to flee. As her gaze reached the makeshift panel headboard, a carving caught her eye — a crescent moon above a cordate leaf. Her head twisted as she leaned in closer to confirm what she was seeing. "Look at this," she said to Breccan without turning from the image.

Breccan met her where she was and Tagwen moved aside to let her lean in.

"Like the tree," Breccan said with furrowed brows. "New faction of some kind you think?" she asked.

"Protectorate symbol more likely," Tagwen paused, "look." She pointed Breccan's attention to the other small bed, the same symbol carefully carved upon the headboard.

Breccan pressed her lips together in contemplation. "Can't say I recognize it. Though I didn't pay much attention to Lucas' lessons," she admitted, slightly embarrassed.

Tagwen let out a small breath. "It's not one I know either." In her mind she rifled through the images she did know: the sigils of the kingdoms of men, the Mark of the Outriders, the Horn of the Rogues, and the Crest of the Sea — none bore a significant resemblance.

"Your Majesty," Lachlann addressed from the front door.

"Any sign of them?" Tagwen asked.

"There are tracks that seemingly lead North away from the homestead — toward the mountains. I didn't have Ruiseal go very far."

"Is there any sign someone is following the children's path?"

"There does appear to be a third accompaniment; walking with them, not behind them, Your Majesty," Lachlann answered.

Hopefully someone who is there to protect them.

"Thank you, sergeant, please prepare yourselves to depart momentarily."

"Yes, Your Majesty," Lachlann bowed and then left the steading.

"Who do you suppose? Family? A friend?" Breccan asked.

"I can only hope," Tagwen replied. "Mairi must be nearly fourteen now, and Artur about eight, so, they can handle themselves if need arises, but still," she paused, "they're just children."

Tagwen took one last glance around the home. She removed the pot from the fireplace, and stoked the cinders slightly. Satisfied, she fitted her glove back onto her hand and walked with Breccan outside. Down the town road she caught sight of the same farmer who had given her directions staring at the regiment with ire. His thin frame stood isolated against the backdrop of the all-gray sky and his worn work-clothes clung to his bones in the rain.

"Yeacralans, move out," she commanded, readying herself upon Seasaìdh. For a moment the man's eyes seemed to directly meet hers, and she felt a chill creep through her spine.

Seas deliver us from here.

***

After a total of eight days, they arrived at Francus Castle in Westvein in the late afternoon, under an increasingly heavy rainstorm. They saw the banner of Oburim — a blue flag bearing three stalks of wheat surrounded by a laurel, flying beside the banner of Middling — a yellow flag bearing a crest of a circle of mountains with a bear in their center.

Breccan leaned over to Tagwen. "It seems we're late to the party."

"It would appear so. Let us not keep them waiting."

2
THE ELVEN PLOT

It had been four years since Tagwen had visited Westvein proper, or Francus Castle. It was not incredibly large. From afar it would be mistaken for a manor house, as it was overshadowed by the surrounding mountains. The castle still maintained a platform to the front egress hovering above an overgrown moat, though there was no longer any water. The gates were hardly representative of the fortress that King Roìbert Dùghlan claimed his estate to be. However, what Francus Castle lacked in stature, it made up for in craftsmanship. Each stone was laid as if it were a mosaic built from the earth itself, and the interior was just as meticulous. The meeting hall housed ornately carved teak beams across the ceiling, and hanging from the centermost point was an intricately designed wrought iron chandelier that depicted the Mistvale.

Unfortunately, the king's tastes detracted from all the natural beauty. Roìbert Dùghlan was notorious for expending his wealth in manners that, to Tagwen especially, made him look foolish. Extravagant furs blanketed the floors, covering their timeless baroque patterns; sizable portraits of Roìbert, his children, and his late wife hung garishly on nearly every wall; and his manner of dress was comprised of the most expensive dyed silks and linens. His son, Jaelan, had taken to the same excesses as his father, while his daughter, Mòrrea, kept herself in the background.

Roìbert sat at the head of the elongated dark oak table, with Jaelan to his right, and King Daïdh Arasgain of Oburim to his left. Standing at attention in the corner of the room nearest Arasgain was his captain, Hubertus Tolmach — a stately fellow with neatly cropped sandy hair and kind brown eyes.

Seated beside Jaelan was a man who looked as if he had walked out of a crypt. His skin was pallid and nearly blue, his eyes were sullen and red-rimmed as if from sickness and they were distinctly gray, almost silver in color. They felt somehow familiar to Tagwen. The man's hair was ghostly white, stringy, and fell to his chin, which did not flatter him. His robes were a rich plum color that were a dramatic contrast to the whole of his physique. He possessed an air of importance at the table.

"Ah, Tagwen, so wonderful of you to come! You've grown quite since I was last in your father's kingdom!" Daïdh hollered, his face flushed, round, and red, and framed by a thick salt and peppered beard — though more salt than pepper, for the king was in his late fifties.

Tagwen bit her tongue and bowed to each of them, rainwater dripping from her hair down her face as she did. "King Arasgain, Prince Jaelan, King Dùghlan, we have come by the Road and thank you for your patience. I hope my delay has not caused any issue. And forgive me, but I do not believe I have had the pleasure to make your acquaintance, sir," she said, turning her attention to the specter who sat beside Jaelan. None seemed to take any care that her and Breccan were rather disheveled.

"The pleasure is mine, Queen Braithe." His voice was strangely full and deep. "I am Goraidh, Sage of the Dùghlan House," he said as he offered her a handkerchief.

Tagwen was pleasantly surprised at the formality but could not escape the chill that his utterance of her title had elicited. "My thanks," she replied, taking the cloth cautiously and blotting at her face before handing it over to Breccan.

Daïdh gave Tagwen a puzzled look before his eyes darted away in realization that he had forgotten Arlon's death.

"You would do well to sit so we can get on with the matters at hand." Jaelen, with his lanky frame and boyish face, attempted to establish a presence at the table, though he only managed to look foolish. He appeared much like his father with the same squared jaw and aquiline nose, but his hazel eyes were from his mother. He paused a moment before uttering, "Queen Braithe," as though it was the punchline to a joke.

Tagwen stifled an exasperated breath.

"Yes, Braithe, as we are relieved to all now be in the same room, the matter at hand is most pressing." There was something different about Roibert's voice at that moment — it was lackluster, stoic. He had not the boisterousness nor flamboyance previously associated with his speech when he etched out every vowel or emphasized words unnecessarily. Breccan pulled out Tagwen's seat for her, which unwelcomely sat at the other end of the table. After taking her seat, she glanced back at Breccan to dismiss her with a look of concern.

The divergence of King Dùghlan's tone and mannerisms from his dress was startling. Clad in a royal blue mantle, and decorated in medallions and rings, he looked as if he were hosting the banquet of the century, but his eyes were unfocused and somber, and his sentences stunted.

"Now that we're all here, it is time to fully discuss this heinous affair. The elves of Brierhïl have at last emerged from their isolation and decided that the lands of the Greyrest are their birthright. They have already waged unprecedented attacks against my lands, and we have reason to believe this is just the beginning. They've wanted this land for ages and now they're moving to strike. I am sure of it," Roìbert reported.

"My friend, the elves are nowhere to be found!" assured Daïdh. "By my laurels, we don't even know if they exist anymore! As I said when we first arrived, your lands appear untouched as far as the eye can see. I had worried that there would be no one home when we entered your lands, given the fright you instilled in your call to arms. We should celebrate that there's nothing to worry about!" Daïdh's clearly inebriated gesticulations nearly knocked over the goblet of wine he had been drinking from.

"Are you going to remain insistent on calling my father a liar, Arasgain?!" Jaelan nearly sprang from his seat before Goraidh put a hand on his shoulder.

"Once again, I do not think our friend in Oburim means any offense, young Dùghlan. It is a strange situation for those who have yet to experience the truth. It is true the elves have been isolated, thankfully due to the foresight of great men," Goraidh calmed.

"Daïdh, I beg you to believe." Roìbert pointed to a section of the continental map on the table, which Tagwen could not see from her seat. "They struck here and covered their tracks. My citizens of the bordering farmland have attested to this."

"Then perhaps the elves regretted their mistake and made amends to the lands! Those strange devils might have some honor after all."

The men all but ignored Tagwen, but she watched them, took note of their mannerisms, and listened carefully to their words.

Roìbert sighed, "My friend, you are blinded. The elves are looking to take the Greyrest and then Middling. I know it. We have seen it." He looked to Goraidh, who stood and closed his eyes to speak.

"They will strike under cover of night and spread their seeds of
deception across the lands so that it might ensnare the legs of
man.
The lands will be untenable; the waters will run dry.
The elves' desire for the borderland is only the beginning.
The whole of Vostheloren is in their eye."

Tagwen watched the men's eyes fixate on the Sage at this revelation, each with a different expression. Jaelan appeared to beam with pride and puffed out his chest, as if he had been the one to prove Daïdh wrong, the smirk dropped from Daïdh's face and his expression turned to one of horror, and Roìbert's shoulders sunk in defeat as he cast his eyes downward to his feet

— a look Tagwen had never known the king to exhibit.

Regardless of their respective countenances, Tagwen discerned that they believed this man's words. To her, it sounded more like an ill of the old "religion" — poetic propaganda crafted by Olwenna's son and used in large part to demonize the dwarves.

Dangerous claims of distrust, greed, and vengeance were not what she had expected in coming here, and her stomach twisted at the thought.

"What do you make of this foretelling, Queen Braithe?" Tagwen had been so busy looking at the men that she did not notice Goraidh staring at her, his expression stone-cold.

Stunned, she replied, "Where exactly is this information coming from? The agreement between elves and men is well known. Would it not be unwise for the elves to go up against an entire continent for the sake of lands that would not serve them? Nor have they been widely seen for centuries now. Are we sure they've not fallen into legend?"

Goraidh paused as if to study Tagwen's very soul. She held still and matched his gaze, clearing her head of any thoughts, as if he could read them.

"A very logical response. Though I can assure you, they have indeed lasted the ages… despite the odds." His gaze hardened subtly before slowly shifting back to his king. "We should bring forth those citizens to bear witness to the truths I have set before this council, Your Grace," he suggested.

"That did not answer my—"

"Your words should simply be believed, as should my

father's! The lot of you would do well to get off your high horses and act!" Jaelen sneered at the visitors. Goraidh raised a hand to speak, but Jaelan stormed out of the room as a child would when they did not get their way.

Roìbert sighed. "Forgive him, Goraidh, he is passionate, as you know, and worried, as am I." He bowed his head in apology to the Sage before turning to the others. "I need rest now. We shall reconvene in the morning to discuss the plan."

"You are most right. Let us retire for the evening, my king. Your strength and wit are necessary for us to move forward. I trust Sir Tolmach here can direct you to your rooms, seeing as how you're all being housed in the same wing." The Sage shifted to Roìbert's side with movement reminiscent of a man a third his probable age, and Tagwen's eyes followed in curiosity as he and the king departed. At this, Daïdh's captain, Hubertus, took his king's arm and escorted him to the door.

Tagwen thought to protest, demand answers, and to inform them about Gòrdan, but an uneasy feeling came over her in watching this meeting's conclusion. That, and her desperation to be rid of her rain-soaked attire called her to hold her tongue for the moment.

Quite the welcome, that.

The hall that led to the eastern tower was lit only by flashes of lightning from the storm outside through stained-glass windows, projecting corrupted images along the dark-stone walls and floors. Depictions of trees and mountains became monsters with tentacles and wings, and there seemed to be eyes everywhere. Tagwen was bewildered by one painting of the late Lady Dùghlan. The queen was looking away from the viewer and donned a sable gown whose collar came all the way up her neck, highlighting a large, silvered necklace with a sizable locket hanging from the chain. The locket was in the shape of a bear similar to the one the kingdom had chosen to represent it, except this one possessed glistening yellow gemstones for eyes, which appeared to blink violently in the light of the storm. Lady Dùghlan held the dangling locket against her chest with one hand while the other appeared to be opening a cracked drawer of a dresser.

Tagwen dismissed the oddity and continued to run one hand along the cold stone to keep a sense of space. The other was placed on Breccan's shoulder as they stopped at King Arasgain's room, where Hubertus deposited him on his bed, and he promptly passed out. Tagwen and Breccan were then led down a flight of stairs, which thankfully held a lit torch at its base above the door to their room. Unsure of what they expected, the two were pleasantly surprised with the comfortable accommodation. In their lodging was an alcove with a proper bath that looked to have been recently drawn for them, a large bed fitted with fresh and luxurious linens, and a lit fireplace along the wall.

The women tended to themselves in preparation for an evening of reasonably good sleep, for once, when there was a soft knock at the door. They turned to each other and sat for a moment in silence to listen. It was nearly midnight and casual visitors seemed unlikely.

Another knock.

Breccan rose from the floor in front of the fireplace, where she was drying herself, and grabbed the dagger she kept under a pillow.

"Who is it?" She leaned against the door to listen.

"A friend. Hurry please, I've not got much time," a hushed voice said from the other side.

Tagwen nodded and Breccan opened the door slowly to reveal a petite, cloaked figure in dark robes. They lifted their hood to unveil themselves — it was the king's daughter, Mòrrea.

"Please can I come in? I need to speak with Queen Braithe." Her angelic voice trembled as she whispered.

With another nod from Tagwen, Breccan let the girl inside, checked for anyone watching, and quickly closed the door.

"Mòrrea my goodness, I have not seen you in some time. What are you doing here at this hour?" Tagwen embraced the girl then motioned her over to the fireplace to sit.

"It is wonderful to see you again, Tagwen. I was most delighted to learn you had accepted the throne in Yeacralas. I apologize for darkening your doorstep at this untimely hour, but I need your help." Mòrrea's delicate blue eyes and long tawny hair glowed in the firelight. The apples of her cheeks rosed at the warmth they received, almost likening her to a cherub. Tagwen had met her when she was fourteen and was grateful to see that, though now grown, she had remained as sweet as Tagwen remembered.

"What is troubling you, Mòrrea?" Tagwen leaned forward in her chair and gave the girl her full attention.

"Well, certainly you've heard of the preposterous claims

my father has about the elves. I suspect this is even why you are here. He does not know that I know, but these halls do echo. In any case, there's this man… an elf." Mòrrea paused to look at both women. "You'll not speak of this to any of them, will you?"

Tagwen and Breccan glanced at each other for a moment and shook their heads.

"Good. Well, I'm in love with him. The elf. His name is Tasar Vanelis and I am in love with him. The elves mean no harm and I know this goes against the agreements our forefathers set out, but they are not bad creatures. He is beautiful and kind. He has the sweetest little freckle on his cheek…" A tear welled in her eye that she could not contain, and Breccan offered her a drying cloth.

"Thank you. I'm terribly sorry but I can't believe what is happening. There is something wrong here and I can't figure out what it is. The king you knew is not the same man he was — though thankfully quieter, he is not the father I grew up with," she cried.

Tagwen and Breccan's eyes flicked over to each other at the same time.

"What? Have you two seen something? Heard something?" Mòrrea pressed.

"I cannot say that we have figured out what it is, but your discomfort is shared here. The tone your father carries alone is… well, seems shockingly disturbed." Tagwen reached to take Mòrrea's hand in hers. "Thank you for trusting us with this. We swear we will not betray that trust," she pledged.

Mòrrea smiled as she broke into a full cascade of tears, and then finally took a deep breath. "Please don't let them hurt the elves. I swear on my very life there's not a chance they would hurt a soul," she promised.

Breccan knelt by the girl's side and looked her in the eyes. "We will not let them. I am curious, though, do you recall when this shift in your father occurred?"

Mòrrea shook her head. "I could not say. I feel as though these thoughts somehow crept their way into my father so as not to terrify him or anyone else with their outlandish nature. I wish I had seen them coming."

"What is important is that you have steeled yourself against them," Breccan replied.

Tagwen sat up in her chair and looked away with slightly furrowed brows. "Do you know from where this Sage hails or receives his premonitions? I've not known your father to be a religious man, so to seek that kind of guidance struck me as rather odd."

Mòrrea gasped, "Goraidh! I told him I was headed to the kitchen for something. I need to go. He cannot know I was here." She stood, wiped her face with her dress sleeve, and smoothed her hair with her hands.

"I do not know where he gets his information, but I do not believe it to be a specific god or religion. I've heard him on occasion mention 'a world beyond' and I just assumed he was alluding to some kind of afterlife. He is, however, strange. My father brought him in a couple of years ago and I can't say I've ever liked him. Though, I will say he is adamant about keeping this family secure after what happened to mother, which of course is a welcome feeling." She walked toward the door. "I sincerely thank you both. Please remember I was never here. And please, please find a way to save the elves," she pleaded before slipping out of the room.

"Well, that was weird," Breccan said, turning to Tagwen after closing the door.

"She is young. Reminds me of Rhona at eighteen," Tagwen recalled through a deep breath. She leaned over, propping her elbows on her knees, and rubbed at her temples with her fingertips. "A 'world beyond', the elves, this Sage… What is happening here?" she ruminated.

"May I?" Breccan asked as she approached, gesturing to Tagwen's hair.

Tagwen's face softened. "I would certainly appreciate it," she replied, and pulled her unpacked wooden comb out of the cracked drawer in the cabinet next to her. She stroked the crack as she closed the drawer, trying to recall the feature's familiarity. It was a deep wound in the wood and charred black. She thought back to the remnants of soup at the MacCaibe house and the eeriness that seems to have followed.

Do they even think Gòrdan's missing? Tagwen cringed and pulled her hand away as she remembered the image of his torn body. She was not a stranger to death, but that sight made her stomach churn.

"We shall see what tomorrow brings by way of information. There is bound to be more of the truth divulged in this plan that Dùghlan supposedly has," Breccan assured.

"Having an answer to any of this would be a decent start."

"For now, having a decent night's sleep should suffice," Breccan countered.

She softly untangled Tagwen's long, flowing brunette hair before gathering it into a braid. "There, feeling better?" she asked, handing the comb back.

Tagwen pulled the braided tail over her shoulder and admired Breccan's handiwork. "Much, thank you," she smiled.

As they finally retired for the evening, Tagwen found no rest, as she drifted into a familiar dream:

She finds herself in a murky, shadowed, mangrove estuary with a glinting pale blue light summoning her through the trees. She makes her way through the mossy brush and roots only to find herself at the edge of the world, where the horizon of storms rests. Below the precipice, hundreds of feet below the earth, are rivers of fire and the howling of beasts that strike fear into the hearts of men. Across the chasm lies a ship, and the source of the pale blue aura steps into view. The most beautiful woman Tagwen has ever seen coalesces out of the light. Her hair is coiled above her head like the storm clouds that surround her, her skin is as dark as midnight, and her eyes glimmer like a pale, wintry morning. Then, as she does every time, just as Tagwen tries to reach for her, Tagwen slips from the edge and falls into the chasm.

She startled awake and gasped for air just as morning had begun to peek through the small window. She held her face through ragged breaths and looked around to find Breccan missing. Before she could panic, Breccan slipped through the door with two cups of tea.

Tagwen took a deep breath and placed a hand on her chest.

"Same dream again?" Breccan sat beside her and handed her the tea, then rubbed her upper back. Tagwen only ever awoke frightened when she dreamt this dream. It had plagued her since the start of her career as a soldier. She had dreamt it so often that she began to believe that there may be something beyond the horizon of storms, though no ship would ever carry a man that far.

Tagwen nodded while bringing the cup to her lips in hopes that the tea would calm her nerves. But unable to drink, she held the cup in her lap and stared at the amber liquid within.

Breccan sat in front of her. "What's wrong? Was this one different?"

Tagwen cringed, "Her eyes."

"What about them?"

"I did not realize it before. He has the same eyes. I knew that color was familiar."

"Tagwen, what are you talking about?"

"Goraidh. The Sage. He has the same eyes as the woman in my dream — like silverlight. The hue is unmistakable."

Breccan straightened and paused for a moment. "Well from what I remember you telling me, they don't bear any resemblance to each other, right?"

"No, they certainly do not, but how many people do you know with those irises?"

Breccan shrugged. "I'm pretty sure both of us have only met the one."

"I know what you think, but she has never changed in the near decade that I have dreamt of her. She's always the same, always just out of my reach, and always above the pit of hellfires. And Goraidh has her eyes… though they're not as bright as hers."

It had been a difficult dream to explain. The few Tagwen had told about the dream neither believed that it was possible to reach the world's edge nor that a mythical woman on a ship stood on the other side of a chasm of hellfire. Though Breccan was her fiercest supporter, even she could not be fully swayed.

To combat the uneasiness, and pass the time, Breccan suggested they train in the courtyard. The queen and her captain had been practicing swordcraft for nearly two hours when the belltower struck eight, indicating it was time to convene for a second session of this clandestine council.

Breccan bent over, out of breath, and put her hands on her knees. "I'll never understand how you do that." She looked over at Tagwen, who was still pacing through parry and thrust movements with her eyes closed.

Without skipping a beat, Tagwen replied, "It is thanks to the years of practice you've put in with me." Finally, she paused, opened her eyes, and blinked a few times to regain her focus in the daylight. As her sight returned, she caught a glimpse of a figure looking down at them from the northern tower of the castle — it was Goraidh. But before she could note his presence, he disappeared.

"We should go," she said, and they made their way back to the meeting hall. Upon arrival, Tagwen saw that Jaelan was seated in his father's chair, which made him look much smaller than he was. Daïdh sat in his chair silently, seemingly staring at nothing.

Tagwen looked around the room. "Good morning, gentlemen. When will the king and Goraidh be joining us?" she asked.

Jaelan unclasped his hands and gestured to Tagwen's designated seat.

"Sit. You're late," he said through clenched teeth.

Confused, Tagwen was ready to protest when Breccan squeezed her arm. It was then she noticed Hubertus standing in the corner, very slightly shaking his head in caution.

Tagwen sat.

"My father is not fit to be leading these discussions this day, so I am here in his stead. We have moved to the decision to strike at Brierhïl in three weeks. The army of Oburim has pledged their allegiance and we expect the Yeacralans to do the same. After tonight's signing of the agreements, you will make for your homelands in preparation for the attack. We will meet in the Greyrest fork in a little over a fortnight. You have your orders and I expect you to follow them," Jaelan directed.

Before Tagwen could utter a single word, Jaelan was up and out of the room, slamming the door behind him. Daïdh Arasgain remained unmoved.

He can't be serious.

"Cannot believe that cretin thought he had a chance to marry you," Breccan sneered under her breath.

Tagwen scoffed as she looked over to Hubertus, who checked the door to see that Jaelan was truly gone. "Does Middling somehow think they have the right to *order* the rest of the realms? Did Oburim actually agree to those insane terms? What proof has been given for any of this?" Tagwen interrogated, her blood thumping in her ears.

Ignoring his king, he came over to the Yeacralan pair. "If the Northlands have agreed, I was not privy to the discussion. King Arasgain wasn't in his room this morning, so I went out to search for him. It took me the better part of an hour, but I finally found him coming out of the North tower. He seems catatonic — he eats and drinks but hasn't uttered a word. He stares beyond me whenever I ask him something. Prince Dùghlan was here when we came in, but did not say a thing until you arrived. And as far as truths go, I have seen nothing presented," Hubertus explained.

"Yet Oburim feels the need to act upon these baseless accusations?" Tagwen pressed.

Hubertus pointed to his king. "Do you really think he made that decision of his own volition?" he asked.

Tagwen unclenched her jaw and called out to him, "King Arasgain?" She walked over to him while waving her hand, but he would not stir. He sat listlessly, his eyes looking tired and his posture drooping. He moved to prop his head in his hand.

She turned back to Hubertus and Breccan. "Perhaps he is *really* intoxicated?"

"If he is, this is new, even for him," Hubertus replied.

"What do we do now?" Breccan asked.

Hubertus motioned for the women to come close to be out of Daïdh's earshot. "I cannot answer that because I do not know — just be on your guard. We were here three days prior to your arrival and the situation continues to devolve," he replied.

"Well that's less than helpful." Breccan's eyes rolled as she crossed her arms.

"I am sorry, Kenefick, but it's the best I have to go on."

"It is fortunate you seem unaffected by this… clouded judgment," Tagwen noted.

Hubertus breathed a sigh of relief and nodded.

"Yeah why are you so not… whatever he is?" Breccan asked, motioning to King Arasgain.

"I'm hoping it's because I don't drink," he responded.

Tagwen eyed him inquisitively before her gaze shifted back to Daïdh. "Do you need assistance with him?"

Hubertus shook his head. "No. I'll be alright. We all need to prepare for the evening. Stay vigilant," he warned.

Tagwen and Breccan left the room back through the southern corridor, one of many whose walls were lined with oversized portraits of the royal family.

"He knows more than he's letting on," Tagwen pondered aloud.

"Tolmach? I mean… he's unhelpful, but he might be the only one we can trust in this godforsaken place," Breccan said.

That's not exactly saying much, Tagwen thought before she stopped abruptly by the painting of the late Lady Dùghlan that had perplexed her the night before. It was easier to see the queen's beautiful tawny hair and hazel eyes in daylight. She reminded Tagwen much of Mòrrea: angelic, which made the stark contrast of the bleak gown so strange. Tagwen could not place what made the whole of this painting so bewildering but became fixated on its composition and specifically the cracked dresser drawer the queen was opening. Tagwen eyed it closer, certain it was the dresser in their room and wondered at the coincidence.

"She was quite the woman, was she not?" The voice sent a familiar chill down her spine as she snapped to turn and face Goraidh, whom neither had heard approaching.

"Did you have the pleasure of knowing Lady Catrìona?" he asked as he stared at the portrait.

Before Tagwen could respond, she was caught by the sight of his left ear. The spread in his hair did not cover it as it had in their first encounter. It was scarred across the top, as if it had been cut and sown at one point, but its shape was comparable to a normal ear.

He started to turn around to face her and Tagwen quickly replied, "I did… actually. She was a wonderful woman, from what I remember, and she was very kind to me." Tagwen recalled meeting Brìghde the last time she had been in Middling. The Lady had welcomed her and accepted her as a daughter, even after Tagwen had presented her rejection to Jaelan. She remembered then a peculiar habit the Lady had of always keeping a hand upon her chest — about where a locket would rest.

She was protecting it.

"Good," he said. "Terrible what happened to Her Majesty. The accident was a most tragic affair for the family. We were blessed that the children were spared the same fate," he grieved. Goraidh finally turned and bowed his head toward Tagwen. His silverlight eyes sent shockwaves through her veins, as if she were seeing a ghost in the flesh.

"Well, I am so glad I found you, Queen Braithe. I wanted to apologize on behalf of His Majesty, King Dùghlan. He was feeling rather ill, and I was tending to him this morning. I urged him to refrain from the council's discussions, knowing Jaelan would be more than capable of sharing our decision. I trust you have heard the call the Kingdom of Middling has made to the Men of Vostheloren?"

Tagwen nodded. "I have been made aware of the… requests." She choked out the last word, feeling that this Sage was the least of whom she could trust to present her grievances.

"Good, good. In any case we'll not keep you long tonight. Formalities, really. I estimate the king to make a recovery by this evening and be ready to put plans into motion. Jaelan may wish to be, but he is not king… yet." He met her eyes. His thin red lips spread into a sly smile.

Tagwen was unsure what to make of the expression and attempted a smile as well. "I thank you for the information about King Dùghlan. I am relieved to know he will be well soon. My captain and I shall not keep you, but we look forward to seeing you again at this evening's dinner."

They bowed to each other and turned to go their separate

ways when Goraidh stopped and turned around. "By the way, Queen Braithe, I must say I had the privilege of viewing your training this morning as I was tending to His Majesty, and I am incredibly impressed with you and your captain's performance."

Tagwen and Breccan, both regarded him. "Thank you, Sage. We appreciate your… words of admiration," Tagwen replied, the hairs on the back of her neck prickling.

"I was also dazzled by your blade. That is quite the weapon you carry. Its striking edges beg to be viewed in the light," he chuckled. "Tell me, you must certainly have a name for a piece of craftsmanship such as that, do you not?"

Tagwen swallowed and nodded. "Thank you, sir. It is an incredible thing of beauty, I must agree. And as a matter of fact, I have named it. 'Mercy' is its name, sir," she said, hoping that having answered his question would permit their leave.

"Mercy. My. Well! I will leave you to the rest of your day. I shall see you both this evening." Goraidh bowed deeply one last time before turning down the opposite hall, his long flowing purple robes trailing behind him, creating the illusion that he floated across the floors.

"Is everyone here just kind of odd?" Breccan asked rhetorically.

"Hurry, I need to check something," Tagwen said as she shoved Breccan along the halls, down the stairs, and back into their room. She quickly closed the door behind them.

"Easy! What's going on?" Breccan's eyes went wide, seeing Tagwen behave like a hound searching for prey.

Tagwen rushed to the tall teak dresser, opened the drawers,

and rifled through their contents, pulling out all her packed belongings and dumping them onto the floor.

"Tagwen? What is going on?"

Tagwen turned and ordered, "Keep an eye and ear on that door."

"What are you looking for?"

Tagwen ran her hand along the inside of the drawer she had seen in the picture until she finally felt it — a latch hidden in the upper right corner. As she pressed it open, the drawer clicked, and the base of the drawer popped up to reveal a hidden compartment. She reached inside and gently lifted the late queen's locket out of the drawer and held it in the light. The bear glistened and its yellowed eyes shimmered along the walls and floors.

Breccan gasped, "By the seas… how'd you know that was in there?"

"I did not know for certain, but once I recognized the dresser's imperfection, I thought it was too close to be coincidental." Tagwen closely inspected the trinket. It was a large, well-crafted silver locket with a snap clasp that came undone as she pressed it, revealing an aged piece of folded parchment. She set down the locket and carefully removed the paper, unfolding it to reveal a collection of characters that she had never seen. It appeared to be some sort of journal entry, or letter perhaps, but none of it was comprehensible.

Tagwen brought it to where Breccan was posted at the door. "Take a look at this. Have you ever seen anything like it?" Her expression was twisted in confusion as she continued to pore over the fragile note.

Breccan shook her head. "What would the queen have been doing with this? And hiding it, no less?"

"Not only that, but why hide its location in a cryptic painting?" Tagwen thought for a moment. "There must be someone who can read this."

"Perhaps it's some sort of family secret?" Breccan suggested.

"Would she not then just bequeath the locket to her children or her husband, at the very least? I think she was hiding it from them all." She looked up from the letter and Breccan shrugged.

Tagwen gently folded the yellowed vellum back into its former configuration and placed it back into the locket. "Mention this to no one, understood? I cannot explain it, but I feel strongly that we need to take this with us." She looked squarely at Breccan, who nodded dutifully.

"I *will* find a way to make sure Mòrrea gets the locket," Tagwen said.

"What locket?" Breccan joked.

Tagwen smiled, then went back to the drawer, and reset the compartment.

After a moment of contemplation, Tagwen spoke again. "Prepare our men to leave at a moment's notice. Be sure you are not followed. When you return, we will make our appearance at tonight's dinner," she instructed.

Breccan's eyes were saddened. "Would you stay here until I return?"

Tagwen's head tilted in puzzlement.

"I ask because there is some danger in the oddity of this place, and I would prefer to have you safely here. I have a duty to your safety, both as my queen… and as my closest friend."

Tagwen nodded after a moment. "I shall remain here in anticipation of your arrival. May the guidance of the sea follow you where you tread."

Breccan smiled. "It always does," she bowed and took her leave.

In the hours that followed, Tagwen readied their belongings, hiding the locket among them, and prepped herself for the evening. She wore her bronze dress armor — a gilded lattice chest plate bearing the sculpted head of a lion — to every affair she attended. Her hair was always pulled back into a neat bun, and on only the most important of occasions did she wear the kingdom's diadem — a thin silvered circlet of dwarven iron. During those times, her likeness was much like that of her father's — plain yet fearsome. She shared Arlon's dark hair, pale face, and coffee-colored eyes, so much so that oftentimes her reflection beckoned a second look, as she almost thought she was seeing him.

Dusk neared and Tagwen became anxious, as Breccan had not yet returned. Then, as if she had known, Breccan slipped through the door. "The traveling party is ready, should we need to leave immediately. I'm glad to see you still here," she said.

"Likewise," Tagwen replied. "Let us get this dinner over with."

Neither had dared utter a word as they walked to the western wing.

A small comfort was found in the walls' lack of portraits, but it quickly vanished as they plodded through the narrow corridor. At the end of the hall stood a large pair of wooden doors, guarded by a yoke of enormous knights.

Tagwen studied their forms as she and Breccan approached. The two soldiers were clad in full, black-steeled armor (which was rare for the region), and their faces were fully obscured under menacing helms. They stood at attention and gripped large morning stars in front of their chests. They appeared almost like statues, but of a most foreboding sort.

Without a sound, the sentries turned to the doors and opened them to usher the queen and her cavalier inside.

The room was lit warmly by a multitude of candles upon sconces and on the square dining table. No furs or grotesque art were present here. It was, however, peculiarly decorated. No banner of the kingdom was present — the table's cloths and runner a stark black against the bright spruce wood.

There, already seated, were the kings, Dùghlan's two children, and the Captain of Oburim. At the southern end of the table sat two empty seats reserved for the Yeacralan pair.

"How are we late — *again*?" Breccan whispered.

Tagwen swallowed and urged Breccan into the seat beside Hubertus.

"Precisely on time!" Goraidh exclaimed from his place beside King Dùghlan. "Welcome all to what we hope will be a fruitful dinner, right, Your Majesty?" He turned to Roìbert, offering him the floor as he returned to his seat.

King Dùghlan did look better than when they had last seen him, but his eyes appeared entirely unfocused as he spoke.

"I appreciate you all having joined together. Such a cause is unavailing without full and deliberate cooperation. I…"

His words blurred into background chatter for Tagwen as Breccan leaned over and whispered, "There is no way he's steering that ship."

Tagwen took a deep breath as she kept her eyes marked on the king. He was lifeless, unanimated. Her gaze flickered over to Mòrrea, who was visibly cringing as she watched her father.

Jaelan sat staring at a dinner knife to check his reflection, seemingly unimpressed with his father's monologue.

King Arasgain sat aloof from his own captain, which was unconventional in the long tradition of kings and their paladins. Seeing this made Tagwen pause. She had not witnessed Roìbert accompanied by anyone other than this Sage.

"… and we will descend on them like wolves. The elves will not win," Roìbert concluded.

The phrase snapped Tagwen out of her reverie, the words searing her ears as the recognition sweated her brow.

"Wonderfully said, my king!" Goraidh praised.

The king dropped back into his seat as if the task of the speech had been a costly ordeal.

The Sage continued, clapping to summon the staff into the room. "Let the feast of our collective crusade commence!" He smiled a wide smile, contorting the folds of his face to look like the ghouls Tagwen had witnessed in records of mythos.

A trio of clearly overworked staff members, all dressed

in grim-colored attire, moved in unison to present the meal of the evening: a lamb cawl, broiled figs, and wine. They seemed anxious to Tagwen, moving with less grace to accommodate for their lack of assistance.

Tagwen stared into the soup and cautiously turned her eyes upward to see if anyone was partaking. Even Breccan had not begun to eat.

"Lamb cawl — made specially for our dear Yeacralan allies," Goraidh grinned at them from the head of the table.

Tagwen noticed Jaelan roll his eyes.

"Surely you must be starving. Do enjoy. We hope it exceeds your expectations." Goraidh raised his glass to them in mock salute.

Tagwen smiled back. "This is… so thoughtful of you all. We have not yet discussed all the plans, though. We were under the impression that this was perhaps more of a… strategic dinner," she said.

She saw Mòrrea take a bite of food, then another. The girl looked up and gave a half-hearted smile, and Tagwen figured herself paranoid.

"Yes, yes, dear queen! There will be plenty of time to make our arrangements. No need to spoil such a marvelous meal with talks of hostilities," said Goraidh.

Tagwen reached for her spoon and dipped it into the bowl. *It's fine*, she thought. As she raised the spoon to her mouth, King Dùghlan slumped over in his chair and then thudded to the floor.

Everyone, aside from King Arasgain, jumped from their seat to help the king.

"Papa!" Mòrrea cried.

"Now, now. He is alright — likely still fighting through the recovery is all. I will take care of him," assured the Sage.

"I will help," Jaelan said, for a moment appearing genuinely worried.

They helped the king off the floor. He flopped around like a doll, but groaned enough to convince Tagwen that he was still alive.

"He will be just fine. We will see to his rest. Please do not let this ruin your meal. We will return shortly," Goraidh said.

Tagwen sat slowly as she watched Jaelan, Mòrrea, and the Sage carry Roìbert from the room. She looked around counting the exits, trying to map in her mind where they all led.

Daïdh continued eating.

"We need to get out of here," she whispered to Breccan who nodded slightly, also seemingly minding the doors.

Hubertus stood and moved behind Tagwen and Breccan. "Don't eat the soup," he said.

"You don't say?" Breccan retorted whilst dropping the spoon she was idly twirling onto the table.

"What is happening here, Sir Tolmach? And where is Captain Trahern? Has Oswallt retired from Roìbert's service?" Tagwen asked.

Hubertus shook his head. "I wish I knew. All I know is that someone needs to get out of here to warn the elves before we all succumb to this mindlessness," he explained.

"Don't have to tell me— warn the elves?" Breccan asked, boggled.

"No man has ever spoken to the elves, let alone announce an attack while trespassing on their land," Tagwen protested.

"With all due respect, Queen Braithe, I would rather try to prevent a war from their cells than watch the world fall to ruin, or turn into him," Hubertus argued, gesturing to his unflappable king.

"I did not say I disagreed, only that it has never been done, Sir Tolmach," Tagwen replied.

"Sure, yeah let's go warn the elves, that may or may not exist, but we've gotta get out of here first," Breccan added.

Hubertus bowed. "I am relieved to know some sense reigns in at least one of the kingdoms of men. I am going to inform your company that you intend to depart while you both go and gather your things. Follow me — those brutes outside are unlikely to let you leave."

At Hubertus' direction, Tagwen and Breccan followed him through a passage away from the guarded door. He guided them through the labyrinthine hallways and pointed them to the corridor that would take them to their room. The torches were no longer lit, and Tagwen's breathing became rapid.

"Stay with me," Breccan instructed. She quickly escorted her queen to their accommodation, gathered their belongings, and then escaped the castle to the barracks.

Hubertus accompanied them, and Seasaìdh whinnied loudly as Tagwen approached.

Ready to ride, Tagwen looked to Hubertus — he bore neither pack nor horse. "Do you not intend to leave with us?" she inquired.

Bowing his head, he responded, "My sworn duty is to my king. I must remain here and fight at his side, but I could not sit idly without trying to do the right thing."

Tagwen nodded, noticing torches were making their way towards them from the gates of the castle. She looked back at Hubertus and saluted him with her right hand in a closed fist across her chest. For all the uncertainty she felt about him, she was thankful for his help.

"Be safe, friend," she cautioned.

"Until we meet again," he replied, as the Yeacralans turned to make the unprecedented journey to the elven lands of Brierhïl.

3

A RIDE OF WARNING

The party raced in a record three days to the borderlands of the Greyrest. Strained and weary, they decided to set up camp, about a two-hour ride from the Road's fork. Even Seasaìdh had begun to slow. There was no security in the lands that surrounded them, but Tagwen determined that being within the bounds of the unclaimed land was safer than remaining inside Middling.

The uncomplicated path of this part of the Road was cause for both relief and worry. The lands were flat, trees were rare, and the Road was unbothered for miles, which made for a smooth journey, but which also meant very limited, if any, options for cover. They settled in a clearing of meadow-grass that had begun to yellow in patches underneath the darkening gray skies, and arranged themselves in a circular pattern to ensure they could maintain watch on all sides of their makeshift border.

Whispers of the land became shouts. The caw of birds boomed like the howls of wolves, and the howls of wolves carried on the wind as if they were the gods themselves speaking.

The men were tired and easily startled. Reports of eyes

encircling the camp made their way to Tagwen, who, despite all efforts to shake her concerns, had begun to believe they were being hunted. She demanded rest for each man and took over their hourly shifts, with Breccan as needed, to get through the longest night thus far in their entire odyssey.

Taking a moment alone by the campfire, Tagwen pulled out the page from Lady Catrìona's carcanet. The glyphs it contained still read like nonsense, but their scrawled facets danced enchantingly in the firelight. Tagwen wished desperately to know their secrets — to hear their words. The wind whistled quietly in answer. The breeze rustled the paper and caused the blaze to flicker violently, casting grim shadows along the grassy floor that unnerved her in her exhausted state.

A twig snapped in the distance, and Tagwen was shaken back to the present moment. She quickly refolded and hid the document in a pouch at her belt, then stood to check for the source of the sound. She looked around but saw the other soldier on watch did not appear to be alarmed. She thought for a moment that she had been mistaken and the sound had only been the crackle of the firewood.

Another snap.

Tagwen whipped her head southward and unsheathed her sword. Underneath the moonlight, she beheld the sight of an eerily veiled figure about twenty meters away. At its side was a beast vaguely reminiscent of a hound, though its size and the timbre of its growl was suggestive of a warg. The figures made no movement as Tagwen remained bewitched by their presence, but she knew they were looking directly at her. Her heartbeat pulsated through her ears as she stood, uncertain of her next move.

Callon Hellig, the soldier designated to take over Tagwen's post, approached her from behind.

"Your Majesty, I—"

Before he could finish, Tagwen had her blade pressed against his neck. He froze in fear. Tagwen caught herself and gingerly lowered her sword, stepping back.

"Hellig. I am deeply sorry. Are you alright?"

"Yes, Your Majesty. I am sorry to have frightened you," he gulped and stroked his neck, relieved that she had not drawn blood.

"I did not hear your approach. I was watching—" she paused before turning back to find that the creatures had vanished. She scanned the horizon manically, trying to determine where they had gone but found nothing.

"Your Majesty? Is there something wrong?" Callon held the hilt of his sword in preparation for her command.

"I cannot say for certain, Hellig. Please relay to the others that I want to be gone from this place at first light and stay alert as best you can."

"Understood, Commander." He saluted and went to deliver the message to the other guard on duty.

Adrenaline left Tagwen wholly unable to find any rest in the hours that followed. She paced the camp whilst constantly keeping watch to find any trace of the stalker she had seen. The morning twilight highlighted the storm clouds that threatened them from above, and the party got underway. Light winds pelted their faces with rain and dampened their hair. The lands further into the Greyrest became more abundant in foliage and the smell of fresh earth filled their lungs. This part of the continent was largely untouched by any beings — its soils nurtured only by Nature itself. The spread of wildflowers coated the Greyrest hill like a coronet, and to the East of the Road laid the wilds of the Brierhïl Forests.

Beyond the Road's fork, there were no maps to guide them into or through Brierhïl. There was no need for men to know the layout of the elven lands because no one dared venture through them. Even Outriders themselves were known to remain on the familiar parts of the Road. Tagwen knew that all they could do was to keep moving toward the forest.

The problem of continuing in a straight line arose around the fifth day, when they reached the peak of the Greyrest hill — the slope down the other side would be too steep for the horses.

Tagwen sent out Corporals Ruiseal and MacCullach to scout around for better paths. Upon their return, they reported that the best way would be to venture South, as the incline was less steep, but that would put them even further behind because they would come face to face with the Irrihead, one of the arms of the great Terrishire River. Tagwen chose this course, since they would still be days ahead of the Middling and Oburim cavalries, and they were quickly running out of resources to sustain themselves.

It took the group the remainder of the fifth day to arrive at the base of the Greyrest hill — in a small cluster of full pines that provided an abundance of cover and a place to camp for the evening. The rush of the Terrishire River could be heard a great deal more than before, and it meant that they were closer to Brierhïl than Middling, which was all Tagwen cared about.

Breccan helped Tagwen pitch her tent for the evening and the two sat for a while in silence, enjoying the music of Nature.

"Do ya think there's any way to get across the Irrihead?" Breccan asked, breaking the quiet.

"I think my father talked once of an old bridge that used to cross all three veins of the river. It was assumed that each had been destroyed in the War of the Midlands and the Lunennette was the only portion reported to have been rebuilt." She paused for a moment. "A long way to say, I am unsure."

"Well, I suppose some of us could just swim across," Breccan joked.

Tagwen tittered, "Yeah, I'm sure that would hardly pose any threat. It's only the largest and fastest moving river in the world."

Breccan chuckled. "This arm's the smallest of the three! And I'll wager I'm faster," she boasted.

Tagwen laughed at Breccan before falling again into silence, preoccupied with the fears that the road ahead posed.

"It's going to be alright, you know?" Breccan assured, looking at her queen.

"I wish I had as much faith as you do. No one has gone this far into their lands. I know we are coming in on, at the very least, admirable circumstances, but I know nothing of the elves apart from what Adrelghard has said of them, and I'm not sure I've ever believed the stories," Tagwen admitted.

"Exactly! Even good ol' Addie has sung their praises in

kindness and generosity and culture. He'd never lie to you. Even though I guess he's never actually told us they still exist — always made them sound long gone."

"You know he despises that moniker," Tagwen redirected, whilst mulling over that truth.

Why didn't Adrelghard ever tell me they still existed?

"Nonsense! He's simply jealous that he cannot think up one as easily remembered as mine." Breccan laughed, nudging an elbow into Tagwen's arm.

The queen sighed. "That does remind me, though, I need to find a way to get a message to him. Maybe his name will even ring in good faith among the elves — if we find them."

Without warning, shouts began to erupt from outside the tent, a clattering of steel rang out and both women bolted from their rested positions into the fray. Those of Tagwen's soldiers on watch were squared up against a single man, whose adept footsteps and quick movements thwarted their attempts to best him. The remaining soldiers began to spring from their tents, but he made no aggressive actions toward them, though, as he took on a merely defensive posture. He backed away from their sure-striking blows, dodging as he seemed to try and reason with them.

Tagwen's voice thundered across the camp. "Halt!" she ordered.

All paused and turned toward her. The soldiers stood back and at attention, and the stranger raised both of his arms without dropping his blade.

"My queen, this man happened upon our camp and refused to state his business," Corporal Ailbert Roid explained.

"You're not exactly where you're supposed to be, either. This is a long way away from the Road for a company of men," the outsider said, panting.

Tagwen walked up to the intruder with Mercy drawn and pointed the end of her blade at his neck. "State your business."

His shaded, timeworn eyes met hers. "Though I do not answer to you, I do not wish to die today, Queen Braithe. I am Ualan Ambarsan, son of Eoghan Ambarsan. I am an Outrider and I mean you and your men no harm. Your camp was merely in my way, and it should be noted that you are not in a safe location," he explained.

"Have we met, Sir Ambarsan?"

"No ma'am. It is just not difficult to recognize the queen daughter of the Benevolent Lion."

Tagwen narrowed her eyes and pressed the blade under his chin. He did not flinch. She looked over his armaments: a small dagger in his right hand, a bow strapped to his back. The insignia of three crossed arrows atop a leaf was burned into his leather cuirass — the Mark of the Outriders. A slight wave of relief washed through her. "Let us talk," she replied, sheathing her sword. She then motioned to Breccan to take control of the camp and reorganize the men.

"Right then, back to yer posts! Brought ten of ya and he bested the lot," Breccan guffawed.

Tagwen brought Ualan to an edge of the camp where a log had been set and motioned for him to sit, which he did. His appearance was austere, but his warm copper skin enriched in the glow of the firelight, and the indiscriminate strands of grey in his long, rugged, umber hair and beard glinted sporadically, giving him a rather youthful cast despite the creases around his eyes.

"What precisely is your business out in these wilds?" he asked.

"You mentioned that we are not in a safe location. Why?" Tagwen replied in answer.

Ualan relented. "I have been sent to hunt someone, some… thing. It has plagued various parts of this continent and has been rumored to have traveled this way toward Brierhïl."

"What is it, exactly?"

"No one is sure. It has been described as a man, though less so if you have the misfortune of living to tell the tale. It is mostly man, with eyes like the blackest night — no whites in them. He is said to travel with a sort of animal — think a wolf, though larger, and with no remorse — a 'warg', should you be acquainted with those beasts."

Tagwen scratched her brow. "I did not see its eyes, but I did witness such a pair, Sir Ambarsan. They stood for but a moment under the moonlight and stared in my direction, making no movement, and as soon as I turned from them and back again, they'd vanished."

Ualan stood and looked at Tagwen in disbelief. "You have seen them? They left you and your men alone? When and where?"

Tagwen looked up at Ualan's puzzled gaze and nodded. "I saw them two nights ago on the hill of the Greyrest a few hours' ride away from the Road's fork. They made no advance toward me or my men, though my men did report seeing dark figures quite a few times during our journey. I tried to be reassuring that it was merely the plague of exhaustion that was casting these nightmarish figures, but now I fear we may have all seen the pair," she replied.

"What are the men of the sea doing so far away from their chosen terrain, Queen Braithe? Why are you out here?"

Tagwen motioned again for Ualan to sit, and he did.

"How well do you know these lands, Sir Ambarsan?"

"They are as known to me as if they were the lines on my own hands."

"Are you aware of a means of crossing along the Irrihead?"

"Why? What interests do you maintain? With no disrespect, I feel that I have answered your questions but received no such acknowledgment of my own."

Tagwen took a breath before responding. "The elves of Brierhïl, should they even still exist, are in danger, Sir Ambarsan. My men and I have endured the Road from Marez to Middling and to where we sit before you at present. The kings of Middling and Oburim have reason to believe that the elves have made advances to claim the territory of the Greyrest, and furthermore, the whole of Vostheloren. I did not believe these accusations and we escaped from Westvein to forewarn the elves that cavalries are making haste toward their home. Your arrival may be the first turn of luck, Outrider. I sit before you in hopes that your knowledge of this land extends somehow into a part of the world unexplored by man, so that I may try to save them."

Ualan looked away for a moment and hooked his hand on his cape's collar, taking a deep, contemplative breath. Tagwen watched a pained expression come over his face as he closed his eyes in seeming reverence.

"My familiarity extends beyond their borders, Queen Braithe." He pulled on the brooch that was holding his cloak together and handed it to her. The gold metal glittered in her hands as the light highlighted its intricacies. The breastpin was in the shape of a symmetrical weeping willow surrounded by a ring with twelve cordate leaves etched in a radial pattern. The roots of the willow wound down and formed the elongated pin, and along its length, a method of characters was engraved that Tagwen did not understand but recognized.

Ualan continued. "I am one of three Outriders chosen to protect the elven lands. I have lived amongst them, learned their tongue, and shared in their culture. They are amongst those closest to those I have had the fortune to consider my brethren. I am risking the whole of my Order in disclosing this information to you. If what you say is true, I will bring you and your men through Brierhïl and to the elven valley. What evidence do you have of this alleged treachery?"

Tagwen rifled through the satchel she kept on her person and produced the secret journal entry from King Dùghlan.

"This is the only proof I possess, other than the words of myself and my captain, as we were privy to the council's discussions. There were only representatives of the kingdoms of men present. The dwarves had been excluded from the meeting for their supposed relations to the elves — or so I now assume," she said.

Ualan took the letter and read in the king's own handwriting the open call to betray the land's treaty. His expression changed to one of disgust.

Handing it back, he said, "Mortifying the gall that men possess. It is a great fortune that Yeacralas holds you at the helm, my lady. I will guide your men into the valley of Thrindūl. I cannot make any sort of promise that we will be well received. The elves may not take kindly to one they have trusted now bringing in a band of outsiders to their sanctuary, regardless of your intent."

Thrindūl, she repeated in her head, intrigued by the utterance of a name she had never heard.

Tagwen bowed her head in thanks. "I expected no such promise. I am grateful and indebted to you for your assistance, Sir Ambarsan."

"I share in the gratitude, and please, call me Ualan, Queen Braithe." With a smile, he stood, bowed toward Tagwen, and continued, "If you'll permit me, I would like to remain within your camp to keep watch. Because you have been sighted by this Hunter, I can only assume it has targeted you and your men. It is likely to show up again if you appear vulnerable, and I now have the duty to safely deliver your company to Thrindūl."

"Of course," she nodded. "I would appreciate your presence, given your knowledge of the entity. Though I must extend an apology — my men and I have not had means for resupplying ourselves much since our abrupt departure from Westvein. We are approximately set for two additional days, provided we observe the rationing we have implemented."

Ualan extended his hand to retrieve his pin, and Tagwen handed it back. He took her hand in his to help her stand. "I have no need of being cared for whilst in your company, Queen Braithe."

"You do not answer to me, Outrider. You may call me Tagwen."

Ualan bowed once more and dismissed himself to take a position amongst Tagwen's men for the remaining hours of the evening watch.

Tagwen stood alone as she watched the Outrider peruse their camp. Her men eyed him warily, but Ualan seemed to pay them no mind. She took a deep breath, the billowing fog of her exhale drifting toward the night sky. She watched its dissipation and pulled her cloak more tightly around herself.

Breccan approached and offered a plate of dinner: dried haddock and bread with a skin of wine. "Hungry?" she asked.

Tagwen took the meal happily and sat upon the log at her feet. "Thank you," she nodded.

"What's his deal?" Breccan asked, gesturing toward Ualan.

"He's going to help us find the elves," Tagwen answered between bites.

"That seems wildly convenient," Breccan said with suspicion. "Can we trust him?"

Tagwen set her plate upon her lap and looked out to the camp. Ualan was now chatting with Lachlann, the soldier on duty.

"He bears the Mark, and I know Outriders do not take kindly to impersonators," she said. "He claims to have lived amongst them. Called their home by a name I've never heard." She swallowed a gulp of the wine and leaned close to whisper in Breccan's ear. "And he has a pin of theirs… and it's got the same sort of symbols like the letter we found."

Breccan looked at Tagwen. "You think it's elvish?"

Tagwen shrugged. "If he's not lying, it is."

Breccan leaned away. "Hmm — maybe they do still live. I mean, men still live, ya know? I guess if they were to interact with anyone other than Addie, it would probably be an Outrider. Doesn't explain Lady Dùghlan, but we don't have much else to go on."

Tagwen finished her meal and sighed contentedly. "I hope you're right," she agreed.

"Well, I'll keep an eye on him, anyway. Never had a problem with Outriders before, but ya can never be too careful." She then took Tagwen's empty plate. "You should find some sleep. We'll be alright," she reassured.

For the first night in a long while, Tagwen finally found rest and woke to Breccan informing her that the party was ready to depart. She quickly dressed herself and emerged from her tent to be greeted by the full chill of the morning. A light dusting of snow was circling through the frosty atmosphere, and the sky was filled with clouds. Tagwen breathed in the fresh cold air, stretched out her arms, and embraced winter's presence. She looked to see Ualan returning from around the hill's bend.

"It would behoove you and your men to cross the river instead of going around it. There is a bridge about ten miles Southeast of here which will prove to be faster, provided we can actually get across," he said.

"Why would we not be able?" asked Breccan.

"It was not built to carry a company of men, horses, and wagons, but we may manage if we take caution."

Many of the men looked quite unsure, but Tagwen nevertheless said, "Take us to it and we will find a way."

Ualan nodded lightly to the queen. "Follow me, then, and remain vigilant. Snowfall is likely to gather, and it will hinder the path ahead. Stay focused."

Tagwen repeated the instruction to her men, and the party formed a line to follow the Outrider, with Tagwen at the head and Breccan bringing up the rear guard. Within the hour, the snow began to swirl around them in a flurry, which distorted their view of the terrain. Ualan moved to lead them along the Irrihead's length to maintain a better sense of their surroundings. The charge of the rivers was near-deafening as their waves crashed upon the rock beds that made up their basins — it was dizzying to the outsiders. Tagwen looked behind herself and halted the procession when she saw Sergeant Catach losing grip on his reins.

She dismounted Seasaìdh and gently helped Lachlann down from Baringr, his horse. Lachlann stumbled in the collecting snow on the ground and heaved into a cluster of frosting reeds.

Ualan walked over to them and looked at Tagwen. "Help me prop him up against something."

Together they laid him against a boulder.

"Here, drink," Ualan insisted, handing Lachlann a flask.

Lachlann shakily drank from the vessel and color appeared to return immediately to his face. He sat up and sniffed the mouth of the bottle. "What-what is this? I've never had anything like it."

Ualan smirked, "Elvish calming remedy."

Tagwen looked over to Ualan and mouthed, "Thank you."

Ualan smiled and procured a small pouch from his knapsack. "Now this is not the most comfortable solution, but it will help," he said, as he broke off a piece of beeswax and split it in two, chewed on both pieces to make them malleable, and fit them to Lachlann's ears.

"What a relief! Thank you!" Lachlann shouted and Ualan put a finger up to his own lips to caution the soldier to remain quieter — to which Lachlann nodded sheepishly.

Tagwen and Ualan helped the sergeant up and onto Baringr and ordered those around him to be mindful and guide him as they continued.

"If anyone else begins to feel the same, speak up. Waiting until it is too late is only going to cause more of a delay and potentially put us all at risk," Ualan warned the company.

Breccan pulled up next to Tagwen. "If I say I'm feeling ill, do I get a swig of whatever was in that flask?" she whispered playfully.

Tagwen snorted under her breath and nudged Breccan back into line, though she too was curious of its contents.

Fortunately, during the ensuing hours, no other members became addled by the noise of the rivers, as it muddled itself into a dull hum for most of them. Snowfall also contributed to the dampening of the noise, which they were grateful for, despite the sting of the cold.

As they neared the fifth hour, they at last came upon the bridge: a modest timbered construction whose planks were deteriorating in the center, thanks to the relentless beating of the river's waters.

Ualan addressed Tagwen, "I shall cross first to test the boards. It has seen some harsh weather since my last traversal."

Tagwen nodded.

He leapt onto the first board, eliciting audible gasps from some who were watching. He kept in this fashion across the whole of the bridge, and it held. Though impressively timeworn, the bridge hardly shuddered at Ualan's forceful crossing. It was not a large overpass — as this width of the river did not call for an extended length — but its duty was heavily challenged above the Irrihead's roar.

Ualan made his way back to the onlookers. "A bit unorthodox, but I suspect it will hold if you do not linger upon it. We'll take one man and wagon across at a time, to be prudent," he suggested.

Tagwen turned to the company. "Alright then, we'll start in order with Grannd and Eldropp. Everyone else will follow suit one at a time." She looked at Sergeant Catach to confirm he had heard, and he nodded.

Ualan crossed again and guided each member along from

the other side. First the Queensmen: Beitris Grannd and Thesden Eldropp. Following them were the Corporals: the MacLeòir brothers, Daniel and Brian, Callon Hellig, Ailbert Roid, Iòsaph Ruiseal, and Samuel MacCullach. Sergeant Lachlann was followed by Breccan, and Sergeant Sìne Matharnach was the last of the guard to cross with the final wagon.

Sìne had made it to the halfway point of the bridge when suddenly one of the wagon wheels snagged in a crack in the wood. Her horse, Aelin, began to struggle against the impediment and whinnied in distress.

"The wagon's caught!" Sìne cried, looking to Tagwen behind her. Tagwen leapt from Seasaidh and stepped delicately onto the bridge.

"What are you doing?!" Ualan shouted, but Tagwen could not hear him. She moved briskly to reach Sìne, whose horse was now in a full panic. Tagwen approached the wagon and saw that the wood was beginning to splinter under the wheel. The weight was degrading its integrity, threatening to send the whole bridge and those on it into the water.

"Let her go!" Tagwen ordered, and Sìne unlatched Aelin from the carriage. Aelin promptly took off across the remainder of the stretch, leaving the two women stranded in the middle.

"Help pull forward when I say!" Tagwen yelled, and Sìne nodded, the water's spray catching her in the face as she held onto the wagon's arms.

Tagwen crouched by the lodged wheel and affixed her hands around its felloes. "Pull!" she called out and attempted to hoist it out of the crevice. Both women simultaneously lifted and pulled, but as they did, the mangled plank fractured under the stress, sending half of the board rushing into the rapids. The resulting free water began to flow up through the hole, causing the other wheel to begin slipping.

"Go!" Tagwen yelled at Sĭne.

"My queen! I—"

"Go! Let go!" Tagwen bellowed, the echoes of the whitewater blurred with the shrieks of Seasaìdh behind her as she held onto the wagon to let Sĭne move out and away.

Sĭne dashed across the bridge, the sounds of planks squeaking against the strain following her stride. Ualan and Breccan pulled her onto land and into safety, and Breccan grabbed her by the shoulders.

"Why did you leave her?!" she screamed.

With water from the river mixing with tears, Sĭne replied, "Captain, she ordered me to!"

Breccan moved the sergeant aside and made for the bridge, but Ualan grabbed her as the water rushed with a sudden force, causing the rapids to haze around the entire passage, obscuring the view of her queen.

Tagwen closed her eyes and braced for the onslaught of waves, determined to release the wagon once it passed, or if it threatened to drag her from the bridge, but the waves did not come. She felt no water coursing over her person, though she heard the rapids misting about. She opened her eyes to see the water swelling to hold the wagon in place, enveloping the two of them as if they were in a sort of capsule. She let go of the wheel to see that it was holding and stood up to see that the bridge was no longer buckling under the weight. She looked around in amazement when she caught sight of a vaguely glimmering light behind her, beside what she barely perceived as Seasaìdh. The mare then emerged from the rolling spray and nudged Tagwen to encourage her onward. With a delicate push, the wagon drew itself forward, the water appearing to carry it along.

After a few agonizing moments had passed, the wagon, Tagwen, and Seasaìdh emerged from the haze and the waters calmed to their natural state. The company on land parted so they could finish crossing, and Breccan raced to her queen's side. "Are you mad?!" she shouted as she looked over Tagwen to find any signs of distress.

"I am quite alright, actually. Is everyone okay?" Tagwen asked.

"What happened out there?" Ualan asked, his gaze alternating between Tagwen and the river.

"I-we nearly lost our queen, that's what happened," Breccan snarled.

"Captain, I am fine." Tagwen laid a calming hand on Breccan's shoulder. "Please. I am here. We are all here. By some gift, it appears we have survived."

Breccan took a weighty deep breath and avoided Tagwen's gaze. "Yes, Your Majesty," she finally responded, taking a step back to assess the carriage and assist Sìne in harnessing Aelin.

Tagwen reached out to beckon her back but refrained midway to give Breccan space.

"In all conscience," Ualan interjected as he looked at Tagwen directly, "what transpired out there?"

"Should we have all the time in the world, I do not think I could conjure an answer for you," she said, looking across the bridge, but the light she'd seen was no longer present.

Sergeant Sĭne approached. "Your Majesty. I wish I had not abandoned your side. For that I beg your forgiveness," she said, her head bowed as she knelt in front of her queen.

Tagwen knelt in front of her. "You serve me better when you stand, Sergeant Matharnach, and especially so if you continue standing amongst us." Tagwen held out her hand and Sĭne looked up and placed her hand in Tagwen's. Her bloodshot eyes allowed the tears to fall.

"It is alright, Sĭne. We are alright," Tagwen reassured her. Sĭne nodded. Tagwen helped her sergeant to her feet and looked to the rest of her men. She saw their uncertainty as they all stood awaiting her next order. "The guidance of the sea follows us where we tread, and we must tread onward to warn our elven neighbors. Because we are Yeacralans, it is our oath to stand and protect all men and lands of Vostheloren, even if they are not our own. Are you with me?"

A collective "Yes, sir!" rang out from the gathered company and Tagwen nodded with satisfaction.

"Ualan," she said, "let us continue."

Ualan took the lead once again and the party formed a line once more — this time away from the rivers and toward the canopy of the Brierhïl Forests.

The wall of trees that comprised the entry of the elven lands was much larger up close than the men had expected.

Colossal trunks of reddish-brown fibrous bark greeted them in a formation that appeared much like ancient sentinels. A baldachin of boughs was created by two trees that were a single shade lighter than their counterparts, and their bark formed complicated arrangements of twining vines that one would need to study intently to notice. The pattering of snow stopped at the forest's edge, leaving a clear line of demarcation from the lands of men.

Ualan stopped at the obscure archway and turned to address the company. "Magnificence can give way to bewilderment. The land is unknown to you, and it is aware of this advantage. Stray not from your place in line in either thought or footsteps. We have a ways to the proper path to Thrindūl, as this weald will attempt to remind us that we do not belong. Remember why you are here, and we may be granted a pleasant entering."

"Take care of your fellow man," Tagwen added, and looked at Breccan in the back line whilst addressing everyone. "No one will be left behind."

Breccan bowed and smiled.

Through the archway, a rush of warmth that reminded Tagwen of Marez in spring swept over the company. The thick of the forest was laden with brush and varietals of mossy ground cover. Rich emerald grasses glinted in bright patches of sunlight that complemented the rust of the redwoods, as if painted by the greatest of masters. The band found themselves journeying on a smoothly paved loam path through the maze of trees. The ground was firm enough for the trample of hooves and wide enough to accommodate a procession of pairs, which helped the group feel more secure in their chances of avoiding becoming lost. Each pair of soldiers held a rope at either end — if one strayed too far from the other, the other was tasked with reining their partner back in to safety.

The air bore a noticeable petrichor, though the earth that surrounded them did not appear to have seen any recent rain. Occasional gusts of wind stirred through the boughs several meters above the forest floor, making it sound as if the grove was speaking in grumbled articulations.

Several members became spooked at the unexpected hoots of owls that rang out as if they were riding alongside the caravan, but none were ever seen. Deer, squirrels, and other small animals appeared in waves — never once being bothered by the foreigners in their domain. It seemed as if the animals had already known of the group's arrival and were watching to make sure they all kept in line.

Scattered pockets of skylight peeked through the canopy, which one would expect to give a sense of the time in the outside world, but despite the company being sure they had been in the forest the better part of a day, the sky had the distinct look of midday.

The strain of what felt like hours finally eased, as Ualan led the party into a clearing — a welcome change from the barrage of trees. Relief quickly faded, though, once they realized there were three passages before them, formed from white firs which stood shorter than the sequoias that had followed them but appeared to be much greater in number. A cover of snow laid fresh on the ground in only the glade, and a familiar chill once again wrapped itself around the entire company.

Tagwen saw that Ualan appeared stunned at the scene before him — as if this development was unexpected.

After a moment, he turned around and approached Tagwen. "We are being tested, I'm afraid."

"Tested?" she asked.

"Only one of these paths leads to the Thrindūl valley. They are never the same, and I only encountered them once in my first venture to the elven lands. Luckily, I was accompanied by an elf at the time, so the passage was made known. I fear now that my invitation into these lands is not extending to you and your company. Otherwise, I would be able to discern the true course. Each path is guarded by one of the ancient guardians of the weald. They require obedience from those who dare to enter, but I cannot recall how we make that known to them," he explained.

Tagwen pondered for a moment. "No reason to raise the alarm quite yet then. We shall rest here momentarily whilst you refresh your memory."

"Do not get comfortable — I do not trust this part of the Brierhïl, as it is known to shift."

"It does not seem to trust us either, Ualan. Please relay what it requires of us once you recollect this information. I must tend to my company," Tagwen said.

Ualan bowed and sat in front of the three pathways in quiet contemplation.

Tagwen returned to the group. "Be at ease for the moment. Eat, drink, and respect the land around you. Do not wander."

As the camp settled in the snowy clearing, Breccan came

over to Tagwen. "What's he doing? Should we not press on? Though I can't say I don't welcome the break," she said while stretching her back and nodding toward Ualan sitting idly in some type of meditative state as powder began to accumulate on his person.

"He is hopefully being granted insight into which path serves us to the elven valley," Tagwen answered.

"Is it not through the third arch?" Breccan asked.

"How do you mean?" Tagwen looked to the arches which all were thickly shadowed — no light penetrating their borders.

"There's no path down the other two, but there is in the rightmost entrance."

Tagwen narrowed her eyes to focus her sight through the portal but yielded no image of a pathway. She turned back to Breccan. "You actually see something?"

"Do you not?" Breccan countered with a raised, furrowed brow. Tagwen shook her head.

"I-I don't know if this is one of the forest's tricks, but it is as clear as your presence before me," Breccan stammered.

Tagwen held for a moment and stared at the entries. She bit at the insides of her cheek and her leg began to bounce as she sat in reflection. She steadied herself and deeply breathed in the frigid air to sober her uneasy thoughts. As she readied a response and turned back to Breccan, she was interrupted by the dulcet tones of a tenor voice rippling behind her.

Ú'alerūn u'atèro
Atèro ihlèn alœränlèn

Ú ènū arèf alè bèlïa u'tælah
Úlufèlèn œt orèbän

Ualan stood before the openings in a stance of reverence, the lucent lyrics softly flowing from his person to the adumbral gateways before them. A sudden wind howled through the clearing, and, in the song's conclusion, the shades faded to reveal the only remaining path — the third archway. Gentle hues of azure and lilac glowed within the portal, as if to another world, highlighting a cobblestone road.

With a satisfied grin, Ualan presented the revelation to the party. "We have been welcomed. The valley of Thrindūl lies just ahead."

"Glad to know I wasn't seeing things," Breccan said quietly.

"Your sight is a marvel, my friend. Forgive my distrust of my own," Tagwen apologized.

"Nothing to forgive! Better to be safe in this wily forest, eh? Are you ready? Elves. Tagwen, we're actually going to see the elves."

Tagwen tensed her shoulders, took a deep breath, and held it in her cheeks before letting the air out while nodding. "Let's hope the forest's reception of us extends inward."

"Friends of Yeacralas! Let us not find ourselves stagnant in this clearing when the way has been made known to us!" Ualan proudly insisted.

With obvious wonder, the company made themselves ready, and with apprehension, followed their queen and the Outrider through the arboreal moon gate as the first interlopers welcomed into the valley of Thrindūl by the Forest's guardians themselves.

4

THRINDŪL

Crossing through the threshold revealed a vast valley that appeared larger than the known border of the Forest, though no man of the outside world could be certain. The atmosphere shared the same weather as the rest of the continent, but the snowfall in the vale shimmered softly here. Ahead of the party, on a cliffside, stood a citadel with a sizable set of stairs winding up and behind the cascading waterfall to the entrance. Water from the falls collected in a substantial, and remarkably clear, pool below the precipice of the acropolis — its hue that of an astonishing ottanio blue. Small trees, comparable to wisteria, were in full bloom, despite it being the outset of winter. Swaths of their pastel lavender spread throughout the land; the blooms vivid against the white of the surrounding snow. Around the flora were innumerable stretches of white firs that the party had already become acquainted with. As they made their way to the base of the stairs, it appeared that there was no one in the valley.

Tagwen instructed her men to remain together while she, Breccan, and Ualan went ahead to meet with the elves. The hope was that their presence would be less intimidating than a full company of armed men knocking at their door. The soldiers were warned not to venture beyond this post, and not to respond defensively should they be confronted. Sergeant Catach was set in charge, and the three made their way up the earthen steps.

At the entrance, they were met with towering iron-smithed doors that bore patterns of abstracted plant life and nature, with sinuous and flowing motifs mirrored between them. Ualan stood closer to the doors and unpinned the brooch from his cloak. He inserted the pin like a latchkey into a hidden lock amongst the metal vines. A cacophony of hundreds of bolts began to release, and he took a step back so as not to be in the way of the marvel that was unfolding before them. The doors glided open inward to reveal a foyer set as a garden. A grand, circular stained-glass window, depicting the same ring and leaves as Ualan's brooch, was set into the domed ceiling, resembling a halo above the centerpiece of the room — a weeping willow.

The tree stood approximately seven feet tall and was just as broad at its widest spread. Its leaves were a soft grey-green and toward the tips of the drooping branches became an ashen white. The bark was a beautiful, muted taupe with the lines of its deep furrows glinting like dainty veins of silver. The tree's roots were oddly symmetrical in pattern. They wound as if plaited from the base of the trunk and stretched across the ground. Encircling the tree's plot on the floor were stone pathways that created connections through the whole of the nursery. All manner of flowers and verdure were decoratively grown along the tended earth in the floor. Vines crept their way up the thick marble columns that served as partitions. The walls behind the columns were floor to ceiling windows — nearly fifteen feet tall — which invited an ample amount of sunlight.

Tagwen and Breccan stood just inside the opening, completely dumbfounded. Ualan smirked at their expressions, knowing all too well how it felt to see Thrindūl for the first time. "Would you believe me if I told you the rest of the keep is even more marvelous?" he asked.

"More so than all… this?" Breccan asked as she gestured wildly with her arms.

"This is the matter of dreams. I cannot comprehend that this exists," Tagwen remarked, staring up at the mosaic in the planchement.

"Well, then, that makes us neighbors in the land of disbelief." A profoundly deep bass voice spoke from the mezzanine in the northern part of the room, startling them, and the trio looked up.

In the balcony stood a tower of an elf. His enormous physique was draped graciously in rich viridian robes that matched his similarly emerald eyes; long pointed ears cut through his shining gray hair that cascaded down his shoulders in alternating curl patterns, framing his face. He looked as though he was carved of the finest polished obsidian; each facet of his features reflecting the glow of the light that surrounded him. If the three of them had not felt small in this room, they certainly now felt small in his presence.

Stunned into silence, the two parties stared at one another.

"Well?" he finally demanded.

Ualan took a step toward the veranda where the elf stood, presumably to provide an explanation for their presence, but the elf raised his hand to stop him. "Ú ènū alœr æs üv egèïl," he said sternly, causing Ualan to back away as if he had been reprimanded.

The elf then turned to look at the two women. "I prefer to not be kept waiting by those who dare enter my house uninvited."

Tagwen stepped around the willow to be in a proper view and knelt on her right knee in a formal salute, her right hand in a fist across her chest. "Forgive our unwelcome presence, sir. I am Tagwen Braithe, Queen of Yeacralas and Daughter of the Benevolent Lion. I am here to request an audience with you and your people so that I may thwart the efforts of other men who seek to bring destruction upon you."

The elf straightened, his facial expression unchanged. "Do you know not whose house you have entered, queen of men?"

Tagwen's mouth lingered open for a moment. "I did not think myself privy to such information in relying on the graces of this Outrider's guidance," she answered meekly.

"But you think yourself privy to step into our territory?" he asked calmly.

"No disrespect intended, sir, but we've been on the run, at her behest, to provide the elves with a warning that men are coming with armies because the other kingdoms live in delusion," Breccan interjected as she stood next to her kneeling queen.

The elf tilted his head slightly as he looked at Breccan, then turned to Ualan. "Færūn èlasïl?" he asked.

Ualan turned to Breccan in confusion and quickly scanned her person before turning back. "Œnè tèūlæhœv," he answered.

Breccan spoke once again. "I'm not sure of the custom here, but I would generally assume that speaking of people in their presence when they do not share your tongue is… well, boorish."

Both Ualan and Tagwen (who had stood), slowly turned to Breccan, eyes as wide as saucers, barely breathing in anticipation of the wrath they were certain her words would incur.

Instead, the elf grinned. "The Forest spoke of your fire, Captain Kenefick. It does not disappoint."

Breccan bowed. "And may my queen and I be made aware of whom the Forest has spoken to?" she asked.

"You stand in the House of Eilfaren. I am thusly Faldïr Eilfaren, Twelfth Son of the name, Lord of Thrindūl and Protector of the Ebrïhèïlè … or 'Brierhïl' in the unlearned tongue of men." He turned to Tagwen. "Your captain serves you well, Champion of the Sea, as do the rest of your men."

"I am incredibly grateful for them all, Lord Eilfaren," Tagwen agreed. "I apologize for bringing a band of men to your door, uninvited and in violation of a treaty long enacted, but I did so with the intention of providing support to the elves. I believe the men of Oburim and Middling to be mistaken about your people and the situation at hand. In asking for your forgiveness, I also ask for your reception of the company I have brought here today, if for no longer than the evening — merely to catch our breath before removing ourselves from your land. They have traveled a long and arduous way at my command."

"Then you will be delighted to join me, your men, and my house for a feast in the courtyard."

Faldïr turned to Ualan with a smile. "You really should have just skipped the stairs, old friend," he teased, and Ualan grinned. He looked again at Tagwen. "I had been walking the vale with my wife when we came upon your companions. It is fortunate for your men that she was there, as I was less than pleased to see a rogue horde of armed men in our realm. In her wisdom, she saw they were weary, that somehow, they had been accepted by the Forest, and when they spoke of Ualan and your quest, we knew they were to be cared for. It was simply a matter of finding where you three had gone. I hope you'll forgive my cheek in our acquaintance, but I cannot have men walking about thinking there would be no consequence — regardless, that one of our own had brought them." He nodded toward Ualan.

"Thank you, sir, and there is nothing to forgive," Tagwen replied.

Faldïr clasped his hands together then spread his arms wide to gesture to the curved staircases on either side of the balcony. "Shall we?" he invited, then left through the doors behind him.

Tagwen let out an audible puff of air, as if she had been holding her breath the entirety of the conversation and placed her right hand on her chest to slow her racing heart.

"Did I not say everything would be alright?" Breccan quipped.

Tagwen inhaled slowly, and on exhale, whispered, "We made it."

"Quite the relief to see him so amicable. Come then, friends! An elven feast is something not to be missed!" Ualan shouted, already halfway up the rightmost stair.

Before ascending the marbled steps, Tagwen grabbed Breccan's arm. "We truly would not be here without you. Thank you. If the Forest knew anything of your fire, it would tremble in your wake." She smiled with gratitude.

Breccan saluted out of habit and then snorted, realizing that her gesture seemed silly. "Now, don't put me out of sorts, we've only just arrived," she blushed.

Tagwen bowed her head with a smile and gestured for her captain to walk ahead of her. Elegant, blond oak double doors, with a hand-carved depiction of the land's sigil and foliage, met them at the landing. Its border was surrounded by all manner of sprawling ivy that thoughtlessly covered what Tagwen swore were runes of the dwarvish language, Krarnolim. A delicate turning of a knob released both doors and they swung open to unveil an adorned garden courtyard filled with elves and the men they'd left outside all now in lifted spirits. Most were feasting, many danced to the tune of lyres, and others appeared engaged in deep conversation.

Tagwen and Breccan beamed as they stepped into the open air and onto the flagstone-patterned walkway.

"Now this, this is Thrindūl. It is a marvel to see men sharing in this moment. The significance of your presence here is… historic," Ualan reflected as he welcomed Tagwen and Breccan.

The footpath was bordered by spherical hedges and well-trimmed trees of the wisteria plant they had seen earlier. Both plants lined the stretch that led into the wider opening where the crowd had been gathered. Trellises in the main courtyard were decorated with little glass baubles that held small lighted candles in them, and across their tops and sides, climbing hydrangea caressed their framework, shielding the party from the snow. Bordering the enclosure were other various palatial buildings, all unique from one another, and one for each of the cardinal directions — the structure they'd entered from being the southern. Sitting in the center, where everyone congregated, was a sizable live-edge white oak table positioned lengthwise from East to West, filled with a rainbow assortment of prepared dishes and bowls of pristine fruits, vegetables, grains, and breads. A variety of glass and metal goblets and pitchers sat filled with water and a gorgeous, effervescent, rosate liquid. At the western head of the table sat Faldïr, and next to him, a fair, graying, golden-haired elf maiden — presumably his wife.

Faldïr spotted the latecomers while in mid-conversation and smiled. "Alas! Our most-awaited guests have arrived! Your Grace, Captain, and my dear friend, please join us," he gestured to his side.

For a moment, the conversations lessened, as all stopped to witness their arrival. Two seats sat vacant to Faldïr's right, and to the left of his wife sat a singular seat for Ualan. The three approached eagerly and sat. Faldïr stood, and in his silence, commanded the regard of all the crowd.

"Today is a feast unlike any that we have partaken in, or that any of our forefathers have known for many generations before us. The Forest, and those who guard it, have accepted an unlikely company into our midst. I, personally, after some reflection and discourse," he paused to beam at his wife, "have come to consider this extraordinary moment as a sign of a better future, for elves and mankind — a collective future, of sorts."

Faldïr reached down for his chalice and raised it, evoking the same response from all at the table. He then turned and held out his free hand to Tagwen, who accepted, and she stood. "In the face of uncertainty, we have seen a leader of men bravely disregard the prejudices of old to help those whom they have never met." Raising his chalice higher, he turned to Tagwen and toasted, "To Queen Braithe and her men, and to all the elves of the Ebrïhèïlè, may this meeting be fruitful for all our peoples, Úel anelū, atèro, alè ebæl." He paused to translate, "For love, forest, and family," and smiled at Breccan, who raised her glass and returned his smile.

The elves at the table replied to the toast with, "Ètalæg u'atèro!" and the company offered a pattering of "Cheers!" or "Here, here!" As they all drank, Tagwen and Faldïr sat.

"Goodness!" Tagwen marveled. "This wine has the most enchanting taste. Might I inquire as to what it is?"

Faldïr laughed, "It amazes me how others experience this!" He leaned in conspiratorially. "We call it 'adagèsè o'rüla' — 'a calming remedy'." He chuckled. "Truly, though, it is delightful. It is from the Ètūgūr Úcèsah that grows in the valley. 'Healing purple flower', as it is known in your tongue. It has many uses — most notably this honeyed concoction."

"Elvish calming remedy, is it?" Tagwen eyed Ualan, who pretended not to hear her as he drank.

"Our vintner is quite gifted at preserving the craft. He follows a precise recipe that hasn't changed in the near thousand years since it was perfected here," Faldïr's wife leaned in to explain.

"Where are my manners?!" Faldïr shouted, setting down his glass and grabbing his wife's hand. "Queen Braithe, allow me to introduce my life's light, Lady Ylerïan Eilfaren," he cooed, taking her hand to his lips.

"Oh now, the flowers have sweetened you markedly this evening," Ylerïan giggled, her cheeks emulating the color of the wine against the rest of her porcelain face and revealing the gentle folds of skin around her motherly eyes. Her exquisite gown, though simple, effortlessly mirrored the same green of her irises and grandeur of her husband's robes. She looked at Tagwen and smiled. "Forgive him, Queen Braithe. It is so wonderful to meet you. Your men have spoken so highly of you and your admirable captain here. 'Breccan', is that right?" she asked the captain, her gaze holding Breccan's.

"Yes ma'am," Breccan nodded.

"Nala'èvanegtas, dear ones. Many beautiful greetings," Ylerïan hailed to the two women.

"It is a privilege to be welcomed into your realm and your house, Lady Eilfaren, and an honor to make your acquaintance," Tagwen said. "Though, I do wish it were under better circumstances."

"None of that now, my friend," Faldïr interrupted, while

topping everyone's glass around him. "Let us revel in this beautiful moment. All too soon it will be time to discuss the darkness that lies ahead."

"We shall find the light together," Ualan raised his glass to initiate an intimate toast amongst the five of them.

"Better than that, mærhïl. We will *be* the light," Faldïr responded, and the rest fell in agreement with raised glasses.

Festivities went on into the eve and, toward the winding down of the banquet, Tagwen noticed Ylerïan pause and wince as if caught by pain. After a moment of regaining composure, she stood and regarded her dinner companions. "This truly has been a magnificent meeting, and I hope you'll excuse my abrupt departure. I've merely become rather tired and think I'll withdraw for the evening."

"Ú'anelū, are you alright?" Faldïr asked with concern. "I shall accompany you," he added, beginning to stand.

"Darling, please. I am quite alright. Tired is all. Please, stay and enjoy this time with our newfound friends," she said, resting a hand on his shoulder to encourage him to remain seated.

Ylerïan excused herself and walked to the eastern building, and Faldïr watched as she left, turning back with knitted brows. He leaned over to Ualan and said something in the elvish language that Tagwen could not hear, which prompted Ualan to follow Lady Eilfaren.

"Your heart carries more troubles than it needs to hold, queen of men," Faldïr said to Tagwen. "Think nothing of it. If something is wrong, it will be mended," he assured her.

"I do hope we have not overstayed our welcome, Lord Eilfaren," she said.

"It would be made known if you had. As it is, I am insisting that you and your company retire here for the evening. Your horses have all been stabled and the western manor holds plenty of accommodations that dream of finally hosting long-awaited guests. I do not wish to end the evening on a somber note, so we will commence discussions in the morning. Hope tells us we have some time to spare, yes?" Faldïr asked.

Tagwen nodded and looked out to the courtyard where both men and elves were sitting around a fire, teaching one another songs, and telling tales of their respective lands. Even Breccan and Callon were relating stories of Kirion Rovicus — the fabled Captain of the Yeacralan Navy — and how he bested Bhaudr the Slayer, chief of the Rogues of the Black Isle. The crowd applauded at the conclusion of their story, and the next participant, an elf, sang a tuning note to prepare their voice, which felt as spellbinding as the wine tasted.

Faldïr leaned over to Tagwen and pointed to them. "Ahh, see what you would miss if you left? That is Ègúlet, the finest song keeper of our time. Listen," he said, leaning back in his seat to take in the melody.

In times where all were one
Storms and darkness sat at bay
The waters, then, flowed peacefully
And all flourished in light of day

No man, nor elf, nor dwarf sat alone
No fear of the cold gripped the eternals' souls
Beings of fire called this land their home
Creatures of gloom hid in their shadowy holes

In times where all were one
We did not fear the sound of drums
And the inseparable had, not yet, come undone
Warned to hide when the storm finally comes

Quaked, the land then frayed
Darkness, storms, and fire
Destroyed all in their way
Sowing the seeds of needless ire

When the walls of hatred break
Finally ending the futile war
The lands will once again quake
And all will be one, once more

Ègúlet had begun in their native tongue, whose name had been revealed to Tagwen as "Lènagïlen." They then translated the song with the same fervor and panache as their first performance for those of their audience who spoke the common language.

"I would like to think, queen of men, that this may be the start to ending the war between our peoples," said Faldïr.

"The war between elves and the Yeacralans ended with

Ellingrath's Treaty, did it not?" Tagwen asked, affronted by the thought that this was untrue.

"Why then, over two-hundred years later, do men and elves still hold ambivalence in their hearts?" Faldïr asked.

Tagwen hesitated, relieving her tongue's need to defend her people as she weighed Faldïr's words. "Your question challenges me, Lord Eilfaren. I fear my having held no opinion of elves may count as the same as those who hold hatred, forefront. You were but myth and legend. Nearly every man I knew had little to believe of elves, for none had been seen in the entirety of my life — nor my parents' or their parents' lives. I was moved to protect after hearing men's call for injustice, but I must now admit I was unaware of what I was protecting. I regret that it is only my witness of your existence that has changed my heart," she confessed.

"Perhaps our being neighbors in the land of disbelief is precisely where we needed to be to see one another," Faldïr suggested, and held his chalice toward her, eliciting one last intimate salutatory gesture. He swallowed the remainder of his wine in a single gulp and set the cup on the table. "Well, I think the night ends here for me. Your men have been welcomed to the western wing as provided. Any room is available to you, so long as it has not been claimed, I suppose. Though, I do recommend the last one on the left of the third floor — most beautiful of the house, in my opinion," he offered.

"I appreciate your kindness in allowing my men and I refuge," Tagwen smiled and nodded.

Faldïr bowed his head slightly, then stood and made his way to the eastern building. It was only then Tagwen noticed they had been the last in the courtyard, aside from two elves who were still tending the fire and gazing up at the moonlight. She stood and stretched, her body aching from the wear of the day, and made her way into the manor.

The building stood three stories tall. Columns entangled in grapevines bordered the entrance. Carved stone steps led up to a set of doors similar to those installed in the southern observatory, and as Tagwen suspected, the border surrounding them held runes of the dwarvish language, Krarnolim, that translated:

NO HARM MAY ENTER WITHIN

She entered freely and smiled in relief that all her men had passed through this way.

Windows of mosaicked colors lined the western half of the first floor. They maintained no discernible pattern, but the moonlight shining within shed their prismatic glow upon the interior. Tagwen was faced with a line of doors, which she assumed to all be rooms, and a set of stairs on either end of the hall. She ascended the rightmost steps and noticed the second floor was much like the first, though slightly smaller. She finally reached the third floor and saw that it held but four rooms. At the end of the hallway, at the room which Faldïr had recommended, stood an elven guard. Tagwen approached and, in silence, the guard handed her a key. He looked young. His long reddish hair was braided ceremonially, his face rather slender, with soft eyes, despite their attempt at displaying an indifference toward the human's presence, and a single freckle nestled on his left cheek.

"Thank you, I do hope you have not waited here long," she said.

The guard did not acknowledge her.

"I understand," she said. "Thank you for caring for us in your home."

He turned and left.

Tagwen inserted the key and entered a clean and open space. A single bed with plush bedding was set in the northern part of the room, which looked to have her belongings already set upon its edge. Subtle lamplights and foliage adorned the bedside tables, and bath accommodations could be seen through an archway in the eastern wall. The magnificence that Faldïr hinted at was hidden behind a set of curtains alongside the western facade. Behind the shades stood a wall of windowed balcony doors, revealing a breathtaking view of the internal forest beset with snow. Though fatigued, Tagwen could not resist the moment of serenity. She grabbed a lamplight from the nearest table and opened the doors, stepping into winter's night. She set the lamp on the balustrade and enjoyed the twinkling glow against the passing flakes. Rustling of the trees did not demand worry here. She welcomed the gentle sounds as she closed her eyes and breathed in the harmony.

However, rustling then became shuffling, and Tagwen

opened her eyes to see below her three individuals emerging from the Forest — two of which looked to be carrying the third. She held up the light and squinted in an attempt to see more clearly. One of the men was Ualan.

Tagwen rushed inside and closed the balcony doors. Taking the lamplight with her, she ran out to the courtyard. Snowfall made it difficult to see the surrounding area as she scanned for the trio's whereabouts. Shadows of tracks that were quickly disappearing caught Tagwen's light and they led her to the eastern estate. The structure was a castle in its own right and much larger than the others in the shared courtyard. Up close, the manor was rather antiquated. Its construction resembled ancestral high and well-fortified builds of Man in the early Reconciliatory Age. Stonework and woodwork intermingled to create what Tagwen realized, to be an impregnable palisade. The illusion of a building faded as she entered through the stockade gate that had been left unlocked. Beyond was a darkened tree tunnel enclosing a path. Tagwen saw that the footpath's tracks led inward, so she followed.

The tunnel, to her relief, was not long, and she was met with the true estate at the crest of a hill. Lights emanated from inside, and as Tagwen approached, she noticed the door slightly ajar. This estate's construction was like the grandeur of the faux facade — embattled and towering with massive moss-covered stone and woodwork. What vexed her, though, was the inescapable thought that this magnificence inspired the baronial nature of Francus Castle, as if the mansion in Middling was this palace's miniature. Their architecture was identical, from the four towers to the pattern of the rock-laying. This estate was simply larger… much larger.

Tagwen carefully edged her way through the door as quietly as she was able and entered the castle's enclosed atrium. Along the square floor lay a tiled sigil of the Eilfaren house. The opening was bordered by carved stone arcades on all sides.

How is this possible? she thought as she caught glimpses of the various walkways leading to different castle wings. Though mystified, she was comforted by the walls' lack of garish paintings.

A faint, bloodcurdling scream gripped Tagwen's spine as she crept in search of the elusive party. The sound echoed from the passage to the northern tower. She blew out her lamp's candle and left the lucerna on the floor by the entrance. Wails intensified as Tagwen drew nearer to the base of the tower.

"You must hold him down!" she heard Ylerïan command.

"I am trying!" That voice belonged to Ualan.

With caution, Tagwen ascended the twisting staircase to the fourth floor, struggling to keep her winded breaths and wobbling legs from revealing her presence. Peering through the crack in the door, she saw Ualan and Ylerïan struggling to pin someone to a table. The individual's howls as Ylerïan attempted to cleanse their wound pierced Tagwen's heart. Intense pain caused the man on the table to rip away from Ualan's hold and Ualan stumbled backward and fell to the ground, revealing the injured party.

"Tolmach?" she gasped.

Ualan heard her and turned. "Well, don't just stand there, come in here and help!" he shouted at her.

Tagwen burst through the door, helped Ualan to stand, and rushed to Hubertus' side.

"What do you need?" Tagwen asked Ylerïan, who was frantically attempting to clean a profusely bleeding gash on Hubertus' shoulder.

"Hold him down!" she demanded, and Tagwen pressed Hubertus' free shoulder and chest to the table.

"Pin his legs," Tagwen said to Ualan, who moved to comply.

"Braithe," Hubertus whimpered as his unfocused eyes attempted to hold her image. "You made it," he rasped, falling faint and limp.

"Tolmach?" She leaned down to check his breath. "He's still breathing," she said with urgency.

"Quickly then, help me cleanse this," Ylerïan requested, handing Tagwen a soaked cloth.

Tagwen dabbed at Hubertus' shoulder, whose congealing wound revealed itself to be several gouges reminiscent of massive teeth — a warg's bite.

"Good, now take this and spread it evenly to cover," she instructed, handing Tagwen a small wooden poultice bowl.

Tagwen slathered the mixture over the entirety of the wound and Ylerïan followed it with a wrap, directing Tagwen and Ualan to maneuver Hubertus' body to better expose the shoulder. Once she was finished, she had them carry Hubertus over to a prepared bed in the next room. Tagwen and Ualan sat in silence around the bedside for a moment, hoping Hubertus would regain consciousness. Two minutes of eternity finally passed as he mumbled something inaudible.

"Æpèlad arog atès," Ualan said, standing over his body.

Tagwen's brow raised at Ualan's elven words to Hubertus.

"Braithe," he rasped.

Tagwen moved to his side. "I am here, Sir Tolmach."

"He… comes." Hubertus struggled to string the words together.

"Rest, friend," Tagwen and Ualan said in unison.

"I'll get Lady Eilfaren," Ualan said, and left the room.

Tagwen held Hubertus' free hand and noticed the additional wounds along his arms and the black eye that was beginning to bloom.

What in the dark depths happened to you? Tagwen thought.

Hubertus gingerly squeezed her hand as Ylerïan entered the room with a glass of herbed water. She came up beside him, had Tagwen prop him up, and helped him to drink. Slowly he began to regain more of a presence, but before he could say anything, Ylerïan demanded that he rest, and he obliged. She then escorted Ualan and Tagwen out of the room.

"He will be alright. You found him in time," she nodded to Ualan.

"It is with fortune that you came, Queen Braithe," Ylerïan remarked. "His condition was worse than what I had hoped."

Tagwen's face flushed as she swallowed. "I was on my room's balcony when I saw Ualan carrying Sir Tolmach, so I hastened to find them to see what was wrong. I had not intended to trespass here," she said sheepishly.

"Why do you call Eachann, 'Sir Tolmach'?" Ualan asked.

Eachann? Is he… Muireall's son? Tagwen wondered, her

brow furrowing as she looked at him.

"I am afraid there is much to discuss, mærhïl," Ylerïan said. "You both should rest. There are spare beds in the next—"

"Lady Eilfaren. Forgive my interruption. Why was Eachann attacked? W-why is this Hunter after us? First my husband, now this? Does he even know?" Ualan interrogated her, growing more agitated with each question, but stuttering in his attempt to conceal his fear.

"Please tell me there is a good explanation for the commotion at this hour," Faldïr responded from the door, rubbing at his temples.

"Eachann. It — it was worse than I thought," Ylerïan explained, her tired eyes welling with tears.

Faldïr's eyes widened, his stance stiffened. "Is he alright? What happened to him? Where is he?" He blinked for a moment as if adjusting his view. "Why is our guest here?"

Tagwen shuffled to face him, the weight of her wearied legs nearly giving way underneath her. "Forgive me, sir. I saw them bring him here. I did not know who it was at the time, and truth be told I'm still not entirely sure, but I came to help, Lord Eilfaren. I apologize for treading about your house yet again uninvited, but Sir Tolmach is fine now," she reassured him.

Faldïr sighed with relief. "Your selflessness is admirable, queen of men, especially given the exhaustion I am sure you are under. We will take care of him from here. Please help yourself to—"

"Faldïr, what is going on here?" Ualan interrupted. "And why do you call him by that name, Braithe?" His face flushed and his hands were unable to find a state of rest at his side.

"Both names are mine, brother," a voice quaked from the far end of the room. Hubertus stood unsteadily in the archway, attempting to push away a separating curtain with his unbandaged arm.

"Eachann!" Ylerïan shouted, rushing to his side, with all following behind. "You must rest, mærhïl," she insisted, wrapping her arms around his torso and propping her shoulder under his arm.

"Please, my lady, I am alright," Hubertus protested, as his battered body disobeyed his will to stand and his weight fell on her shoulder.

"Nonsense, dear boy, look at you. You will rest," Faldïr commanded, helping Ylerïan bring him back to bed.

"Lord Eilfaren, I must explain. There is much you all must know," Hubertus grunted, wincing as they helped him settle back under the bedclothes.

"There is time for that, my boy." Faldïr clasped Hubertus' hand in his, his eyes brimming with tears.

"I am afraid there is less time than we thought," said a resonant voice from the main room — where stood an elderly elf in forested robes. His face was adorned by a long, twisted gray beard, his equally long hair was tied neatly behind him, and beneath his bushy ashen brows, beset by skinfolds of age, stared a pair of silverlight eyes.

Tagwen's throat closed, and gut clenched as she looked at

him, hoping somehow this was a hallucination borne of fatigue.

Faldïr pressed the tears from his eyes as his face tightened on hearing the voice.

"Mærênar," Ylerïan uttered, as if seeing a long-lost son. She clasped her hands together and held them against her chest. "What happened?" she asked breathily.

"You've come to be proven right, then, E'ruleïl," Faldïr said without looking at the elf.

"I have long known the warnings I've set at your table to be true, Son of Uhèrad. My presence now is borne of urgency to see that Sir Ghuinne is cared for, and to prepare your house for what is coming. Additionally," he paused to look at Tagwen, "I am here for you, Queen Braithe."

The confirmation that this — Eachann — was Muireall's son was not distraction enough for Tagwen. The man before her was not of the spectral nature that she had seen in the Sage of Middling, but there was a familiarity in his presence that tied them both together.

Witnessing Tagwen's apprehension, he said, "Be not afraid, queen of men, for I am not he whom you've already seen, though regrettably he is of my kindred."

Faldïr looked up and to the gentleman. "What do you want with her?" he asked.

"Would anyone be so kind as to explain what is going on here?" Ualan grumbled, his arms folded across his chest as he glared around at those assembled in the room.

"Faldïr…" Ylerïan said softly, "we need to tell them."

Faldïr took a breath as he released Eachann's hand. "Firstly," he began, his sullen eyes looking at Eachann, "Gòrdan is dead. Ualan found him in the Enbron Woods."

Gòrdan? He can't mean Gòrdan MacCaibe, Tagwen thought with alarm. The idea that somehow both were involved in this seemed impossible. *But what are the odds?*

"Gòrdan's dead?" Eachann asked piteously, his expression alternating between despair and anger. He turned his eyes to Ualan. "I am so sorry, brother. Mairi and Artur, are they safe?"

"You did mean Gòrdan MacCaibe!" Tagwen interrupted. "The children were—" she sputtered, and then gasped. Her thoughts caught up to her as she stared at Ualan.

"You… you're his husband," she said aghast. "The carving. The leaf and moon. That was you?" she asked.

"I did not have time to bury him properly. I had to leave him there… strung like a criminal," Ualan paused, tears in his eyes, "I had to protect our children." He wiped the tears from his face and cleared his throat to regain composure. "But Mairi and Artur are safe," he answered. "They are at an Outrider stead. I did not want to risk their lives crossing the continent to bring them here — not alone."

"You've been missing. Near a decade… or were you not really missing?" she asked.

"Both men have been members of our house for nine years, queen of men. Because of this, they needed to present a certain amount of secrecy. I understand this must all be very strange to comprehend," Faldïr answered.

Her head spun a moment as she tried to process this revelation, then remembered the day she found Gòrdan's body.

"The king's letter I showed you," Tagwen said to Ualan. "I found it in a pack that I think belonged to Gòrdan."

"Why would he have had that?" Ualan asked.

"That is what I shall now explain," Faldïr answered. "There was reason to believe that we were in danger," he began. "Eachann and Gòrdan were part of an effort to extract information from the kingdoms of men." He stopped and met Tagwen's stunned gaze. "Though armed with the information that there was a chance that men were against us, your arrival was wholly unanticipated, but its occurrence may inevitably prove that there is truth in this seer's words." He gestured toward the one they called E'ruleïl. "Which is more than I care to admit," he murmured under his breath.

5

Navigating the Truth

Faldïr had commanded all to retire the conversation for the evening on the promise that everything would be made clear in the morning. Tagwen and Ualan vehemently insisted upon staying with Eachann, should he need anything, and were thusly offered the spare cots in the healing room.

Tagwen awoke to Ualan sitting at the edge of his cot staring at Eachann as he slept. The gentle rise and fall of Eachann's chest breathed hope into Tagwen as she swept the dust from her eyes.

"He lives, but I fear our luck may be running out," Ualan said without turning.

Tagwen twisted and stretched as she pulled herself to sit upright, every muscle twinging with discomfort. "You did not strike me as a man who believes in luck," she said.

"Truthfully, I think it's the only thing that's kept me alive this long," Ualan confessed.

Tagwen stood. "It must still be serving you if your lives, and your children's lives have been spared."

Ualan sighed. "Perhaps you are right, but I would sooner

exchange my place to bring Gòrdan back."

Tagwen frowned. "Do not rob Mairi and Artur of both their fathers."

Ualan turned to her. "You looked for them," he noted.

Tagwen nodded. "I wanted to tell them of Gòrdan's death, but you all were gone when we arrived. My only hope was finding their tracks in accompaniment of your own, I now know."

"Thank you. It warms my heart to know that you cared for him and them in such a way." He smiled a pained smile.

"I trust Eachann is well?" Faldïr entered the room with E'ruleïl at his side.

Ualan stood and bowed. "Yes, my lord. He has lived to see another sunrise."

"Good," said E'ruleïl.

"Come. I realize you both must have many questions, but allow me to first divulge what I know," Faldïr said, motioning for Tagwen and Ualan to follow him. He led them through the castle's series of halls, and Tagwen recognized the route to be the one that led into the meeting chamber. She did not, however, anticipate the size of the room — it was closer to a banquet hall, with a sizable round table in its center. The table was ornately burnished with radial root-like patterns leading to a palm-sized, white center stone.

They all seated themselves, and Faldïr began.

"About a calendar quarter past, we received report from our dwarven allies that there had been what appeared to be a company of men trespassing through the Ebrïhèïlè. Scouts sent to canvass the area determined that the Forest had routed these intruders back from whence they had come, which we concluded to be the West. At first, we posted guards along the borders, in hopes of finding these men to assess their motives, but when a near month passed with no sign of them, I had the guard duty pulled back. But, as if the men knew this, they attempted to enter the Forest once more, thankfully to no avail, but in their apparent fright, they dropped this.”

Faldïr unrolled a scroll he had been carrying to reveal a type of map, which he passed to Ualan and Tagwen.

“They were trying to map their way through the Forest?” Ualan looked up with a mix of confusion and anger.

“It would appear so,” E’ruleïl confirmed.

“We also found this,” Faldïr continued, displaying a torn piece of yellow fabric. “It was tied along a branch as a means of a path marker, we think.”

Tagwen took the piece of fabric, whose ochre hue she recognized instantly to be part of the Middling uniform. The texture was the same as the capes the knights donned.

“Thus, I was convinced of the treachery afoot and that is when I sent for the Order,” Faldïr explained.

“And I wanted no part,” Ualan said somberly. “I’ve been a fool, my lord.”

“You held to your convictions, mærhïl. I do not begrudge you that.”

“I could have protected Eachann, protected my love,” Ualan said, sounding sad.

“That is where I believe you to be wrong,” E’ruleïl offered. “It may have been wise to refrain from taking part in this investigation. The darkness seemingly does not know there are three Hallows of Ylerïan."

"Hallows of Ylerïan?" Tagwen asked.

"It is the name of our Order," Ualan explained. "We are all connected through the grace of the Matron of Moonlight, our Lady Eilfaren. That carving of the crescent moon and dheldora leaf is our sigil." His eyes were saddened. "To protect us," he muttered.

"Had you gone with either of them, I fear you would have been found and likely targeted by the same assassin who claimed Gòrdan's life, and who subsequently tried to take Eachann's," E'ruleïl said.

"Do we know yet who that is?" Tagwen asked.

"If I am right," E'ruleïl said, "I fear the danger extends beyond this fabricated quarrel between elves and men."

"Fabricated?" Tagwen's gaze became stern.

"I fear so, Your Majesty," replied E'ruleïl. "I witnessed this corruption once before, in an age long forgotten by men, elves, and even some dwarves — a time when the world was whole. For I have walked the land of Vostheria."

Tagwen looked puzzled. "Vostheria?"

"Yes," E'ruleïl said, as if recalling a dream. "Agus ò athèr alè elagen. The land of the Age of Fire and Gold, and I am one of the last Heralds of the First Elves."

"But that would make you… what, nearly four-thousand years old? Do elves live to be of such an age?" Tagwen asked, dumbfounded.

"It is a gift that has been long removed from this part of the world. The land Erul speaks of is that which has long passed into legend — the joined world — the one that was lost to the sea of storms. When our connection to the birthplace of elves was severed, we were also removed from our endowment sown into the lands — immortality," Faldïr lamented.

Tagwen's brows knitted as she sat wholly perplexed. She did not know what question to ask first.

"I must admit," Ualan said, trying to relate to Tagwen, "this all was — is — incredibly difficult to believe."

"Unfortunately, there is not a way to prove my claims other than attempting to fatally wound myself, and I'd much rather not sully this meeting with such a display," Erul commented.

Faldïr thrummed his fingers upon the tabletop. "That is also not the purpose of this conversation." He looked at Tagwen. "How long is it since you've departed from the Midland kingdom?"

"A week, sir," she said. "Given that, their plan will likely be set in motion within a fortnight."

"Hmm," Faldïr grumbled. "And we have not found what you were looking for, Erul?"

"What were you seeking?" Ualan asked.

"In addition to Gòrdan and Eachann's infiltration to the realms of men, I sent them in search of something of great value. A token of the First Age that I believe would help us figure and thwart this plan of theirs, but alas we've come up empty-handed," Erul revealed.

Tagwen moved instinctively to her pouch and felt for the tender piece of vellum she had carried from Middling. She procured it from its safe-keeping and held it up. "Would this be at all what you sought?" she asked.

"A piece of paper?" Ualan asked.

Erul's eyes widened and he motioned for Tagwen to pass it to him, and she gingerly set it in his open palm. Erul then delicately unfolded the note and Tagwen watched in awe as his eyes pored over the letters she could not read. "This is it!" he exclaimed. "Where did you find this?"

"It came to me in Middling. I find my actions unsavory in this matter, but I dared not leave it behind. What is it?"

"This is the last letter of Yacendïl. His only surviving script," Erul explained, breathlessly. "This, my dear company, is said to contain the last known location of the Quill of Avantèas, an extremely valuable relic of the dawn of the First Age, but one that is potentially treacherous, should it fall into the wrong hands."

"That name — Yacendïl. I've heard it somewhere before," Tagwen said, looking at Erul.

"Yes, yes. Yacendïl is the father of Yeacralas, in that he established its kingdom of men. The very name Yeacralas is derived from the elvish 'Yaceralan', meaning 'Yacendïl's creation'. Though, he did not name it himself — his son Ærèg Èlasïl bestowed it to the land. But I digress," Erul finished.

"Well, what does the letter say?" Ualan questioned.

"Ah, yes, well let's see, this appears to be in the earliest of elvish, and my Avœlèn is not quite what it used to be," Erul admitted as he straightened himself in his seat. He flattened the letter out on the table and gently ran a finger along the characters, pausing in places as he mumbled to himself. In those pauses, he would shut his eyes and recite the word under his breath. Tagwen sat still and expectantly, her heart racing, knowing she would finally learn the contents of the bewitching page.

After a few moments, Erul gasped and snapped his fingers, causing Tagwen to jump.

"Much is illegible now, but this much I could discern: 'In my dark she shines for all, away in her light truth remains'." He stopped, his brows knitting. "It is a lament," he said solemnly.

"A lament for who?" Tagwen asked.

"The love of Yacendïl's life, the Blessed Southern Star. Otherwise known as the elven maiden, Anabeh. It is said that when she completed her task of bringing forth the first elves of Vostheria, she failed to return to our birthplace — the elven isle of Ardenïl — because she fell in love with the mortal, but the very source of her power and light would eventually bid her return to the heavens," Erul explained

"It tells us not what we had hoped then?" Faldïr asked with a frown.

Erul stood abruptly and paced behind his seat for a moment. "It must! It cannot have survived under such perilous circumstances all these years! Through all the stewards who were sent to protect it. It doesn't make sense." He stopped to point at the parchment. "I have searched too many years for this letter after foolishly letting it slip my grasp." He began pacing again. "No, no, it must mean something. I must think on this. Faldïr, there may still be records of your great grandfather's here that could tell me something. If you need me, I'll be there," he finished hurriedly before leaving the room through a passage in the eastern wall.

Faldïr tried to reach for him to beckon him to stay but sighed as the elf sped off.

Tagwen worried that somehow in her journey she had disrupted the integrity of the paper. She pulled it close to take another look and breathed with relief. The page was the same as she remembered. *What were you supposed to say?* she wondered to herself.

Ualan shook his head and rubbed his forehead. "This… quill… is it as threatening as he contrives?" he asked Faldïr.

"From what I know, the Quill of Avantèas is said to be a gift from the gods who created our very world. The legends speak its name as 'Varucïel', 'true thought', and say that it was the very instrument that penned the first words of the world. According to remaining accounts, it was only capable of writing the truth, hence its name, and would also be able to provide the writer with prophecies for the future. In the wrong hands, the prophecies would change, and the written words would turn into truths bent through malevolent means. It was thought that the quill would serve as a conduit, by virtue of its wielder. So, yes, should the myth be found tangible, it very well could change the course of our world, as it supposedly did long ago," Faldïr replied.

"Who is he afraid of acquiring the quill?" Tagwen asked.

"I should not be surprised that you do not know. The great folly of man was in the destruction of Mïrabasia," Faldïr lamented. He looked up to the ceiling. "May my forefathers forgive my utterance in these halls." He continued, "He was known as the harbinger of the world's destruction, the onetime inheritor of all elvendom, and the only demigod to have walked the earth — the Forsworn Daemon, Ruèhnar. E'ruleïl fears that the signs of his return are upon us, and they've only solidified with your presence here, Queen Braithe." Faldïr stopped and looked at Ualan with mournful eyes. "We believe also that the assassin appointed to cause the demise of Gòrdan, this… Hunter… was once a man, now molded into a Warden of Ruèhnar, a mœrdeth. A tormented and twisted soul whose being no longer represents the life it once held, and who will not rest until his task is completed. If he discovers his attempt on Eachann's life has failed, he will try again."

"Forgive me, the world's destruction? Are you implying that this world is not whole?" asked Tagwen.

A moment of silence passed, as her question hung in the air.

"Once men and elves felt it was their duty to protect our histories, but that was long forgotten as they began squabbling for lands left over and kingships not rightly earned. We elves had the gift and misfortune of watching generations of people pass. Men who were undeserving of the powers they amassed died alongside the few who were honorable all the same."

"Have I brought these ill omens upon you? Has destiny betrayed our hand? I meant only to help. Had I known—" Tagwen began.

Faldïr raised a calming hand. "No, queen of men. I, like my ancestors, was warned that the darkness was not truly at bay," he explained. "We were told that the lands would be sown with distrust and malevolence beyond our control. What little preparation I sought began to reveal sinister truths. When Ylerïan felt the departure of Gòrdan, I knew we were already too late," he bemoaned. "E'ruleïl warned us that we could not hide in our Forest when the time finally came. But it was you, queen of men, who brought us hope. Hope that perhaps we need not hide anymore," Faldïr said with a sad smile.

Tagwen bowed her head to him. "I am glad then to have followed my conviction, but I do not know how much time it has granted us. When I left Middling, they were prepared to strike in three weeks."

"What is there to do now? Surely, they must be making their way, having had a week's time already," Ualan said.

"For now, we prepare with the information we have. Let us gather our allies so we may make a better-calculated effort," Faldïr instructed.

***

The belltower struck six and thus the council ended. Faldïr sent Ualan to call on their dwarven allies in the North, and Tagwen was bid to return to her men. It was estimated that the Middling and Oburim armies would arrive within the sennight, and without knowing precisely what to expect, all were sent to prepare as best they were able.

Tagwen approached the gate leading to the central courtyard and heard yelling on the other side. "She is not under our guard! We cannot be held at fault for your lack of attention."

"I'll only ask once more. Where is she? I demand to be made aware of my queen's whereabouts!"

Tagwen recognized Breccan's voice and ran into the fray. "I am here! It is alright, everyone please calm down. I was in discussion with Lord Eilfaren. I apologize for my disappearance."

"Best learn to keep your men under control," an elven guard warned.

Breccan moved to step at the elf with her unsheathed sword when Tagwen shifted between them. "Forgive them, I did not alert them of my departure," Tagwen counseled.

The elf huffed and was escorted by his partner away from the encounter. Breccan choked down the adrenaline as she relaxed her sword arm and pressed the wild flyaways of her hair from her reddened face. Before she could speak, Tagwen waved away Callon and Sĭne, who had followed her out. All three looked as if they had awoken from a nightmare and had immediately raced outside, the rush of blood the only thing keeping them warm.

The captain dropped her head with embarrassment as she realized she had not yet caught her breath.

"What were you thinking?" Tagwen asked.

Breccan stabbed her sword into the freshly powdered ground and sat on one of the garden walls. Her linen tunic was sweated through, and her flushed face burned bright against the glow of the snow.

"I — It was so dark, and I couldn't — I couldn't save you."

"What are you talking about?"

"A dream I had. There was a plain devoid of life, and it

was dark and cold, though it was engulfed in flame. I couldn't reach you, and I couldn't see what happened, but you fell." She stopped and looked up. "That's when I woke and ran to find you — waking Hellig and Matharnach in the process. When I saw your door ajar, and no sign of you, I panicked. This isn't home and I didn't know where to look."

"You cannot worry if I am not always in your sights, Captain."

Breccan raised her posture and lowered her head. "Understood, my lady."

Tagwen cringed at having to scold her oldest friend, but she knew being a guest in these strange lands did not leave room for missteps. She unearthed Breccan's blade, Saìde, and handed it over. "Ready yourself and the company. We await orders from Lord Eilfaren on preparations for Middling and Oburim's arrival."

Breccan bowed and accepted her sword. "Yes, Your Majesty," she said, departing and leaving Tagwen alone in the garden.

Tagwen waited until Breccan was out of sight before making her way back into her abandoned quarters. Upon the edge of the still-made bed, she sat listlessly, staring at the opposite wall. Much had been learned but nothing had been made clearer. It was a sobering realization that despite everything her father had prepared her for, this was not among the possibilities.

A meek knock at the door startled her from her thoughts, and she looked to see Breccan standing in the doorway. "Forgive me, my lady. I came to inform you that the company has rallied themselves in the courtyard and are performing drills until further instruction. What would you like me to tell them?"

"I wish I knew," Tagwen replied, staring at the floor solemnly.

"My lady?"

"Breccan… I don't know what we're doing here," she admitted, looking up at her friend.

Breccan approached, kneeled before Tagwen, and looked her in the eyes. "We're here to help the elves. There's nothing more to it."

"Sir Tolmach's name is Eachann."

"What?" Taken aback, Breccan's face twisted with confusion.

"Also, he and Gòrdan were part of an Order of Outriders who have been helping the elves for years. Ualan, too, is a member of their rank — and Gòrdan's husband."

Breccan stood and stepped away from Tagwen until her back was pressed against the wall. "What-What does that even mean? That — How do you know?"

Tagwen stood and began wandering around in a circle. "That's where I was last night. Tolm-Eachann," she stopped herself. "Eachann was severely injured. Before I went to bed, I saw Ualan and Erul dragging a figure, which I now know was Eachann, to the eastern manor. I followed to see what the trouble was, and the manor is exactly like Francus Castle… except massive. And—"

Breccan cut her off, "Wait, wait, I'm sorry who is Erul and

how is that possible? And Tolmach is injured? Is he alright? Ualan is Gòrdan's husband? But I thought he was dead er- missing." Her eyes were transfixed on Tagwen as she paced.

Tagwen stopped in her tracks, took a deep breath, and quickly exhaled. "Eachann," she emphasized, "is recovering. As far as the rest of it goes, there is… so much, and so little that I understand."

A moment of silence passed before Tagwen exclaimed, "The letter!"

"Letter?"

"The paper we found in Lady Catrìona's necklace. It was a writing of some ancient elven that only Erul could read. They had been looking for it. And it was a letter — or rather a lament, he said."

"A lament about what?"

"Well, it was from the father of Yeacralas, Yacendïl, and it was a lament for… I forget her name, but Erul called her 'The Blessed Southern Star'. He was upset that it didn't tell us what he was looking for."

"Blessed Southern Star?"

"Yeah. That's what he called her."

"My mother used to call the moon that."

Tagwen's eyes narrowed as she asked, "How do you mean?"

"She taught me a poem for if I ever got lost," Breccan explained before reciting it.

"Beialdan's light is North and bright.
But should he hide, seek the maiden of night.

> Though sometimes not near, she is never far,
> For our coast holds the Blessed Southern Star."

"Moonlight," Tagwen breathed. "Away in her light, truth remains."

"What does that mean?" Breccan asked.

"I am unsure that it means anything, but perhaps Erul will know."

"Who is this Erul, again?"

"Come, we need to find him."

Passing through the quad, Tagwen stopped and hailed Lachlann over.

"My queen is there news of the coming armies?" he asked.

"We've determined that the likelihood of their arrival will be about a week," Tagwen replied. "I want you to see to it that everyone is properly fitted and that our equipment is adequately repaired. I know we did not prepare for an outcome such as this but make do with what we have."

"Yes, Your Majesty," Lachlann bowed and left to rally the group.

"We really were not prepared for this," Tagwen admitted to Breccan.

"A single of our soldiers is worth five of Oburim's and easily worth ten of Middling's. Fret not — we also have the elves," Breccan reassured.

With a comforted nod, Tagwen glanced toward the northern estate. From the corner of her eye, she saw a robed figure making its way along the road that led to the stables. "I think that's Erul. Quick!" she exclaimed to Breccan.

Down the cobbled path that ran alongside the northern building stood the stables. Tagwen and Breccan pushed through the open door and were greeted by a choir of whinnies. There, Erul stood in front of the paddock that held Seasaìdh and was softly stroking her face. This stopped Tagwen cold, as she watched her mare so calm in the presence of a stranger.

"I have never seen her like that with anyone other than myself," she said.

"Oh, she and I go way back, don't we, beautiful?" Erul cooed at the snorting horse.

"You know Seasaìdh?" Breccan asked.

"Indeed, I do, Kenefick," Erul replied, continuing to stroke Seasaìdh. "I named her."

"Adrelghard said he named her," Tagwen said, almost to herself.

Erul chuckled, "Did he now? Well, I'm sure it would have been difficult to explain that an elf was gifting a horse to a queen of men he had never formally met." He then turned to the women, and Breccan grabbed at the hilt of her sword.

"I mean neither of you harm, dear Breccan. Though I'm unsure why both of you are here. I must be going, time is of the essence, as it were," he said.

Tagwen noticed Breccan's defensive stance and put a hand on her shoulder. "Breccan, this is Erul. Erul, you clearly know Breccan somehow, but I'm sure you can understand her apprehension, as she does not know you. Regardless, I think we might know something that connects to the letter. Her mum used to tell her a poem—" Tagwen stopped, looking to Breccan to fill in the details.

Breccan relayed the poem again to Erul, who was silent for a moment. "Moonlight" he finally whispered. "Your mother was a wonderful woman, and so very brilliant. Yes, moonlight. That confirms where I must go."

"How do you know my mother?" Breccan demanded.

"Where must you go? Oburim and Middling are going to be here soon," Tagwen said.

"I have much to tell you both, but now the fate of this world rests on finding the last — hopefully alive — caretaker of the letter." He muttered the last bit as he unlatched the lock on Seasaìdh's pen.

"You can't leave now! Faldïr said you would be able to help us. And why are you taking Seasaìdh?" Tagwen asked with alarm.

"Fear not, Seasaìdh and I will return as the armies arrive," Erul explained, mounting the horse in one swift movement. "Look for me at dusk on their arrival. Hopefully I will bring good news and the man we seek."

"Who is so important that you are leaving now to find him? The fight is here!" Breccan yelled.

"The man I seek… is your father," Erul replied, looking down into her eyes.

Both women stood with mouths agape as Erul reassured them, "I do wish I had time to tell you more, but I promise I will arrive before the end. Onward Seasaìdh!" he ordered, as

Seasaìdh carried him out of the stables, leaving the two women behind.

"Did he—" Breccan stopped. She stood staring at the open stable doors, unable to grasp the words she needed. Flakes of snow drifted inward, but the chill did not register.

Tagwen looked between her captain and the entrance, looking for some clue to help her speak. "I — he's alive?" she finally managed to utter.

"No." Breccan shook her head. "He wouldn't know him — my mother never even spoke of him. He must be mistaken."

"Breccan. What if it is… him?" Tagwen cautiously posed.

"No. Lucas is my father." Breccan strode toward the opening. "And so, he shall remain."

Tagwen opened her mouth to try and reason with her friend, but the distant sound of horns caught her attention — horns and drums. Breccan looked worriedly to her queen, and Tagwen stood with her eyes closed for a moment to listen. A second later, a faint echo of bagpipes carried on the air and her face twisted into a smile. "The dwarves are here," she announced.

Dwarven culture was fascinating to Tagwen, and the grandeur of their music was a favorite of hers. The grandiose nature of everything the dwarves of the Dholdron'lièr Mountains did was captivating to her. She had the fortune of being introduced to their society and customs through the relationship cultivated by dwarven liaison Adrelghard Tugrom and her father. The other kingdoms of men fell to xenophobic tendencies and rejected alliances with the dwarves. As a result, Yeacralas held advantages in armor craft, stonework, and blacksmithing.

The accompaniment of dwarves was of incredible size, and in attendance was the King of the Mountain himself, Pàdair Barindroun. A stout man, as all dwarves are, but with a distinctly silvered and decorated beard in his elder years, and a scar that ran across his face from his right temple to his left cheek. The procession gathered in the main square and Tagwen and Breccan made their way to the meeting. The elves and all Tagwen's men joined to witness their arrival. Faldïr and Ylerïan stood at the center. Tagwen motioned for Breccan to join their soldiers and then she walked to Faldïr's side.

"We may yet have strength enough to defend ourselves," he whispered as she approached.

Tagwen smiled and stood at attention to welcome the dwarves. Ualan walked in step with the King of the Mountain and bannermen held at their sides. Many years had passed since Tagwen had last seen King Barindroun, but he was just as elegant as she remembered him, though she was now significantly taller. The musicians broke and surrounded the courtyard, continuing the anthem of their people, "Girean's Call." Flourishing notes amassed as the song ended, and in the breaking of their formation, a familiar face stepped to the front line — Adrelghard. Tagwen exhaled an excited sigh of relief and failed to conceal the smirk that formed in the right corner of her mouth.

"Kingdom of Dholdron'lièr! Welcome! Your presence is a solace in these times," Faldïr greeted.

King Barindroun stepped forward, followed by two iron-clad knights. "Analek khradiin, my friend!" he bellowed as he moved in to hug Lord Eilfaren, who eagerly knelt and accepted the gesture.

"And the Matron of Moonlight, it is wonderful to be in your graces again." He bowed to Ylerïan.

"It is you whose spirit we are so fortunate to have in attendance, Your Grace." Ylerïan curtseyed as he took her hand to give it a customary kiss.

"A pity these are the circumstances that merit our reunion," Pàdair lamented.

"Indeed, but my people and I are ever grateful for your support. As well as the support of the Yeacralan realm," Faldïr said, gesturing to Tagwen.

"My goodness, you must be Tagwen Braithe. It is an honor to be rejoined after all these years, Your Majesty. My sincerest condolences for your father's passing. He was an honorable man." Pàdair bowed to the queen and Tagwen returned the formality.

"It is very good to see you again, King Barindroun. My father always spoke highly of you. I am glad to get to know you in my present position," she said.

"Brave of men to enter these lands. He would be proud of you," Pàdair winked at her.

"Thank you, Your Grace," she smiled.

"Well then!" Pàdair shouted. "Shall we? Seems we have a bit to discuss." He motioned to both Faldïr and Tagwen.

Both nodded in agreement and Faldïr began to lead them to

the eastern manor when Pàdair objected. "Not yer meetin' room! It's been a time since I've seen the Osècero!"

With a smile, Faldïr corrected their course and led them all toward the arboretum.

Tagwen waited for a beat behind them and trotted into the open arms of Adrelghard. "I am so glad you are here," she huffed into his shoulder.

"Aye lass, so am I, but what on earth are yeh doin' here?" he asked.

She pulled back and said apologetically, "I meant to send a letter."

"Well, come, explain on the way so I'm caught up," he smiled through his thick auburn beard and mustache.

As they made their way toward the willow garden, Tagwen briefly shared the request that had come from the King of Middling, how their stay had been less than ideal, and how the journey to this point had been even less so. She made no mention of the painting or the locket.

Adrelghard shook his head. "What a mess these men have become. Have yeh managed to send a letter home?"

Tagwen took a deep breath. "No," she replied. "I had thought to do it during our time in Middling, but that proved to be short-lived. And since we've been here, I've not had a way to do it without sending one of my own men, which I'm not about to do. I also meant to send a letter to you, but there was little chance of that either."

Adrelghard nodded. "Not a worry, lass, I'll see what I can

do. I'm sorry you've been caught in this debacle."

"Did you know about any of this?" she asked with mournful eyes.

Adrelghard nodded once again. "Middling think their treacheries have been unobserved, but we hear a lot from under the mountain. I never thought to mention it because they'd seemed so unorganized. Should've suspected otherwise. King Barindroun was right, though, it was mighty brave of yeh to come here."

"I am starting to think it might have just made matters worse," Tagwen sighed.

Adrelghard put a hand on hers. "No good thinkin' like that, Yer Majesty."

They were guided inside the atrium to convene with the others. Pàdair took in an audible breath and exhaled into a wide smile. "Is this not a sight for sore eyes!" Stepping toward the willow, he gazed up into its boughs in awe. "I remember this was a wee little seedlin'! It's grown quite well, it seems," he marveled.

"Indeed, it has," said Faldïr with pride.

Suddenly, the animated king became quiet, and his shoulders slumped ever so slightly. His eyes, which had been filled with joy, now darkened from the kind of sadness that is only ever felt deep inside one's chest. Without taking his gaze from the tree, he addressed the party behind him. "So, he was right then? This ancient wickedness… is real?" he asked.

Tagwen watched Faldïr hang his head, as Ylerïan reached to

take his hand.

"We are afraid so," Ylerïan confirmed.

"Hmph," Pàdair grunted. "Well, where is he? Might as well know what under-workings are at play here."

Faldïr and Ylerïan looked around the room, realizing that Erul was not amongst them.

Tagwen spoke up. "He's gone."

"Gone?! What do yeh mean, he's gone? Where's he gone to?" Pàdair turned around and stared at her.

Tagwen looked to Faldïr and replied, "He went to find the last known caretaker of the letter. He didn't say where."

"Mæranedïl?" Ylerïan's eyes lit up.

"You know him?" Tagwen asked with urgency.

"Mæranedïl… is my brother," Ylerïan said.

"He's… an elf?" Tagwen frowned, struggling to understand.

"But of course he's an elf! And now we've got two missing elves who seem to be somehow key to this whole mess," Pàdair said. "What exactly do we have to go on?" he asked.

Faldïr stood straighter. "From what we estimate — given Queen Braithe and Eachann's testament of what they saw — the armies of men are set to arrive within the week. The Midland men are somehow the ones in charge of this assault."

"Well, I can tell yeh the Northmen have already made their crossin' into the heartland. Near three days past now," Pàdair reported.

"Three days past?" Tagwen exclaimed.

"Aye, and a good lot of 'em, too," Pàdair replied.

Tagwen turned to Faldïr. "Then this has been planned much

longer than I knew."

"If I had to guess," Pàdair paused to count on his fingers, "these men are likely due at the Forest's wall by tomorrow night."

Faldïr's brow furrowed in the first covert sign of agitation Tagwen had seen from the elf, which worried her.

"Then we will be ready," he proclaimed.

"I can set up my force at the Path. We can cut off any potential routing from the North," Pàdair offered.

"I and my men will go where we are needed," Tagwen promised.

Faldïr nodded at Pàdair. "Yes, blocking the North also secures the Path for us, should we need it. Not that I intend to run." He turned to Tagwen. "Your men will join my own at the Western front."

Tagwen nodded.

"We will meet them as they arrive, so we must be ready. I want all companies assembled in their locations by nightfall. We will make camp within the Forest. It is the best vantage point we have," Faldïr explained.

"I'd like to see these cowards try to enter the woods," Pàdair said with a grin.

"Let us meet in the central yard at dusk. Your men have a better chance of not being lost if we go together," Faldïr said to Tagwen.

"As you wish," Tagwen replied.

"Do we intend to try and reason with them?" Adrelghard asked all those assembled.

Faldïr steadied his breathing and slowly nodded. "Yes. I do not wish to shed the blood of anyone on this land. Enough of that has been done by our forebears. That being said," he paused and glanced at Tagwen, "I will not hesitate to cut down any man who wishes harm to my people."

"Understood," Tagwen agreed, her expression unchanging. She held no love for anyone who wished harm to another. As a soldier, she knew it was either her life or theirs, and if lives could be spared, that was preferred, but if they struck first, she struck last.

Ualan had been standing dutifully silent in the corner, listening, his manner changing only after the last exchange between Tagwen and Faldïr.

Tagwen saw a sense of approval wash over his face in seeing her so willing to defend the elves, who he called his brethren. As the party broke apart to begin their preparations, he left with the dwarves and Tagwen was left with the Lord and Lady Eilfaren.

"I do not support these men in their actions," she began, "but I do not wish to see them cut down." She wavered a bit as she tried to hold her stance. Battle was not a discomfort to her, but she often thought of those she had lost along the way to the blade.

Faldïr approached her and set a comforting hand on her shoulder. "I have stated that it is not my wish to see them destroyed, queen of men," he assured her. "I will reason with them as best as they will allow, and I will not forget the fortitude of the Southmen."

Tagwen took a breath and bowed her head. "Thank you,

Lord Eilfaren."

"We must be getting ready," Faldïr urged.

Upon Tagwen's return to the lodging of her men, she was approached by Corporal MacCullach.

"Your Majesty," he bowed. "May I have a moment?"

Tagwen motioned him over to a quiet section of the hall. "What is it, MacCullach?"

"Permission to speak freely, my queen," he said.

"Granted."

"We have alliances with these kingdoms. I have a brother who lives in Middling, who, like me, is also a knight. I had never considered the possibility of facing him as my enemy. Are you sure we are doing the right thing?" Samuel stepped back and looked at his queen. "I apologize, Your Majesty. I am just — unsure."

"This is not a situation any of us were ever prepared for, Samuel. Facing our own brethren was a reality we had hoped would never come to pass. But sometimes it is our own who we must combat to protect what is right, what is just." She saw the uncertainty on his face building. "I do not want to fight them, Corporal. It is not my intention to take up arms against the men of Middling and Oburim, but I will not sit idly and watch them inflict pain upon the elves."

Samuel did not appear comforted by her words. Biting at the insides of his cheeks, he nodded.

"I will do everything in my power to prevent any bloodshed, Samuel. Just as much as I do not want to fight them, I do not want this company harmed," she added.

Samuel straightened; his discomfort softened almost into a smile. "Thank you, Your Majesty. I am grateful for your leadership and your grace in speaking with me as you have."

Tagwen bowed her head and Samuel offered her a formal salute to be dismissed.

Sunset had descended upon the valley of Thrindūl. The snow caught the last of the rays and danced them around the company of men, elves, and dwarves who had gathered. Faldïr stood in the center of the congregation and addressed the crowd. "We are witnessing an unprecedented time. May we count the fortunes we have been blessed with, as I will not forget the kindness and strength of those before me. To those who have come to our aid, your actions have forged in me a new hope — one that extends beyond this current threat. I cherish the kinships that have been offered in these darkening days. May we be the light, together. Alud èlal arulavè!"

"Vefrak dhondri!" the dwarves shouted in answer.

"For Vostheloren!" Tagwen led her men in response.

As ranks were forming a line to begin the descent into the Ebrïhèïlè, Tagwen overheard Faldïr's parting words with Ylerïan and Eachann, who insisted on being present. "You don't understand, Lord Eilfaren, I must come with you. You haven't seen—" Eachann protested.

"No, Eachann. I will not risk your life. As selfish as that may be. And since you have been targeted, we can only assume that if that assassin is in their midst, he will make another attempt on your life. No, you both will remain within Thrindūl, where you are protected," Faldïr commanded.

"Faldïr—" Ylerïan began.

"I will not have it. That is my final word," Faldïr said sternly. He began to turn and walk away when he returned to his wife and kissed her hand. "I could not bear to lose either of you. Please," he begged.

"We will await your return, u'anelū," Ylerïan said as she stroked Faldïr's face.

With a nod, Faldïr put a hand on Eachann's shoulder for a moment and then turned to lead the elven line. He was followed by the dwarves and Tagwen waited, as her small accompaniment of men would take the rear of the line. While waiting, she was waved over by Lady Eilfaren. She turned to Breccan, who was at her side. "I'll be back in a second. Lead on, and I will catch up."

"Yes, Your Majesty," Breccan nodded.

Tagwen approached Ylerïan and bowed. "My lady." She then turned to bow to Eachann. "Eachann, it is good to see you in better health."

"You have done us all a great kindness, Your Grace," Ylerïan said with a thankful smile. "As such, I wish you to carry this — a token of my house. May it serve you greater than its former master." She handed over a golden pin — one Tagwen was familiar with — Gòrdan's key.

"My lady, I cannot take this. Ualan should have it," Tagwen objected.

"It is mine to give to whom I will," Ylerïan said. "The Forest is greater protected having you within. I wish to honor that."

Tagwen delicately grasped the pin and held it to her chest. "I will return the honor by accepting it, and I will do my best to be the steward of Gòrdan's emblem."

Ylerïan smiled, and without opening her mouth, Tagwen heard her voice inside her head. *Be safe, queen of men, for dangers grander than this present threat are eager to make themselves known.*

Tagwen's breath was stolen from her lungs as the shock of this exchange took hold. Ylerïan continued again telepathically, *Do not be afraid. Should you need me, you need only call.*

Tagwen bowed shakily in thanks and Ylerïan returned the gesture. As Tagwen moved to catch the end of the line, she felt a hand on her shoulder and turned to see Eachann.

"Be wary, Queen Braithe," he warned.

"So, I've been — told," she said, looking past him to the image of Ylerïan making her way to the eastern manor.

"More so than that — that Sage is going to be among them. He's managed to get Roìbert and King Arasgain to reach a state where they're unable to see reason. They are in worse condition than when you last saw them. Perhaps if they're not within his sphere of influence they might be revived," he suggested.

"Thank you, Eachann. I will see what I can do," she assured, saluting him.

"I am sorry I could not tell you the truth of myself. I have always considered the kingdom of Yeacralas to be decent people, and it felt dishonorable, but I hope you understand now why it was necessary."

"Are you Muireall's son?" Tagwen asked.

Eachann smiled. "Indeed, I am, though regrettably it has been some time since I have been home."

"Well, know that she is well and that she misses you," Tagwen shared.

He held the hand of his uninjured arm to his heart. "Thank you. It delights me to hear good news of her after many years," he said gratefully.

Seeing the armies finishing their departure into the Forest, he bowed. "Be safe, Queen Braithe."

Tagwen smiled and left, catching her men just as they crossed through the moon gate from which they had first entered. The serenity of Thrindūl fell behind them as they stepped once more into the wilds of the Forest.

6
BATTLE ON THE MIDLANDS

Tagwen held to the end of the line until the entirety of the three armies arrived at a central glade. It felt to have taken at least the better part of two walking hours to get to this point. A communal fire was started briefly to give everyone a moment's rest before the forces would split to their designated locations.

Breccan approached Tagwen. "Everyone so far accounted for — much easier to navigate this time with two full armies ahead of us," she chuckled.

"Good," Tagwen said absentmindedly.

"Are you alright?"

Tagwen pressed her lips together and squinted for a moment. "Something about this doesn't sit right."

"Are you having second thoughts about helping them?" Breccan's eyes went wide.

"'No. Nothing like that." Tagwen held out the pin that Ylerïan had given her.

"Is that… his?" Breccan gaped.

"Gòrdan's, yes. Lady Eilfaren insisted I take it. And then… she spoke to me — inside my mind." Tagwen shook her head as she looked at the trinket.

"Inside your head?" Breccan looked stunned.

"She told me there was a bigger threat ahead. That this opposition is somehow insignificant."

"What does she know?"

"If anything, she didn't say. It just felt like a gut feeling sort of warning. Then Eachann told me to beware of the Middling Sage. Which, truthfully, I felt the moment we met him." She shuddered.

"That one I can believe," Breccan nodded. "Have you told Lord Eilfaren?"

"I will when we reach our position," Tagwen said. "It seems they're getting ready to depart. Take the rear with Catach, would you?"

"Yes, Your Majesty," Breccan bowed.

The three heads of houses met in the center of the glade. Faldïr unsheathed his blade and held it on its side toward Pàdair and Tagwen.

"Though forged for times such as these, I care not to use such a weapon, but I vow to protect these lands and those who protect it alongside me, so long as I draw breath."

Pàdair then followed with the kingly greataxe he had strapped to his back. The glinting edge caught the sliver of moonlight shining above them, revealing the runic engravings that Tagwen could read:

BE NOT THE DELIVERER OF FAIRNESS BUT THE

PROTECTOR

"Forged from the great Durifrael himself and gifted to many kings long lost. Bequeathed into my hands from the hands of my father, I vow to protect these lands and those who protect it alongside me, so long as I draw breath," Pàdair pledged.

Tagwen then drew Mercy and held it much like Faldïr had held his sword. The intricate etchings of three-petaled drooping flowers along the fuller glowed in the light and a beam lit up Tagwen's face. Her darkened eyes seemed to hold the stars.

"Though its story is unknown, the blade long belonging to my house and wielded only by my hands, I vow to protect these lands and those who protect it alongside me, so long as I draw breath," she swore.

At this, they departed one another's company, the dwarves heading somewhere to the North, within the Forest, that Tagwen did not know, and the rest following Faldïr to the front. How close they would be to the edge of the Forest, Tagwen could not tell, but she knew her only hope was ending the conflict before it even began.

A long stretch of torches carried by the elven soldiers helped guide the band of men through the ever-winding path of the Forest. The once-widened road felt much narrower to Tagwen, capable of only comfortably allowing two men abreast of each other. She walked with Sïne, whose eyes darted continuously through the cold darkening woods. The foliage, too, was much thicker than the men had remembered — though Tagwen harkened back to Ualan's warning that the Forest had a tendency to change. She could barely see him ahead of the archers. She looked around as she walked and clasped the pin that now held her cloak. She thought of Gòrdan, and the horror that followed him.

Rest in peace, dear friend, she thought.

"Your Majesty," Sĭne's voice brought her back to the moment.

"Yes, Matharnach?" she asked.

"Do you really think we can reason with them?"

"It is my sincerest hope," she responded.

"What if we can't? And what if… what if they're lying to us?" Sĭne's voice lowered. "What if the elves really do mean to take over?"

"Lord Eilfaren and the elves have my full faith and support, soldier. I expect the same of all of you," Tagwen cautioned.

Sĭne looked ahead and away from her queen. "Yes, Your Majesty. My apologies."

Tagwen could see the trepidation upon Sĭne's face — it was a look that all her company seemed to share as of late. Engaging in preparations for war with an army they had never fought alongside — especially a people who were thought to not exist — had never been a requirement in their training. After all, the elves had been only characters of fables to them until now.

The line continued until they came upon a change in the trees and Tagwen knew they must be close. Sequoias began to tower over the company, shielding them from the shadowy night sky, but encasing them in their own ghostly darkness. Nearly another hour passed and a new clearing that the men had not previously encountered opened to hold the entirety of their camps. The men set up in the southeastern pocket — their few tents and stations taking up very little space in comparison to the garrison of elves.

A few of the elven soldiers approached the collection of men and offered shares of their provisions, blankets, and armaments. Tagwen gladly accepted these gifts in thanks. She recognized one of the soldiers to have been the guard of her room and bowed her head in acknowledgement of him. To her surprise, he returned the gesture and offered the salute of her people, and she reciprocated. After preparations were made, the men and elves mingled around a campfire, much like they had upon their arrival. Tagwen's nerves calmed as she watched while polishing her armor.

Breccan came out from prepping the final tent.

"I thought I tasked one of the MacLeòirs with polishing," she said.

"You did. I sent them to join the others. Besides, I miss cleaning my own armor sometimes," Tagwen smirked.

Breccan sat beside her. "I never would have believed you if you had told me we'd be sitting here after receiving a wild letter from Dùghlan."

"Neither would I," Tagwen agreed.

"Wait 'til we tell this one to Mercher," Breccan joked.

"I hope we get to." Tagwen looked down at her armor, the light of the distant fire gracing the edges of her kingdom's crest — the lion of her father rearing against the dark.

"We will," Breccan reassured, nudging Tagwen's shoulder. "You should join them."

"Why don't you go," Tagwen said. "I think I need a moment. I want to be ready for anything tomorrow."

Breccan nodded and gently patted Tagwen's knee as she rose. The queen watched her captain jump into conversation, eliciting smiles and laughter from the rest of her men and even some elves. Breccan always had a way of making everyone feel welcome.

In her periphery, Tagwen could see Faldïr approaching. He no longer donned his signature green robes, but rather was clad in a similar emerald hauberk with his house's insignia embroidered on his left breast. As Tagwen stood to greet him, she noted he seemed taller in this knightly garb.

"I hope I am not interrupting," he greeted.

"Not at all. Is there something you need?" she asked.

"My scouts report that both armies have set up camp across the river. They're assembling a bridge to make their crossing, but it looks like it won't be complete until dawn. There are men stationed along the river's edge, but no one yet on our side of the water."

"We're ready for them," Tagwen nodded.

"I hope you're right," Faldïr replied. "There's something I want to show you. Bring a cloak," he instructed.

Tagwen set her armor and shining cloth on the table and retrieved the cloak she had brought — a chestnut wool fabric with the initials "N.R." embroidered on the lapel for "Netta Ròsach," her mother. Faldïr handed her a lantern as they set out together, and she followed him back into the Forest. Through trees and no discernible path, Faldïr navigated them for the better part of an hour. Tagwen became concerned at the possibility of getting lost — or worse, having her men think she'd abandoned them. She cautioned herself against that line of thinking, and as she did, she found herself standing at an overlook.

The sky opened and the expanse before her was breathtaking. Waves of the mouth of the Terrishire River rushed below her and the crash of the sea sounded to her left. Tagwen could see the near entirety of the Southern land, and for a moment she thought she could make out the faint glow of Marez far beyond in the West.

"Beautiful, isn't it?" Faldïr asked.

"This — is magnificent."

"I have not been out here in decades, I am afraid, but it is as wonderful as I remember," Faldïr lamented.

"Thank you for sharing this with me," Tagwen said.

"Ahh. That is not all I wish to share," Faldïr said, directing her gaze to the right. Behind him stood a tree of such grandness — the likes of which Tagwen had never thought possible. Roots of the tree extended beyond the cliff as if reaching toward the open air, the tallest boughs hung nearly seventy feet above the ground. Silvery veins, much like the weeping willow Tagwen had seen in the arboretum, ran throughout its trunk. Her awe beckoned her hand to grace its bark, and to her surprise the tree was strangely warm, and within it an energy pulsated like a heartbeat. She pulled back and looked at her hand.

"What is it?" she asked in shock.

Faldïr chuckled lightly. "This is the tree of Eecrelêne. Would you care to hear her story?"

Tagwen nodded and Faldïr motioned to a stone bench that had been placed nearby. He cleared his throat before beginning.

"Long before the time we now know, our history tells of the first elves. They were brilliant, and honored as such with ancient gifts of immortality, grace, and craftsmanship. But they were also loved by the progenitor of all life in the world — the god we call 'Ehlïf'.

"Now, notably amongst the first elves were Eecrelêne and her partner, Guódnè. Artists, they were. Eecrelêne was a painter. She marveled at the world and sought to cherish it in moments that would be untouched by time. Guódnè was a poet. Together, they penned pictures of our people and our history. Their works are lost to us now, but that is not what this tale is about.

"Though their love of art was what they were most known for, and what history has sought to remember them by, Eecrelêne and Guódnè's love for each other was what captured the eyes of Ehlïf. Stories tell that at the end of the First Age, when the demon came, Ehlïf sought to preserve the love of Eecrelêne and Guódnè amid the darkness that was befalling this earth. It is said that the lovers gathered here and embraced as they watched the shadow consume the skies. Ehlïf found them here and began to turn their form into winding trees. New life out of the decay, as it were.

"During their transformation, the earth began to crack and split apart. Their metamorphosis had not yet completed when Guódnè began to slip from Eecrelêne's grasp. Unable to catch her partner, Eecrelêne's form finalized into the fashion we see today, her arms the roots outstretched, trying to reach for

Guódnè."

"Where is Guódnè's form then?" Tagwen asked, fully absorbed in the story.

"The river your people call 'Terrishire' has a true name — 'Na'ægūl Guódnè' — or 'Guódnè's Rivers', in your tongue. When Guódnè fell, the sheer force of their new structure broke the earth, creating the river you see today. It is surmised that Guódnè may have rooted to the bottom of the river where it meets the sea, but none have been able to confirm this, as the waters are far too deep."

"Why are you telling me this story, Faldïr?" Tagwen asked quietly.

"To perhaps remind myself that there is a bigger force than all the darkness that may find us."

"And what is that?"

"Love, dear queen. Love."

"But their love did not save them," Tagwen frowned.

"On the contrary. It is their enduring love that changed the face of the world as we know it, and though we may not see Guódnè, we know their presence is still with us — as is Eecrelêne's, and the growth birthed of their love blooms within my halls. Love is not beholden to impermanence."

Tagwen sat back and mused. "Is it your love for this land that has carried you this far?" she asked.

Faldïr nodded. "Perhaps." He chuckled, "I had always thought it was obstinance, but I prefer your interpretation."

A sweet moment of silence passed between them before Tagwen was moved to speak. "Do you think they will reach the wall before dusk tomorrow?" she asked.

"The river is the smallest of the branches, but they've seemingly set themselves up at its widest point — for what purpose I cannot discern. Why? Do you?" he asked.

"I certainly hope they do not. Erul just promised to return upon dusk of their arrival," she said.

"Hmm," Faldïr contemplated, "I will have my scouts—" he stopped, stood abruptly, and listened.

Tagwen jolted to a stance and began to look around. Her sword was stashed at the campground, which made her vulnerable. "What is it?" she whispered.

"We must go — something is wrong. I can hear a worry at the grounds."

Running in haste back from whence they came, jumping over brush and root, Tagwen was relieved she had not yet fallen or that her cloak had snagged any branch. They came to their encampment to find their members silent, backing away to the walls of the glade that encompassed them. Three figures stood central to the gathering. Their presence alone suffocated Tagwen as she looked at their branched faces and limbs. Lights flickered in sockets that Tagwen assumed were their eyes in bright flashes of blue and lavender. The armor donning them was intricately wound steel plating that looked as if it were part of their bodies, and the helms they wore appeared as extensions of their tree-like forms. Two of the figures stood in front of the third, and Tagwen could faintly make out that it was holding something.

Faldïr, too, stood as if the words had been stolen out of his mouth. His body moved uneasily toward the figures, who stood silent and still. Tagwen willed her body to follow. Her limbs attempted to root themselves where she stopped, ineffectually. The slow approach she and Faldïr made did not cause the figures to stir. They remained as if they were statues that had sprung from the earth they now occupied. Tagwen was not unconvinced that this is how they came to be.

Faldïr and Tagwen finally stood in front of the figures, and Tagwen witnessed Faldïr wince and hold at his forehead.

"Don't hurt him!" she exclaimed as she helped Faldïr stabilize his balance.

"It is alright. Just do not look them in the eyes. I will handle this," Faldïr told her, stumbling back to correct his stance.

Following his order, Tagwen backed away and directed her gaze below theirs, but still the voice beckoned in her mind. "Eïluèl," it said in a raspy whisper. She fought against the temptation to lift her eyes, but the voice repeated the call until her will failed. As she looked, the vision of their fiery eyes flashed in front of hers and she was back in the dream that haunted her.

She exited the shrouded fen and came to the edge of the world. The view of the ship and the maiden aboard were in front of her once more. Only this time, she could hear the woman call, "Eïluèl." The word floated on the air as a whisper but felt thunderous in her mind.

Instead of falling into the earth as she had done so many times before, Tagwen responded. "I do not know what that means! Who are you?" she shouted across the void.

The woman repeated the call as the earth split further open, and Tagwen fell in as she always had, arriving where she now stood in the camp. Her body was overcome with nausea, and she fell to the ground and retched. Picking her head up, she looked around and noticed all the elves and her men were catatonic, staring at nothing. Faldïr was at least wincing animatedly, and Tagwen assumed they must be doing the same thing to him, but perhaps he knew what they meant.

Moments passed as Tagwen wrestled herself from the ground. The two figures who stood in the front parted to reveal the third. In its arms was a spiritless figure cloaked in a torn gray and muddied gown; it was King Roìbert Dùghlan's daughter, Mòrrea.

"What did you do to her?!" Tagwen wailed as the third figure approached her.

The figure stopped in front of Tagwen and offered her the girl. It was the tallest and brawniest of the three, its eyes continual azure flames. Tagwen managed to avoid its face and noticed Mòrrea was still breathing.

"Thank the seas," she exhaled as she accepted Mòrrea into her arms. "Thank you," she said to the being.

The strange presences reformed a line and disappeared into the Forest. Rustles of wind and snow followed them, breathing life back into the fort.

The faint hum of chatter returned as the soldiers resumed their business, apparently oblivious to recent events.

Faldïr turned to look at Tagwen. "Are you alr— Who is she?" he asked.

Tagwen blinked a moment and looked down. Mòrrea's angelic face had a faint scratch that looked like it was from a branch, and her hair was besmirched with leaves and dirt. Tagwen looked up at Faldïr, who was rubbing his head. "This is the Princess of Middling," she revealed.

Faldïr looked panicked. "Bring her to my tent. Quickly."

Tagwen followed and scanned the glade. It seemed the events that she had witnessed were not known to anyone else.

Inside Faldïr's lodging, Tagwen laid Mòrrea on the makeshift bedding and covered her in blankets. "She's so terribly cold. Can we get some hot water?" she asked Faldïr.

"Yes, I'll fetch some," he said and left.

Tagwen began to remove the leaves from Mòrrea's hair and brushed away some of the dirt. "What are you doing here?" she muttered to the girl.

Faldïr returned with a bowl of warmed water and grabbed at a nearby cloth. "Here," he said, setting them both on the table beside Tagwen.

She took the cloth, dipped it in the water, and proceeded to pat at Mòrrea's face and forehead, cleaning the small spat of blood on her cheek and the dirt from her brow.

"Who were they?" she asked as she worked.

"They—" Faldïr shook his head in disbelief. "They were the Naovïlrūn. The Guardians of the Forest."

"The Guardians of Obedience?" Tagwen asked, seemingly shocked.

"Yes. How-how did you know that?" Faldïr quizzed.

"Ualan spoke of them when we first arrived," she explained.

"Yes, well. They have never shown themselves in the entirety of my house's existence. There were records of them making themselves known in times of dire need, but this? Why is she here?" Faldïr's countenance was unreadable to Tagwen. She had assumed this was true elven shock, but she could not be sure.

"Did you hear them?" Tagwen asked.

"I told you not to look into their form!" He scolded and rubbed his face. "It is a miracle you are not a bumbling animal right now! Their method of communication is severe; no human and hardly any elf is known to have survived it. Are you sure of yourself, do you remember who you are?" He looked into Tagwen's eyes and carefully scanned her person.

"Yes! Faldïr, I am fine. I was sick for a moment, but I came to quite easily enough."

"What did they say to you?" he asked.

"They whispered a word or a name. It seemed elvish so I could not tell. But they took me somewhere. I was living through a dream I have had in the past," she explained.

"What did they say?" Faldïr pressed, his expression stern.

"Eh-ee-loo-ell, Eïluèl," she shared. "I apologize for my unlearned pronunciation, but what does it mean?"

Faldïr leaned away and his stature slackened. "In Lènagïlèn, it means 'earth's smile'. I do not know the significance of that. They are not known to be very... clear," he explained.

"What did they tell you?" Tagwen asked. "It looked as if it wasn't very pleasant."

"It wasn't," Faldïr confirmed. "But alas, they told me nothing. It was only dark. I feel their presence may strangely have been… well, meant for you."

"Tasar?" rasped a weak voice behind them.

Their attention diverted to the delicate individual in their care.

"Mòrrea! Thank goodness. It's me, Tagwen. Are you alright?" She took the girl's hand.

"Tagwen? Wh-where am I? I was — running. It was dark and cold. What is this place?" Mòrrea fought to string together her words.

"You are in the Ebrïhèïlè," Faldïr answered.

Mòrrea's eyes widened, and she tried to sit up.

"No." Tagwen stopped her. "No, you need to rest."

"You must be the Lord Eilfaren!" Mòrrea exclaimed.

"How do you know of me?" Faldïr approached and stood at her bedside. "Have you been sent here by your father?"

"No! Please. I — that's where I was! I was running into the Forest to try to warn Tasar that they were coming," she explained to Tagwen.

"Tasar? Tasar Vanelis?" Faldïr asked.

Mòrrea gulped as her hand gripped Tagwen's tighter and she looked back and forth between the two of them.

"I will handle this," Tagwen assured her, as she patted her hand. She stood and motioned for Faldïr to follow.

"How does she know one of my scouts?" Faldïr asked, clearly confused.

"I think perhaps we should let him explain," Tagwen suggested.

Faldïr looked out across the camp and spotted Tasar at a

bench nearest the fire. "Scout Vanelis!" he shouted, causing everyone to turn to him.

Tasar Vanelis stood, and Tagwen recognized him once again as the guardian of her room. "The freckle," she whispered under her breath.

Tasar approached and bowed to them both. "Yes, my lord?"

Faldïr gestured for him to enter his tent and Tasar stopped abruptly as soon as he was inside.

Mòrrea gasped as she saw him. It was then Tagwen noticed a single tear falling down the Tasar's cheek.

"Would you care to explain how this girl of the Outlands called you by name?" Faldïr commanded.

Tasar swallowed and another tear followed the first. "My lord, I —" he started but could not continue.

Tagwen sensed Faldïr's frustration but looked to Tasar. "This is the Princess of Middling and she has had an unsettling night. Please see that her needs are tended." Tagwen urged the elf forward and he moved instinctively to his beloved, kneeling by her bedside, and holding her in his arms, as if he were no longer able to bear being without her.

Faldïr's stance straightened, and his eyes widened as he watched the scene unfold. He moved to protest, but Tagwen turned and held a hand to his shoulder.

"Love, dear Lord. Love," she whispered.

Faldïr's stern face softened as his shoulders relaxed. He looked back to the image of their embrace, and then slowly looked away. "Remind me not to tell you any more stories," he quipped. No smile came over his face, but he was no longer vexed by the encounter. He backed away reverently from Tagwen and bowed to leave the tent.

"Is he going to send me away?" Mòrrea asked Tagwen.

"Not as of yet. You have some explaining to do, though," she said, then paused before adding, "The both of you."

Tasar looked at Mòrrea and held her face in his hands. "I will speak to him. This is not your fault. He will know that," he comforted.

Mòrrea's eyes welled with tears as she pulled and held Tasar close. They let go of each other and Tasar stood and bowed to Mòrrea. Before he passed Tagwen, he bowed to her as well. "Thank you for protecting her," he said, sounding deeply grateful.

Tagwen bowed her head in response and the elf left to face his fate. She then turned her attention to the girl. "Why are you out here, Mòrrea?" she asked.

The girl wiped the tears from her face and began. "I snuck away as my father's army set out. I couldn't sit by and do nothing. I tried to get through the Forest, but I kept getting lost. All I remember is laying down for a moment and falling asleep. When I awoke, I was here."

"But how did you cross the river?" Tagwen asked.

"I knew my father's army would avoid the bridge further South along it, and so that's where I went."

"Mòrrea, that was an incredibly dangerous thing for you to do," Tagwen scolded.

"I knew what I was doing," Mòrrea snarked. "I have gone that way before. It's the bridge where…"

"Where you two first met. Isn't it?" Tagwen realized.

Mòrrea's cheeks flushed. "I wanted to see how close I could get to the Forest. All the talk of elves made me curious if they did still exist. Tasar was scouting the southern bridge the night I decided to cross the river. I couldn't believe what I was seeing when we met, but he was just as interested. We have met there ever since — every full moon or so. Father and Jaelan hardly ever noticed I was gone, and if Goraidh knew, he never said anything."

Tagwen walked to her bedside and sat on its edge.

"You're going to have to fight my father, aren't you?" Mòrrea's voice quaked as she choked back tears.

Tagwen turned to the girl, who, in that moment, reminded her so very much of her sister, Rhona, as a child. She felt her chest expand as if she had taken a breath, but the relief was short-lived. "It will not come to that," she said forcefully, as if trying to convince herself.

"There's a lot of them, Tagwen. A thousand men at least from Oburim."

"A shame they have come all this way for nothing," Faldïr's voice entered the room, Tasar trailing behind him.

Tagwen stood, a light smirk on her face.

Faldïr motioned to the tent's opening. "Would you allow us the room, Queen Braithe?"

Tagwen bowed in response. "Certainly."

Tagwen reached one last time for Mòrrea's hand and squeezed it with a smile. Faldïr stopped her as she began to brush past him.

"You were right," he whispered.

Tagwen gave a brief nod in answer and pushed through the opening back into the frigid night air. The clamor of the camp had died down, and she noticed most of her men had gone to find some semblance of sleep.

When she entered her tent, she saw Breccan passed out while sitting against the crude bed. She grabbed the blanket and laid it over her captain. She sat next to Breccan against the bed and pulled her cloak around herself. Looking around the tent, she thought of her father. She wondered what he would do in moments such as this — what kind of preparations he would be making, if any. She was unsure there were any arrangements she could make for this unprecedented situation.

The candle on the improvised table was near its end. The wax overflowed its brass handle and onto the stump. The light shook violently when a breeze snuck its way through the tent cloth, but it was not a wind that finally snuffed out the flame — it had simply reached its end, and Tagwen tried, then, to sleep.

Dawn made a dark and hazy approach a few hours later and Tagwen was nudged awake.

"Tagwen. Tagwen. Time to wake up," Breccan's voice urged.

Slow blinking and pained expressions met the impromptu alarm. "Is it morning?" Tagwen labored herself upright, every movement arduous.

"I am not sure. It still looks quite dark, but I hear movement outside."

Tagwen stretched and pulled her neck and back to an

adequate sitting position and rubbed her eyes. There was indeed rustling outside, and Tagwen did not want to appear off guard. She turned to a kneeling position and hoisted herself up from the floor using the edge of the bed. Standing, she twisted her body to loosen her muscles and reached a hand to Breccan, who accepted the assistance.

"I'll go see what's happening. Feel free to take a moment," Tagwen said.

"Don't have to ask me twice," Breccan said, plopping herself down onto the bed.

Tagwen snorted and left. Looking up to the sky, she could tell it was somehow morning, but the gloom felt akin to an unfortunate portent.

A few elves were scattered about, rekindling the central fire, assembling armory stations, and even a few prepping a morning meal: tea and bread with some kind of soup variant. Tagwen approached the tea makers and bowed.

"Is the Lord Eilfaren about?" she asked.

They nodded and handed her a cup of tea. She motioned for a second and they obliged. She cautiously entered Faldïr's tent, expecting to find Mòrrea sleeping, but found only Faldïr and his squire helping him into his armor. A worried look fell over her face and Faldïr dismissed his assistant.

"She is fine. She is in the healing tent with Scout Vanelis," he assured, and Tagwen breathed in relief, handing him the second tea.

Faldïr accepted the drink and motioned for Tagwen to sit. "They have finished constructing the bridge. I am not sure what they are waiting for in crossing, but it seems cowardly to come at us in the night. I think, however, that is precisely their aim," he reported.

"I am not sure why they would even think they have a better chance of navigating this Forest in the night," Tagwen pondered aloud.

"Neither do I," Faldïr agreed. "But I had a thought."

Tagwen waited with anticipation as Faldïr continued, "We ride out and meet them," he suggested.

"Meet them?!" Tagwen cried.

"Yes, give them a chance to turn before they make the mistake of defiling the Forest's floor."

"Might that not be their hope? To lure you from this safety?" Tagwen suggested.

"Is that a strategy of theirs?"

"It seems to me that it would give them the best chance. It would choke our armies along the bridge that they've constructed. Who knows what they have rigged it to do," she said.

"Hmm. I had not considered that," said Faldïr.

"I am… conflicted, Lord Eilfaren. I appreciate the idea of meeting them and giving them a chance to turn, but I am scared to lose any advantage that may save the lives of our men. They also include a counsel whom I believe to be the instigator of this dangerous effort."

Faldïr cooled his tea and took a long drink. "E'ruleïl forewarned of his like. I fear him not. As for the moves we intend to make, I will decide within the hour."

Tagwen nodded and stood to make her way to the opening.

"I would appreciate, queen of men, if the decision is made to meet them, that you will be at my side," Faldïr added before she left.

Tagwen turned and bowed. "I will be where the Ebríhèïlè needs me," she promised.

Faldïr gave a soft, grateful smile and Tagwen returned to her own tent to find Breccan still sprawled on the bed, twirling Saìde in the air.

"Deep in thought, are we?" Tagwen chuckled, causing Breccan to snap into a seated position.

"Warn someone, will ya!" Breccan huffed.

"It's a little cold, but here," Tagwen said as she offered her captain her untouched tea.

"Thanks," Breccan said. "Anything going on out there?"

"Lord Eilfaren is considering meeting them at the bridge they've made."

"An interesting choice."

"That's what I thought."

"Well, maybe it's a good decision. Gives them a chance to run," Breccan snickered.

"The only problem would be if that Sage is there, which I am most certain he is," predicted Tagwen.

"Just don't let the creep speak," Breccan said and was met with a snort from Tagwen.

"I worry that he may know Mòrrea is here," Tagwen said.

"Mòrrea's here?! How on earth did she get here?" Breccan shouted.

Tagwen put a hand on her shoulder. "I'll tell you once we get out of this mess."

Breccan shook her head and gulped the remainder of the tea. "That girl's a wild one."

Tagwen nodded as a soldier of the elven guard requested entrance to inform her that Faldïr had made up his mind to meet the armies where they stood before they could get too close to the elven lands. Tagwen confirmed she understood and proceeded to prepare for the confrontation ahead.

Tagwen and her captain armored themselves by midday, though the darkness above indicated otherwise. Distant crackling of lightning and the soft boom of thunder echoed as the skies were encompassed in a storm. Luckily, the rain had been scant, but Tagwen was not convinced it would hold.

They approached the center of the encampment to see Faldïr accompanied by Pàdair, and the two of them were followed by their captains, Èhalūs Odægūl and Gelandric Kikdreth, respectively. To Tagwen's relief, Ualan and two additional knights of each party were also present, but she did not catch their names. She had chosen Lachlann and Iòsaph to join her and Breccan. The dozen of them set out at late noon to begin the hour's ride to meet their opposition head-on. Faldïr insisted they do not ride fast. He did not want the horses exhausted should they need to heel back into the Forest. Tagwen rode a mare of Faldïr's house, who felt as balanced and well-mannered as her own, but her heart ached at not knowing where Seasaìdh or Erul had gone.

Onward they rode, the rain picking up as if to urge them back inside. Yet Faldïr pressed on, unwavering in his determination to meet the challenge ahead. Tagwen admired the tenacity but leaned to Ualan to quietly ask, "What do you think of this plan?"

Ualan's brooding nature was only enhanced by the onslaught of rain dampening his face. "I do not trust these men," he huffed. "But I trust Lord Eilfaren."

"As do I," Tagwen agreed.

The delayed approach felt excruciating, as Tagwen could begin to make out the line of men waiting on the other side of the Irrihead. In the ever-growing darkness, she saw the traitorous banners of Oburim and Middling lit by struggling torches, their wetted pennants fighting to fly freely in the storm's winds. A horn sounded and she watched the line of men reform into a shield wall — some extending to the middle of the bridge.

Cowards, she thought.

She saw the archers nock and hold their bows, arms shaking from the cold. These armies had not seen war in decades. It was Tagwen's men who'd fought against the menaces of the Black Isle. Middling's men were untested, and there was no chance they knew how to fight against both the elves and the dwarves.

The small troop approached the edge of the bridge cautiously and Faldïr called out, "Will those who have authority over your regiment meet with us?"

Silence was their answer, except for the faint stretch of bows and the occasional clink of armor and steel. Then, Tagwen saw Roïbert, Daïdh, Jaelan, and Goraidh emerge from an opening in the front barricade. All upon steeds, they crossed over the bridge and stopped at its edge. Something about King Dùghlan was unsettling to Tagwen. He was fully armored in an uncharacteristic black armament, and his gaze was stern and distant, as if he were not really looking through his own eyes. King Arasgain had a similar countenance, but his stylistic appearance was very much still his own, though now donning traditional Oburim steel plating.

Prince Jaelan mimicked much of his father's dress, but his look was even more sinister than Tagwen had ever known him. He glared malevolently at the elves and dwarves — as if he were ready to spit on the ground where they walked. Tagwen had not liked Jaelan much, but this was a disturbing evolution for any man. Finally, the master behind the curtain, as Tagwen was now convinced, Goraidh. His plum robes were now a rich black, embroidered with a silvery thread that created an emblem that Tagwen did not recognize as part of any house. Its vague outline looked like that of a flame and a winged creature, but she could not be certain.

"What traitor is so bold as to approach and attempt to entreat with the kingdom of Middling?" Roìbert demanded.

"Traitor?! Why, you ought to know all 'bout that—" Pàdair began shouting before Faldïr held up his hand to silence him.

"I am Faldïr Eilfaren, Twelfth Son of the name, Lord of Thrindūl and Protector of the Ebïhèïlè. You stand here in what seems to be a preparation of war — a long avoided encounter between the men and elves of this land."

"It was you who began the treasonous assault on the lands

of men, you duplicitous coward. Elves have hidden in their hole like vermin for so long, we are simply here to destroy a pest," Jaelan spat from beside his father.

Tagwen could see Pàdair seething underneath his helm and felt herself fighting to reach for her blade to cut down this pathetic excuse for a prince. Roìbert pushed his son behind to silence him and then pulled out a scroll, from which he read.

"You, the elves, have been accused of faithless deeds against the lands of men in an act that directly violates the Treaty of Ellingrath. You have decimated farmlands and harmed civilians in your pursuits of the lands you have long claimed are your birthright, hereby known as the Greyrest. How do you plead?" he demanded.

"This is not a trial!" Tagwen shouted. "You have no proof of these allegations, as I have seen your lands and can attest that no harm has come to them."

Suddenly, the Sage trotted forward, and light felt stolen from the world as his silverlight eyes pierced hers. Tagwen attempted to rebuke his presence, but her words caught in her throat.

He pulled out his own scroll and read.

"Tagwen Braithe, you are hereby condemned as a traitor to the kingdoms of men, the lands of Vostheloren, and are relieved of the crown you have stolen. It has been decided by the great kingdoms of Middling and Oburim that Yeacralas is in violation of proper attendance and will thusly be put in the charge of Prince Jaelan Dùghlan."

"Say the word and he dies," Tagwen heard Breccan behind her hiss through gritted teeth.

The Sage continued, "Tagwen Braithe, you and your men who have joined you are thusly banished from the kingdoms of men, as it is clear you have found solace in tying yourselves to the likes of conspirators such as those you stand with today."

"You gutless skulkers! Yukanskei drofiindahk!" Pàdair shouted as he unsheathed his greataxe.

Tagwen watched as the bows raised and Roìbert held up his hand to lower them. "You all have until midnight to retreat into the hovels from which you came, and then formally resign any unfounded claim you think you have on the Greylands. If you do not comply, we will cut you all down and the Forest with you," he proclaimed.

"We shall meet you in battle then," Faldïr replied.

Thunder cracked above them as the skies highlighted the tense silence, but hoofbeats coming from behind Tagwen redirected her attention. Upon an elven mare rode two figures, and Tagwen's heart sank. Mòrrea and Tasar rode through the meeting party.

"Father, you must stop this!" Mòrrea screamed as she dismounted the horse. Tasar dismounted too and followed behind her.

"Mòrrea, what are you doing with these animals?! Come here, now," Jaelan instructed her.

"Oh, shut up, Jaelan! You're even more oblivious than they are," Mòrrea scowled.

"Mòrrea, your brother is right, come join us, my dear," Roìbert pleaded, and for a moment Tagwen thought she saw his eyes flicker, as if the true part of Roìbert was being brought back to life by his daughter.

Standing between the two parties, Mòrrea stood proudly and defiantly against her father. "You are wrong about them. They've done nothing wrong, and you know it, father. You know it truly in your heart. You've been poisoned to think of them as these monsters, but it is you who has turned into the monster!"

"Mòrrea, you are too young to understand. Please, listen to me," Roìbert begged.

"No. I won't stand for it any longer. Father, I have seen their goodness. I am in love with an elf," she protested, pulling Tasar's hand to hers.

"Accursed scoundrel!" Jaelan screamed at Tasar and drew his longsword. Tasar drew his also, prompting the remainder of each party to react in kind.

"Enough!" Faldïr shouted. "No blood is going to be shed here and now. You should listen to your daughter, king of men. You fight the wrong war."

Flashes of anger, confusion, and hurt blinked in King Dùghlan's eyes, and Daïdh was as stoic as Tagwen had last seen him. His movements did not even look like his own.

"They cannot be reasoned with," Goraidh hissed at Roìbert. "Your daughter has become corrupted as well, it seems."

"Snake!" Mòrrea accused. "I thought you cared for our family, but now I see. You've done this to him! To all of them! You probably lied about my mother too, didn't you?!" Mòrrea moved toward them as she screamed.

In her step, the world stopped, until the thrash of flesh broke the silence.

Tagwen watched in slow motion, her breath roaring in her head as she saw an arrow cut through the space in front of her and into Mòrrea's chest. Scarlet drops mixed with the wetness of the rain, saturating the ivory linen that soaked her gentle frame to the bone. Tagwen dismounted her borrowed steed as fast as she was able, but still felt the strings of time holding her back. Mòrrea began to fall to the earth, as all assembled watched the inexplicable unfold. Tagwen managed to catch her on the way down and held the darling in her arms. Mòrrea sputtered and choked on her own blood as Tagwen looked down at the arrow. It was not of any make she had known. Its shaft was like that of bone, its fletching looked to be some kind of scale, and it was black, like darkness, black like death.

She looked toward where the arrow had been released and saw a lone bowman on the horizon to the South.

It was then that Faldïr's gaze caught up with hers, and the single figure became many.

"Mœrdeth!" Faldïr bellowed as he drew his sword.

The kings of men were shaken, something had broken. Their gaze became their own and it was overtaken with fear. Roìbert was stunned in silence as he stared frozen at his beloved daughter.

Tagwen looked up and screamed, "It's an ambush! Rally your men!"

The words did not seem to register, and the horses began to fight against the anxiety they were sensing.

Tasar fell to his knees as he watched in horror the life slowly fade from his lover's eyes. Tagwen looked at his mortified expression and instructed, "Take her back, now!" But Tasar did not move. "Now, Tasar! You need to get her out of here! Now!"

Blinking wildly as he tried to refocus, he nodded and Tagwen stood with Mòrrea draped in her arms. More arrows began to slice through the air, and she heard the screams of the Middling and Oburim armies being knocked down. Tasar remounted the mare they'd ridden and Tagwen draped Mòrrea gently over the horse's back and into his arms.

"Go! Now!" she commanded, and he rode back to the Forest.

Looking around, she saw Lachlann, Iòsaph, and Breccan scrambling to avoid being hit. Ualan was firing his bow toward the mœrdeth army. Pàdair and his knights were holding shields in front of their collective group.

"Fall back!" she yelled to Faldïr.

"We must fight!" he responded, but looked back in worry as the line of archers grew into at least a thousand foot-soldiers strong. All were clad in black and bone.

"Faldïr, we need more men!" Tagwen pleaded and he finally nodded.

"Fall back!" he ordered his men and the dwarves.

"What do we do?! There's so many of them!" Breccan shouted at Tagwen.

"I'm going to try to get Middling and Oburim to form up! You need to go back and secure the Forest with the others!" she shouted in the rain, amidst the crash of thunder.

"I'm not leaving you!" Breccan insisted.

"Go! Now! Ruiseal, Catach, head back into the Forest, now!"

"Your Majesty?" Ruiseal protested.

"That's an order!" Tagwen yelled.

"You heard her, ride!" Breccan ordered the two of them, and before she turned to leave, she looked at Tagwen. "You best know what you're doing!"

"Go!" Tagwen yelled again.

Breccan urged Arofel onward and followed the other parties back into the safety of the Forest.

Scrambling, Tagwen ran over to the king of Middling, who was yelling at his men.

"Run! Run while you can!" he screamed over and over to a crowd of soldiers who were struggling under the onslaught of arrows, confused as to what to do or where to go.

"Roìbert! You dog-headed idiot!" Tagwen screamed.

Roìbert turned around and looked to see where the insult had come from, and Tagwen could see the malice that painted his eyes had been washed away. "We must run! We will die out here! There is no hope! What have I done?" he lamented.

"Pull your men into rank. We need to form a wall," Tagwen said.

Roìbert looked as if the instructions were in a language he did not understand.

Daïdh, too, was lost when it came to instructing his men. He looked at Tagwen. "What are we to do?"

Tagwen grabbed her elven mare as she was rearing about and pulled her down. "Easy, easy," she soothed. "We must fight, dear one."

The horse calmed long enough to let Tagwen mount, and the

queen unsheathed her sword to help draw notice to herself.

She rode to the seeming front of the scrambling lines of Middling and Oburim.

"Men of Middling, of Oburim! Hold your position! Hold… Your… Position!" she commanded. The knights that heard followed her order, and the rest fell in line with their companions. Many stepped over accumulating puddles and the bodies of fallen comrades. Others trembled breathlessly in fear of the unfolding situation.

When Tagwen had finally garnered the attention of most of them, she gave the next command. "Archers! Ready! Aim! Fire!"

Arrows of Middling and Oburim spewed in the air and caught some of the oncoming foot-soldiers, who were advancing on their position. Tagwen repeated the same order, and Roìbert rode to her side, sword drawn.

"What can I do?" he asked her.

"Lead them!" she shouted at him, and he nodded, raising his sword in the air. In a battle cry, he howled, "Knights! To arms!"

"To arms!" Daïdh echoed.

So, the push began, Tagwen, Roìbert, and Daïdh led the charge onto the lowlands, into the affray of an army none of them recognized.

The clash became a blur to Tagwen as the figures she was fighting against shifted around her like shadows. Glimpses of bone masks, and what she could swear were red eyes, made her feel like she was battling ghosts of a nightmare. Roìbert and Daïdh had kept up well enough, but Tagwen could tell the men who remained were being torn down too quickly. Between felled foes she would look for any signs of hope or relief, but none yet revealed themselves. Fraught with anxiety and exhaustion, she knew her only hope now was to cut down as many of them as she could. Leading them toward the Forest was another thought, but she had to be sure the internal armies were ready, and she had not yet heard dwarven drums or elven horns.

"We are being overrun!" Tagwen heard Roìbert cry above the clash.

Tagwen saw the two kings but suddenly realized she had not seen King Dùghlan's petulant son or his Sage. Beyond the battlefield was Tagwen's answer. Two dark figures were making their way South to claim the helm of Yeacralas. Newfound waves of anger swelled in Tagwen, and she cut through a line of opponents to reach a small hill of the lowlands. The numbers did not favor the men, and it was getting darker. Dusk was upon them, and the storm already obscured much of their vision.

Before Tagwen could realize the significance of the hour, a beacon was lit on the highest part of Greyrest's peak — a pale blue aura, like the one she had seen on the Irrihead's bridge. She squinted to try to make out its source, but the continued surge of enemies would allow her no adequate reprieve. The light grew brighter as it appeared to be getting closer and the armies were momentarily transfixed. The aura's heavenly glow enveloped the skies and elicited fear from many on the battleground, most notably the unknown attackers. In what sounded to be a harsher version of the elven language, many began to yell at each other, pulling out of the fight.

They're retreating, Tagwen realized with relief. She looked up again at the light source. The light began to pulsate, and though it pained Tagwen to see, she was grateful that it was more of a hindrance to the aggressors.

"What is that?" Roìbert yelled toward her, shielding his eyes with his arm.

At that moment, Tagwen knew.

Erul.

Relentless rain beat down on the survivors, and Erul approached with Seasaìdh and a shrouded stranger alongside. Seasaìdh whinnied in delight in seeing Tagwen, and Tagwen's heart was full in seeing her mare's safe return.

"We must move into the Forest — I do not know if that will be enough of a deterrent," Erul called above the roar of the rain.

"What was that?" Tagwen asked.

"The light of the Èlavïl," Erul answered.

"The what? Why did that work?" Tagwen pressed as a crack of lightning ripped through the sky that caused her to flinch and the horses to cry out.

"Come I will explain, we must move into the Forest. I do not know that they will not come back," Erul urged.

Tagwen nodded, and looked to Roìbert and Daïdh, who were assessing the horror that had befallen the grounds.

"Gather whoever is left. We must make for the Forest and out of this storm. They may return," she said.

"We can't go in there," Roìbert said. "Not after what we've done."

"That wasn't a suggestion," Tagwen warned.

With an uneasy nod, Roìbert proceeded to follow her instruction, and Erul took the helm of the line.

"Follow carefully! And sheath your arms. You are not welcome here, but we have little choice," Erul instructed.

The path through the Forest was unwelcomely dark, but Erul's staff cast the pale blue light as before to guide them. It did not take long for the group to enter the campground that the elves and Tagwen's men had occupied. She caught sight of Faldïr and Pàdair, who stood aghast at their approach.

"Stay here," Erul instructed the uninvited guests, and he and Tagwen addressed Faldïr.

"What are they doing here?" Faldïr snarled.

"The dark army has gone for now, Lord Eilfaren, but I know not if they will insist upon their pursuit. No one is safe out there at present," explained Erul.

"Seems no less than they deserve," Pàdair scoffed.

"I agree," Tagwen said, "but we are meant to be the protectors of fairness, are we not?"

Pàdair huffed, "Read Krarnolim, do yeh?" He then nodded. "Well, of course she's right. And they tried taking your throne from yeh!"

Then Tagwen remembered. "The Sage, and Jaelan. They're making their way towards Yeacralas!"

"As I assume was always their plan," said the shrouded figure Tagwen had forgotten had accompanied Erul.

"Name yourself and answer how you come to know of this," Faldïr demanded.

"Surely, you must remember me, mærhïl," the mysterious

visitor replied.

The elf then revealed himself. His long, gingered hair and striking green eyes elicited a gasp from both Tagwen and Faldïr. For Faldïr, it was the recognition of the elf himself. For Tagwen, it was the sight of Breccan's features.

"Mæranedïl, home at last," Erul announced.

7
Uniting Vostheloren

Faldïr looked over Mæranedïl and exhaled with satisfaction and unbridled relief. "We feared you might have been dead after all this time. Ylerïan mourned for years. Where have you been?"

"He was not easy to find, but I had heard rumor of a man matching his description in the North, near Stoneheim Grove," Erul explained.

"I am not here for good," Mæranedïl said. "I have been brought forth to assist my brethren and I shall, but the walls of Thrindūl will not be my end."

Faldïr looked upset at this but nodded. He then looked to the company of intruders that they had brought with them.

"What of them?" he asked.

"We may yet need them, Faldïr," Erul said.

"For what purpose? So they may be close enough to cut us in our sleep?" Faldïr retorted.

"Something changed, Faldïr," Tagwen said. "It is as if they have awakened out of a dream. They are not the same men we met out there."

"Sure look the same to me," Pàdair argued.

"This human is right," Mæranedïl looked to Tagwen. "Forgive my informality, but the two you spoke of earlier heading to Yeacralas, I surmise that had always been their plan — to lead the kingdoms of men, elves, and in their luck, dwarves, into the trap that you all... well... fell into," he explained.

"Ahh, yes, this is Queen Tagwen Braithe," Erul introduced.

Mæranedïl bowed. "Queen Braithe, an honor."

"I am not so sure I will be able to claim that title much longer if they intend to filch it and my kingdom," Tagwen replied.

Tagwen noticed the crowd that had surrounded the camp. All manner of elves, men, and dwarves were watching the central party, awaiting word from their leaders.

"We should talk somewhere more private to discuss what to do next," Tagwen suggested.

"Fortifying ourselves in Thrindūl for the time being would be the wisest option, I am afraid," Erul said to Faldïr.

Faldïr's shoulders tensed, and he swallowed before answering. "Those men will go no further than the vale. I do not want them near my house or my people."

"As you wish, dear lord," Erul nodded.

Faldïr turned to the onlookers and addressed them kindly. "Members of all houses, we have been met with even stranger times than we set out with. Prepare yourselves. We journey further into the Forest."

Tagwen finally caught sight of Breccan, whose eyes were

glued to Mæranedïl in curiosity, anger, and wonder. The men behind her of Tagwen's accompaniment were tired. Tagwen could see their sluggish movements and weary expressions — loyalty the only thing carrying them at this moment. A pang of guilt ran through her, as she wanted to ease their burden but was unaware of what she could even do for them.

"What of my daughter?" she heard Roìbert shout from the post where he was tasked to heel. He dismounted and attempted to approach Faldïr, but a circle of elven knights held him at the end of their readied bows.

Faldïr met him where he was and bid his archers to step away. "I have had her sent into the healing house of Ylerïan, my wife," he explained. "It would not do well to hope, king of men. mœrdeth arrows are not trivial shots," he consoled.

Roìbert's eyes seeped with tears as he tried to maintain his composure. "Will you allow me to see her?"

"I have no intention of barring you from your daughter, but neither you nor your cohort will trample upon my house unsupervised," Faldïr informed him.

Roìbert bowed in acceptance of Faldïr's decision and stepped back to take his place in the line of journeymen into the elven vale.

The ride was shorter than Tagwen had expected, and she found herself thanking the Forest for their expedient passage. Tension was heavy throughout the marching line. No matter who she glanced toward, their expression was one of great discomfort. Reaching the open vale of Thrindūl was at least a welcome breath of fresh air for those who had already been embraced by the elves.

Faldïr instructed that all men of the opposing armies were welcome to make some semblance of a camp in the vale but reminded them that they are not guests of this land and thusly were not free to wander. Tagwen noticed childish sneers of some men amongst both Oburim and Middling but was relieved to hear Roìbert and Daïdh repeat the command. The heads of houses then made their way into the eastern manor. Roìbert stood astonished at the resemblance to his own estate.

"It is true then?" he asked, seemingly amazed.

"Once our houses were aligned against a common threat, king of men. Generations of our peoples have forgotten that the stones laid on our grounds were placed by the same hands," Faldïr explained over his shoulder as he led them to the North wing.

Roìbert hung his head in shame, and though Tagwen felt some satisfaction in seeing the king put in his place, she also pitied him.

Faldïr, Erul, Mæranedïl, Roìbert, Daïdh, Tagwen, and Pàdair ascended the steps into the open door of the healing room that had only recently held Eachann. Through the door, the celestial visage of Ylerïan was bent over Mòrrea. She looked up at the party and Tagwen could see she had been crying.

"Mòrrea!" Roìbert cried out and ran to his daughter's side. His hand reached for her face and Tagwen saw the pause as he looked up to Ylerïan, who gently shook her head. Everyone else remained at the door, but Tagwen slumped against the nearby wall and put her hands over her face as she wept into her palms. Pàdair placed his hand on the forearm of the young queen.

"I'm so sorry, lass," he consoled.

"She's gone?" Daïdh asked.

Roìbert wailed and laid his head on his daughter's chest as he cried. Daïdh walked over to him to whisper his condolences, and Roìbert turned to his long-time friend and embraced him. Daïdh held and tried to soothe the grieving father as Roìbert wept into his shoulder, his body shuddering like a hound in the rain.

The pain of losing Mòrrea cut deep for Tagwen, as she saw the lifeless darling upon the table. She wanted to reach for her, to nudge her awake. Tagwen could hardly accept that the girl was gone.

Ylerïan moved over to the onlookers to give the grievers a moment alone.

"Let us convene in the atrium," she said quietly to the group.

King Barindroun offered Tagwen a handkerchief. Her trembling hands accepted it and she wiped at her face.

"Be at ease, Your Majesty," Pàdair calmed. "Why don't we get yeh some fresh air, eh?" he suggested.

Tagwen nodded, and he put his arm around her to lead her down the tower's steps.

They approached the main foyer where their companions had gathered. There, Tagwen witnessed the first embrace of reunited siblings, as Mæranedïl unveiled himself to Ylerïan. More tears fell as she thought of her own siblings.

"Afūsad!" Ylerïan exclaimed.

"Ylerïan," he smiled sadly. "I am sorry it has been so long."

Tagwen stood a step or two away from the others, and Erul approached her. "I am sorry, Queen Braithe," he said.

"She was too young to die, Erul. I should have saved her."

"It was not your fault, Tagwen," he counseled.

"I led them here, didn't I?" She turned with anger toward the ancient elf.

Erul looked at her with sadness and sighed, "I did not see it at the time, this plan of his."

"Who is he, anyway? And you — you're the one who saved me on the bridge, aren't you? What are you?"

The room fell silent as all those gathered looked at the pair. Tagwen rubbed her arms to ease her anxiety. Erul lowered his voice, "I know I've not been as forthright with you as much as perhaps I should have been, but time now beckons that we tend to these matters first." He turned to the crowd. "If there is any hope of saving our world, best we all be in agreement, yes?"

"A girl just died, for mountain's sake!" Pàdair objected.

"And more may die if we do not act swiftly, Master Barindroun," Erul responded.

"Many have already died. Not just my daughter," Roìbert interjected as he and Daïdh entered. He looked in shame at the room, but to Faldïr especially. "I have no right to speak in this house, or any place of this land because of my actions. I beg that you accept my only defense — that the serpent who infiltrated my house filled my dreams and waking eyes with a wicked darkness. Weak as I was in steeling myself against those thoughts, part of me still toiled to try and bring myself back." He approached Faldïr. "I beg your forgiveness, sir. All that was precious to me is lost, and I have naught anyone but myself to blame, but if you shall have it, I will serve your house as mine once did to any end that may find me," he pledged.

Faldïr's impassive countenance dissipated as he reached a hand toward the broken king. "Your daughter will not have died in vain," he promised.

Accepting Faldïr's hand, Roìbert nodded, still tearful but clearly grateful.

Faldïr looked to Erul to indicate he should continue.

Clearing his throat, he resumed his speech. "Goraidh, as you may know him, was once a kindred elf to me. Then he was known as 'Gegènlïf'. He has since gone by many names, none of which bear any importance to now. Most notably, however, he has long been corrupted by the daemon, Ruèhnar. He served him, unbeknownst to me, in the very beginning of this world. So much so, in fact, that at the battle that severed this land from its counterpart, he attempted to kill me, and nearly succeeded. With him, he took something of incredible value, but luckily only half of it. Its name has long been lost amongst your peoples but was known as the 'Afegèlœf ò Æselūnelèr'."

"Tome of Collective Memory, for our non-elven guests," Mæranedïl interjected.

"Quite right," Erul said. "The Tome of Collective Memory, as it were, served as the accumulation of histories from every kingdom of the world: elves, men, dwarves, and dracari."

"Dracari?" asked Daïdh. "What manner of creature is that?"

Erul lowered his head and closed his eyes. "They were a creation of Ruèhnar's that he thought would serve him, but the elves of the South found the first birthed dracari before he did and taught them the ways of the world, their language, and customs. There is much about them that would take too long to tell you now, but I can say the dracari's story does not end well. I have not been able to find any who have survived on this continent… until today."

Tagwen's eyes widened. "The wardens. They were soldiers unlike any I had ever encountered. I thought for a moment they were part of the Rogues, but their eyes—" she stopped herself.

"Red, like fire," Daïdh finished for her.

"Yes, it seems he has finally bent them to his will after countless centuries of being trapped with him. In manners of which I shudder to think," Erul confirmed.

"Why were they afraid of your light?" Tagwen asked.

Erul replied, "The light of the Èlavïl aids in casting out Ruèhnar's corruption. I cannot wield enough to remove it completely, but deterring them was better than nothing I would guess."

"Is this, Goraidh, then — is he after the other half of this book? And if so, why?" Ylerïan asked.

Erul nodded, remembering to return to his story. "Ah, yes. All stories, prophecies, and important accounts or decisions were made in that book. The caveat of it was that only selected Sages of each kingdom were allowed to write in it, with the Quill of Avantèas. Once, Goraidh and I were the keepers of the text, if you will — not Sages, but more so its guardians to ensure those who were permitted to utilize the book were the only ones who did. Goraidh is not after the other half of the book, as he could not acquire it if he tried — at least that is my hope. It was the last thing I managed to wrestle from him in what he believed to be my dying hour."

"You have it then?" Faldïr asked.

"No, thank goodness. With any luck, it resides far beyond the storm, in Ardenïl," Erul replied.

"I am sorry, but this seems like nonsense," Roìbert interrupted, confused. "Wielded light? A demon? A land beyond the storm? The storm guards the edge of the world. There is nothing beyond it."

"Many lifetimes I have seen come to pass, and with each generation our histories and the lands of the East became nothing more than fairytale. The everlasting storm that your kind has so long feared, and for good reason, is not the edge of the world, but rather the wall that divides us from its other half," Erul revealed.

"An entire other half? Are there people over there? How can you be sure?" Daïdh asked with astonishment.

"Once, the wall broke, when the monstrous sea serpent, Œdêrèg, thrashed through it," Erul explained.

She claimed it's a scale from the giant sea drake 'er great, great, great-grandfather or so encountered on a voyage once at teh beginnin' of a bygone age, Tagwen recalled the words of Blàr in The Siren's Whistle — what seemed like years ago now, and placed her hand on her chest plate, where underneath lay the trinket she had forgotten she had worn around her neck.

Bludrynd was… real?

"I had been on a voyage to find some manner of keeping the opening viable. Too many men, elves, and dwarves had given their lives for it. The only glint of hope I had was seeing a ship on the other side. Until it, too, suffered under the wrath of that primeval beast. Nothing else have I to go on. The storm stitched itself together to form the impenetrable wall you all see on the horizon, but I must believe that there are still those out there as there are here," Erul said.

"What hope is there of getting through now?" Tagwen asked.

"None that I know. Though this is not yet our quest," Erul answered.

"What is, then?" Roìbert asked.

"We have come to suspect that the reason Goraidh orchestrated all of this was to find the quill," Mæranedïl took up where Erul had left off.

"He regrettably has the latter half of the tome that contains the pages that were left blank for the prophecies of the future. I now see his plan was to write Ruèhnar's strength back into existence, to finish what he sought to do so very long ago — claim the world for his lord's own," Erul warned.

"Does he know where it is?" asked Tagwen.

"He is presently heading toward his best guess, I fear," Mæranedïl replied.

"The quill is in Marez? My kingdom holds no such novelty. If so, it has been long hidden from my family's knowledge," Tagwen said, beginning to feel a sense of panic.

"Seeing as how Yeacralas was the kingdom of Yacendïl,

it is the closest possibility. The location of the quill was never revealed to either Goraidh nor I. Yacendïl, in his later years, stowed the quill away, permitting knowledge of it to only those Sages who had been ruthlessly trained and matured to utilize the tool. Many agreed at the time to enforce the separation of the book and quill so none with malicious intent would have an easy time accessing both," Erul explained.

"From what E'ruleïl has told me, it was lucky that the last letter of Yacendïl had not fallen into his hands. I regret that its steward met such an unfortunate fate. Brìghde's brilliance, though, had kept it safe, right under his nose," Mæranedïl shared.

"Brìghde? Brìghde Catrìona?" Roìbert's face was pitiable: eyes red with sorrow and now quivering lips at the mention of his late wife's name.

"Yes. She did the world an incredible service — unknown and unthanked. A task she willingly accepted at my request to satisfy my own selfish desire," Mæranedïl lamented.

"You? You're the reason my wife is dead?" Roìbert's gaze became hardened and angry, and his fists clenched.

"King of men, Mæranedïl is not the reason your wife is dead. He is an unfortunate actor, perhaps, but their collective decision was for the good of us all. It was the traitor in your midst who could not break her, and thus took her life," Erul said.

"I will kill that worm if it is the last thing I do," Roìbert spat.

"Though I do not wish to imply that Lady Catrìona's actions were in vain, the letter does not tell us what we had hoped," Tagwen addressed Mæranedïl. "Surely you must know this."

"I fear there are few left who have the eyes to see its true message," Mæranedïl said, regarding Ylerïan.

"Me?" she asked.

"Heirs of Ærèg Èlasïl," he explained, solemnly.

"Oh," Ylerïan lowered her gaze in seeming disappointment.

Tagwen thought of Breccan for a moment, how she had been able to see things that Tagwen could not, and wondered if this was the explanation for it all. That somehow the friend she had known most of her life was… elven. That this man who bore her resemblance was the father she had thought abandoned her and her mother. Instead, Tagwen began to see that he was trying to save them.

"You involved my wife easily enough," Roìbert scoffed.

"She did not know of its contents either, only its importance. She knew as little as I could tell her, and I am sorry it wasn't enough to protect her." Mæranedïl bowed in apology.

"This 'feather' had better be worth the lives of my house! I have lost everything, everyone I loved. Gone! Even my son! My son has become one of them! One of the very traitors who killed his mother and sister. My dear Mòrrea—" Roìbert cried in pain.

"This 'feather' is worth the lives of many more than just your house," Erul said softly.

"Well, let's get on with it then. One of yeh read the thing," Pàdair urged.

Mæranedïl and Erul looked at each other. "There is… a bit of a condition with regard to that," Erul said.

"The letter can only be read on the pedestal from which it was penned, and Yacendïl had one forged specially. And, the writings can only be seen under a full moon, no less," Mæranedïl added.

"A full moon is due near three days from now. Where is this pedestal?" Tagwen asked.

"In a cave of the First Age known as the 'Fire Cave', 'Athœvab', which was once part of a series of caverns connected to the volcanic mountain of E'batheron. If it survived the destruction of the world, it would be within the island now known as 'The Black Isle'," said Erul.

"This has got to be some cruel joke," Tagwen scowled. "The Black Isle?! Full of bandits, murderers, and if you believe the rumors, vile creatures of a most horrid nature are said to lurk in its depths. My men and I have faced those enemies. They scarred Breccan and took the vitality from my own brother! Are you positive this is the only way?"

Tagwen was overcome with panic and anger. She had put her men through so much as it was, and hearing now that this nightmare was not yet over made her feel relentless guilt. Worse, she was now also having to fight the urge to rush into Marez with the flames of vengeance. The thought of the two traitors bringing their depravity and shadowed horde to the serenity of the coastal city enraged her. Worry weighed in her chest as she thought of Rhona, Enania, Elnan, all those of her house, even Mercher. She did not know what the occultist who ensnared the house of Dùghlan was capable of. However, amidst her anger, she softened as she saw Mæranedïl's fist clench at her mention of Breccan.

"I regret, dear queen, that this is the only way we have found," Erul answered. "The pedestal forged for Yacendïl, the light of the love of his life, and the eyes of an heir to their fated child. It is all we have determined."

"Erul told me it was your mention of 'moonlight' that helped bring it all together. It seemed so simple, but we had not considered such a mundane answer," Mæranedïl said.

"Well, it was actually Breccan who helped me come by that thought. You should be thanking her," Tagwen said.

Mæranedïl bowed. "Perhaps I shall," he replied.

"Are we off teh storm this Isle then?" Pàdair piped up.

Erul's expression became slightly pained at the thought and Tagwen realized that he had not meant for everyone to make the journey.

"Who do you mean to send?" she asked him.

He took a big breath and leaned slightly on his staff. "I do not think it wise to send our collective forces to a single location, when now we have a prominent threat looming in the South. And you, queen of men, may have a much larger role to play, yet," he told her.

"I will not leave my city to burn or be corrupted by his evil," Tagwen said.

"Perhaps," Roìbert began, "if we redirected our forces to Marez, to try and stop his madness, it would stay any chance of his knowing where this fated party is headed. He is likely expecting your hasty return to your kingdom."

"I would not ask any to fight for me without my being there," Tagwen stated.

"You need not ask, queen of men," Faldïr said. "You came to my house to protect it and protect it you have. The elves will honor our newfound partnership."

"Aye, yeh have the strength of Dholdron'lièr at yer back too, Yer Majesty. Yeacralas is our ally, and they are being threatened. We will answer the call," Pàdair added.

"Oburim owes you a debt, Queen Braithe." Daïdh bowed. "You were the only kingdom of men who were wise enough to try and prevent a war. Your house will not pay for our misdeeds."

Roìbert approached Tagwen. "My wife loved you as a daughter, and my daughter loved you as a sister. My son, too, loved you. Though I see now, perhaps in wisdom beyond your years, did you stay yourself from joining our houses." He then crossed his right fist over his chest. "I will fight for you. Middling will fight for you."

Tagwen moved to be in the middle of the surrounding company. She saw their sorrow, their uncertainty. Despite their heroic promises, she knew that this now was larger than them all. "Goraidh and Jaelan already have the upper hand and their army is not one to be trifled with," she started. "We'll need everyone well armored, as many suitable soldiers as we can muster. Their numbers hauntingly outmatched our own, but they likely do not suspect our cooperation with each other." Tagwen saw the hesitation and worry, but their gazes never broke from her. She continued, "We may have broken the treaty of this land, been misled, hunted, and tested at every turn. We have lost ones dear to us, and more are being threatened as we speak. I feel, friends, that traveling together, fighting together, perhaps even dying together, is now our destined road."

She unsheathed Mercy and held the blade aloft.

"I have sworn, to those of this land and the Seas that guide me, that I will lead faithfully and truly to any end."

One by one, each member held either a hand or their own weapon into the air, and Tagwen's heart began to race.

Father would be proud, she recalled Elnan's words, and now seeing those around her, believed them.

"Let us be the light in defiance of these darkening days!" she hailed.

"Let us be the light!" the room echoed in answer.

A moment of silence followed as they all reveled in this collective unity, and Tagwen felt hope being born anew.

Your people are lucky to have you, dear queen. She heard Ylerïan's gentle voice in her head, and smiled.

"Good! Settled then. We leave for Yeacralas as soon as we're able," Pàdair announced.

"First light would be best," Erul proposed.

"Even better! Always love an unreasonable timeline," Pàdair mocked, as he readied himself to depart.

"Let us go and make our respective preparations, then," Tagwen said.

Roìbert bowed to Tagwen to excuse himself and he approached Faldïr. "My daughter," he said. "I wanted to bury her with her mother, but I fear we will not have the means of escorting her there. Knowing now that they both shared a love for your people, would there be any chance that she is welcome to rest among them?" he asked with tears in his eyes.

"The Forest brought her here. There is no greater honor to those of this realm. We will embrace her as one of our own," Faldïr promised.

Roìbert nodded, and mouthed his thanks to the elven lord as he turned in haste to compose himself. Tagwen looked at Faldïr and smiled in thanks, and he bowed his head to her. She then approached Erul. "What is it I must do?" she asked.

"Not all is clear to me, I am afraid," Erul answered.

"Why then must I go to the Isle and leave others to fight in my stead?"

"I suppose I cannot make you, queen of men, but King Roìbert is right, Goraidh and Jaelan will expect your return. Marez is undoubtedly to turn into a trap for you. Letting a full army clear the path may be the safest plan we have."

"Is it not then a trap for my family already?"

"Likely, yes, dear queen. I regret that truth, but I feel keeping you away is better than potentially giving those monsters every advantage."

Tagwen turned away from him. She felt a burning in her chest as she considered the logic of the elf's words.

But I am supposed to protect them.

Erul continued, "It is my plan to join you. Mæranedïl also, since he is destined to be our eyes for this mission. I know only that we should bring a small accompaniment — just enough to keep us all protected. And a dwarf, they are masters of the underground so it would make sense to have one of them with us."

"I do not want to risk anyone else's life," Tagwen said, her gaze snapping to him.

"Your care is admirable, dear queen, but alas, we cannot do this alone," Erul reminded her.

Tagwen took a deep breath, attempting to calm the building frustration.

He is not wrong, Tagwen.

"Who should we bring?" she finally asked.

Erul stroked his beard in thought. "I feel Ualan would be a wise choice given his knowledge of the lands in general. Your captain too is a very admirable option."

Tagwen nodded, apprehensively. "I will consider your suggestions. For now, I need to inform my compatriots of my departure," she said.

"Of course, yes. They have served this land and its people well. They have all our thanks," Erul said.

Tagwen bowed and departed as the rest had, finding themselves back amongst those who were now their allies, though unsure of their next moves. She looked around the vale and reached her hand out to feel the sprinkling of rain from the tail end of the storm. Echoes of bustling and chatter hummed in the background of her thoughts as her heart sank thinking about the tasks at hand: sending away her men under the care of another and burying Mòrrea. A tender nudge pushed her shoulder, and she turned quickly to find Seasaìdh, led by Breccan.

"Oh, darling!" Tagwen exclaimed as she wrapped her arms around the mare's neck, and Seasaìdh draped her head over Tagwen's shoulder. The mare's whickering felt like home.

"Least Erul brought her back in one piece," Breccan quipped. "How… is she?" she fumbled for words.

Tagwen released Seasaìdh, and without looking at her friend, hung her head in sorrow. Tears welled in her eyes again as she recalled the girl's passing. Her head lifted slowly, and as she looked into her best friend's eyes, she could tell Breccan already knew.

"Mòrrea's dead."

Breccan let out a sharp breath and bit the inside of her lip to try and refrain from crying. "Those bastards," she spat. She aggressively rubbed the tears from her face. "What are we going to do about it?" she fumed, a deep crease forming on her forehead.

Tagwen glanced around for a moment, wondering what fate would befall those she surveyed. They were going to be sent to the Southern realm for her kingdom, and she would not be there to show them the way, or to explain to her family what was happening. She did not even know if they were presently safe.

"Tagwen?" Breccan tried to pull her attention back.

"Middling, Oburim, Dholdron'lièr, and Thrindūl have vowed to protect Yeacralas in my absence."

"Absence?" Breccan's face fell.

"Goraidh and Jaelan are headed to Marez because they think there is a token to be acquired from my house. They certainly must assume I am racing toward them, but they do not know that it will be an entire collective army that meets them. I do not think Erul is wrong that Marez may now be a trap for me. But more so, he thinks we may have an advantage with that letter we found. Apparently, there is more to it than we can see, but to reveal its truths requires us to go to the Black Isle."

"What on earth for?! Does he know who lives there? That place is awful," Breccan argued whilst unconsciously scratching at the scar etched across her lips.

"There are incredible things at stake, Breccan. If there is any chance I can help stop them, I must try. From what Erul has said and the things I have learned, I do not believe I have a choice. To accompany him potentially keeps more lives safe, and I can be moderately useful."

"What about our home? Our people?" Breccan asked.

"There may be no one left if I do not go. I have faith in those who have sworn to me their protection of Yeacralas. As I have faith in the fate that has found me."

"You really think this is what we need to do? In your heart?" Breccan asked pointedly.

Tagwen knew the question was not one Breccan took lightly. "In your heart?" meant everything, no argumentative questions asked afterwards, and even each following blindfolded if that is what was required.

With a nod, she answered, "In my heart."

Breccan stood attentively and nodded. "When do we leave?" she asked.

"I leave at first light."

"Nice try. Who is to join us?"

"You need not come, Breccan. I do not wish to risk your life in such a way. Especially not again upon that wasteland."

"Best of luck getting rid of me," Breccan scoffed. "So, I'll ask once more, who is to join *us*?"

"You would join me to the land you despise? For a journey that may lead to nothing?"

"You believe in it, don't you?"

Tagwen felt a rush in her chest. She could not determine why, but something about this quest called to her. She nodded.

"Good! Then yes, I will be joining you. But, please tell me we're not the only ones going out and stumbling around over there?"

Tagwen shook her head. "Erul and Mæranedïl will be in accompaniment. Erul has also suggested Ualan to come along as his knowledge of the lands will no doubt prove useful, as well as a dwarf to navigate the caverns on the Isle."

"There's actually caves there?" Breccan's brow raised. "Well I'll be," she chuckled. Her jovial nature then faded. "Shall we tell the others?"

Tagwen nodded reluctantly and gestured for Breccan to accompany her to deliver the news. With Seasaìdh beside her, Tagwen was imbued with a bit of courage and met her men as best she could without breaking down — telling them of the fate of Mòrrea, the truth of the army she had fought, and the decisions that now had to be made. Many, though exhausted and dreaming of home, protested to continue their service to Tagwen wherever she needed to go, but she assured them that home is where they were needed most. She told them of Goraidh and Prince Dùghlan, and what they intended to do. Confused glances brought worried questions that she fielded as they came, explaining that she, too, did not understand how these histories had been lost, or how the truth of the world had been so concealed. She assured them that they would not be alone — that all companies they had been amongst in this fight were to back them still.

In an unprecedented act, Tagwen gathered them together in a hug. "I will miss you all, but by land or sea I will come home," she promised.

Because duty demanded, Tagwen knighted Lachlann as Captain to lead the remainder of their small band:

By land and sea

To guide and to lead

I knight you, Lachlann Catach, son of Alenia and Colum Catach

Captain of the Yeacralan Guard.

May you serve our people well in this stead

And may the guidance of the sea follow you where you tread.

Lachlann proudly accepted this new position and pledged to secure their kingdom or die trying. Tagwen hid her worry at the thought that she may return to more of those she cared about not being there anymore and encouraged them all to take care of one another.

***

Midnight had nearly come upon them when Faldïr and a

procession of elves, all dressed in silken silver robes, entered the vale. With lanterns and flowers in hand, Tagwen saw the center of their entourage, pallbearers carrying Mòrrea. Her body had been cared for, cleaned, and oiled, and she was dressed in a finery of white silk embroidered with white crystalline jewels. Her long, tawny hair was draped perfectly upon her shoulders and was decorated with a crown of tiny white flowers that mirrored the stars. In her hands she held a pair of elven gloves, and Tasar's bare hands carried one corner of her burial cot.

Faldïr approached Roìbert, who had changed into a mantle of Middling's signature ochre hue. He donned no adornments and held his crown in his hands. The two bowed toward each other without speaking, and Faldïr gestured for Roìbert to walk alongside him. So, the line began with their lead — the elven cortege proceeding behind. Everyone joined as they saw fit, and in silence they all walked along the vale, through a thick curtain of flowered vines that were tied against trees to create an opening. Beyond the drapery was a mounded garden, each with a different pattern of flowers atop.

There was already a small gathering at one of the mounds near the front of the garden. Erul, Ualan, Ylerïan, Eachann, and Mæranedïl each held a lantern over an opening in one of the grassy knolls: Mòrrea's final resting place.

The gathering that had come to honor the princess spread out evenly around the garden, and Mòrrea's keepers brought her to the center, slowly and reverently, whilst the hum of dwarves mingled with that of the elves. Men fell silent in watch, kneeling in the salutes of their kingdoms to pay respect as the princess made her way past. Tagwen stood amongst her men, allowing the grieving father to speak his last unheard words to his daughter. He laid his crown at her side, and touched her hand as if afraid she would shatter. Tears stained his face as he bent to kiss her forehead. He held for a moment before breaking away, and then turned to Tasar with an extended hand. The elf took the king's hand and was led to his lover's side. Roìbert backed away to allow them one last moment together, still wiping his eyes. Tasar placed a hand gently on Mòrrea's and stared at her as if looking long enough would bring her back to life. Finally, he bent and kissed her cheek, so as not to take from her father's kiss, and uttered something Tagwen could not hear. He then returned to his post, to deliver his love to the earth.

Tagwen finally came forth and offered the locket of Lady Catrìona, laying it delicately near the crown. "I'm so sorry, Mòrrea," she whispered before moving away.

No words were spoken in prayer over Mòrrea's body. Everyone knew the angel had returned to the heavens. There was no need to try and secure her passage. However, song came from a voice Tagwen had not heard since she was a child. King Arasgain, in the ancient tongue of Oburim, sang the protection song of the Northlands. The baritone of his operatic voice carried effortlessly throughout the gathering as Mòrrea was placed in her chamber. Tagwen had forgotten the king was so adeptly trained and thought it beautiful that Mòrrea had brought out the best in everyone. The harmonizing of the elves and the bass of the dwarven hum created an orchestra of sound — all honoring a girl whose only transgression had been love.

With her love, though, came the greatest gift anyone could have given their world: the uniting of Vostheloren.

Perhaps she was 'Eïluèl', Tagwen thought. If there was anyone who could embody the earth's smile, it was Mòrrea. Though her light had now been carried with her into whatever fate followed this, at least it could no longer be stolen.

Mòrrea was laid to rest, and the mourners dwindled, though Tagwen remained behind.

"She rests in the sanctuary that was reserved for Lord Eilfaren, you know," Tagwen heard Erul say as he approached.

"I did not know that. Though I can think of no place more worthy to hold her for eternity."

Erul walked up and placed a hand on the knoll above Mòrrea's crypt as a sign of mourning and respect.

"Was she 'Eïluèl'?" Tagwen asked.

Surprised by the utterance, Erul beheld her strangely. "Who spoke that name to you?" he asked.

"The Guardians. They delivered her here, and I heard them speak that name repeatedly. I did not know what it meant until Faldïr told me," she explained.

"The Naovïlrūn? They spoke to you, and you lived to tell about it?" He blinked at her for a moment. "Did they say anything else?"

Tagwen shook her head. "Well, no, but they did take me into a dream."

"A dream? Of what sort?"

Tagwen, who had been kneeling beside Mòrrea's resting place, stood. "I have a recurring dream that I reach the… middle,

I suppose… of the world, but there's a chasm in between full of fire, screams, and death. On the other side there is a ship, a ship with a light like I have seen from you. Out of the light steps a woman. She is beautiful, though terrifying like a storm in the night, and usually she tries to reach out to me, but that time I heard her say that name. And her eyes — they look just like yours, and Goraidh's."

Erul took a breath as he leaned back, taking in all Tagwen had told him. He put a hand on the hill for a bit of balance as he squinted whilst searching for a response. Finally, he said, "Her name is Avourel. She was the daughter of the elven king of Ardenïl."

"Is she alive?" Tagwen asked softly.

"It was my sincerest hope that she had survived, and now I think I may have my answer. How long have you had this dream?" Erul asked.

"For near a decade now. The first time was when I became a soldier of my father's guard."

"When you were gifted your sword?" Erul asked with a raised brow.

"Actually — yes. Why? Is that significant?"

Erul stared at Tagwen in silence for a moment, then said, "After the goddess of Water, Lïflèn, dispersed her destruction upon the world in grief for her lost son, she created the five maidens of light, the Èlavïl, and wept. Her tears spilt upon the land of Ardenïl, creating something she did not intend, a gift that only the elves could ascertain."

"Immortality?" Tagwen asked.

Erul nodded. "Precisely. Now, this immortality came in the form of a flower that became known as the 'Tenaloetor Lïflèn' or 'Tears of Lïflèn'. Anabeh, the most gifted of maidens Lïflèn had created, had the ability to guide the roots of the plant across from the island of Ardenïl into the land we walk today. What was significant about this plant, as many came to find out, was that it was not to be plucked from the earth or have its roots cut. Thus, when the lands were split apart, the gift was removed."

"How, then, have you remained alive so long?" Tagwen asked, mystified.

Erul gazed off in apparent disappointment as he answered. "I, like Goraidh, was born to be a guardian of Anabeh and her sisters. This… *gift* was instilled in my being since the beginning, along with the magics you have seen — being able to harness the light of the maidens and manipulation of water."

"So Goraidh is immortal too," Tagwen said nervously.

Erul nodded.

"Does he possess those other powers as well?"

"No. His command of beasts was his endowment. Though, now, I have no way of knowing what sorts of power his service to Ruèhnar has granted him."

Tagwen wrapped her arms around her torso and her glance wavered.

Erul cleared his throat and spoke again. "Avourel," he said, "was a young princess. Naively, she plucked a flower from the mother plant and had it pressed into a blade as a gift for the love of her life, Eïluèl. In doing so, the sword could be wielded only by Eïluèl's hand, but it placed on her a curse.

"You see, Eïluèl was human. When presented with this flower, if they accept it, a human's soul is captured with it, and until the plant is returned to the earth, their soul is cursed to never rest. Their souls also return in many iterations of life, though completely unaware of who they had previously been. Many, by happenstance, I assume, found rest as the plant fell into the ground out of pockets, ignorance, or through the natural process of decay. But Eïluèl's gift lives because the blade it was pressed into also lives."

Tagwen did not understand, but unsheathed her sword anyway and held it outward. The flowered etching glinted in the light of the lanterns, illuminating Mòrrea's barrow. "No one else could ever carry it," she said, examining each of its facets as if for the first time. She traced the lines of the drooping three-petaled flowers along the fuller with her eyes — they looked like tears to her now.

"Because they cannot. Because they are not carrying the soul of Eïluèl with them," Erul explained solemnly.

"Should we melt it down then? Put her to rest? Or would—" Tagwen stopped, staring at Erul hopefully.

"I do not know," Erul shook his head. "I have suggested against it for many years, but selfishly, because I believe it may yet serve a purpose."

"How many people before me have brandished this weapon?"

"Many. Unfortunately, all unwilling to believe my words. There were many who cast it away, losing it for decades at a time. It has been stolen, buried, thrown away, used as a trophy, among other fates."

"What purpose do you think it serves?" Tagwen asked.

Erul paced around for a minute, stopping to look at the sporadic patches of starlight through the breaking clouds. "I believe that perhaps, because of this sword's imbued nature, that it may be a weapon that could bring about Ruèhnar's demise."

"We… I am meant to face this… demigod?" asked Tagwen, alarm in her voice.

"I do not mean for you to go alone, but none other than you can carry that blade."

Tagwen held the sword toward the sky, studying its balance, its weight, the way it had never seen a dulled edge. She wondered for a moment how she had not noticed its peculiarity before and paused in worry. "Goraidh noted the blade whilst I was in Middling and asked its name. Does he know its significance?"

Erul shook his head. "I doubt he does, or I feel he would have tried to purloin it from you. This sort of weapons-craft was not thought possible, and was considerably foolish to have been created — may its creators forgive my tongue. So, I do not suspect he would have reason to assume its nature. Let us hope he was simply enamored with the elven steel, hmm?"

"Does it have a name?" Tagwen asked.

"It was long ago known as 'A'elūdèr', 'forevermore'. A promise of love that Avourel and Eïluèl made to one another."

"A'elūdèr," she repeated. "That's beautiful. So it shall be called again — to honor her," Tagwen proclaimed, as she gently sheathed the blade. She looked at Erul and asked, "What was she like? Eïluèl?"

Erul smiled and picked up a lantern. He motioned for Tagwen to follow as they began making their way back to the main courtyard of Thrindūl. Along the way, he told Eïluèl's story.

"Eïluèl was a woman of the ages. A poet, swordsman, lover, adventurer — there was nothing that she feared except losing Avourel. She was also one of the youngest in training to be a Sage of the Tome of Collective Memory. She had a panache and liveliness about her. Which made her perfect for Avourel, who had always been so quiet and observant. I was Counselor for the House of Itelūnèl, Avourel's father. He and I always marveled at how merry the girls were with one another. Brings me joy to remember."

He stopped as they reached the center of the courtyard and lowered his gaze. "When Ruèhnar cast the entire middle of the earth into shadow, Avourel and Eïluèl were separated. I know because I found Eïluèl dying in Avïria. While she lay dying, she gifted me the sword, and told me to find her in the next life. I did not know she had been aware of her eternal fate until that dying breath — a moment that will never escape my memory," he said, looking grief-stricken.

Tagwen frowned.

"I left the blade in Avïria to be found by her soul's subsequent carrier. For many centuries afterward, I roamed this land, taking stock of the blade's location, trying to reason with its keepers to listen to my truths and heed the warnings that darkness would return. When I thought that perhaps Ruèhnar may never return, after nearly two-thousand years of believing he would, I gave up," he admitted.

Tagwen regarded him. "What made you try again?"

Erul took a long breath. "The signs of darkness had finally returned." He paused a moment. "But more than that, I knew Eïluèl deserved to find rest. So, I scoured any lingering record to see what, if anything, I had the power to do. It was in finding you, the first beacon of hope I had encountered in many long years, that helped me believe salvation of Eïluèl, and indeed the world, was possible."

He put a hand on Tagwen's shoulder. "I am sorry that the burdens of the past have fallen to you, Queen Braithe. But I truly believe there has been no other more capable than you."

Tagwen swallowed, trying to hold back tears. "I do not know how to believe the same."

"The greatest amongst us almost never do... until they do."

Photography by Annie Splatt on Unsplash

Photo by Johannes Plenio on Unsplash

PART TWO
BEFORE THE STORM

8
Fated Company

The dreaded hour had arrived. Finally enjoying some amount of sleep, Tagwen woke peacefully, the light peeking through the curtained balcony. The elven bed was of great comfort, and she wished she could sneak but a few more minutes just as there was a knock at the door.

"Tagwen?"

She grumbled slightly at Breccan's bid for her to wake, but she called out, "Come on in!" before burying her face into a pillow.

Breccan's fresh and bright face appeared before her, along with a tray of tea, which coaxed Tagwen to at least sit up and accept that the day had begun.

"Morning," Breccan smiled as she set the tray on the bed and offered Tagwen a cup.

"You're cheerful this morning," Tagwen scowled as she blew on her tea to cool it. The rich purple-amber liquid warmed her thoroughly.

Breccan took a deep breath, her demeanor becoming somber. "I am trying to tell myself this is just another part of an adventure that we're having, but the reality is altogether different. I fear for our comrades, and the people of our home. I try to tell myself that I am not leaving them, that I am working to help them, but it's hard. That's all," she said.

Tagwen nodded and took another sip of tea. She looked through the crack in the curtains and watched as light glistened off the snow that had accumulated on the balcony overnight. "I must believe we're doing the right thing. This is so much bigger than anything we had considered," Tagwen reminded her.

Breccan walked over to the curtains and pulled them open to let the light fully grace the interior of the room. "Then we best get a move on, eh?" She smiled at Tagwen who rolled her eyes but smiled in agreement.

Breakfast preparations had been made and were being shared in the largest banquet that Thrindūl had seen in centuries. Men, dwarves, and elves all gathered throughout the courtyard and down into the vale to share one last meal together. Jovial conversations, despite the doom that was both behind and ahead of them, mingled in the air. Tagwen could see that even Roìbert smiled, if only for a moment, amongst his men and Daïdh. Seeing their respective leaders interact with one another gave the men the courage to put aside their prejudices, even if just for the sake of becoming a temporary cohesive unit. Tagwen was grateful for their efforts, and she knew that this nature would need to be maintained if they were to rescue her city.

My city, she thought. Marez was the only home that Tagwen had ever known growing up, and now she was being compelled to ignore its call for aid.

A delicate elven horn blew and Tagwen could see Faldïr and Ylerïan gathering those destined to make the journey to the Black Isle with her: Mæranedïl with Erul, Ualan — who looked surprisingly eager this morning — and Adrelghard, the dwarf who had been chosen to guide them through the caverns. Comfort washed over Tagwen at seeing a party so capable.

Remembering that she was part of the group she was admiring, she jolted, excusing herself from the company she was eating with, and ran to join them. Breccan, too, with what appeared to be a bread roll being stuffed into her pocket, hurried to join as well.

Everyone was present, and the Lord and Lady Eilfaren smiled to greet them all.

"Never before has such a fellowship been formed on the lands of my house. Regrettably, the need for such a companionship is dire, but I believe that I speak for us all when I say that there are none I would trust more to deliver the success of this quest than all of you," Faldïr proclaimed.

"As such," Ylerïan began, as she gestured for the elves who accompanied her to present the gifts she had brought, "these, as some of you already have, are the keys of our Order. I present them in these times so that you all will have some manner of protection outside of these walls."

Thus Adrelghard, Breccan, and Mæranedïl were presented with the pins that Tagwen and Ualan already donned on their cloaks.

"They will repel certain sicknesses, purify water, and allow for my connection with you all," Ylerïan explained.

Tagwen felt at the brooch and was intrigued at learning of its remarkable capabilities.

"Please take this gift of our house as a token of goodwill and luck, wherever this journey takes you," Faldïr added.

Each member, as they received their pin, bowed in thanks, and Faldïr and Ylerïan gave them each an uncustomary hug.

"I, too, wish you all luck, though regrettably I have no token of my house to give in thanks for the undertaking you have tasked before you," Tagwen said.

"Lest you forget, queen of men, your unselfish determination to protect and aid my home is your gift. You have gone, and are going, above and beyond the call of your post. For you and your people, we would risk everything," Faldïr said.

Tagwen appreciated the sentiment, but her throat closed at hearing anyone pledging to imperil themselves on her behalf. Despite her inhibitions, she paid her respects to the Lord and Lady of the Forest with the Marezian salute.

Erul then addressed the group. "The Lord and Lady Eilfaren have offered to ride with us to the shores where Guódnè meets the Lerïacūl Sea. From there, we will be on our own." He raised his bushy ashen brows at the small group to confirm they had all heard and understood. He then motioned for them to convene where the horses were being prepped. Seasaìdh was draped in a beautiful emerald regalia with the emblem of the Eilfaren house sown in gold thread along the sides. Tagwen marveled at how majestic she looked, and a small tear escaped her eye on seeing the mare that she had not been sure she would see again.

Each member mounted their respective horse, and they were led through the courtyard by Faldïr and Ylerïan. As the party made their way through, the waiting masses created a channel that led to the Ebrïhèïlè's outlet. Men, dwarves, and elves dropped flowers at the hooves of the passing company, and offered tears, salutes, and well wishes. Roìbert and Daïdh both bowed to Tagwen as she made her way through. The faces of her company all looked to her with pride, worry, and some sadness.

Eachann, too, was in the crowd. He wished the best for the group but was sullen because he was not yet healed enough to join them.

Tagwen nodded at him as she passed. She wished to thank him for rescuing her and her troop from the clutches of Middling and regretted that she had not done so. *I will if — when — we return*, she thought.

About an hour's ride from the vale, the group was shown an opening to the shores; along their edge were two rowboats that looked as if they had been cleaned but had not seen any use in some time.

"I realize this is not the kind of vessel you may be used to, warriors of the Southlands, but I hope they will serve you well enough across this threshold," Faldïr said.

"I've sailed worse, believe me," Breccan responded, eliciting a smile and chuckle from him.

Tagwen took a moment with Seasaìdh as she had done so often before any journey they had made. Foreheads together, she whispered the prayer of her people, and hugged the mare to bid her goodbye. Seasaìdh, as if she was aware of the situation, did not whine as she usually did when Tagwen had to leave — as if she understood that there was nothing that could be done.

Tagwen embraced Faldïr and Ylerïan, as well, wishing them safety and success in whatever lay ahead for them in Yeacralas.

"We will all be here when you return, as will your home," Faldïr promised and Ylerïan nodded.

Tagwen chose to believe them and joined her designated boat with Breccan and Ualan. Looking behind at their farewell party, Tagwen made a promise to herself that it would not be the last time she would see them, and she sincerely hoped she could keep such a promise.

Pushing across the largest stretch of the Guódnè River was unfortunately the fastest way across from the elven shores. Fighting the rapids that pushed into the ocean was tiresome. Two hours of grueling rowing finally provided the relief they sought on the other side. Haverlow Woods now stood in front of them, and they pulled their boats to the bank, no longer needing them. The afternoon sun provided a modicum of warmth in the chilly autumn air, and Tagwen was grateful for the sky's lack of storm.

"Yeh know, yeh could've used yer arms! Got to stay young somehow in yer ancient age!" Adrelghard teased Erul.

"But you've done so well, Master Tugrom! This old elf truly appreciates your contribution," Erul quipped back.

A mild grumble came from the dwarf as he rolled his eyes at Tagwen and Breccan, who both smiled.

"A moment's rest I think would be warranted. That was — quite a bit of rowing," Mæranedïl answered, soothing his wrists and forearms.

"Let's keep moving," Breccan countered, avoiding the elf's gaze. Tagwen had noticed Breccan was determined not to acknowledge Mæranedïl. Glancing between the two of them, the resemblance was surreal, and it was taking Tagwen all her fortitude to keep from demanding that Mæranedïl explain to Breccan what happened all those years ago. She hoped the conversation would happen in its own time, but the looming threat of their voyage did not lend itself to spare time, as they were now chasing moonlight.

"The captain is right," Erul agreed. "If we are to make good time, we must at least be through to the other side of the woods by nightfall, if not to the Outrider camp that is our immediate destination."

Mæranedïl took a breath and nodded as he finished hoisting their rowboat to the shore and grabbing his pack.

Peering into the woods, Tagwen felt uneasy. Lacking armor save for the surcoat she donned, she felt uncomfortably naked.

The woodland looked darker, overshadowed, and in a way, dead. There were trees rich with leaves that still stood at its edge, but Tagwen could see the brush was thorny, the path was unclear if there was any, and the scent of the forest floor was that of mud and decay.

Ualan noticed the apprehension on Tagwen's face. "Outriders do not even like this forest. I am told it was not always this way, but it has been in this state since its separation in the beginning of the Second Age," he explained.

"Not exactly a comfort, but at least I am not the only one who feels its — eeriness," she said.

"This forest indeed was beautiful once," Erul added as he moved to take the lead of the group. "I advise we all stay close and watch your step. Murky waters and unpleasant things are said to skulk in here."

With that, they began their delve into the adumbral grove. Tagwen pressed her hand to her chest as she entered. The tokens of love and luck from both Blàr and the Eilfaren house positioned over her heart made them all feel closer to her.

The first few steps into the woods were graced with sunlight, but soon after, the overgrowth began to snuff out the illumination. Erul cautioned against utilizing too much light, as he did not want to attract any unseemly eyes, and lit his staff, to Tagwen's amazement. Pale blue light emanated softly from its crown of twisting branches as he waved his hand over the top.

"How does he do that?" she whispered to herself.

Mæranedïl, who had heard her, explained. "He is an exemplar of the First Age — one of the Viethèl. A guardian set out to oversee the genesis of the first elves, the Naladhïl. He and others were all said to have some manner of gift, whether it be craft or a form of magic; they were all uniquely blessed."

"He told me of his origin, but seeing the conjuration first-hand is incomprehensible. How do you know so much of all this?" Tagwen asked.

"I made it my duty to know. I have long trusted Erul and have learned much from him about our world and the world that came before."

They heard Breccan scoff in front of them and Mæranedïl

lowered his head. "It took me away from much that I loved, but there was little choice, as the information I knew would have put anyone around me at risk. So, I hid, perhaps for too long," he said to Tagwen, but hoping to reach the heart of his daughter.

"I can only hope that my people understand the same when they do not see me in Marez to defend them. But I must also learn to accept that many probably will not, regardless of my intent," Tagwen said, and Mæranedïl gave her a sad smile in understanding.

No sound came from Breccan then, and Tagwen refrained from trying to meddle any further. "I had seen Erul's light once before, and again at the battle on the midlands, but I never knew how it came to be. Its source looked so natural and unnatural at the same time. But the idea that it is some ancient sorcery has not exactly helped it make more sense," Tagwen said.

"Dwarves tried a manner of recreatin' it once — did not go so well," Adrelghard interjected. "Seems it really is some form of unattainable magic, after all," he mourned.

"You know I would be able to focus much easier if you all weren't chatting about trying to pick apart my very being," Erul grumbled, and Adrelghard snickered.

Haverlow became denser after about fifteen minutes into their traversal. The underbrush was tangled in vines and thorns, random marshy puddles littered the floor, and the overgrowth of the trees hung in all manner. Many of the plants were dead or dying, and very little sunlight managed to wriggle its way through.

"Is there some sort of path through here, E'ruleïl?" Ualan

asked.

"Are you telling me the Outriders avoid the Darkened Woods? How peculiar, Master Ambarsan!" Erul quipped sarcastically as he poked his head in various directions. He added, "I am sorry dear boy, but if you would give me just a moment, I should be able to guide us all through." He then mumbled under his breath, "Theoretically."

While they progressed, Tagwen, though uncomfortable in such a dank environment, was intrigued by various broken stone structures that were scattered throughout. Some plausibly had once been statues, others seemed to be of pillars or the like. They were unimpressively gray in color, but remarkably polished. They glittered like mirrors in Erul's light as the group passed by them. Tagwen could make out carvings in some of them: images of weaponry, dwarven runes too worn for her to fully read, dwarven faces, and one of a mountain on fire and a dragon — the sigil taunted her as she tried to recall where she'd seen it.

She turned to Mæranedïl and asked, "What are all of these from?"

Mæranedïl looked as if he were about to answer, but Adrelghard piped up instead. "These look to be ruins of the first settlement of the 'hill dwarves'. Made their way about the land instead of the mountains. Incredible farmers they were, and stonemasons. Some lived within the hills, others built atop, but their community was known to be very tight knit. When the elves took control of the Great Forest, it spread and the hill dwarves did not want to live in the woods, so they moved to the Eastern reaches of the continent in the First Age... so at least the story goes."

The rock forms faded into shadow as the group proceeded through a tangle of vines and trees, delving deeper into a darkened patch of the forest.

"Those ruins, specifically," Mæranedïl added, "are part of the hill dwarves who would later move to living in the Uhodor Mountains because of the first dragon, Ūlagenol — if memory serves me correctly. The daemon birthed the dragon with the obsidian stones of the fire god Vostheros—"

"The Dragonhide Obsidian that he *stole* from the first dwarves, by the way," Adrelghard interrupted.

"Dragonhide Obsidian?" Breccan asked, finally interested in the story.

"Mere legend," Adrelghard clarified. "Supposedly it's a beautiful black stone, darker than the night sky, but with a vein of light running through it — like fire. There were notably only three of those stones given to the first dwarves: Urèc, Værèc, and Ïorhèl. That power-hungry child of the gods charmed Værèc and Ïorhèl into giving up their stones easily enough, but Urèc wouldn't break. The halfwit then threw the stones into a volcano to try and create a dragon that he could control and didn't realize he couldn't until it was too late."

Coming upon another set of stones, Tagwen saw the same carving of the dragon and fire. "Is that what that carving is about then?" she asked, pointing to the slab as it glowed briefly in the blue light.

"It certainly would seem so. Ūlagenol was known to reside inside of the volcano, E'batheron, as he was birthed within it and from its fires. The dwarves of this place must have had some reason to record his presence," said Mæranedïl.

"I believe Urèc was part of the company of dwarves who resided here. It would make sense, since they'd journeyed into the East to save their people from the wrath of the dragon, who also vied for the stone, I might add," added Adrelghard.

"Did the dragon ever find the third stone?" Breccan asked Mæranedïl, whose face lit up from her acknowledgement of him.

"No," Erul answered. "Ūlagenol searched for the better part of the First Age for that stone, but somehow Urèc outwitted both the drake and the forsworn paragon. None ever knew where the stone ended up as far as I am aware, but many at the time surmised that it served as a beacon for the Dracari people before they became… well, you know." Erul paused. "If that has answered your questions for the time being, it might interest you all to know that I am in fact, lost."

Convinced they had been wandering for at least a few hours, Tagwen looked around and spotted the same collection of ruins, and the etching of the volcano and dragon wavered as Erul's light moved around.

"We've gone in a circle?" she asked.

"Something — or someone — does not want us to reach our end," Erul finally said with narrowed eyes spying into the wooded depths.

"Some — one?" Tagwen repeated, as she tried to refrain from the instinct of drawing her sword.

Breccan did not share the same restraint, and unsheathed Saìde with alarming speed.

Mæranedïl marveled at the sword he recognized. "I remember the day I gave that sword to Deìrdre," he remarked.

"Many patrons gifted trinkets to my mother. Don't think because you know her name that somehow, you're special," Breccan snarled, without looking at him.

"Quiet," Ualan said to all. "I think I hear something."

"Lost, are you?" a voice asked, but no one was around.

"Did one of yeh say that?" Adrelghard asked, as his eyes darted around manically.

"No," Tagwen whispered.

"Come now, show yourself," Erul commanded the voice. A crow then landed on the top of his staff. It was unlike any crow Tagwen had ever seen. Its eyes were blue and soft like the shallow of the sea and the tips of its wings were iridescent.

"Strange aggregates of adventurers attempt to pass through these woods often, but none so interesting as you," the voice said, seemingly coming from the crow.

"Is — is the crow talking?" Ualan asked.

"So, it is true!" Erul exclaimed, to much the surprise of all present. "You must be one of the fabled Heralds of Avantèas. I had never the fortune to meet any of your kind," he said happily.

"There are few of us left. They call me 'Afesal'," the crow said.

"Avantèas? The Great Heron?" Mæranedïl marveled and the crow nodded.

"Why then do you come to us in such an hour?" Erul asked.

"You are lost in search of Truth. Such an errand calls to us," Afesal answered.

"Are we really talking to a bird or am I dying?" Breccan asked, blinking wildly at the sight before her.

Erul extended a hand to the crow, and it eagerly accepted the perch.

"My friend, will you help us find our way? It seems we've wandered about ourselves."

"Dangerous path you walk. More dangerous still your destination," Afesal riddled.

"Well, we can't just stay holed up in this soggy forest!" Adrelghard exclaimed.

"Safest here you will be during the light. Path becomes clear in the night."

"Dear crow," Tagwen began, "we really must be going. We need to be at the Black Isle by the full moon. There is no time to linger here."

"Time you have, Guardian of the Tear. Shelter now you must make to avoid mistake," Afesal rhymed. With a gentle flap of its wings, the bird vanished into the shadows.

"Marvelous," Erul admired.

"No one else freaked out about a talking bird?" Breccan asked, looking at her cohorts.

"Guardian of the Tear?" Mæranedïl pondered.

Erul cleared his throat and addressed the party, "Well, it would seem we are making shelter here for the day. Best to eat and sleep while we can, and head out when the moon is highest, I suppose."

"Because a bird told us to?" Breccan asked, eyes wide and brow raised.

"Precisely, Captain. A Herald of Avantèas is an incredibly rare creature. I was not even sure they still existed… or ever existed, for that matter. They are harbingers of fortune if their words are heeded. It is reckless to ignore their portents," Erul explained.

Breccan blew a held breath and eased, sheathing her sword, and looked for a spot to set her pack. There was little room around the encircling ruins that they had found themselves in, but all managed to find for themselves a corner of space. Adrelghard started a small fire and Mæranedïl made tea. Ualan paced around, on guard, as Erul drifted to sleep against a tree. Breccan and Tagwen sat on a fallen pillar that now served as their bench. Nibbling on a dried fruit from her pack, Breccan stared at Mæranedïl.

"You should talk to him," Tagwen urged as she watched Breccan's snacking become increasingly aggressive.

"I don't even know if he's really him," Breccan said.

Tagwen rolled her eyes. "Breccan. You two look like twins."

Breccan sneered, not taking her eyes off Mæranedïl. Finally, she sat up and looked at Tagwen. "What would I say to him anyway? I can barely look at him without imagining him abandoning my mother."

"What if he could explain what happened?" Tagwen asked.

Breccan shrugged. "I'm not sure I would see it as anything other than excuses."

Tagwen knew there was no pushing her and that she had every right to be upset with him. Tagwen wanted to explain on Mæranedïl's behalf the truths she had learned of him, but stopped as she knew full well it was not her place.

"Don't worry about this. We need to try and rest," Breccan said, as she patted Tagwen's knee.

"I think I might stay awake for a bit and keep watch or discuss plans. I'm not really sure when we will be allowed to leave here and it's making me anxious."

Breccan rubbed her friend's shoulder. "Let me know if there's anything I can do. For now I'm gonna try and sleep, okay?"

Tagwen nodded and went to sit next to Adrelghard, who patted the ground beside him in welcome.

"Yeh should try to rest, yeh know. Take a page out of that one's book," he said, looking over to Erul deep in a slumber.

Tagwen shook her head. "I wish I could."

"Trying times make poor bedfellows, it would seem," Mæranedïl said.

He was taller than Breccan, but his eyes and the color of his hair were plainly hers. Her smile, though, must have been her mother's. No facial hair caressed his face, as was common amongst the elves, and his skin was impeccably clear, with a similarly freckled finish as Breccan's. Tagwen noticed that he shared the same cheekbones and jawline as Ylerïan — both soft yet distinguished.

"I'll say," Adrelghard huffed, taking a sip of the tea Mæranedïl had brewed.

"Trying times are the only bedfellows I've known for some time now," Ualan shared as he joined them around the fire.

"Well, we're happy yer here, lad. Sorry it's been quite a bit fer yeh," Adrelghard smiled sadly at the Outrider.

Ualan nodded, served himself some tea, and added a speck of tinder to the fire.

"How are you doing?" Tagwen asked him.

"As well as can be expected I suppose." He paused to take a drink of his tea. "I do not wish to dwell. I know Gòrdan would not want that for me. My children are safe and I am seeking to destroy the evil which has broken my heart and home. That is suitable for now."

"Aye, that's mighty good thinkin'," Adrelghard toasted with his mug.

Ualan smiled as he returned the toast, then addressed Mæranedïl. "May I ask you something?"

"Certainly," the elf said, seeming intrigued.

"Where were you all this time? Ylerïan spoke of you often with such reverence. I had never thought you anything other than dead, I am afraid. To see you are alive after all this time I have been in their service, it was… curious," he said.

Mæranedïl stopped as he was about to sip his tea and gazed beyond Tagwen's shoulder, where Breccan lay.

"I could not return to Thrindūl," he admitted. "There was much at stake when I became the steward of Yacendïl's letter, and though it was a task I relieved myself of, the target it would leave on me, and anyone associated with me, would be a grave one. There were many I did not intend to leave, but Ylerïan and others alike needed to assume I was dead to ensure their safety." He regarded Tagwen. "I just do not think some of them ever understood." He paused for a moment and glanced away. "I suppose I cannot ask them to," he lamented.

"Some of them may never have been told," Tagwen said.

Mæranedïl's brows furrowed in thought as he beheld the ground.

"How did you come to be in possession of such an item?" Ualan resumed his questioning.

Mæranedïl's gaze softened. "There was… a woman," he paused, "eyes like the clearest pools of Thrindūl's waters, hair like threads of gold, and a heart worth more than all the trinkets of the world. She had been given a box full of random tokens, but most notably there was a book. It was terribly old, with ratted pages and worn binding, and out of it fell the letter. Luckily, I knew Erul at the time and I showed it to him, but I almost wish I had simply thrown it away."

"Thrown it away?!" Adrelghard choked.

Mæranedïl nodded, looking again at Breccan's back as she seemingly slept.

"When I showed him the letter, he told me I needed to leave Gilèdo, and everyone in it. That someone must have planted the letter to find me — to confirm I was elven. So, I left, told the love of my life as little as I could, and went North." He stopped and looked around at the fireside company. "Ylerïan only knew that I was venturing across the Southlands — which alone the Lord and Lady weren't very fond of. I never returned to Thrindūl to tell her otherwise. Come to find out, Erul had informed her of my charge, but I never returned to anyone… until now. And for some it is too late."

"Why then, if you left and told no one anything, did you

need to involve Lady Catrìona?" Tagwen asked.

Mæranedïl hung his head as he stared into the swirling bits of leaf in his cup. "It was an unfortunate happenstance that I met Brìghde. I was passing through Middling when a little boy fell into one of the local rivers. I dashed in to save him, and it turned out to be Brìghde's son, Jaelan. I failed to conceal my countenance as an elf, but despite her shock, she treated me with no malice, no other-ance, but simply gratitude for saving her son."

"Bet yeh wish yeh hadn't done that now, don't yeh?" Adrelghard said with a smirk.

"The thought had crossed my mind, but he was a boy then, a sweet child. I would do it again if I were given the same chance with what I know now," Mæranedïl replied. "Brìghde asked me many questions, most notably why I was so far from home. I do not know why, but I was compelled to tell her everything, as I had just lost all I held dear to me, and her comfort was moving. She told me then that she may never be able to repay me for saving the life of her beloved child. So, she would use her own life to protect me and my people, and she saved us all."

Jaelan unknowingly saved us all, Tagwen thought, realizing that the boy at the time had set a series of decisions in motion that would change the course of history — all by the hands of a people he now detested.

"Even then, you still decided to never return home. Why?" Ualan pressed.

"I was still too afraid. More so I was ashamed I had relieved myself of the burden into the hands of a woman I did not know. I was sure no one would understand why I did what I did. So, I hid as far away as I could go, settling around Stoneheim Grove for the better part of nearly three decades," said Mæranedïl.

"Did you ever consider coming back?" Tagwen asked softly.

"Always. Every waking moment was an internal battle in deciding whether to return, and because of my sheepishness, I never got to say goodbye to Deìrdre," Mæranedïl answered.

There was a long moment of silence. Tagwen knew there were no words of comfort she could provide to the elf. She wondered still if he ever would tell his story to Breccan, as she deserved.

"Well," he paused to stand, "best to try and get some sleep." He bowed to the gathering to excuse himself, then made a pillow out of his pack and nestled on top of the driest bit of moss he could find.

"Uncanny, isn't it?" Adrelghard asked, whilst looking at Mæranedïl.

"Hmm?" Tagwen muttered.

"She looks just like him, don't yeh think?" he asked.

"Lord Eilfaren must have seen it," Ualan added.

"Seen what?" Tagwen tilted her head at the Outrider.

"Remember entering the arboretum? When he caught us?" Tagwen nodded. "Well, he asked me if she was half-elven, and I told him I couldn't tell," Ualan relayed.

"She's always had such keen senses. She could even see the path into Thrindūl," Tagwen marveled.

Ualan blinked at Tagwen for a moment with a look of disappointment. "And she never said anything to me?"

Tagwen snorted. "She didn't know you. And from what you had told us of the Forest, she was convinced it was a sort of illusion."

Ualan nodded and poked at the fire with a stick for rekindling. "Why don't you two get some rest. I'll take the watch for a bit," he offered.

"I'll sit with yeh, laddie," Adrelghard said as he pulled a rolled piece of paper from his pack. "Maybe yeh can help me make sense of this ragged mess. Erul tells me it's a map from the dwarves, but I don't think they knew the area that's now the Isle well enough."

"Perhaps I could help," Tagwen proposed.

"By all means! If yer not gonna sleep I suppose," he teased and handed her the parchment.

Tagwen smiled at the jest and peered at the drawing for a moment. Its outline was vaguely like that of the Isle, but its depictions were much different than how she remembered the desolate land to be.

"How old is this?" she asked, flexing the drawing toward Adrelghard.

"Pfft. Beats me. Got teh be Second Age at least — hardly anythin' left of the first since the great library burnt."

Ualan clicked his tongue. "A shame, that. The elves revered Mïrabasia. So, not surprising that The Tyrant saw to its destruction."

Tagwen cringed at the mention of Olwenna's son, Reese Glas-Bowen. She looked back at the map to distract from her thoughts. The chart was more a sketch than a formal cartographic depiction of the elder landscape. The steppes were drawn as grassy hills but the mountains she remembered that rose above them now were shown to have been the smallest end of E'batheron's ranges. A line was drawn vertically upon the face of the lowest peak, but no inscription was left of its purpose. No distinctive marking indicated a path or landmark, other than the lost volcano. The parchment was old, and stains of wear and ink blotted the page. Every dot could have once been an important icon but had now been blurred with age.

"Fascinating to see what this land ostensibly once looked like," she commented. "But alas, I'm not sure what this is trying to convey."

She handed back the map as the urge to yawn overcame her. "Goodness," she paused, "I think I will take up the chance to sleep. I'll try to remember anything peculiar I can about the isle. It's been a few years, but it's hard to forget such wretchedness."

"No worries. Plenty of time to figure this out. I'll bother the Outrider with it for now," Adrelghard said, grinning at Ualan.

Tagwen agreed and lay next to a fallen pillar, where she could still view her companions. Fighting the initial tiredness that came over her, she traced the lines of the carving on the pillar. It was the same depiction of Ūlagenol and the fiery mountain.

What happened to you? she wondered as she followed the image of the dragon's form falling into the flames. A flash of memory came across her eyes, and she pulled back her hand. She turned away from the pillar and tucked her hands to her chest, stifling her rapid breathing. She wished then that her curiosity had not gotten the better of her, as she made the haunting realization: Goraidh had been wearing the emblem.

***

The music of crunching leaves and chirping crickets woke Tagwen. The atmosphere was noticeably darker, but she could not tell the hour from inside this murky keep. Worried she had slept too long, she looked around frantically, but noticed Adrelghard and Ualan were still asleep. Erul and Breccan were sitting around the dwindling fire, but Mæranedïl was nowhere in sight. She gathered herself up and sauntered over.

"Evening, sunshine," Breccan smiled.

Tagwen smirked and asked, "Where is Mæranedïl?"

"Gone to scout a bit — to be sure the hour is near," Erul answered.

"Is it not dangerous to have gone alone?" Tagwen asked, as a strong rustle of leaves in the bough of the tree nearest her made her jump.

Mæranedïl hopped down from a branch and onto the decaying forest floor. "The moon approaches her highest point," he reported.

Tagwen looked up into the boughs and back at Mæranedïl. "Well, I suppose that was always an option." She then looked at Erul. "Does that mean we should be going then? I don't really see a path anywhere. Do any of you?"

"The path will be made known to us all, queen of men," Erul responded. "Best wake everyone, though."

Ualan woke in a startle, grabbing Mæranedïl by the wrist as the elf tried to nudge him awake. He promptly apologized and collected himself and his things. Adrelghard awoke in a grumble, insisting on at least a few more moments, and was irked at the insistence of Erul's staff poking him in the back.

Once the entire party was assembled, Erul snuffed out the remainder of the fire. All became hauntingly dark, and Erul instructed everyone to be completely silent. Tagwen waited and tried to control her erratic exhale, realizing she had been holding her breath for too long. Few minutes more passed and suddenly the grassy floor became luminescent. The darkness finally permitted the glow of the path.

"Well, I'll be," Breccan whispered in awe.

"Quickly and quietly," Erul instructed, and the group followed his lead in a straight line.

The bioluminescent path wound for what felt like hours, twisting and turning through all manner of muddy forest floor. Despite the light that the path offered, it was not enough illumination to see hazards ahead. An occasional branch or wily vine would catch the passersby, but Erul insisted they not produce any light for fear that the way would no longer be visible. Tagwen held onto Breccan's shoulder as she always had in darkness such as this. Adrelghard's breathing and occasional dwarven curse at a branch or root that seemed sent to torture him assured Tagwen that he was not far behind. As they all moved, she listened carefully to hear Mæranedïl's soft shuffle and Ualan's delicate footfalls. Erul had rather quiet steps to Tagwen, but it was the consistent thump of his walking staff that let her know he was still with them.

Hoots and cricket chirps still seemed to be the loudest sounds within the forest, until there was a sudden "shush" from Erul. Everyone froze and Tagwen could hear, and nearly feel, thousands strong marching to the West. Her hand subconsciously clenched onto her captain's shoulder, but she was comforted by Breccan's hand reaching up to take hers. She could feel the rage flushing in her face; her city was not ready for anything such as this, despite its defenses. She feared for the innocents who could potentially be hit first on the cliffside of Logrosca. No warning would be sent to them. She could only hope that enough of them survived to warn the rest of Yeacralas. The thought sent her hand clenching again and was met this time by a gentle pat and a thumb rubbing it softly. Echoes of the passing army dwindled, and Erul seemed convinced enough to continue their journey.

The group stepped out of Haverlow into the moonlight, shielded from view of the army by part of the Aurilon Peaks.

"Lucky we listened to that bird then," Breccan observed.

Erul raised his brows and nodded at her.

"Why is it we should be spared, when there are thousands, whose lives are now at stake? No warning will come to them, they cannot possibly prepare for the wave of darkness crashing onto their doorstep," Tagwen grieved.

"With hope, the messenger I managed to send will prepare Marez, lass. I had a note sent to your house tellin' them to prepare for anythin', including war, when we first arrived in Thrindūl. Admittedly, I hadn't known the scope of what was to come, nor that we wouldn't be there at the time I sent him,"

Adrelghard confessed, "but he was hopefully well ahead of this mess to give them some sort of warnin'."

Tagwen looked gratefully at the dwarf and hugged him. "It is more than I thought they had. I can only hope your messenger will be safe."

"Plus, the Horsemen are decent in a fight if they need to be. Yeacralans are hardy; they won't go down easy," Breccan added, and Tagwen nodded.

That they should need to fear being cut down at all is a tragedy, Tagwen thought.

"Let us make use of the moonlight whilst we have it," Erul interjected. "We must reach the Outrider post if we are to make the most of our time."

Pressing on through the night, the party walked along the land like shadows. Grateful for the range's protection from where the armies were marching, it looked that the path to the camp was clear.

Three more hours passed in their travel, and the moon still shone brightly in the sky. Sunrise would not be for at least another few hours, as the company managed to take full advantage of the night's cover. Without pause, they arrived at Aurilon Point, named for its adjacency to the small mountains. The outpost was surprisingly larger than most Tagwen had encountered and appeared more a full-fledged garrison than an Outrider stead. Complete with a stone guard wall, the party walked along it until they reached the front gate.

"There may be other Outriders here, let me take lead,"

Ualan cautioned as he tapped rhythmically upon the gate's thick timbered door. No answer came and he tried once more, to no avail. He looked around and placed his ear upon the entrance.

"No one home?" Breccan asked.

Ualan's mouth twisted. "It wouldn't be uncommon, but this is one of our best defensive holds — someone has to be here." He reached for a chain at his neck that held two keys, using the shorter of the two to open the gate's door, and ushered everyone inside.

Targets, dummies, and racks of shackled weaponry were sprawled throughout the open area. Watchtowers posted at the southeastern and southwestern corners loomed over them but did not appear to have anyone at their stations. There was, however, a light emanating from under a door in the interior of the building in front of them. The timber and stone construction held no windows along the walls, so it was impossible to know what was inside.

Ualan closed the gate behind them. "It is not usual, however, for the towers to be empty. Stay shadowed a moment whilst I see who's here. The gate was locked, so someone of the Order who has a key must be present," he said. He performed a similar knock on the door to the knock he had used upon the front gate, and footsteps could be heard shuffling inside.

After a moment, the door cracked opened, and a man cautiously peeked through the opening. "The pass of Okerfair…" he prompted suspiciously.

"Is the word of our edict," Ualan answered, sighing with relief.

With that, the door opened widely, and the man's expression grew wondrous, "Ambarsan?!" he exclaimed.

Ualan lifted his hood to reveal his identity. "It is good to see you, old friend."

The men embraced, and the man suddenly became aware of the company Ualan had brought as they were lit by the interior illumination. "Are they *all* with you?" he asked, puzzled.

"Yes, we have important business ahead, we looked to this post for rest. May we come in?" Ualan asked.

"Of course! Of course! Please. These nights grow curiouser, and I see your presence here only adds to that. Come." He gestured for the party to join him indoors. Once they were all in, he looked cautiously around the yard before closing and locking the door.

As he turned around, his surprise became even more notable. "Can it be?" he asked, looking at Mæranedïl and Erul.

"Indeed, Outrider, we are elves," Erul confirmed.

"And you—?" He began to ask Tagwen.

"Peric," Ualan paused and gestured, starting from the member closest to him. "This is Adrelghard Tugrom, Mæranedïl, E'ruleïl, Breccan Kenefick, and Queen Tagwen Braithe. Everyone, this is Peric Deyne of the Outriders."

"You do look remarkably like your father, Queen Braithe," Peric bowed as he addressed her.

"Please, call me Tagwen. It is a pleasure to make your acquaintance, Peric." She returned his bow.

"What brings together a fellowship such as this?" Peric asked Ualan.

"Perhaps if we could rest and find a warm meal, we may indulge in your questions, yes?" Erul suggested.

Peric nodded to the elf. "There are plenty of accommodations for each of you. It is lucky your journey has brought you to the most obliging of our outposts. I will have a manner of stew started for you all as you settle in. It has been a while since we've shared this space with members outside the guild."

"We are most grateful for your hospitality," Erul said with a smile.

Each of them found a small room on the second floor, each room containing a modest bed with worn, but clean, linens. Tagwen set her pack down on the floor and laid on the bed for a while. It was not as comfortable as the elven bed she had woken up in the day before, but it was a welcome respite from the damp and cold ground of Haverlow's forest floor. Scents of a stew wafted through the air and Mæranedïl knocked on the frame of her open door.

"Seems dinner is ready," he informed her.

"Thank you, Mæranedïl," she said. "Mæranedïl?" she stopped him as he turned to leave.

"Yes, Queen Braithe?"

Her words caught in her throat. "Nothing, sorry. I'll be down momentarily."

Mæranedïl bowed and turned again to leave.

"Don't meddle," she scolded herself before heading downstairs.

Everyone was gathered around the large communal table, and Tagwen was thankful that they had all made it this far. She sat across from Breccan and next to Adrelghard.

Peric brought a large pot to the center of the table and began to ladle what looked to be a suitably made vegetable soup. "Ualan let me know that you elves don't partake in the consumption of animals, so I hope this is suitable for you all. I've got a cured goat leg for any who are not so opposed."

"You can send that haunch right on down, laddie!" Adrelghard exclaimed, and Peric obliged.

Ualan brought out bottles of mead from the cellar and poured to each member's content.

Tagwen was pleasantly surprised at the quality of the soup that Peric had prepared but was more appreciative of the salted meat that had been provided. It felt like ages since she'd had a meal of the sort — not that she was knocking the elven food she had enjoyed. "Thank you, Peric. This is a wonderful gift for such a journey," she complimented.

Peric raised his tankard. "It is my pleasure, dear queen. It has been some time since I have been able to cook for such a gathering." He then turned to Ualan. "You're grayer than I remember," he said with a smirk.

Ualan snorted lightly. "It has been some time, dear friend; two years at least."

"And Gòrdan! Gosh, it's been ages since I've seen that handsome man of yours," Peric laughed. "How are he and your children? They must be quite grown now, yes?"

The gathering around the table went quiet, and Peric's eyes

darted about, but no one met his gaze.

"My children are… safe," Ualan said still not looking at him.

Peric slowly set his mug upon the table. "What's happened, brother?"

Erul piped in as Ualan struggled to reply, "Gòrdan's life has been claimed by one they call 'The Hunter' — beastly thing that he is."

Tagwen saw the muscles in Peric's throat tighten. He looked as if he were about to set a hand upon Ualan's but he refrained, and she wondered why.

"Ualan, I…" Peric could not find the words.

Ualan shook his head. "I'd prefer to refrain from invoking my husband's name, as he is regrettably not yet put to rest."

"Are you the only one out here? Why is this outpost so deserted? Ualan said the towers at least should not be empty," said Breccan trying to assist in moving past the conversation.

Peric took a drink and set down his mug, wiping the excess from his thin black mustache with a tablecloth. He shook his head and cleared his throat. "My companions Avelson and Crag were here not two nights ago. There's been talk in the Order of routing more of our forces to the southern outposts, but we first must gather everyone from the region. I assume you all have seen the Dreaded Army? That can be the only cause for a camaraderie such as this."

Tagwen looked at Peric upon hearing the name of the dark force and in her periphery saw Ualan's brow furrow. *How does he know of them?* she thought, unnerved.

Erul spoke up. "Promise of answering your questions was

made in exchange for a meal, and quite a pleasant one you have provided. Yes, we have seen the army. We faced them head-on in the lowlands of the Greyrest."

Peric's eyes widened. "For what purpose had they to go so far North of their source? Assuming you know they've been coming from the Black Isle, no less."

Tagwen saw Peric's hand reach for a pocket underneath his vestment, but stop and simply pad the fabric as if trying to pat his chest.

Ualan peered through narrowed eyes at Peric. "We had not yet found their source, but that is peculiar to know."

"When did you first notice them? That might answer even more of the questions I have had since witnessing their arrival," Erul asked.

"It was another of our Order, Thorfin Quine. He had business that brought him down this way near a month ago now, and he reported activity coming from the shores of the Isle. A horde like none had ever witnessed. We had not realized the force of the Rogues had grown such," Peric said with alarm.

"That's not the Rogues yer seein', lad," Adrelghard told him, taking a drink of the ale.

"Not the Rogues?" Peric looked at Ualan, confused, and Ualan looked to Erul to discern how much to reveal. Erul nodded to signal that Ualan could share the whole truth.

"They're known as 'mœrdeth'," Ualan began. "They are entities who serve the dark lord of a time long forgotten. 'The Hunter' is allegedly one of them."

Peric grimaced as his leg began to bounce upon the floor.

"So, the stories are true then? The world splitting and the rift?"

"How do you know about all that?" Breccan asked, her eyes piercing through Peric's.

Tagwen, at this point, paused from eating. She noticed sweat beginning to accumulate on the temples of Peric's forehead, and the anxious leg habit they both shared made her stomach tighten.

Why is he so nervous?

Peric leaned forward and sat his arms on the table as he drummed his fingers for a moment. "There are texts in the ruined library, really old things, some in the ancient tongue, others in languages I've never seen. Many of them talked about this dark entity you speak of. 'Death's embrace' is a phrase many of them cite. It all seemed so strange to me, as scary stories you'd tell a child to correct their behavior. Do you mean to tell me this is the cause of your journey? That they are not tall tales?" he asked, as he swallowed apprehensively.

"You seem curiously frightened, Sir Deyne," Tagwen commented. "What do you know of all this?"

Peric thumbed his tankard for a moment before taking a long drink to muster his courage. "These texts did not only speak of the destruction that this demon created, but of the devastation that would come again — that the earth would shake, the land would fray. Darkness, storms, and fire would follow, cutting down everything in his wake." He took another gulp before continuing. "Crag told me I needed to stop reading those stories," he chuckled nervously.

Tagwen caught him eying the door behind her.

"Sorry," he apologized, as he wiped the sweat from his brow

with a cloth.

"Wait," Ualan said, looking accusingly at Peric, who winced under his gaze. "There would be no stories told in the common tongue in Mïrabasia. It was an elven temple and records chamber."

Tagwen saw Peric reach again for his breast pocket whilst his gaze flickered over to the door, and she stood. "Who knows we are here?" she asked.

Peric looked at Ualan with tears. "He threatened Ina. He said I was to keep you here until they could arrive."

Erul stormed up to the man and grabbed him by the collar. "Who, boy? Who told you?" he bellowed.

Peric winced again. "The one with black eyes, The Hunter. He held me in his beast's jaws until I complied. Please, you must listen to me now and leave."

Peric's pleas echoed around the hall but were broken by a loud crash outside. Panic-stricken and angry, Tagwen glared at Peric. "Is there another way out of here?" she demanded.

Peric nodded, still in the clutches of Erul's grasp. "Through the cellar below. Ualan knows. There's a trap door that leads outward."

Tagwen looked to Ualan for confirmation, and Ualan nodded. "You all go to the cellar; Breccan and I will grab packs. Go! Now!"

Everyone followed her command as she and Breccan ran up the stairs. Growling and howls came closer to the door, and the sounds of vicious claws raking against the wooden construction met them as they descended. Ualan stood in the dining hall and motioned for them to follow quickly.

Through the kitchen, into the pantry, there was an open trap door on the floor. Peric stood at the entrance and ushered them all inside. Tagwen and Breccan threw packs down onto the floor before jumping in, and finally Ualan descended the steps. He looked behind himself to help Peric down, but his friend did not follow.

"Peric! Now!" Ualan yelled.

Sounds of the entrance door splintering in the front room rang throughout the whole building, as the snarls of the wargs came crashing through. Peric looked behind before handing Ualan a paper.

"Please find Ina and tell her I'm sorry. Okerfair guide you, brother," Peric cried as he shut and locked the trap door behind them.

"Peric! No!" Ualan howled as he tried to push the trap door open. In the pitch-black, Breccan pulled Ualan away. "Let him go! We need to go!" she implored.

Screams heard above chilled Tagwen to the core, as the sounds of crunching and ripping grasped at her throat. Ualan fell silent and all held still for a moment, listening to the scratching and growling of the wargs, and mumbled utterances from their masters. Erul then softly lit his staff, casting the pale blue aura into the cellar. Behind them sat a door that opened into a tunnel. Packs were gathered, and Ualan hurriedly guided the group through before sealing the door behind them.

9

Cornering Darkness

Lachlann called for everyone to be ready before sunrise. Queen Braithe and Captain Kenefick were set to be headed to the Black Isle for purposes that Sĭne did not fully understand. Nonetheless, she woke and readied when she was ordered, as Lachlann was now captain of their leaderless guard.

Surrounded by numerous unrecognizable faces as she entered the main courtyard, Sĭne looked around for some familiarity, squeezing her hands as she stood alone. She spotted a seat amongst the men of her company at one of the many banquet tables that had been prepared. Fixing her posture, she approached, ostensibly confident, as she walked through the crowd of Oburim and Middling's men, the elves, and dwarves. Callon waved at her as she approached and patted the open bench seat between himself and a dwarf she did not know.

Sĭne sat and let out a brief exhale. "Morning, Hellig," she greeted.

Offering a plate of fresh fruits and cheeses, Callon smiled. "Mornin', Sergeant," he returned.

"Sleep well?" she asked.

Callon shrugged. "Probably same as you — so no," he joked.

Sine chuckled at the truth. She had not slept well or much since leaving Marez. Between the silence and the eeriness, the rush out of Middling, and being here in the elven lands, restful nights were few and far between. "Have you seen Queen Braithe?" she asked.

Callon shook his head. "No. I think she's meeting with the other nobility about who gets to take care of us," he laughed and then sighed.

Sine took notice. "It may not look like the right thing, but Queen Braithe is wise. There must be some bigger reason for her leaving," she said.

Callon leaned in close. "I just keep overhearin' the Middlin' chatter. They saw some right wicked things out there, and we're headed toward 'em," he whispered.

Red eyes, bone masks. Sine had heard all the rumors too but tried her best not to think about them.

"Middling and Oburim haven't seen war in decades, Hellig. Though the tales seem outlandish, we're well trained and trusted by Queen Braithe. We'll do fine," she reassured.

Callon nodded to show moderate acceptance and motioned to her plate. "The cheese at least is divine here. Please eat, Sergeant," he smiled.

Sine grinned and picked up a piece of the aged wedge that gave an aroma of fresh cream and herbs. Biting into the slice, she sunk slightly in her seat in delight. Flavors of this land were wondrous to her. She missed much of the Marezian cuisine, but the delicate and curated nature of the elven food was so refreshing and sustaining that she could not help but feel satisfied.

An elven horn sounded, and all turned to the center of the quad. Sīne saw Captain Kenefick and Queen Braithe making their way toward its source — the elven Lord Eilfaren and the beautiful Lady Eilfaren. Sīne had been fascinated with the lore of creatures like elves for some time. She feverishly read any text she came across, learning about these mythical beings who were acclaimed as both beautiful and remarkably intelligent. Now, speaking to them, she'd found that the tales were true. The elves were all so beautifully sculpted, and their language and conversations were so elevated that she felt lost in wonder.

Sīne watched as Captain Kenefick received a token from the Lord and Lady, as did the strange (but kind) Outrider, Liaison Adrelghard Tugrom, and two other elves. Queen Braithe appeared to already have one of the emblems and Sīne wondered at their purpose.

Callon tapped her shoulder, and she jumped in her seat. He pointed to Captain Catach, who was gathering their company together to prepare for the sendoff of their queen and captain.

"Duty beckons," Callon jested and Sīne nodded, taking one last bite of what appeared to be a type of fig.

Their regiment had encircled Lachlann. Sīne and Callon nudged their way into line and Lachlann nodded to acknowledge their presence.

Gesturing to those gathered, Lachlann said, "I have been informed that we are to be under the order of the elven guard.

Queen Braithe has granted Lord Eilfaren our aid, but we are to be the shepherds of this army, as only we know the Yeacralan lands. In a moment, we will be preparing to line the vale to bid safe travels to our queen and captain." He paused. "Are there any questions?"

Silence ensued, save for the clamor of the environment, and he nodded.

"Right, good. Please then begin preparations for our departure into the valley," he said, dismissing them.

Lachlann stopped Sïne as she turned to leave. "Sergeant," he said.

Sïne turned around and regarded him. "Yes, Captain?" she answered. Lachlann stood about a head above hers, his long blonde hair tied neatly in a tail. He could be mistaken for an elf at a distance, given his stature, but his crooked nose showed him to be a man.

"May we talk?" he asked.

Sïne nodded. "Certainly. About what?"

"Am I doing alright? This role feels… strange. I worry it will affect camaraderie," he confessed. He shifted uncomfortably. His eyes softened and his posture slackened. Sïne had known Lachlann since they were children. They were not the closest of friends, but through knighthood they had become advocates for each other. Both had moved up the ranks simultaneously, but this is the first time one had the upper hand.

Sïne was moved by Lachlann's concern and knew he was being genuine in his question. She placed a hand on his shoulder. "We need you at your best, Captain. I trust you not to abuse your post," she said simply.

The new captain bowed his head and crossed his right arm over his chest. "Thank you, Matharnach."

"Any time, Catach," she replied with a nod.

Sĭne looked once again out at the vast array of faces around her, seeking one she knew. Callon's voice surprised her.

"What did Catach want?" he asked.

Jumping slightly, then turning to face him, she answered, "That's Captain Catach, soldier."

Callon rolled his eyes. "Trying to get used to that. What did the… captain want?" he asked again.

"If it concerned you, Corporal, I'd have let you know," Sĭne said with a smirk.

Callon raised his hands in surrender. "Fine, fine. I see how it is," he joked. "Some are headed into the vale already for the departure. Wanna head down?"

Sĭne nodded, since it was a better offer than sitting alone, and followed Callon into the vale where they had first entered the elven lands. Memories of that journey felt years ago now. Entering the lower valley, she saw lines formed of both elves and dwarves, all standing neatly at attention, even as they chatted with one another. Middling and Oburim's company had assembled themselves opposite of them, though much less dignified.

"Can't believe Queen Braithe actually trusts Dùghlan or Arasgain," Callon whispered.

"If anyone overhears you, we'll be tried for treason, you

know that?" Sīne snapped under her breath. She stopped for a moment before continuing in a whisper, "Me either."

Much of the situation did not sit right for Sīne, as she felt the other armies of men possessed few redeeming qualities. She had run for her life on account of their efforts to bring destruction to the elves. She was not keen on believing they had turned over a new leaf. Nonetheless, she held to her belief in Tagwen's words the evening before: "The kingdoms of Middling and Oburim have pledged their service to our home. They will be your brothers in arms to secure Yeacralas." As she continued to look over the line of Middling's men, she sighed. *They are just soldiers — just following orders.* Her distaste toward them felt misdirected as she continued observing them. They were hardly to blame for their leadership's missteps.

Sīne theorized that the death of the Princess of Middling must have changed their hearts. She did not know much of Mòrrea, or the role she had played in the liberation of the kings' minds, but the death of a princess was significant all the same.

She and Callon approached the place where others of their company had gathered — along the line of the kingdoms of men. Beitris, the MacLeòirs, and Thesden stood chatting amongst themselves. Across from them, she noted some elves who nodded kindly as her gaze met theirs, and she smiled at their grace.

Beitris Grannd stood next to her. "Seem's like someone has an eye for you, Sergeant," Beitris said playfully.

Confused, Sīne glanced around.

"A little to your left, but don't make it so obvious!" Beitris whispered.

Then she saw him. Standing amongst the elves, in a long charcoal cloak covering a bandaged shoulder and arm was the captain of the Oburim Army. Sīne fondly remembered his help in prepping their departure from Middling, and wondered why he stood separate from his own people. He smiled at catching her attention and she quickly turned away.

"Thanks for that, Grannd," she said, her face flushed.

"Oh, come now, you're the only woman I get to converse with, and he's quite handsome," Beitris smirked mischievously.

"He is likely just being friendly at recognizing we are the ones he helped escape," Sīne said.

Beitris let out a sarcastic snort, then asked, "Do you think they all mean to help us? Without Queen Braithe and all?"

"What do you feel?" Sīne asked.

Beitris paused and her mouth twisted a bit. "I think so," she concluded. "I certainly hope they do."

"Then hold to that," Sīne instructed. "We must have faith in these new allies, though it may seem unrealistic," she counseled.

Elven horns sounded again in the distance, followed by the trumpeting of dwarven bagpipes. The remainder of her company filed into the line as they stood at the front edge awaiting the procession. Captain Catach ensured they were all accounted for and instructed them to stand proudly for their queen. Sīne watched as the beginning of the fated party entered the vale.

Upon beautiful steeds their company rode. First, the Lord and Lady of the Forest led the advancement. Royally outfitted in dazzling emerald ensembles, they embodied the majesty of the woodlands. The Outrider, the dwarven liaison, the old elf whom Sìne did not know, and another unknown elf who looked strangely like their former captain, then rode by with an equal air of impressiveness. The Yeacralans' queen and captain followed behind. Sìne was awed most by Seasaìdh and Arofel, upon whom Queen Braithe and Captain Kenefick sat, respectively. The horses were immaculately cleaned and brushed, and the regalia that draped their backs was a similarly rich green that mimicked the earth, with the elven sigil embroidered in bright golden threads.

Sìne offered them a small smile as they approached, and the gesture was returned by her queen. Her company then moved to salute in unison — a final honor to their commanders. The fellowship disappeared into the forest and the parade ended, leaving those behind to prepare for their own journey.

"Our arrangements must be complete by Lord Eilfaren's return," Lachlann informed the remaining members of their regiment. "Report to Sergeant Matharnach once your name and belongings have been submitted to the elven quartermaster, who you will find in the central courtyard amongst the carriages. You have one hour," he said.

A collective "Yes sir" was issued before Sìne and her fellow soldiers made their way back to the quad. She walked with Beitris into the western manor to their room on the ground floor. Inside were two modest beds, and Sìne lay for a moment on the one she had claimed. Beitris sat on the side of her own as she looked at Sìne. Pawing the bedding, she spoke, "Going to miss this. My own back home isn't nearly as comfortable as this one."

"Likewise," Sìne agreed, staring up at the ceiling.

"Don't go on getting too comfortable, now. You heard the… captain," Beitris said.

Sīne sat up and stared at Beitris through narrowed eyes. "Why are you all doing that?" Sīne asked.

"Doing what?"

"You and Callon at least have paused when referring to Catach as 'Captain'," she said.

"Well—" Beitris started, "we just don't want to upset you," she confessed.

Sīne shook her head. "I have no problem with Lachlann becoming captain. Queen Braithe had to choose, and he has excelled in his posts." She paused and tore away from Beitris' concerned gaze. "Besides, I've not exactly proven myself on this expedition," she admitted.

"Nonsense! You were just doing what you were ordered to do!" Beitris exclaimed, in an attempt at comfort.

Sīne exhaled a sharp breath. "That is not justification enough."

"But—" Beitris interjected.

"No. Gather your things. We must be going," Sīne said with finality.

Beitris nodded, turning her attention to the sprawled manner of her belongings.

Sīne was relieved that had been enough to end the conversation but found herself folding and refolding the same linen tunic as she thought of an apology. Before it could come to her, though, Beitris finished collecting her items and headed to the door.

"I'll meet you out there, Sergeant," she smiled back at Sĭne, her curled black hair bouncing effortlessly around her tan face and dark eyes.

Sĭne nodded at her, and Beitris left.

Grabbing the end of her long, tied-off, light brown hair, Sĭne marked its straightness and the slight fray of its ends. She tossed the tail behind her head and finished packing her effects. She then made both borrowed beds and took in the view of the room one last time. The light wooden floors and mixed stone walls, the intricate elven lantern on the live-edge center table. This little space had been home to Sĭne for the time she'd spent here. She silently thanked the area and left to report to the command.

Crossing through the makeshift garrison that had been deployed in the once peaceful garden, Sĭne approached the elf who looked to be the quartermaster. He stood a head or two above hers, his golden hair was plaited down the length of his back, his skin as pale as snow, and like all the elves of this land, he bore viridian irises. His lips pressed together in a mild look of disdain until his eyes caught the crest upon Sĭne's chest.

"Ahh. You are one of the Southland queen's men, yes?" he asked.

All their voices too were lyrically enchanting; the stories Sĭne had read of them did not do their kind justice. She nodded and bowed politely. "Sergeant Sĭne Matharnach," she said, spelling her surname so the elf could add it to the record.

"Nala'evanegtas, Sergeant. I am Master Mæraca," he greeted, bowing deeply toward her.

"Nala'evanegtas," she returned, her throat tightening in hopes that she had not mispronounced the greeting.

To her astonishment, Mæraca beamed at her. "Your pronunciation is impressive!" he exclaimed. "It is nice to see some men learn; many, I fear, do not care enough to try," he said, seeming disappointed.

"It's a beautiful language. I only wish I knew more," she replied.

Mæraca nodded at her and proceeded to continue the registration process. "As I've informed many of your regiment already, you are to ride with the Lord Eilfaren, King Barindroun, and the leading men of the other domains. Thus, you'll be gathered over there." He gestured toward a group where some of Sĭne's mates were congregating, and near them, huddled in their own circle, were the heads of houses.

"Thank you," Sĭne said.

"Êadura üv," he educated.

"Êadura üv," she repeated.

Mæraca smiled in appreciation. "Üv ean æpèlad."

Sĭne repeated the last phrase in her head continuously as she moved to join her companions.

Callon and Thesden greeted her as she approached, but she was absently mouthing the expression to herself.

"Somethin' on yer mind, Sergeant?" Callon asked.

Sĭne became aware of herself then and cleared her throat. "No, no, I'm fine. Everyone ready for this?" she asked.

Thesden nodded. He and Beitris were the youngest of the collective tasked with this expedition. Sĭne wondered why

Captain Breccan had chosen them but supposed she could not have known how this voyage would evolve. Barely two decades old they were, and Sïne admired how intrepid they continued to be throughout this journey — wishing the same for herself.

"Captain Catach went with the MacLeòirs to bring the horses. They'll be 'round any moment," Thesden told her.

Pulling up behind their assembly, right on cue, came the three tasked with wrangling the horses. Sïne rushed over to help, but really to be reunited with her mare, Aelin.

Aelin whinnied in delight when she saw her, and Sïne soothed her face. Her sorrel coat and mane were typical of the Logroscan region's horses, but the singular white patch on her chest made her unique. The Matharnach family had been gifted the mare from a widow in Torrerìn who could no longer care for her. Though intended for Sïne's brother, Emyr, Aelin became attached to Sïne — thus it has been ever since.

"Hello, my dear," Sïne greeted.

The horse shuffled her snout in response and Sïne chuckled.

"Seems she missed you," a resonant voice spoke behind her. Sïne turned, stunned as she beheld Lord Eilfaren. He stood next to her whilst extending a hand to Aelin, who accepted his affections.

"Lord Eilfaren! I — yes. I-I missed her, too," Sïne stammered.

Faldïr stood as a great statue. The vestments he wore of elven steel glistened, despite the overcast skies, and his countenance appeared carved in marble. He turned his gaze to Sïne and offered a salute that she returned.

"Forgive me, I am an old elf, and it has been some time since I first met your company. Remind me of your name," he said.

"Sergeant Sĭne Matharnach, sir — Lord," she swallowed.

Faldïr gave a hearty laugh. "Sir does just fine, Sergeant. Thank you," he smiled.

"Êadura üv — sir."

Faldïr stood tall and proud at hearing Sĭne's words. Grinning, he bowed deeply to her, and she half-bowed in return, unsure of the customary response. He then took his leave to meet with Captain Catach. Preparations were nearing completion, and the hour of departure was near.

"We must prepare," she said softly to Aelin. Bringing Aelin around to the readying area, Sĭne found her saddle. Mounting and filling her bags with the packaged order of rations and water, she overlooked the mare one last time to confirm the straps would hold. She then untied the belt of her sword holster and affixed it to the saddle, hiding it underneath the draped blanket.

Satisfied, she patted Aelin and walked her to the front line, where Captain Catach was awaiting them. He sat upon Baringr as he surveyed the crowd to take account of all the men under his care. Spotting Sĭne, he regarded her and mouthed something to himself as he continued glancing around.

Sĭne, too, looked around. The elves formed perfect ranks as they awaited their lord's order. The armor and bows of the archers were all uniformly laid upon the soldiers — the air of perfection made them appear the quintessential army. Dwarves, too, though more brash in their armaments of steel and more relaxed in nature, were in perfect order.

Glancing around at her own men, Sĭne realized she was standing next to Thesden, who sat upon a gracious elven colt, and next to him was Iòsaph upon a similar steed. Realizing she was the only one remaining on the ground, she climbed onto Aelin and adjusted for comfort.

Trotting up on her right was Callon, who was excitedly pointing to the horse he was riding. It was blessed with a gorgeous light charcoal mane and tail that Sĭne swore were nearly blue in color. The animal's mannerisms were exceptionally well-behaved, and its stride was effortless and graceful. Sĭne shook her head in surprise at seeing Callon upon such a creature.

"Isn't he a beaut?" Callon bragged.

"He certainly is," Sĭne agreed. "You're hardly a fit for such a majestic animal," she teased.

Callon snickered and stroked the horse's neck. "She's just jealous, mate," he soothed the steed.

Sĭne rolled her eyes at him and gave Aelin a pat. She was not envious. Sĭne loved the mare who had served her so graciously these past five years.

Drums from the dwarven army sounded. A crescendo of elven horns followed, and Lord Eilfaren beckoned their attention. Standing beside him was the dwarven king, the kings of men, and Lachlann, all aligned as equals.

"We journey now to a fate unknown," Faldïr began. "We hold that those who stand beside us today are counted as brethren of our company. We ride not for the saving of a singular city, but for all Vostheloren. Discard your prejudices, stand firm in your resolve, and may the gods have pity on us all. To Marez!" he proclaimed.

The leading men all raised their weapons to the shouts of the troops. Sĭne shouted along with them but held no sword in the air. Instead, she raised her fist then crossed it along her heart.

Thus, the march began. Oburim's army was perhaps the largest battalion among them, at nearly eight hundred strong, despite the loss they had suffered on their arrival. Elves counted as the second largest, at two hundred archers and four hundred foot-soldiers. Dwarves, and the Middling Army, came in third, at approximately four hundred mixed combatants, total. Finally, nine — nine of Sĭne's division remained — the whole of their army sitting at home, unaware of the situation at hand.

Through a great portion of the Forest, they rode. Views of Thrindūl were swallowed swiftly by the Forest's dense foliage and tree cover. The pathway leading out of the Ebrïhèïlè's safety was the widest it had been, providing the necessary space for the unconventional legion to quickly make their way through. Sight of the Outlands broke through the Forest's tree line about an hour after the frontline had begun the journey.

Sĭne squinted as they were birthed from the forest into the early afternoon light. Grounds in front of them lay still frosted from the previous night's chill, having not yet melted away. At a decent pace, another hour passed, and the leading party reached the bridge that Sĭne recalled hearing about in rumor. There she saw the truth. Carnage spattered the landscape. Scattered bodies lay strewn about the lands with a crust of frost encasing most of them. As they passed, Sĭne caught sight of a fallen adversary. Their hood had fallen from their head, revealing a flowing mane of raven hair. Their skin, too, was a light tan, despite having frozen during the night.

King Dùghlan and King Arasgain broke apart from the frontline and directed some of their company to join them as they took the next few hours to gather the bodies in piles to be burned. Black cloaks, masks of bone, and strange weapons, too, were part of the collection to be given the same treatment as those who wielded them.

A soldier of Middling came to grab the body that Sĭne had noticed. As they dragged the corpse, the mask fell slightly from the creature's face, revealing the countenance of a beautiful woman. Sĭne was taken aback. The woman looked not unlike the elves in features, but the hair was not one of their traits. She seemed peaceful in this deadened state, much to Sĭne's discomfort.

She's hardly a monster, Sĭne thought.

Silence, apart from the dropping of bodies and the sizzling cracks of flames, was all that could be heard. Lord Eilfaren and Sĭne's band held back from the men of Middling and Oburim as they put to rest their men and those who had cut them down.

Sun broke through about midday and the associated warmth was welcome to many of them. Though the skies in the distance told a tale of pending storms, it would be long until they and the armies met.

Pressing on, the directive became to reach the Road, cutting across the bloodied lowlands of the Greyrest to reach its southern stretch. The hope was to garner the whole army across the Terrishire Bridge and find a patch of land suitable enough to hold them in South Drÿs.

Beside her, Sĭne could overhear Thesden talking to Brian MacLeòir. "Could you believe it? All that talk really was true — bones and whatnot," he said.

"Not really much o'a dead army though, eh? Mean they are dead, but not like Sam's brother was sayin' 'bout them bein' undead," Brian said.

"Lucky for that, innit?" Thesden replied.

Sĭne heard Brian's affirmative response as their conversation ceased and then noticed the grip on her reins, easing her clenched fists around the leather strap. She flexed her neck and shoulders too, as she realized their stiffness. A caw of a crow caught her attention as she witnessed a singular bird fly overhead. It was flying away from their destination, and Sĭne once again seized her reins, which had become an impromptu crutch.

Crows often were portents for the men of the Southlands — considerable omens of virtue. Their presence in singularity, however, often proved a sign of ills. Sĭne's father had warned her all her life that "a crow alone means no good's to come." Even now, in her early third decade of existence, she could not shake the superstition. Squawks ebbed behind her, as it searched for other ears to bend, and Sĭne faced forward, coming upon the muddied grounds of the marshlands of Drÿs.

Faldïr sent scouts ahead to survey the path's integrity, considering recent storms. When they returned, Faldïr relayed information to Lachlann and messengers of the other units.

Captain Catach approached his men. "Marshes are overrun, the path is stable enough, but it is imperative that you remain diligent upon the Road," he warned. "Sergeant, please take the rear guard to keep everyone in line," he charged Sine.

"Yes, sir," she nodded.

"Should be a smooth process if everyone follows our lead. We'll all be through and over the Lunennete Bridge by sundown," he promised.

After seeing their collective nods, Lachlann returned to his place and the procession continued. Approaching the bridge, the mire surrounding the Road was thick. Mounds of dirt had been created in the slide from the small hill of North Drÿs and Sine kept a close eye on her companions ahead. Nearly to the edge of the bridge, Sine noticed a shift in a pile of sludge next to the path.

Ignoring it, she continued, until Aelin reared in a panic, sending Sine into the mud. A chain reaction of frightened horses fell down the line, as soldiers tried to calm their beasts. Panicked herself, Sine shuffled to try and get up, until she confronted the source of Aelin's alarm. A figure, clawing out of the mud, had reached an arm out and touched Aelin, and was now trying to grab at Sine. The muck's thick grasp did not allow for an easy escape as the humanoid figure grabbed at her leg. Sine screamed for help, as a pair of blood-red eyes peered at her. Glazed in mud, the creature could barely keep hold, but kept trying to use Sine as leverage to free itself.

The creature's mouth opened to reveal a set of fanged teeth

as it rasped the word "andarïè" just before Captain Catach rendered the being lifeless. Sïne stared for a moment, the sounds of the environment blurred into unintelligible echoes until Lachlann pulled her up from the ground.

"Sergeant, can you hear me?" he asked, scanning her person.

Sïne nodded and shook her head to refocus. "Yes. I'm sorry-I… what was that thing?" she faltered.

Lachlann regarded the still figure on the ground. "Seems it was a straggler of their army," he guessed.

Then who was she? Sïne thought, recalling the maiden on the battlefield. It was impossible to imagine a being of such beauty holding the same attribute as what she had just seen.

Surveying the rest of the chaos that had ensued, Sïne saw horses and wagons now stuck in mud, and soldiers scrambling to rectify the situation.

"I'm so sorry," she breathed to Lachlann.

"Was not your fault, Sergeant. Let's move. Aelin is on the other side of the bridge. Take care to regroup and clean yourself off," he instructed.

Sïne bowed her head and took her leave, attempting to shield herself from onlookers, though she was caked in mud and rogue foliage. The ground of South Drÿs was slightly less damp, and thus preparations for camp were being made. Aelin was found tied next to Baringr in the plot where her company would rest. Sïne shuffled through her pack in search of a cloth and a change of clothing.

"Psst," she heard from behind and turned around.

Beitris stood with a bundle of cloth and motioned for Sïne to follow. She went behind an already-fashioned tent, where no one was around, and helped Sĭne out of her fouled armor.

"I'll get this cleaned up," Beitris said kindly.

"No, no, I can take care of this. I appreciate the offer, though," Sĭne replied.

"Don't be silly — I'm not going to do it. I was going to task Daniel with it. He owes me a favor, anyway," Beitris smirked.

Sĭne laughed. "You can tell him I requested his service — seems like a silly waste of a favor," she said.

"Oh! Brilliant. Thanks, Sergeant," Beitris beamed.

Once Sĭne was out of her armor, Beitris led her inside the tent, helped her to change, and assisted in cleaning the mud out of her hair. "A good rinse in the river will clean these right up," Beitris said to the pile of soiled clothing.

"I will manage that bit," Sĭne said. "Thank you for your help, Grannd."

"My pleasure, Sergeant," Beitris returned, then paused. Her expression became concerned as she continued looking at the laundry.

"Something wrong?" Sĭne asked.

Beitris shrugged. "Was it really one of those creatures that attacked you?" she asked.

Sĭne took a breath. "I think so," she finally said, not quite meeting Beitris' gaze.

Beitris scratched at a seemingly phantom itch on her neck. "Got to be wary of everything then, I suppose," she said.

Silence descended for a moment, until they were interrupted. Entering the tent was Lachlann, who stopped abruptly upon seeing the space occupied.

"Forgive me!" he apologized, shielding his eyes.

"Sorry, Captain," Sĭne started. "We were about to depart," she said apologetically.

Lachlann nodded, removing the cover, then asked, "Is all fine now?"

Beitris nodded, "Yes, Captain," as she saluted, and Lachlann permitted her to leave.

"And you?" he asked Sĭne.

Sĭne nodded. "Sorry, Captain, I'll be on my way."

"You must stop apologizing, Sĭne," Lachlann scolded.

She regarded him, grabbed the bundle of clothing, nodded, and bowed before leaving. Acquiring a basket for her garments, she walked to the Terrishire River to clean them. Icy waters rushed through the linens, dragging the stains of terror along with them. Sĭne's hands were stung and reddened by the piercing cold as she wrung her garbs dry. By the time she was finished, most of the army was settled. Rows of soldiers camped by fires and makeshift shelters that lined the Road. She walked down its cobbled length to find the quarters that would be hers. Spotting the Yeacralan banner next to that of the elves, Sĭne was relieved her company were equipped with proper tents. She searched until she found a camp with a vacant cot. Inside was Beitris, Callon, and Thesden chatting amongst themselves.

"Welcome to the chateau, Sergeant," Callon joked.

Sĭne laughed and laid her clothes out to dry at the edge of her cot. "I love what you've done with the place," she mocked.

Beitris scoffed. "If I had left it to these two, the cots would still be awaiting assembly," she jeered.

"We were workin' on it!" Thesden frowned. Their shared laughter drifted into a brief silence.

"So, is it true then, Sergeant? The creature you saw…" Callon asked.

Sĭne groaned. "Seems everyone is aware of it. Yes. It was… well, I'm not sure what it was. It was covered in mud and all I could see were its eyes," she recalled. *And teeth*, she thought.

"Red? Like they've been sayin'?" Thesden probed.

Sĭne nodded. She thought for a moment about how it had spoken, and how calling it and the woman "creatures" felt merciless. Pulling her cloak closely around herself, she stood. "If you'll excuse me, I'm going to find something to eat. Can I get any of you anything?" she asked before exiting.

They all shook their heads and Sĭne bowed out of the tent's flaps. Nighttime had arrived. The glow of the scattered fires caused the landscape to appear as though it were ablaze. There was no hiding their location if anyone was watching for their arrival, and Sĭne shuddered at the thought.

Pacing around the encampment, she looked for some manner of provisioning. Nearest the tents of leadership was a crude assembly of cooks, both dwarven and elvish. She made her way into the queue, and as she approached the front of the line, she overheard the elven cooks speaking.

"Æsūd èdūs üv'èterèf?" the taller of the two seemed to ask.

"Üv andarïè ov äh," the second gestured toward a box.

Sĭne recognized that singular word and watched as they both then lifted the box to carry it to another location.

"Can I get yeh somethin', soldier?" the dwarf at the serving table asked her.

Realizing she was in the front of the line; she made a quick request for whatever they had available and was served a bowl of meat porridge. She bowed in thanks as she walked, still watching the elves. They had returned now to their station, and she was desperate.

"Excuse me?" she addressed the one who had said the term.

The elf looked up at her, his honey-colored hair perfectly framing his sharp features and dark skin, and sat expectantly waiting for her to speak.

"Sorry, um, I was wondering if you could tell me what 'andarïè' means?" she asked.

His keen gaze beheld her for a moment, as though studying her intent, but nonetheless appeared intrigued on hearing a human utter his tongue. He turned his attention to the dwarf she had previously encountered and muttered a question.

The dwarf answered aloud, "Üv'acūs, 'help'."

"Andarïè, 'help'," the elf translated for Sïne.

"Help," she whispered to herself. "Êadura üv," she said in thanks.

His mouth turned into a gracious smile as he bowed to her and offered her a loaf of elven bread. She nodded and eagerly accepted, bringing it and her porridge back to the lodging.

Beitris was the only one waiting inside when she arrived. "Are they giving away whole loaves?" Beitris asked, wide-eyed.

Sïne shook her head. "I don't think so, but here," she said, as she tore a chunk off the end and handed it to Beitris.

The queensman smiled. "Thanks!"

Sïne nibbled at another bit of bread she broke for herself, staring absently at the floor. Her thoughts were interrupted as her other roommates returned, trays of grits in hand. Thesden handed a bowl over to Beitris, who beamed in thanks.

"Were they offering loaves somewhere?" Callon asked Sïne, upon seeing the bread.

She shook her head and tore the remaining bread apart for the two of them.

"Perks of bein' a sergeant, I suppose," Thesden laughed.

Sïne scoffed, "Sure."

The four ate peacefully. Her compatriots talked through the meal, sharing anecdotes of their pasts or things they had heard through the grapevines of this aggregate army. Sïne sat pretending to listen but held quiet as she sat haunted by the last word of that… creature.

"Did any of you see what they looked like? This dark army?" Sïne asked suddenly.

All three looked at each other and shook their heads.

"Nah, Sergeant, they've all got those weird masks on," Callon answered.

"So, none of you saw… her?" she asked.

"Who?" Beitris asked, frowning.

"She had black hair, and looked like — like an elf," Sïne answered.

Callon snorted. "An elf? Sergeant, these dracari, mœrdeth things couldn't possibly be as pretty as the elves."

"Pretty, eh?" Beitris teased.

"Awh, c'mon, Grannd, you know it, too," Callon said.

"So, *none* of you? None of you saw her?" Sĭne repeated.

"No, Sergeant, I'm sorry. Maybe their face caught the light wrong if ya did see 'em," Thesden suggested.

"Yeah, there's no way these things are even human, from what I've heard," Beitris said.

Sĭne sat in silence, now unconvinced at what she had seen.

When they were all finished, Beitris offered to return dishes, and the rest prepared themselves to sleep. Upon her return, they extinguished the lantern and dozed off. Sĭne lay staring at the tent ceiling for a time, until the inability to remain awake finally called her to slumber.

Waking to the dawn peering through the fluttering tent canvas, Sĭne felt the windchill on her face. Indebted to the blankets and furs that had been provided, the rest of her body was thoroughly warmed. Her companions remained well asleep, but drones of activity buzzed outside.

Thus, she forced herself from her comfort, grabbed an extra woolen tunic for warmth, and stepped quietly out. Many of the men of Middling and Oburim had begun stowing their belongings. A line of dwarven soldiers were marching through the central gathering, carrying bundles of weaponry, crates, and cloth. She saw Lachlann armored and entering the camp of Lord Eilfaren and took that as the sign to wake the others.

Many woke unenthusiastically, but obeyed Sĭne's order, regardless. A few she came across were already awake, including Daniel MacLeòir, who provided her cleaned and polished armor.

He helped fasten the armaments, and she continued to help the others begin the take-down.

Bits of snow began to fall as the storm clouds had finally arrived. Campfires continued to be lit, and many who were awaiting instruction were huddled around them. Sĭne gathered her effects to pack onto Aelin.

Aelin stood serene against the backdrop of snow, alongside the gray-dappled steed, Baringr. Scooping a handful of feed for them both, she fed them the treat from her hands, to many happy snorts.

In the distance, she noticed a pair of horses and riders approaching from the South. Judging by the russet coats of the stallions, they appeared to be Horsemen of Logrosca. They rode swiftly from the basin of the Clerlūn ruins up and through the encampment, and Sĭne clutched at Aelin's reins.

Not long after their arrival, the elven horns sounded an alarm. Rushing back to the center of camp, orders in all languages were being shouted, and all manner of soldiers were hastening to ready themselves to depart.

"Yeacralas! Yeacralas to me!" Lachlann was shouting amidst the commotion.

Sĭne found her way to him, as he searched for all his companions.

"Lachlann!" she called out.

He noticed and dashed to meet her. "Some Horsemen were traveling along the Wynfjord arm of the river and caught sight of our banners. They said an army is coming from the deserted lands near the Peaks. We're going to try and head them off before they reach Marez — while they warn Logrosca. Find the others and be ready to ride," he instructed.

Sïne nodded quickly. She found Beitris, Brian and Daniel first, then together they found Iòsaph, Callon, and Thesden.

"I saw Sam and Ailbert briefly. I think they're headed to the stables already," Iòsaph said.

The regiment hastened together, meeting the remainder of their company at the front lines. Journeying to Logrosca would take the entire day, and even then, they would have only barely passed the whole of the Enbron Woods, should they not take time for rest.

Faldïr came to the front of the line with King Dùghlan and began the lead South. Sïne saw Captain Catach join them shortly after, racing up from behind their unit after confirming they were all accounted for. Onward they rode for hours. Breaks lasted little longer than five minutes at a time. Enough to relieve themselves, bite at a ration, and remount horses, if they had one. Snowfall, too, quickened its rate as the hours ticked by. Sïne's gloves barely kept out the cold, and she frequently flexed and rubbed at them to sustain any manner of warmth.

Darkness approached sooner than was anticipated as the storm overhead grew thick. They had only then reached the borders of the woodland. Sïne was not keen on meeting that forest again, after their first encounter. Continuing still, they rode past the woods, to her relief, but in the distance, faintly observable, was a moving line of torches and shadow. She felt a chill rend her body immobile as she watched the length of the gloom grow. Where their entirety was being formed, Sĭne did not know, but they were many — too many.

Processions stopped once more for a final rest. The forces were still nearly a half-day's ride from one another, but the proximity felt like a chokehold to Sĭne. Exhausted and energy expended, she wished for respite, but found herself staring afar, as if keeping an eye on the army would hold them at bay. Camps, both makeshift and practical, were built once more, but in a more careful fashion to serve as future infirmaries for the inevitable wounded. There would be no talks, no negotiation of peace. They were told the army could not be reasoned with, as they were, but a drove of mindless servitors.

"Andarïè," Sĭne whispered to herself.

Lachlann approached her from the side and cleared his throat to announce his presence.

"There they are," Sĭne said, not taking her eyes off the shadows.

"You have fought bravely before, Sĭne. These creatures are no different to what we have faced. They bleed as monsters do," Lachlann reminded her.

"But what if we are the monsters, Lachlann?" Sĭne asked.

Lachlann turned his head, confused. "Sĭne, you know that is not true — our company least of all," he responded.

Sĭne took a deep breath. "It asked for help before we cut it down," she said.

"The creature spoke?" he asked. His face turned pale, and his eyes became filled with worry.

Sĭne nodded, continuing to withhold eye contact. "They

spoke a word that I did not know, but I have come to find it's an elvish word — asking for help," she reported.

Lachlann held silent for a moment, and turned to look toward where Sĭne was facing. "Perhaps," he said, "they were abandoned by the horde for holding a sense of self-preservation," he proposed.

This caused Sĭne to break her vision of the horizon and turn to him. "You think so?" she asked.

Lachlann met her gaze and nodded. "The whole of that army was ruthless in their charge against our men, and the men of Middling and Oburim. Many of our native brothers fell by their hands," he reminded her.

Sĭne looked up to prevent the flow of tears. She had forgotten Lachlann had witnessed their first attack, and now felt dishonorable in questioning their integrity.

"Forgive me," she lowered her head.

Lachlann shook his head. "You do not need forgiveness, Sĭne, only faith in yourself to know when and what the right thing is," he said with confidence. Reaching a hand to her shoulder he beckoned her gaze to his. "You are a good soldier, Sergeant. I trust you will remember that truth."

"Did you see… her? Or any of them, for that matter," Sĭne asked.

"To whom do you refer?" Lachlann asked.

"I saw one of their army," Sĭne began.

"The one near the bridge?"

"No," Sĭne shook her head. "It was upon the fields of the Greyrest. She had raven hair and had the countenance of an elf

— truly beautiful, but strange," Sīne recalled.

"Perhaps that is what those… dracari used to look like. But Sīne, their countenance does not provide them with any humanity. I mean, look at them," he said, pointing to the horizon. "They move in swarms and portray a mindlessness so — so inconsolable. Lord Eilfaren has explained they are no longer of this world, that they serve only darkness."

"Why, then, would one of them request aid, Lachlann?" Sīne persisted.

"I don't know, Sīne! I — I'm sorry." He turned away from her for a moment.

Sīne looked out to the army once again. "I just wish I knew what we were facing, Captain."

Lachlann clenched his jaw. "We're facing monsters, Sīne. I know you saw its… fangs," he shuddered. "What manner of creature, other than a beast, holds a feature like that?" he asked.

Sīne shook her head, recalling the hideous, wolfish teeth.

"They appear insistent upon pursuing our home, Sīne. I would rather it be us who is victorious," Lachlann said firmly.

Sīne nodded and wiped away at the rogue tear that had escaped, before turning to Lachlann. "Then we shall be, Captain," she promised, biting at her cheek.

A moment of silence passed before Lachlann was moved to speak. "Are we okay, Sīne?" he asked.

"Yes, sir," she answered as she saluted him to take her leave. Lachlann examined her carefully as he saluted in kind and permitted her departure.

***

Rest was lacking. The sounding trumpets rang to wake Sĭne soon after she had fallen asleep. Adrenaline urged her limbs onward, exhilaration armored her person, and discipline quieted her fears.

Meals were provided and quickly eaten, marching orders were set, and the subsequent march began. Three seemingly endless hours carried them to the battlefront. The line of shadow grew and amassed to eclipse the continent's legion. Low growls sounded through the grasses and wound their way around the front to chill the army to the bone. Sĭne sat stoic alongside the chattering of her kinsmen until she was addressed.

"Sergeant?" Callon whispered as he moved beside her.

"Yes, Hellig?"

"D'ya know what's for dinner?" he asked hesitantly.

Sĭne closed her eyes as her heart sank and gut clenched. She breathed deeply before turning to Callon with a smile. "I hear the dwarves have a marvelous feast planned: cured meats, fresh eggs and bread. And ale! A time-honored recipe, so I've heard," she comforted.

Callon gave a light snort and shook his head in thanks, his eyes not quite meeting her gaze.

"Save me a seat when we get back, understood?" she instructed.

Callon's posture adjusted, and he saluted dutifully. "Yes, Sergeant," he replied.

Lord Eilfaren rode the front line, sword raised to catch the peeking sunlight through the haze. "Brethren!" he called out. "Today we break, and fulfill, the promises of our forefathers! For today we fight as one! Ride! Ride for your homes, for your honor! Ride for Vostheloren!" he thundered as he rode along the line upon his dazzling, golden warhorse.

Sïne, and all the battalion, howled in answer, unsheathing their swords to raise in unison. They were ready, and horns blew to commence their advancement. Sounds of blood rushing in her ears and hoofbeats upon the outer lands of the Logroscan fields were all Sïne could hear — until the crashing screams of the opposition cut through her focus. Batting away spears, thrashing the bows of archers, and dodging rogue knives was a dance, and Sïne its danseuse. Gawky movements abandoned her willowy frame as she contorted to strike down the ghosts that haunted the plain. Aelin, too, rode hard and gracefully, evading blows as though she had transformed into the wind.

Guttural snarls escaped the enemy's ambiguous, skeletal faces. Their eyes, though similar in their crimson hue, were not pleading. Sïne hoped for any shred of benevolence, but recalled Lachlann's warning of their inhumanity, and as they lunged and moved to strike at her, she found his claims to be true.

Sïne and the rest of her men were performing well, despite the adeptness of their enemy. It was the men of the other kingdoms who began to fall heavily under the assault. Sïne caught glances of the elves; the foot soldiers were presently an impenetrable shield wall, and their archers behind flew arrows precisely at the lines ahead. Dwarves were well-known to be stout and hardy in war, and their movements seemed unpredictable to the enemy, which gave the legion an advantage.

However, their numbers still began to prove too little. Every pack that Sĭne drove through, another would seemingly spring up in their place — the darkening of their presence on the land seeming endless. Sĭne began to lose sight of her men, becoming surrounded by hissing and wild flails. An occasional glimpse of maroon vestments reassured her that the Marezians continued to stand. Movement became restrained through the decimation, and Aelin bucked and kicked, thrashing in panic, which sent Sĭne plummeting to the ground. The mare dashed off to find a pocket of safety as Sĭne crawled in haste from the grassland.

"Aelin!" Sĭne shouted as she came upright, but the mare was dashing away. Regaining her wits, she was nearly caught by the spiked orb end of a chain but stabbed into the assailant. As it fell, it bore its incisors at her like an animal underneath the ghoulish mask. Continuing to catch her breath, she approached the deceased soldier and knelt to uncover its face. Hesitantly, she reached for the yellowing bone veil and pulled to reveal another being like the one she had seen earlier. Silken raven hair flowed to his shoulders and his eyes, though still that chilling blood-red, were now soft — and free. His pale face lay before her, his mouth slightly ajar, exposing the beastly canines.

As Sĭne sat mesmerized by his visage, Oburim's horn sounded. King Arasgain was calling for retreat. Sĭne glanced around; the forces of men were dwindling. The elven wall had broken, and all companies were now scattered throughout the battlefield.

"No! We must fight!" Sĭne shouted to those who ran beyond

her. None stopped to listen.

Then shouts from King Dùghlan came. "Pull back! We are outnumbered, Lord Eilfaren!"

Sìne discerned the shouts had come from behind, but she was too far ahead in a clustered fight. Glancing around for an ally, she spotted an unexpected face. The captain of Oburim was struggling to maintain himself against surrounding combatants. Eachann's swings were rigid, as his atrophic shoulder was learning to regain its former dexterity.

"You shouldn't be here!" she yelled at him as she moved to assist.

They circled in tandem with one another, their backs nearly pressed together as they fought the other's blind side.

"I know!" he called back as they twisted through an onslaught. "But I could not do nothing!"

Sìne saw more men following the lead of their kings to retreat and looked for a route of escape. She fought vigorously, snarling back to regain some of her lost fervor.

As she did, a new echo of hooves beat upon the land as the Horsemen of Logrosca finally joined the fight. They were not noted as a military force, but rather a faction of the Southland's men who were the best riders of the continent. Sìne marveled at their arrival as they drove through the crowd of shadow. Many armed with lances, they contended with the confused army with ease. Their stallions were of the most athletic nature, bred for speed and strength; there were none that matched their robustness. Sìne and Eachann watched as their entrapment was broken, the lines of their rivals thwarted. The kings of Middling and Oburim were even caught in surprise, turning to watch their unexpected saviors. The men of their armies were renewed, turning once again to fight.

Faldïr was awed by their arrival, and led a new charge at their side, following their lead of trampling through the opposing army. The grim antagonists, as if held together by a singular motive, continued to press the attack, but they began to fail. Fighting stances became staggered and wild, their balances easily overpowered. Some, however, became wise to the tactic of the horsemen and began specifically targeting the horses. Many steeds gracefully bounded away from their attempted attacks, but a few of the near hundred stallions were caught.

One crashed down nearest to Sĭne and Eachann, who rushed over to the rider's side. His courser had fallen dead upon him, and he struggled to move.

"Push!" Sĭne instructed Eachann, until she saw the rider's head shake, tears welling in his eyes.

"I cannot feel my legs," he cried.

Sĭne overlooked his body, his fair face was already graying; perspiration saturating his golden waves. The entirety of his torso was crushed underneath his stallion, who shared a remarkably similar mane to his rider.

"We'll get you out of here," Sĭne assured him.

The man shook his head again with what little he was able, his strikingly green eyes still brimming with sweat and tears. "No. They look-look to —" he struggled to string together his words.

Sĭne tried to calm him, but he fought against the pained end.

"No — time — they look — to slaughter — the Lions," he breathed sharply at each phrase and spoke with a clenched jaw.

"Tell — Nani—" he stared at Sĭne's face before his grimacing gaze softened and he faded. His expression was not unlike the other soldier she had seen.

Are we all then monsters? she wondered.

Sĭne closed the warrior's eyelids and brushed a hand upon the fallen steed.

Hearing the uproar of the contest, she returned to the terror that besieged them. She stood and tried to make sense of her position, then turned to help Eachann stand.

"I need to warn Lachlann!" she yelled, and Eachann followed.

Running through the riot, it was a harrowing few moments before she found the captain fighting alongside Callon and Samuel, still upon horses.

"Captain!" she called.

Lachlann's worried glance was thrown at Sĭne as he directed Baringr toward her. "What is it, Sergeant? Where is Aelin?" he demanded.

"There's no time, they're headed for Marez! We need to go!" she yelled.

Lachlann scanned the battlefield. "We cannot redirect our forces; we are already outmatched. We risk the city more if we do not cull this swarm," he said.

"Lachlann! We cannot do nothing!" she insisted.

"Sergeant, this is not nothing!" he yelled, as he swung at a foe.

"We can't leave the city to fall," she roared at him.

"Sergeant, you are ordered to fight here!" Lachlann instructed.

Her stare turned angry, she gripped her sword with a newfound ferocity, and she turned to Eachann.

"Are you with me?" she asked.

Eachann nodded.

She ran with him from the men of her company, hearing Lachlann call her name from behind. Whistling at a loose elven mare, she caught her by the reins and mounted, and then helped Eachann up.

So, they rode, breaking away from the ongoing battle, to Marez.

10

THE PASSAGE OF AŪRAÈLON

The Outrider garrison's cellar tunnel exit led to another manner of trap door hidden below a grassy knoll. Ualan was the first to scramble up the ladder to the surface. The echoes of claws raking against the second door followed them outward. He pulled everyone into the open, and then locked the hatch behind.

"That probably won't hold them long, right?" Breccan asked, backing away from the trap door.

"They're not known to be impeded by doors. The ladder won't bode well for them, but we had best get a move on, regardless," Ualan said as the snapping and snarling below began to sound louder.

"How in the world did they know we'd be there?" Breccan pressed.

Ualan breathed sharply, tucking the chain of keys through the neckhole of his tunic. "I do not know, but I am not about to wait and try to ask them. Let's move."

The party rushed toward the eastern shores. They continued walking under the light of the waxing moon, Southeast through hilly grassland and swirls of accumulating snow. The fourth hour of their trek approached as the sun's rays began cresting behind the horizon's storm.

Tagwen looked out at the sight before them — nearly five miles from their present position lay the remainder of the Aurilon Peaks.

Silence befell the group as they gathered their wits. Ualan silently wept as he stared at the sky for a moment, and Erul approached him. "I am sorry, dear boy," he consoled.

"He was a true brother to me," Ualan lamented. "Now his treachery must be forgiven, but he will not hear my words of forgiveness."

"Perhaps when we can find his wife, you can present them there," Erul suggested.

Ualan looked down at the letter that Peric had handed him in haste and noticed it was not sealed. "Ina was his daughter," Ualan clarified.

Erul sighed heavily as he patted Ualan on the back. "She will be alright. It is us this entity is interested in, after all," he said, trying to sound reassuring.

Ualan lifted the letter out of its envelope and looked at the last writing of his lost friend. His brow furrowed with alarm as he scanned the note.

Tagwen had been watching surreptitiously and came over.

"What is wrong?" she asked.

Without a word he handed her the letter.

They have been following you.

> *They know your path leads to the Isle.*
> *Run.*

"Peric had always intended to warn you," Tagwen realized.

The Outrider nodded as he took the note and stowed it away. "We must go. They know where we head, and perhaps even why. We cannot delay any further," he said to the group, glancing behind to see if the beasts had managed to catch up — but thankfully no figures had yet emerged.

Adrelghard was breathily clambering up a rise behind the group as he looked up to the mountains that taunted them. "Well, I bloody well forgot about those," he griped.

Erul, too, breathed heavily as he gripped tightly to his staff. Looking up to the mountain and then behind, he said, "We did not have much choice, Master Tugrom. The Misty Pass is our best hope at getting across in a timely manner."

"The Broken Pass, you mean," Breccan corrected as she brushed flakes of snow from her coat. The passage through the Aurilon Peaks was rumored to once lead to a dwarven stronghold. It has long since been abandoned after the war "The Usurper," Olwenna, waged upon the lands nearly three-hundred years ago.

"Yes," Erul nodded. "That too," he muttered. He walked up to the front of the group as he surveyed the mountainside for an indication of where the pass began. There was a break in the peaks of the mountain that emulated jagged sentries — the jutting of their forms appeared unnaturally carved into the rock. Between the break lay a steep incline covered in snow:

the entrance. Beyond that, the course was notorious for its swift ascents, dangerously narrow chokes, and unrelenting twists and turns as it winds itself throughout the mountain.

"Do you think the beasts mean to follow us up there?" Mæranedïl asked.

Erul shrugged. "I do not know, but there is no turning around now. Hopefully their having to reroute from the tunnel will be enough of a deterrent," he said as he shuffled onward through the frost.

Another hour had gone by when they reached the mouth of the pass, and snow began to fall heavily. Tagwen continually checked behind herself to see if there was any sign of the predators that were stalking them, but the land was quiet, and the flurry unfortunately obstructed her view. Chills distracted her as she urged herself to keep moving. Upward the group hiked, the summit of the initial rise blurred in the snow.

"Yeh know, us dwarves have traversed many a mountain, but this pass," Adrelghard stopped to take a breath, "this one is the worst."

"I have never endured the misfortune of this road," Tagwen struggled to say as she nearly moved to all fours to climb up the rest of the way.

"We're almost there!" Erul shouted from up ahead, shielding his face from a gust of snowy wind. Tagwen looked up and saw Erul disappear into the snow.

"Erul!" she shouted.

A faint echo of her call bounced between the mountain's guards, but no answer came. Seeing Adrelghard struggling through the accumulating banks, she held out a hand and helped pull him upward the ascent.

"Curse this damned snow!" he yelled.

Breccan looked behind herself at them. "Are you alright?" she shouted above the wind.

Tagwen nodded in confirmation but did not waste the air in her lungs to shout back. The winds were picking up now, and she was certain the peak was close, but the incline felt endless. Still focused on helping Adrelghard, she maneuvered him, so he was in front of her and suddenly saw a hand through the fog lift him up and over the ledge. Another hand came for her, and she grasped it, pulled up by Breccan.

Out of breath, the cold biting at her face, she leaned with her hands on her knees and looked up at Breccan. "Thank you," she gasped, as her friend, too, was trying to catch her breath.

At this ledge was a flat patch of ground. In front of them lay a canyon that was the true start to the path ahead, and the blizzard carried on behind them, shielding the ledge in a wall of snow. Erul observed the gathering and counted them all to confirm their number.

Ualan leaned slightly over the ledge to check for any unwelcome followers. "Well, wargs may be fast, but they're not incredible climbers," he pointed out reassuringly. "This might truly be the safest road," he said as he turned uneasily toward the chasm that towered ahead.

"Let us hope you are right, Son of Eoghann," Erul said. "Come, we need to keep moving."

"Girean guide us," Adrelghard prayed under his breath as he

pulled his cloak over his shoulders.

Exhausted by the climb and the cold, the group nevertheless stumbled on. The wind howled through the gorge as they entered, piercing any exposed skin with its chill. Walls of the canyon were covered in strips of ice, and the top of the ravine was now covered in snow. Echoes of the crunch of their steps on the icy ground ricocheted around them. Large boulders were strewn throughout the path, as if the walls had caved in at one time. This part of the pass was welcomely flat, but wound like a maze, and became uncomfortably narrow in random areas. Even some of the corner turns were so sharp that many had to remove their packs and contort their bodies around them to make it through.

Stepping out of the crevasse, they were met with a gap in the mountain, with a drop of at least twelve meters. Iced over and decayed wooden posts with threadbare, cut ropes, marked where there had once been a bridge, now lying at the bottom of the pit it had crossed.

Without enough room for them all to step onto the ledge, Erul stopped abruptly and called back. "We're going to have to jump! Make room behind!" he shouted.

"Jump?! What d'yeh mean we have to jump?" Adrelghard called out.

"Exactly what I said!" Erul yelled back.

Breccan, at the rear, stepped backward, giving room for the rest to follow suit. Ualan, behind Erul, watched as the ancient elf tossed his pack across the break, hoisted his robes at his belt, and gave a modest running start, clearing the rift with relative ease.

Erul looked back at him and chuckled. "Well, if an old man like me can do it, there's little excuse for the lot of you."

Ualan shook his head and smirked, then duplicated Erul's action. Then followed Mæranedïl and Tagwen.

Adrelghard stood next and peeked out over the ledge, and quickly backed away up against the ravine with Breccan behind him. The span was only about two meters across.

"Oh, come now, Addie! You've got this," Breccan encouraged.

"Dwarves are not made for jumps!" he huffed, as he shook himself.

"I could give you a starting push," Breccan joked.

"You!" Adrelghard stammered. "No dwarf is going to be bested by a mountain!" He ran in place for a moment as he gathered his breath and began the run to the ledge. "Fertrath Nundulonok!" he shouted as he leapt, closing his eyes as his body tumbled to the floor on the other side.

Quickly gathering his composure, he brushed himself off, waving away the help that Ualan and Tagwen offered. Clearing his throat, he looked back at Breccan.

"See Brek? I told yeh!" he jeered.

Breccan smiled as she adeptly sprang across the break. "You certainly did, Addie," she smirked. His face became unamused at watching how easily she'd made the endeavor, and Breccan nudged him on the shoulder in jest.

Erul regarded the party again to confirm their number. "Good! One hazard down," he said with some relief as he observed the cave that opened before them.

Its opening was wide, but Tagwen could vaguely make out the path that continued inward, and it was not nearly as accommodating. She glanced around to see if there was some other manner of path, but the only road that remained was the drop they had crossed.

Erul lit his staff as he looked behind himself. "Stay close, not that there's much room to wander," he admitted.

Tagwen glanced at Breccan and noticed she was struggling to strike a flame for a torch, but before she could move to assist, Mæranedïl approached. "May I?" he asked Breccan.

To Tagwen's surprise, her captain accepted the offering of help, and for a moment she saw Breccan regard Mæranedïl without him noticing. Tagwen smiled at the thought that perhaps things would mend for them after all. With a torch lit, and a quiet "thanks" from Breccan, Mæranedïl bowed to her and ushered her inside the cavern.

Stalactites of ice loomed over their heads as the company made their way inside. Further in, the cave was pleasantly warmer, but claustrophobic. Tagwen focused on steadying her breaths as they made their way forward. Flickers of the torchlight behind and Erul's light ahead bounced around the cave walls and the shadows mocked them.

Seeing Tagwen's white-knuckled grasp, Adrelghard tried to comfort her. "It gets wider up ahead, lass, and admittedly quite beautiful," he said.

Tagwen looked appreciatively at the dwarf as he reached a hand toward hers. *This will pass*, she assured herself.

She then heard a faint rush of water that became louder with each step. Smells of fresh rainwater poured through the cave tunnel, until its source became clear.

Stepping out of the initial den, the group entered a large opening with a natural land bridge to the other side. Before them, nearly fifty meters high, a subterranean waterfall poured from the ceiling into a stream below the crossing. Glistening from the illumination they'd brought, the waters reflected shimmering crystals raining down from the heavens, and Tagwen was awestruck. She had not been the only one, as Ualan, Mæranedïl, and Breccan all stood open-mouthed at the natural wonder.

"Behold, an Eye of Mïraglèn," Erul presented.

The shower of the water created a refreshing mist that brushed against their faces, and Tagwen closed her eyes a moment, pretending she was out at sea.

"It was called the 'Misty Pass' once for a reason, and well, now yeh know why," Adrelghard said with a grin.

Breccan took a large breath and exhaled, outstretching her arms, embracing the spray that enveloped them. "Yeah, this is actually nice. We should unwind here for a minute," she suggested.

"I actually agree with that," Ualan added as he rubbed at his right knee.

Erul scanned the other side of the bridge warily, and Tagwen eyed him curiously. "What do you say, Erul? It has been some manner of hours, and I do not wish to meet closed spaces again so soon after such a welcome break," she said.

"For a moment only. May I remind you all, this pass is not known for its kindness," Erul said as he raised his staff to try and shed light to the other side of the bridge.

Tagwen acknowledged his concern and quickly ate at a loaf ration that the Eilfaren house had provided her. She watched as he scanned the water and the cavern walls, pacing cautiously across the natural bridge as if he was expecting to meet something on the other side.

She then noticed Adrelghard peering at the map he had pulled out when they'd been in Haverlow.

"Any luck figuring it out?" she asked him.

Adrelghard tossed his head. "Eh, it's hard to say. Keep lookin' at it to see if anythin' starts makin' sense, but I think I'm just gonna have to wait 'til I see the Isle myself."

Tagwen peered at the drawing again. "Wish we'd not have to see it at all, frankly." She noted Breccan peering over her shoulder, then looking back to the waterfall to take a deep breath.

"Aye I'm with yeh there. We'll find our way and out soon enough, I'm sure," Adrelghard comforted.

A few minutes passed as everyone took to refreshing themselves with food and water, and Erul then insisted they continue their descent into the caverns.

Crossing the bridge, they came to another tunnel opening which proved to be not as crowded as their first entrance had been. Sounds of the waterfall faded behind them as they pressed through another cave that appeared to have been laboriously carved from the rock. The pathway lay flat and smooth, and the walls of the hollow became squared, and Tagwen noticed rusted and broken handles where once had been sconces. Descending deeper into the mountain, the pathway became steep until they reached another opening. This cavity was larger than the one with the waterfall, by tenfold. Rock had been carved into stairs that wound within and around the surrounding wall, down deep into the crevices of the earth. Mazes of staircases twisted like vines throughout the opening, but no sounds save their own steps echoed throughout the lair.

"What is this place?" Tagwen asked.

In a whisper, Adrelghard replied, "The secret mines of King Dheldron. He was said to have gone mad in here in search of Ūlagenol's remains when the beast disappeared from the earth. Myth has it that the remains decompose into a crystal that not only holds immense beauty but could be carved into blades tougher and sharper than any metal known to dwarf-kind at the time. No one else believed it. Sent many a dwarf to their deaths in search of a vein," he gulped as he finished his sentence, avoiding looking down at the boundless pit below.

Tagwen gazed upon the vastness of the open chamber and the silence it held. She heard a rock clatter upon stairs in the distance, the echo of its fall went on longer than Tagwen had thought possible. She was convinced that it had not reached a bottom, that the sound was simply out of her conceivable range.

The wizened elf halted as the stone clacked down the steps, then looked to the group. "Follow me and stay quiet. We may not be alone," he whispered.

Thousands of steps stood between them and their destination: a passageway hidden in the walls on the opposite end from where they came. Shuffling footsteps resounded as they descended and rose upon an endless flight of stairs. Though the craftsmanship of the stairs was sound, the width of their steps was only fit for a single individual at a time. Many were cracked and weathered with age, and indents indicative of repeated use made their footsteps unsteady.

Tagwen's calves and thighs began to burn under the strain of climbing as she tried to keep up with Erul's effortless stride throughout this torturous labyrinth. She gathered herself for a second. A few rocks in the distance fell and clattered as they had before… upon steps that felt miles away, but Erul paused abruptly to sense their origin.

Without warning, a rock flew and Ualan caught it, looking hastily around to see where it had come from. Then another flew and struck Adrelghard in the shoulder, causing him to curse. This time, as they looked to see where the assault originated, dozens of glowing white eyes peered at them from the darkness beyond. Flurries of small pebbles then began to be hurled at all of them as they braced themselves against the onslaught.

"Hurry!" Erul yelled.

Running across the chasm as fast as they were able while ducking and shielding their faces, the six were pelted by assailants they could not see. They reached what looked to be the final ascent just as their attackers made themselves known. Gangly, pale creatures with eyes like alabaster and fang-like teeth landed on the steps both ahead and behind them. Scantily clad in muddied cloths, carrying crude spear-like weapons, they lunged wildly at their targets.

Fending off the aggressors, as well as the continued barrage of hurled rocks, the group struggled to make any forward progress. Tagwen kicked many off the steps as they climbed the pillars below to swat at ankles and stomped on fingers as they attempted to grasp the ledge.

"There's too many of them!" Breccan yelled from the backline. Slicing through the strikers yielded yelps and cascades of clicking sounds that seemed to be coming from all directions. Breccan's cry reverberated throughout the subterrane, and an eerie silence followed as the strange creatures began to click and yelp while retreating. The group stood confused as they watched what looked to be hundreds of shadows climbing the walls, skittering away.

A hiss then, from the bowels of the cave, resonated upward. Tagwen peeked over the edge of the stairs to see if she could see what had made the sound. Only she had no time.

A sudden thrash razed a column of stairs behind them, beginning a domino effect of collapse as the avalanche of rock and stone began. Jolted by the sheer force of the aftershock, the company was nearly thrown clean off the steps, but all braced themselves enough to hold on.

"Run!" Erul howled as he continued leading them to the exit.

Hustling with newfound strength, they climbed to the last flight. The stairs behind them crumbled as they ran. Shrieks of a kind Tagwen had never heard before roared throughout the cavern, rustling the cave's ceiling, and causing bits of rock, rubble, and dust to fall upon them.

Coming to the final step, Erul stopped. There was a gap between the stairs and the wall.

"We'll need to jump! Hurry!" he shouted back as he sprang

across the gap, landing barely within the entrance to their escape. He stood at the doorway as he helped Tagwen, Mæranedïl, Ualan, and Adrelghard across, leaving Breccan the last to jump. She launched herself toward the opening, but as she did, the platform behind her gave way, crumbling under the force of whatever demon was causing the destruction. Her hands caught the ledge of the exit and Tagwen raced to grab hold of her.

Pulling at her pack, Tagwen hoisted her captain over the ledge, but as she looked up, she saw the monstrous horror that aimed to be their end. A colossal slithering body with a scaly, snouted face wound itself to face them. Yellow eyes of a snake, and a reptilian jaw with an enormous set of teeth were nearly upon her as she paused, dumbfounded at its appearance.

Erul seized her shoulders and threw her behind himself. He then lit his staff brighter than he had ever done before, illuminating the creature in its monstrous entirety. The light caught its eyes, and the creature screamed, shaking the earth around itself.

"Be gone, foul creation of the dark! We will not serve to sate your wickedness!" Erul commanded.

Tagwen stood behind him as Breccan tried pulling her backward out of the tunnel. She watched in awe and horror as Erul confronted the beast. Rearing its abominable head, the creature then moved to ram at their stand. Erul backed away as the mouth of the fiend crashed into the wall. Backing away in assumed pain, the monster raged with a ferocity that shook Tagwen to her core, snapping her back to their escape.

Rocks collapsed the entrance behind them as they all ran into the open air. Relief washed over them as they made it out but worry soon fell upon them all after hearing the destruction that was occurring within. The shaking of the earth was tumultuous. The faint wail of the beast echoed through the crashing tunnel, and a final breath of debris rushed from the outlet.

Adrelghard, wheezing violently, yelled out, "What in a devil's name was that?!"

Wiping at his brow and dusting off his cloak, Erul answered, "That was a creature I had long hoped was extinct. I see now I horribly misjudged its lifespan."

"Misjudged its lifespan?! How old is the accursed thing?" Adrelghard asked, aghast.

"It is a creature older than I. How it came to worm itself into the mountains of Aūraèlon, I do not know, but it was one born with the earth and allowed to thrive in its underbelly."

Breccan, trying to shrug off her discomfort, looked to the ancient elf. "Is there maybe anything else we should be aware of, Erul? You know, like giant primordial beasties that no one ever told us existed?" she asked casually, straightening herself to appear less shaken.

"Many, dear Captain, but we've no time to go over them now," Erul replied.

The captain nodded sarcastically as she pressed her lips together, as if his non-answer was exactly what she had expected. She turned her attention to Ualan, who was patching up his hands from being grazed by rocks and weaponry.

Tagwen watched the exchange and remembered the first creatures who had assaulted them. "So, what were those…

things? Their resemblance was markedly — human," she said to Erul.

Erul peered at the opening from which they had fled. "Valœclènè. Forgotten ones. Gnarled beings of men and some elves who turned into the miserable forms you witnessed. They hid in the depths of the world after Ruèhnar broke it. I am surprised they have also survived this long," he said.

Surveying her surroundings as she was catching her breath, Tagwen was relieved that they had at least made it out of the tunneled portion of the pass. They were not, however, completely free of Aurilon's antipathy. Continued paths forked ahead of their location, winding both upwards and down upon the mountain. Blustery winds wound the heights and the accompanying cold was numbing. Tagwen looked at her allies who huddled about, muttering amongst themselves as they affixed their gloves or pulled their cloaks about their faces. Erul, most notably, was looking to the sky, squinting as if trying to find a constellation through the tempestuous mantle of clouds that hid them. Lacking a clear view of the sun's position made it difficult to assess how long they had left to achieve their end, but Tagwen wished it to be late afternoon, hoping they had made good time through the under-dark.

Adrelghard shivered a chill away as he spoke, "Well we can't be sitting here all day, I suppose," he groused.

Shaking his head, Erul disagreed. "I think in fact it would be best to hold here. There is a good chance that collapse will attract attention, and our adversaries may, with hope, presume us dead. If we make it out of the pass too soon, I fear we may be caught."

"You mean for us to camp here? Are we not under pressing circumstances, Erul?" Ualan asked as he finished biting off the tie for the bandage on his left hand.

"Pressing though our circumstances may be," Mæranedïl said, gazing skyward, "this venture may yet be folly if the moon is not permitted to shine through this storm."

Tagwen had not yet thought of that, as she had remained wholly fixated on merely reaching the Black Isle. *If this was all for naught...* she silenced the thought.

Pulling up her gloves and adjusting her askew cloak, she set off to look for firewood. She wandered just up the leftmost pass where a line of dead conifers lay strewn about the mountainside. Gathering what she could, she returned to where the others had set up — under an overhang of cliff with frosted roots weaving throughout the earth like tinsel.

With a fire going, Tagwen realized the extent of her hunger and longed for the meal they had abandoned that morn. She dug through what the elves had provided: six days' ration of bread, a small wheel of hard cheese, a bag of dried varietal fruits, and a skin of the elven wine. She sighed, searching through the contents, cursing herself for feeling picky. She wished for herbs or some manner of fish or critter that they could roast, but the mountaintop was bare of those accoutrements. It was then that she was handed a wrapped handkerchief by Adrelghard, and inside was a thick slice of the cured goat she had thought they had left behind.

Tagwen smiled at Adrelghard, who nodded in response. There was a shared silence among all of them as they huddled by the flame awaiting Erul's prompt to continue their journey.

Ualan was the one to break the silence as he whittled on a warped piece of fir. He was humming. Mæranedïl smiled in recognition of the tune, and put words to the melody, prompting Ualan to harmonize with him.

Òu eïlèc Ardenïl

aèdlen ecūlonè èlal

Mïraelerïa òu naênar

Uceleòl en u abacús

Æten Èlavïl nalïfūr ebsa

Er alè arèf u'edavu

Effortlessly, the song carried along the mountain like a wren calling its family home. Peace befell them all as they listened, grateful for the departure from their current circumstance.

Their ballad ended and Erul took in a hearty breath. "The Èlavïl were magnificent. It is a shame their work here on this earth was so short, but alas their splendor outlasts the ages," he proclaimed.

Breccan leaned over to Tagwen. "I wish I knew what half of what they say means," she whispered.

Overhearing, Mæranedïl offered, "Perhaps there will be time to learn after all this."

"Yeah, maybe," Breccan answered as she rubbed at her scar.

Mæranedïl's face saddened, seeing her anxious habit. "Can I ask what happened? To your—" he gestured to his own lips to mimic her mark.

Breccan realized her quirk and pulled her hand away from her face, straightening her posture. "It was nothing," she answered.

Mæranedïl's eyes fell, and he nodded, excusing himself from the circle. Breccan's hand stirred to reach for him, but retreated to her side as she noticed her behavior.

Tagwen moved to soothe her friend, but Breccan stood and relocated closer to the cliff wall that protected them and lay upon her pack, turning away from those present.

Silence, once again, overtook the camp. Even as Mæranedïl returned, he was not eager to continue any manner of conversation. Erul maintained a constant observation of the paths ahead of them and would occasionally regard the sky to determine its mood. Snowfall answered his inquiries as a steady flurry built a small snowbank around them. Ualan, Adrelghard, and Mæranedïl eventually made attempts to sleep, as Erul remained silent on whether they were to proceed. Tagwen observed him, feeling no need to rest. Erul did not stir. His countenance fell into that of a contemplative state as he sat quietly. She sent no question his way, though she held many that begged to be answered.

Twilight began to show behind the whiteout that wreathed them, and Erul finally spoke, "It is time."

Roused by his declaration, Tagwen gathered her things and began waking the others. All readied by nightfall. Frozen vapor ceased to fall as they made their way to the upward-leading trail.

Peaking at the summit's final height, Tagwen could faintly

see the Ebrïhèïlè in the distance behind. Woodland that had once served as a comfort now bore a closer resemblance to the horde of the nightmarish army. Trees in their unmoved silence stared at her, watching the fated party's every step, and glaring into her soul a warning, though in help or hindrance she could not tell. Though the moon still hid behind heathered clouds, every glimpse of light that was permitted to wash over the sleeping land created new illusory horrors.

Flashes of the disfigured shadows within Middling's castle halls recalled in her mind, her heartbeat quickened as she tried to brush aside the phantoms. Whispers then rasped throughout the mountain's crest, seeming to bite around ankles as Tagwen saw she was not the only one who heard. Murmurs became hisses of air that swept tauntingly through and around them. Frantically taking in her surroundings, Tagwen noticed Erul's face scan the environment and his grip tightened on his staff. The rest, too, with darting glances and tensed shoulders, paced in-line, circling about themselves as they attempted to assess the landscape.

Quickened, the air became blustery winds whose strength became cyclonic. Powder and dirt lifted from the ground, creating an impenetrable wall of debris that forced Tagwen to shield her face. Views of their surroundings vanished, and the intensity of the gale deafened each of them to their companions' cries. Tagwen's hair and cloak whipped around her body, making her stance and vision distressed and unstable.

She screamed for Breccan but could no longer see her. Rapid flying sands scraped at her exposed skin, burning as though they were cinders. Heat rose in intensity as Tagwen held at her face to stop the pain. Peeking through her cover, she saw a blinding light. She peered through her hands to see flames spit and whip within the wall of the tempest. The growing inferno blazoned upon her face as it formed an image of a faceless figure.

Pained screams then shrieked within her psyche, causing her to clutch at her head. Louder and louder, they yelled, until they became discernible. Calls begging for help, children screeching, and wails of agony cried out Tagwen's name.

"Gwennie!" she heard, as if her niece were standing in front of her.

"Enania!" she called back.

Voices of Rhona, Elnan, Mercher, and even that of her father, were crying for her, in fear of being abandoned.

"Where are you?!" she screamed into the fire.

Apparitions of Marez shone through the flames of the figure that now seemed to position itself directly in front of her. The sweltering, scorching heat singed her watery eyes and burned at her throat as she watched a montage of destruction play out.

Blackened and tattered sails upon vessels broke through the endless storm at the world's center, bringing armies of darkness that marched through her homeland. Countless civilians, dead or dying, lay strewn about the streets of Marez. Conflagrations tore through homes and markets of the lower town. Her fleet of ships were swallowed in blazes that the sea could not protect from. She saw visions of her kin, one after the other, being sacrificed by the hand of iniquity.

Tagwen fought against the crushing torment, refusing to believe in the wicked ploy. The figure seemed to recognize

her courage as it grew larger and loomed over her. She could
not see or hear anyone else as this being bellowed inside her
consciousness in the tongue of man.

The age of Men is over.
Your abhorred natures will be cast into the depths and
shrouded in shadow.
The error of your creation will be rectified.
Fires will consume their mistakes.
And from its ashes
I will rise.

Stunned in fear, and trapped in the eye of the storm, Tagwen
could not move. She held no motive to fight or flee, as she
was captive in the stare of this demon of flame. Courage she
once held began to slip, as the thoughts of her family's demise
crippled her resolve. The being raised up a hand as it moved to
strike at her, and she closed her eyes, bracing for the fatal smite.

Suddenly, above the roaring hellfire, a familiar voice broke
through.

"You will not prevail here, Harbinger of Death!
By the light of the Èlavïl,
I demand you dispel this petty visage.
And return hence to your accursed keep."

Tagwen opened her eyes, and Erul stood between her, and
the devil borne of fire. His staff raised, he held it up to the beast,

calling forth a light that struggled to tear through the flames.

Deep, raucous laughter shook the ground they stood on as the flames and light swirled up into the atmosphere, at last disappearing. A scream of wind rushed around Erul and through Tagwen, stealing the breath from her lungs. The force pushed her backward, and the lingering shriek echoed inside her head as her consciousness faded to black.

Momentarily dazed by the encounter, E'ruleïl regained his breath and turned to see that Tagwen had fallen. He dropped to her side. "Tagwen," he said as he shook her shoulders to wake her, but she did not wake.

Breccan, Ualan, Mæranedïl, and Adrelghard ran up to them, all equally shaken and worried.

"Tagwen!" Breccan yelled, as she fell to her knees beside them. Moonlight shining through the clouds highlighted Tagwen's reddened face. "What did that monster do to her?" she demanded of E'ruleïl.

Erul shook his head as he scanned the rest of Tagwen's person. "I do not know," he admitted. He looked up at the others, faint moonlit outlines above him, all seemingly still intact. "Are any of you hurt?" he asked.

Heads shook and he nodded with relief he had not known was possible.

"Did you see it, Erul? Halls of my fathers' burnin', dwarves dyin', Dholdron'lièr crumblin' into dust," Adrelghard cried, patting himself down as if he were still snuffing out the flames, and equally patting his chest to calm himself.

"I saw my brothers torn apart by wicked beasts, lands consumed in the sea, and my children—" Ualan stopped, trembling as he spoke. He held his hand to his mouth to stifle his worried cry. Adrelghard patted Ualan's back to comfort him.

Breccan glanced behind herself at the face she figured to be Mæranedïl. "I saw my mother. She tried to call to me, but she…"

Mæranedïl knelt next to her and put a hand on her shoulder. "It was a horrible deceit. Deìrdre cannot be touched by his vileness."

Breccan nodded and returned her attention to Tagwen. E'ruleïl touched the queen's forehead. Her skin burned at the touch, and the snow that fell to her face evaporated instantaneously.

"Ruèhnar is much stronger than we had known," he said. "The kinds of power he once possessed — should he ever regain the full extent of his might — what we all witnessed will be joyful memories in comparison," he warned ominously.

In Tagwen's senseless state, she held no fear. For timeless moments, her thoughts hung listless in a void of space. She felt no hurt in this endless darkness. In what little cognizance she maintained, she thought that perhaps this was Death's peaceful domain. Then, lucid words that felt like a lullaby entered her subconscious.

"Wake, queen of men. This darkness will not take you. Our journey is not yet at an end, and you must hurry." It was the hushed tone of a woman.

She felt her body begin to fall, and the comfort of this neared end was pulled from her. She slowly returned to consciousness, and laboriously blinked, trying to collect her attention in this awakened state. She brought herself to face Erul and said in a hoarse breath, "We cannot linger here."

Erul exhaled a large breath and nodded. "Quite right," he agreed, beaming in gratitude at the queen's return.

Breccan pulled Tagwen into an embrace, and Tagwen heard her stifle a whimper. She moved her body as much as she was able to return the hug, with Breccan carrying most of her weight.

"Are you okay?" Breccan whispered.

Tagwen nodded.

Her captain held her closer, then pulled her upright and helped her stand. Tagwen took a moment to gather her bearings and looked around at the land that seemed as untouched as when they had first stepped to its peak.

"Was that… real?" she asked Erul.

Erul nodded. "Ruèhnar has made himself known for the first time in over two thousand years. The threat of our company, and presumably our quest, has been realized. Goraidh is no longer unaware of my survival, and he very much does not want us to reach our end," he said.

"What did you see?" Mæranedïl asked Erul.

Erul surveyed the surrounding area. "I am more concerned with what I did *not* see. It would do well for us not to trust in these visions and to make haste toward our quarry."

Tagwen thought back to the terror of the visions she had been shown and shuddered. "We have no time to squander, then," she concluded.

"Are yeh good to continue, lass? There's no shame in holdin' steady a moment after havin' hell thrown right at yeh," Adrelghard reassured her.

Tagwen shook her head. "I want this over with so I can return home to my people," she declared forcefully.

With unsteady nods of agreement, the others collected themselves and continued along the descending path that released them from the clutches of the mountain. Under the cover of night, they pressed onward through to the closing shores of Vostheloren. Across the break of the Lerïacūl Sea lay the Black Isle.

Towering in the center of the island was a structure none of them had ever seen. Grim spires surrounded a central minaret atop a barbarous construction of stone and steel. Smoke billowed at the citadel's base, concealing much of the lowland.

What Tagwen noticed most were the ships docked at its coastlines. From where she stood, she assumed them to be galleons of a monstrous make. Black and tattered sails swayed unfurled, rocking the boats like a child's bassinet. She realized their forms were the very transports she had seen in the flame's nightmare. Her face burned and she balled her fists, determined not to let the taunting frighten her.

"Where did all that come from?" Breccan broke the silence.

"The wound of the world," Erul answered.

11
The Black Isle

Standing upon the cliff's edge of the main continent, Tagwen looked out across the small cut of sea between them and the Black Isle.

"Ruèhnar is sending armies from inside the storm," Tagwen observed.

Erul validated her words while he peered across the landscape. "If this dark army has not destroyed it, the pedestal will be within the southern part of the Isle. That is nearest where the caves were said to be, anyway," he explained.

Desolation Steppes was the hallmark of the lower isle. Swaths of desert hills, where once abundant flora and fauna flourished, now nestled near and around the former volcanic range. Much of the land had become uninhabitable over the centuries of occupation by the Rogues, and now by Ruèhnar's forces.

Tagwen wondered if there were any of the brigands left or if they had joined the Dreaded Army's ranks — willingly or unwillingly. She did not dare hazard a guess.

"Think they'd know its significance if they came 'cross it?"

Adrelghard asked.

Mæranedïl answered, "Hardly any at all knew about the pedestal, though there's no telling what sorts of insight they've been granted after all this time."

Lapping of the shore's waters filled the quiet for a moment. Though the tower appeared to have activity surrounding it, the rest of the land was still.

Though no one had noticed his disappearance, Ualan returned to the group and whispered, "I've found a dinghy. It'll be a bit of a squeeze, but it should manage to the Isle's shore at least."

"Impressive," Erul complimented.

Following him down the rocky bank to the proper shore, the group found the skiff leaning upon the descent. Weather-beaten, and decaying in parts, lay their only hope for reaching the Isle. Flipping the dory right-side up, a family of rats skittered out from underneath, causing Breccan to squeal. Ualan turned to her in surprise, and she glared at him.

"Awh, it's just a coupl'a wee rats, Brek," Adrelghard teased.

Breccan grumbled.

Ualan quickly pretended the encounter had not occurred, and he and Breccan carried the boat to the water. Fortunately, the ferry did not sink.

One by one they stepped onto the approximate three-meter watercraft, Erul first, then Mæranedïl and Adrelghard. When Tagwen stepped on, the boat seemed to have hit its limit.

Tagwen shook her head. "This will not hold us all," she

observed.

"Not a problem!" Breccan exclaimed as she shed her pack, cloak, and boots, tossing them into the boat. "Outrider and I will swim, eh? Plus no one seemed to notice the lack of a paddle," she snickered to Ualan.

Ualan sighed and took off his outerwear, then the two pushed the others further from shore as they held onto the stern. Using all their strength, they swam, propelling the craft onward. Through the dead of night, their expedition lasted little less than half an hour. Silence still met them on the other side. The Black Isle's shore was rocky, and the clamor of the beaching vessel was distressingly boisterous, but it did not attract any unwelcome attention. Trees that crowded the ridge above were either dead or dying. The surrounding land that the company could see, too, was devoid of all life. Soundless was this side of the crossing, save for the hesitant tides brushing along the rocks. Ualan and Breccan changed into a spare set of clothing before the chill had a moment to settle in, leaving their soaked garments behind in the dinghy.

Adrelghard surveyed the land as he pulled out the crude map from his vestments, hailing Erul over for a bit of light.

He circled around himself as he stared between the landscape and the map before waving Tagwen over to take a look. "I think our best bet is teh hug the coast 'til it brings us 'round South. Cavern should be near there if it's as Erul here and this tatty map say it is," he suggested.

Tagwen gazed about the Isle, remembering stepping upon the shores — and the campaign of vengeance that led her here. The strangely arid atmosphere stung her throat, adding to the burning agitation that was smoldering underneath her calm facade.

That fight is over, she consoled herself.

"Based on where we are, the dunes are closest which we can cut across to get to about where those mountains are depicted," she explained as she began leading through the Desolation.

He then followed, matching her steps to the directions on the map. Wandering into the twilight hours, they stepped onto the first sign of dunes formed upon the steppes.

Tagwen glanced behind herself at Breccan as she crossed the threshold, knowing well enough the fight this land had once held. Had she not disobeyed her father's order to bring retribution to the ones who disabled her brother, Breccan would have never been hurt. The captain was looking down at the patches of sand and closed her eyes briefly as she walked over its marked divide, breathing deeply as she opened them, clenching her fists repeatedly. Her eyes then caught Tagwen's, and she nodded to assure her queen that she had control over her fears.

She lives. Elnan lives. You have survived and grown from that mistake.

Light winds would brush by as they walked, wafting the corresponding sands and loose gravel from their footsteps like a mist in the wake of their stride. Already having lost much of its heat, the sands and decimated vegetation also brought a new wave of cold, as the group delved deeper into the steppes. Cover of night was their present savior, as their proximity to the dark tower grew uncomfortably close.

Abruptly, Erul stopped Adrelghard and pulled him and

Mæranedïl down behind a small hill, prompting the others to join them. He held at Adrelghard's mouth when he brought him down. When Adrelghard realized what was happening, Erul released him and held up a finger to his lips to caution all of them.

A faint screech then echoed in the distance, like that of a carrion bird.

Erul peeked over their cover and urged everyone to stand and continue their journey.

"What in Girean's name was that for?" Adrelghard asked.

Erul pointed to the top of the tower. "There was a guard change I noted, and one of them was a falconer — sent his bird up to circle the tower as their watch transitioned. We'd surely have been caught by its keen sight," he warned.

"Must be near the new day, then," Breccan noted.

"It also means they have reason to suspect intruders upon the Isle. They might already have been warned to look for us," added Tagwen.

Gazing to the East, Tagwen carried on trudging through the unpleasant terrain. They traced her steps in silence as they walked, monitoring their balance. Those who could see it, checked the tower on occasion. Coupled hours faded past as they crossed the Desolation Steppes without pause. Facing them now was a small range of mountains, a black backdrop against the wee hours of morn. They were equal in stature to the tower that threatened the entire landscape and were likewise out of place. Worn mostly by the sands of time, there were sheared chunks of cliff-face that contained darker striations and sediment, revealing a truth of their past.

Adrelghard consulted the map again as he switched his gaze between it and the peaks. "Are yeh sure Lord Eilfaren's great-great-grandfather got these from the dwarves?" he asked.

Erul coughed. "No. I said that he made best guesses according to your historians. Fascinated with this sort of thing, he was," he said.

Adrelghard shot Erul a disappointed look above the map's edge. "That's not even near teh what yeh told me," he argued.

"Come now, Master Tugrom, you're well noted for your ability to decipher these sorts of… things," Erul complimented.

Adrelghard groaned at the pleasantry and checked the map again in the dim dawn light. Tagwen came over as he sat with the parchment, trying to imagine what the land once looked like to see if the drawing would make more sense, but she could not picture it. This place was dead to her in every manner of the word.

"Hard teh tell anything on this map — it's such a mess," Adrelghard groaned.

"It's really hardly a map the way that it's drawn. All these random dots and lines, they could mean anything. Look," she paused to point at several flecks, "these all look the same, but they're not even on the landscape. And these lines are on the land but they don't correspond to anything I know."

Adrelghard suddenly jumped up from the boulder he was sitting on and set the parchment upon it. He fumbled around on the ground before he picked up a piece of chalky rock and began drawing upon the vellum.

"Are you mad?!" Erul barked at him.

Adrelghard finished his marking and stepped away, looking up at Erul, who rushed to see what he had done. Erul suddenly paused, gently lifted the map, and gasped.

Tagwen gazed upon the drawing. Five of the dots had been connected to form a large obtuse triangle opposite a smaller triangle of similar dimensions, both connected by a central point.

"What is it?" she asked breathlessly.

Erul chuckled. "Quite clever of the old elf," he remarked.

Adrelghard cleared his throat for attention.

"And you, of course, Master Tugrom. Though I did tell you you'd figure this out," Erul reminded him.

Adrelghard huffed.

Erul smiled. "To answer your question, Queen Braithe, this is the constellation of 'The Anvil' — representative of the great elven maker, Aèdu. It is clever because it was he who forged the pedestal. Without belaboring the point, this mark is likely to be our entrance," he discerned.

"Is it much further?" Mæranedïl asked.

Tagwen swallowed as she recognized the location. "It's just around the shore."

Where I lost the man who paralyzed my brother.

The entrance, indeed, was not much further. Winding behind the first peak there was a worn dirt pathway that led to a cliff-face. Upon first sight, it appeared as nothing more than a dead end.

"Well, that's not ideal," Erul commented. "Are you sure

this is where this central mark leads?" he asked as he pointed Tagwen's attention to the map.

A familiar feeling of despair washed over Tagwen as she looked around. Memory played in her mind of running to this bend, seeing the same rock wall, but her target had vanished.

"It's got teh be here, I *refuse* to believe that Aèdu's mark is coincidence," Adrelghard said.

"Start looking around, let's not be caught in daylight here," Ualan instructed.

Breccan strode up beside Tagwen who seemed frozen in place. "Hey, you doing alright?"

Tagwen turned to face her, her eyes flickering to the scar upon Breccan's lips. "Of course, why?" she answered.

"Your fists are balled into knots," Breccan noted.

Tagwen took a deep breath and tried to unclench them. Breccan had not known that she abandoned her crew amidst the fight to chase the Rogue here and lose him. Tagwen regretted the secret she had kept all these years.

"Look, I hate this place too. We'll get out of here as fast as we can, okay?" Breccan assured and Tagwen nodded.

Tagwen observed the rocks again, angry that there was nothing she could see.

Where in the dark depths did he hide?

Breccan turned to match Tagwen's gaze and squinted. "Hey, wait a minute," she muttered. She cocked her head and walked into the canyon, turned around a rock and disappeared.

Tagwen's eyes widened. "Breccan?" she called.

The captain peeked out from the rock. "I found something!"

she announced.

With a moment of care, and a close enough eye, the illusion faded to reveal that the canyon held a hidden archway. Inscribed upon the archway's stoned frame were runes of Krarnolim that Tagwen read.

NO DAWN WILL REVEAL UPON THE ROCK

He was… she silenced the thought.

Notably at the end of the phrase was a stamped insignia, a combination of the runes that monogrammed "DA."

Adrelghard gasped as he read the phrase. "This is Durifrael's handiwork," he marveled.

"And Aèdu's, no doubt," Erul added. "Quite the pair they were — most genius in their creations."

Adrelghard gave a reverent bow before he crossed the threshold. Within, there was no light source. Erul opted for a torch he found dusted and holstered in a sconce on the wall. Igniting the flame caused a flurry of bats to rush out and elicited a pitched squeal from Adrelghard.

"Aww, it's just a couple ah wee bats, Addie," Breccan mocked, recalling their earlier exchange upon seeing the rats.

"Bet yeh think yer right funny, don't yeh?" Adrelghard grumbled.

Breccan smiled and patted him on the shoulder. "I sure do," she replied.

The dwarf promptly brushed himself off, hoisted his breeches to readjust, and gestured to Erul to continue. Fire lit, the tunnel became clear — fashioned in much the same way as the squared tunnels they had crossed within the passage of Aūraèlon. Blackened stone walls were cut and polished so smoothly that the company could see their reflections in the rock behind the lingering dust. No design was carved onto the walls in this hallway of mirrors. Erul's light created an infinity of paths, though this tunnel only followed straight for a mile before coming to a wall.

"A dead end?" Ualan asked in shock.

Erul placed a hand upon the glassed black stone. No crevice, markings, or keyhole was present, and no push or swipe of his hand yielded any change. Shaking his head, Erul scoffed, "No such barrier has ever been described for this place."

Ualan leaned to Mæranedïl, "Can you see anything?" he asked.

Mæranedïl shook his head.

The endlessness of their presence was daunting to Tagwen. Ceaseless motions and lights flickered around her; she was surrounded again in the illusory fire without the scorch of its heat. She leaned her back against the rightmost wall and slid herself to the floor. When she lay her head on her knees, Breccan came over.

"What is it? Are you okay?" Breccan asked.

Tagwen rested her chin upon her knees with her arms wrapped around her legs. She momentarily made eye contact with Breccan, then looked to the ground.

"We came here for nothing. I abandoned so many… for nothing," she grieved.

Breccan put a hand on Tagwen's arm. "There's probably something we haven't figured out. Don't fret just yet," she calmed.

Tagwen sat up and leaned her head against the wall, looking up to the ceiling. Seeing herself in the reflection, she quickly looked away and began to stand. She and Breccan pulled each other up, and Tagwen nodded with an uneasy smile. Avoiding the gazes of her companions, she turned to Erul. "What are we meant to do here, Erul? Is there another way?"

Erul took a breath and wiped his brow with his sleeve. Shaking his head, he gestured to the boundary wall. "I have not a clue as to the craftsmanship of this place, but this is clearly of intent," he explained. He held the torch closer to the wall to see if there was any hidden compartment or indication of the wall's purpose but found nothing.

"Addie, what do you know of this guy's work?" Breccan asked.

Adrelghard scoffed. "That's the great Durifrael Berunli you're talkin' about! Master craftsman of the First Age forged many great things during his time for dwarves, elves, and even some men. This wouldn't be his first hidden tunnel system, but this dead-end vein isn't exactly a trademark of his. Yacendïl must have asked that this place be near impossible to find, and if it were found, be even harder to figure out," he guessed.

"There's not a mention of a key, or a phrase, or even some form of magic to reveal this place?" Ualan asked.

Erul, Mæranedïl, and Adrelghard all shook their heads, and Ualan groaned. "Are we even certain this is the right location?

Perhaps this is a false entrance?" Ualan suggested.

"Athœvab was noted well enough in Yacendïl's records. It was always assumed the pedestal was here because it was the most central point in the Southland. Additionally, the architecture of this place is consistent with the work of Master Berunli, who would have been one of the only makers Yacendïl trusted," Mæranedïl explained.

Tagwen finally allowed her eyes to take in the whole of the passageway. Boundless halls, shadows, and lights mocked where they stood. She moved her arms in a pattern as she scanned each wall, attempting to discern in the echoes any derivation from her movements. Nothing. She spun slowly in place to look around. "There's something we're missing, then," she determined.

Erul sighed and lowered his gaze to the floor. "I fear I may have led us astray," he confessed. "This path seemed so certain," he muttered.

Mæranedïl addressed the group. "It is still early in the day; we have time to think this over. We should all scan the hall's length. Maybe there's a part of the stretch that holds some information," he suggested.

Breccan shrugged. "Not the worst idea," she concurred.

Each then wandered, Tagwen and Breccan carrying a leading torch down each side of the hallway, in search of a clue. The tunnel had not seen visitors in ages. A film of dust clung to its impeccable facades. Tagwen took a napkin that held one of the elven loaves and started wiping away at the debris to get a better look. Stripes and branchlike patterns in the stone were mesmerizing up close. Her reflection once again served as a haunting familiarity; she did not gaze back at herself for too long. She held the torch at arm's length whilst she tediously surveyed the wall. They stood at a little over two meters in height, and the hall's width was barely one meter wide.

Tagwen glanced behind herself to catch the reflection of Breccan as she was perusing the opposite wall. Realizing she was staring, she shook her head and continued. The walls delivered no answers as they reached the mouth of the tunnel. It was now near-late afternoon outside as she squinted in the light. Relieved to breathe the fresh air, she stopped and stared out at the sea. Snuffing her torch in the sandy ground, she sat for a moment.

Breccan came out of the burrow shortly after and mimicked the queen's actions. "Nothing?" she asked.

Tagwen shook her head. "I have no idea, but it was a decent effort," she said. "We should try to see if there is another way. We have practically lost the day; we cannot afford to lose the moonlight too."

Breccan nodded, taking a breath of the oceanic air.

"Thank you for coming with me — I know this may feel for naught, but it is a welcome feeling to have you at my side," Tagwen said earnestly.

The captain smiled and nudged her shoulder into Tagwen's. "Of course," she said. "Wouldn't let ya go alone — even with the rest of 'em," she winked. "And look, maybe we just need to wait for moonlight, that's been a thing this whole time, right?"

Tagwen laughed then shrugged. "Maybe. Let's get them and see what we can make of the rest of this godforsaken place."

"Aye," Breccan agreed as she disappeared through the archway to gather the others.

Tagwen watched Breccan take her leave and the smile faded from her face.

I will not let this place win.

She looked again at the archway's inscription. "Any hint would have been helpful," she said to herself, thinking of Yacendïl.

About ten minutes later, the remainder of the group arrived at the tunnel's mouth, finding Tagwen waiting alone and staring at the archway.

"Beautiful, isn't it, lass? A shame this is where it ended up," Adrelghard commented.

Tagwen read the dwarvish aloud, "Khradiin elne kel vâ urek venlahsk."

"You remember much!" he beamed. "No light will bring about the rock… roughly," he translated.

"Light?" Tagwen looked puzzled. "Does 'khradiin' not mean 'dawn'?" she asked.

Adrelghard shrugged. "Pretty interchangeable, the two of 'em," he said.

"No light," she repeated, then gasped. "No light! Follow me! Don't use the torches!"

Tagwen rushed past him and ran inside, the darkness swallowing her whole. She refused to touch the walls to find her way, instead continuing straight ahead to confirm her suspicions, hope pounding in her chest. Though she was running, the stretch felt longer than she remembered. She braced herself for impact with a wall but was caught alternatively at the edge of a large conical cave with a hole in the ceiling, revealing the waning day.

There, at the light's center beam, upon the floor, stood the foretold pedestal. Surrounded by a polished floor of obsidian, a stair plinth of squared quartz held a caryatid of the same crystal. Her form was free flowing as a sail catching the wind, and her hands effortlessly held the podium above.

Tagwen stood in awe as the remainder of the group began to file in behind her, assuming similar expressions. Some part of her vainly wished for some proof that her brother's assailant was dead inside this chamber, but the serenity of the room eased her angered heart.

The sun's final rays shone through the pale white stone, catching the cracks and sheen of its natural beauty.

Adrelghard stared in awe. "By Girean's hammer, lass. You're brilliant!" he said.

"Marvelous," Mæranedïl breathed.

The room was empty save for the centerpiece. The walls were of the same earthly rock but carved meticulously to focus the light directly toward the pedestal. No runes or other writings were etched into any surfaces. The surrounding space was incredibly dark, regardless of the brightness of the centered light. Even the tunnel they had just emerged from was difficult to see. Despite its shadowy disposition, and given the Isle that encapsulated it, there was an unnatural calm within this place.

"I had never dreamed I would step within this chamber," Erul said with awe, engrossed by the charisma of the grotto.

"Well, we weren't exactly meant to find this place, right?"

Tagwen asked.

Erul nodded absently as his gaze meandered about the room.

Entranced by the majesty of the central structure, Tagwen approached and ascended its steps.

"Do be cautious, Your Majesty, we know not the entirety of the magics present here," Mæranedïl warned.

Tagwen bowed to the elf and began to turn from the stone when a shadow caught her attention.

Gazing upon the surface of the crystal, it appeared as still water shimmering in the light. She placed a hand delicately on its edge and felt the coolness of its touch. With her caress, the water-like image began to shift. She leaned over to see her reflection, and behind her appeared a woman. Tagwen looked behind herself, but the woman was not there. Returning to the water's image, the woman stood still behind her, and then placed a hand on her shoulder. She was radiant. Her eyes glowed a honeyed amber, and her skin a dazzling deep copper in the brushstrokes of sunlight. Her long, black spiraled hair was tossed about her face in a wind as she smiled at Tagwen. Tagwen reached her hand to the phantom on her shoulder and the vision vanished. Erul's reflection came into view.

Tagwen blinked into the faux reservoir. "Did you see her?" she asked him.

"See who?" Erul asked, sounding mystified.

Tagwen pointed to the surface. "In there, there was a woman," she said.

Erul narrowed his eyes at Tagwen for a moment. "Did you recognize her?" he asked.

At this, Tagwen backed away and stared at Erul. She shook her head. "No. I-I don't think so," she stammered.

"Did she have dark, golden eyes?" he asked.

She inhaled sharply. "Yes," she confirmed.

Erul simply bowed his head as he continued to assess her. Tagwen's eyes fell as she placed her left hand upon A'elūdèr's hilt. She held a moment before she looked back with a smile and nodded.

"I suppose this is now a matter of awaiting the moon's arrival?" Ualan broke the silence that had engulfed them.

The wizened elf looked up to the hollow in the ceiling. "Once again, you are correct, Master Ambarsan. Should not be terribly long now. The sun has already made its departure."

Tagwen walked over to Breccan, who had been standing nearest the entrance, her hand caressing her scar. She seemed unaware of Tagwen's approach, as she was staring at the center statue, until she spoke. "This was here… this whole time. Crazy, isn't it?" Breccan asked.

Tagwen gently grabbed Breccan's hand to pull it from her scar. Breccan realized her intent and chuckled slightly. "Sorry, old habit. You know," she said sheepishly.

"Forgive me for selfishly—" Tagwen began.

Breccan interrupted by shaking her head rapidly. "I won't hear it," she argued, squeezing Tagwen's hand.

Tagwen wanted to object, to finally admit her wrongdoing after all this time. She then heard a rustling of paper and she looked to see Mæranedïl and Erul spreading out the letter. The paper lay upon the stone, and Tagwen saw a light begin to emit from the podium's base, up through the carved maiden, and finally settle into her eyes.

"Um, guys," Breccan interjected, staring at the stone.

Erul and Mæranedïl both gasped as they regarded the page, prompting everyone to slowly approach.

"Shield your eyes!" Erul shouted mere seconds before the pedestal flared in a radiant beam up through the cut in the ceiling. Thunderous cracks of lighting burst throughout the column of light, and then all went silent.

Tagwen peered through her shielding arm to see the light was gone, but her sight remained. "Is everyone alright?" she asked breathlessly.

"What kind of security measure is that?!" Adrelghard frantically asked.

"One we were not trained to subdue," Mæranedïl choked.

Erul cautiously turned back to the page. "This is no mere letter."

Tagwen walked up the pedestal's steps and examined the paper. The yellowed vellum was renewed, its worn edges mended, but no writing now graced the page — it was thoroughly empty.

"It is a severed page of the Æselūnelèr. The light revealed its true form. Had we been Sages of this place, it likely would not have reacted in such a way," Mæranedïl said.

Tagwen looked from the page to the elf, his eyes staring at the paper, but they were not scanning its surface.

"How do you know?" she asked him.

Erul stepped in. "It is a page of a book of power — the moon has not risen, yet it has been revealed. There was no way for us to know, which was obviously deliberate," he explained.

Without acknowledging Erul, Tagwen addressed the silent elf, "Mæranedïl?"

Tears began to trickle from his unmoved eyes, and Erul finally noticed. Erul moved to the elf, who put a hand up to stop him from coming closer.

"What does it say?" Mæranedïl asked.

"Everything alright, lads?" Adrelghard asked from where he stood.

"You cannot see, can you?" Erul asked.

Mæranedïl choked back his tears, and asked again more forcefully, "What does it say?"

Erul lowered his gaze to the table, ignoring the page. "It says nothing that we can see, mærhïl. You know that."

Mæranedïl's face turned away from Erul's voice and his brows furrowed. "How could I have been so ignorant?!" he cried to the room.

Breccan slowly approached from the side and looked at Mæranedïl, whose eyes did not acknowledge her approach. "You can't see?" she asked, aghast.

Mæranedïl's expression fell upon the place where her voice was. Glancing up, but not quite matching her gaze, he shook his head.

"But you can," he replied.

Breccan's face wrinkled for a moment, and then Erul gasped. "Can you see anything on this page, Captain?" Erul asked Breccan.

Breccan swallowed nervously as her eyes glanced over to the paper. There was undoubtedly script written upon its face that looked remarkably fresh, as if it had just been penned and the ink had not yet had a chance to bleed.

"Yes," she said plainly.

Tagwen's eyes went wide. "You can?" she asked.

Breccan nodded.

"You are the last one who can — should you have also required proof of your parentage, you now have it," Mæranedïl said, his visage directed at the table.

"But your daughter does not know the elven tongue, mærhïl," Erul reminded him.

Breccan's eyes flashed at Mæranedïl at Erul's mention of her relation, and a small tear caressed her cheek.

"What about Ylerïan?" Tagwen added.

Mæranedïl shook his head. "Ylerïan is my half-sister. The lineage we share is not of Yacendïl's house," he explained. "If I am right, it should form the tongue of man, given Yacendïl's disposition of being a mortal. The elven, I suspect, was a ruse," he added.

All eyes fell to Breccan as she shuffled the paper toward herself. She saw that the characters indeed were formed for the common tongue, their facets impeccably handwritten.

"I can understand it," she confirmed.

"Would you care to read it then?" Mæranedïl asked.

After a pause, Breccan responded, "Sure," and quietly placed a hand on his.

Clearing her throat, she read:

"For long has Liflèn's son sought to estrange the work of his half-brother, Vostheros. Êdūnar's desire of rule and wish to enact himself a true god has brought about a divide amongst the peoples of Vostheria. Some have heard his call. The seeds of discord, sown.

Because of this, the vision has been gifted to me: to hide both Varucïel and the Athèrèc. There is yet another piece, which will yield a power alike to the two. Born of its antithesis, it will be a weapon much like its counterparts, if those who find them carry them with malice. Varucïel will lay within our kingdom, so that its influence will guide you and your heirs, justly. Athèrèc will be gifted back to the descendants of Urèc — as was always intended. The final piece will reveal in the time of your charge — completing then the instruments of fate.

Be wary, my son; child of the sea and holy light. They will seek to find this truth. Teach it only to those who have labored to learn the ways of this duty. I bear this letter as my final act upon this world. The conclusion of what I must do, foretold.

Should you forget these words, remember your mother, for in my dark, she shines for all, away in her light Truth remains.

Forever your father, Yacendïl"

Breccan's voice cracked as she read the closing regard, gently squeezing Mæranedïl's hand. The act promptly reduced the elf to tears. He wept openly into his free hand as Breccan held his other.

Tagwen, in a fury, banged her fists upon the slab, shocking everyone. "The quill is in my kingdom, isn't it?!" she cried at Erul.

Suddenly, a thunderous crack of lightning rang in the sky above them, and with it a force that emanated from the pedestal, knocking them all backward.

The ground began to shake, and bits of the wall started to crumble.

Pulling herself up from the floor, Tagwen called out, "Head toward the tunnel, now!"

Ualan helped up Erul, Adrelghard scrambled on his own and assisted Breccan in helping her father. Ualan, Erul, Adrelghard, and Mæranedïl rushed to the exit as Breccan turned back to retrieve Tagwen and the letter.

Tagwen grabbed Breccan's hand as she helped pull her forward, but it was too late.

Erul, looking back at them from the tunnel's outlet yelled, "Hurry!" Motioning for them to reach him, a large boulder loosed from the ceiling, creating a cascade of fallen rock. Erul backed into the tunnel, and the two women stepped away to avoid being crushed. The debris now separated them.

"Erul!" Tagwen yelled as she rushed to the settling rock, attempting to remove the boulders from the opening.

Breccan joined to help her, and in the strain cried, "It's

no use! They're too heavy!" Moving to strike at the obstacle, she lost the momentum and instead rested her hands almost reverently on the stones and stood silently.

"Erul!" Tagwen called again but received no response. She smacked her hand upon the rock and recoiled in pain. Screaming at the blockade, Tagwen dropped to her knees in tears.

It took a moment before she realized the silence and looked up to see her friend weeping where she stood.

"Oh, Breccan," Tagwen breathed, as she rubbed her sleeve along her face. She stood and walked over to her friend.

Breccan's shoulders were shaking, as even in this moment she was trying to stifle her tears. "I'm okay," she choked.

Tagwen moved to her friend's side and wrapped her arms around her. Breccan wailed as she turned into the embrace. "He's — he's my…" Breccan cried.

Tagwen gently shushed the captain as she patted her back. "I know, I know," she calmed.

Breccan held Tagwen close and cried.

As she calmed, neither spoke a word. Both disheveled and dusted with rubble, they decided to sit for a moment on the floor. No sound emanated from the other side. Occasional pebbles would shift and clatter to the ground, but nothing else stirred.

Tagwen looked about the once serene room. The polished obsidian floors were shattered and broken where boulders had fallen — the cracks wound like spiderwebs throughout the sharded ground. Regrettably, the pedestal too was fractured, the seeming light it once held was now gone and its quartz construction looked akin to the same wreckage of rock that surrounded them. She stood and sauntered over to the ruined construction. At her feet she found the face of the statue. She knelt next to the piece and placed a hand on the woman's notched cheek.

This is all my fault, she thought. She then looked at the ceiling's fissure and noticed it was much larger than it had been earlier. Following the destruction, she mapped a route in her head. "Perhaps we could climb out of here," she said aloud.

Breccan finally lifted her reddened eyes and followed Tagwen's, seeing the various holds and ledges that had formed. "Might as well try, but we won't be able to carry our packs with us," she noted.

Tagwen nodded and stood, shedding her luggage. She tightened her weapons-belt and tucked her cloak around herself.

Breccan looked to where the page of the tome lay on the floor beside her. Nearly being moved to tears again, she grabbed the paper and attempted to give it to Tagwen.

The queen shook her head. "You keep it," she insisted.

Obliging, Breccan gently folded the vellum into a square small enough to hide in her boot.

Positioning herself nearest the rock wall, Tagwen began the climb. The size of the boulders contributed to large-enough footholds that made the ascent easier than she had hoped, though it was still quite a height.

Near ten minutes of climbing, she reached the final ledge. "I'm almost there!" she called to Breccan, who was following behind.

Grasping at the rocky edge, Tagwen struggled to pull herself up and over, but as she did, she found herself staring at the paws of a monstrous beast.

Snarling above her, Tagwen dared not move, as the bloodied saliva from its jaws dripped in front of her face. Next to the paws she saw boots: dark, sharp-steeled boots caked in mud and detritus.

"Get. Up," a growling voice demanded.

Slowly pushing herself from the dirt, Tagwen stood, her heart racing. Surrounding her were nearly a dozen of the same shadowy soldiers she had seen in the midlands, all armed with bows aimed at her. Their blood-red eyes all seemed to glow in the darkness through the skeletal masks they wore. The grayed paws she'd discerned belonged to the demonic wolf whose razor teeth bared themselves at her. Its master stood at its side, towering over Tagwen. The Hunter's ghostly face was beset with lifeless all-black eyes. His features were remarkably human, even though the blood vessels around his face all appeared to be veins of the same blackness within his eyes. His hair, too, was devoid of all color — the all-white locks illuminated under the moonlight.

A shredded black cloak wisped behind him and in his hand was a mace of enormous size, its blackened steel encrusted in dried blood. The same haunting crest of a dragon being consumed by flame was inlaid between its spiked sides.

Behind her, Tagwen could hear Breccan bring herself up, and her heart sank.

"Glad we made it —" she instantly cut herself off.

Tagwen was silent as she watched the fiend's every move — what little movement he made. Their stance reminded Tagwen of the night on the Greyrest hill — their forms were undoubtedly grimmer up close.

"Your weapons," he snarled.

Breccan laughed. "Yeah, okay," she mocked.

The archers heightened their aim, and Breccan fell silent.

"What do you want with us?" Tagwen asked.

"Your weapons," he snarled again.

"Should we refuse?" Tagwen retorted.

At this, the Hunter raised his hand and the mœrdeth soldiers hissed in unison, revealing underneath their masks sets of fanged, wolf-like teeth.

"Shall I release them?" he asked.

Breccan's resolve slackened at the grisly demonstration, and she acquiesced, handing over her sword. "Fine, whatever, take 'em," she postured.

Tagwen held at A'elūdèr for a moment. Relinquishing the blade to the enemy was foolish, but they were clearly outmatched. Begrudgingly, she unsheathed the weapon born of the promise of love, staring at its etching.

"Tagwen?" Breccan urged.

The queen's chest tightened, her hands betraying her innate understanding that this was not a moment to fight. Finally, she forced herself to surrender after hearing Breccan's plea.

Wrapping their blades in a similarly darkened cloak, the Hunter's hardened expression turned back to them. "Follow me.

Run at your own peril," he warned.

"Where are you taking us?" Tagwen demanded.

The Hunter turned around and headed toward the macabre tower. The two women reluctantly followed.

Looking behind her, Tagwen saw the gaping hole in the ground from which they had just emerged, cursing herself for not expecting unwelcome company. Searching for a moment to escape, she found none, but figured that if he had wanted them dead, they would have been dead already.

Approaching the dark tower, its enormity became clear. Wrapped balconies of watchmen wound around the outside. The falconer sent up his bird, who screeched at their arrival.

Crossing over a moat bridge, Tagwen could feel and see rivers of fire below, sounds of metal screeching, hissing, and clanking echoing around them. Tarnished, thick, barbed steel adornments covered the tower's entrance door, surrounding the harrowing insignia of Ūlagenol.

Within the tower, Tagwen could see a series of staircases spiraling up into the heights. All the spire's construction was singular, charred, eerie metal. Torches lit the columns of every floor, creating the same feeling of endlessness that she had felt in the tunnel.

The Hunter took them through a barred door to the underground.

"What are we going to do?" Breccan whispered.

Tagwen leaned in and lowered her voice. "I don't know, but I'm hoping this is buying the rest of them time to get out of here," she said.

It was then she realized the empty cells lining the walls that confirmed they were to be prisoners.

He took them to the end of the hall to the final cell, opened the doors, and ushered them inside.

Tagwen was relieved they were not separated and concluded that he determined them nonthreatening.

"Hey, what's all this about?" Breccan shouted after him.

The Hunter's soulless eyes bore into her, and he bared his teeth to reveal similarly blackened gums, though he did not share the same beastly canines as the others.

"He wanted you alive. Pity," he snarled quietly. The warg snapped its jaws through the iron bars, causing them both to jump back.

"Come, Ä'bafat," he commanded his beast, and it licked its teeth as it glared at them before answering its master's call.

Soon the fiend and his archers ascended a set of steps beyond the end of the cells. Tagwen tried to watch their route as best she could to remember how to leave if they ever got a chance.

"Well… now what?" Breccan asked.

Tagwen gripped the iron bars as she leaned her forehead upon the metal. Shuffling sounds echoed from the cage across from her, and she realized they were not alone. She peered up to see if she could make out what it was, worried that it was one of her other companions.

"Hello?" she called.

There was little light to aid in seeing through to the inside of the other cell, but slowly a figure emerged.

A haggard man with soiled clothing, unkempt hair and a wild beard made his way to the jail door. He wore neither shoes nor cloak; his tunic was stained in all manner of blood and dirt. Though his face appeared sallow, it did not seem bruised.

"Hello there," Tagwen greeted, relieved that it was not one of the others.

Breccan came alongside Tagwen and offered a slight wave. "How'd you end up here?" she asked.

The man's expression turned wide-eyed, a gasp left his lips and he put his hand up to his mouth. "I — it can't be," he muttered.

The women turned to each other and then back to the man.

"What's your name?" Tagwen inquired.

He began to weep and tried to steady his breathing. "Queen Braithe? Say this is a dream," he pleaded.

"You know me?" she asked.

"Can you not remember me?"

Tagwen looked closely but shook her head. "I am very sorry, sir, I cannot recall your face," she said.

"Seen better days, I suppose," he choked. "I am so sorry," he began to weep again.

Tagwen frowned. "There's no reason to apologize, good man," she assured him.

He stopped for a moment and pushed his face against the bars to look directly at her, still crying. "If I'd known then what it was, I'd have never delivered that letter," he admitted.

Tagwen's hands dropped from the cell door, and she took a step away. Seeing a ghost in the flesh, blood rushed from her face. "Gòrdan?" she whispered with astonishment. Shaking her head, she turned away. "No, no. Master MacCaibe is dead," she said.

"For long now I have wished that were true," he confessed.

"How can we be sure it's really you?" Breccan asked.

"The body you found — poor chap from Oülle they killed. He had my boots and cloak on, did he not?" he asked.

Tagwen turned back to face him. The image of the man in her halls began to form, his tender brown eyes brimming with tears brought her back to Marez, to home.

"It was the boots we recognized, but there was no cloak," Breccan replied warily.

His face turned to worry, and then to surprise. He laughed through the tears. "Oh, thank goodness! You found it! Wait —" he paused. He leaned as far as he could and squinted, then reclined back in shock. "You both… it's true… you've seen the elves," he said.

Tagwen nodded. "And Eachann, and your husband, Ualan," she added.

"You know his true name! You — you met Ualan? Is he alright? By gods, my children! Are they safe?" he asked, worried.

"I feel he'd be better if he knew you were alive. As for Mairi and Artur, he took them to an Outrider stead. They are safe," Tagwen assured.

Gòrdan paced around with his hands on his head, smiling and chortling. The tears in his eyes caught the glint of firelight as he gazed across to them.

"Sir MacCaibe," Tagwen called. "What happened to you? Why are you here?"

Gòrdan scoffed at the title, then rubbed his face and eyes with both hands. "Somehow that devil, Goraidh, figured out I'd stolen a note from the king's hand. I was going to take it to Lord Eilfaren to show that Dùghlan had been manipulated. That this 'Sage' we'd suspected for a time was truly wicked, but they found me before I could complete my mission," he said sadly.

He stopped and looked at the two of them. "I hear little in these halls, save for what that monstrous brute chatters about whilst they think I'm asleep. I heard your name mentioned but thought it simply my mind finally giving way. Now you're here and I —" he stopped, looking down to the floor. "I am so sorry, Your Majesty."

She recognized his voice in the formality, the slight emphasis of the "j". This was truly the former messenger of Middling.

"There is nothing to apologize for, Sir MacCaibe," she assured him again.

"We do, however, need to find a way out of here now," Breccan interjected.

Gòrdan picked his head up and peered down the hall toward where the jailing party had exited.

"Their route is every four hours, I've gathered — so perfectly timed it's unnatural, I tell you. Most of the time, there's no one down here, but at about midday, they serve me some awful lump of bread. You can barely tell, but there's a crack in the wall over there that lets in the sun or moonlight, if I'm so lucky. Seems to be around mid-evening, yes? That is when you were brought here?" he estimated.

Tagwen nodded. "Do you expect them to be around soon?" she asked.

Gòrdan checked the hall again and shook his head. "Unless they're coming back for you, we've got until midnight. But I've tried everything, dear queen. The floors and walls are solid stone. No guard with keys passes through. Thought maybe I'd be skinny enough to crawl through these bars by now," he chuckled weakly.

Tagwen put her face as close to the gate as it would allow her to scan the area. The long hall of cells was to her right, and the open stone lobby with ascending stairs to her left — where her captors had disappeared. No other door existed that she could see, and no windows were carved into the rock. Soundless, too, was their dungeon. She leaned back and surveyed the interior of their cell. Large, rough, stone walls on three sides, and a wooden bucket in the corner.

Breccan was looking at the ceiling, which was not much taller than she was, slapping the rock in hopes of finding some peculiarity.

Tagwen became aware of the closeness of the walls all at once and grasped the cage's bars to steady herself.

"I really am sorry, Queen Braithe," Gòrdan apologized again. "Not a fate you deserved," he lamented.

Before Tagwen could respond, Gòrdan turned away to rest in the darkened corner of his cell, and Tagwen sighed. She tapped her hands on the bars for a moment before she left to sit next to

Breccan against the back wall.

The captain was staring at nothing, and her head instinctively fell onto Tagwen's shoulder.

"Can I apologize now?" Tagwen asked.

Breccan snorted, apathetic. "Maybe," she said.

Tagwen took a deep breath. "I think instead I shall apologize when we return from here," she promised.

Breccan nodded and Tagwen leaned her head against the wall. Tagwen remarked on the oddity in the lack of webs, bugs, or rats within this hall, as if no life at all was able to thrive in this place, the life also being sapped from her beloved friend. She watched a torchlight upon the wall outside of Gòrdan's cell and swore for a moment that the expressionless face from the mountain was within the flame. She looked away to find peace and noticed Breccan had fallen asleep.

Breccan's repose was soothing in this gloom, as Tagwen watched the gentle flutter of her closed eyes. She found herself humming, then softly singing. It was a lullaby she had sung often to Enania to set her niece to sleep — a song her own mother had sung to her and her siblings.

Sea moves gently
Rocking you to sleep
Her waves drift widely
Catching sails their breeze

Float now darling
Be one with the sea

Dream of wandering days
But always come back home to me

Tagwen finished the melody and grabbed a handful of her mother's cloak. Its softness and warmth pacified her, and she rested her head upon Breccan's. Her hand then graced the emblem that held the cape together and she thought of Ylerïan.

We need your help, she silently called.

Sitting in the quiet, hoping for a response, Tagwen figured it to be of no use. Adjusting herself delicately so as not to wake her friend, she tried to find some comfort upon the cold, hard stone. Sufficiently adapted, she closed her eyes, and wished that somehow, she would wake far away from this place.

*****

Rattling startled Tagwen from the depths of her sleep, and she noticed a light coming from the stairs.

Hearing footsteps, she closed her eyes again, pretending to sleep. They came closer and closer before Tagwen could sense that they stopped at their cell door. Keys clinked and Tagwen stirred. A cloaked and bone-masked figure was opening the door and Breccan jumped, putting herself in front of Tagwen.

"What are you doing?" Breccan demanded of the figure.

"Would you quiet down!" they whispered loudly, still fiddling with the keys. Their voice was not brash, it was a tenor that Tagwen was acquainted with, but in her current stupor struggled to place. She peered through narrowed eyes at them, their stature and tone as they grumbled and cursed, trying to find the right match for the lock.

"Ualan?" she said, when it finally registered.

He stopped and looked at her and she saw then the shade of his umber beard underneath the facade. "Yes, now would you both let me figure out these infernal keys? We don't have much time," he grumbled.

"Ualan Ambarsan?" Gòrdan had stumbled slowly to his cell door.

Ualan stopped fidgeting and cautiously turned around. Upon recognizing Gòrdan, he gasped and removed the detestable mask from his face. "Is it really you?" Ualan asked.

Gòrdan began to weep. "Yes, my love. By Okerfair, it is good to see you," he cried.

Ualan ran over to Gòrdan and hugged him through the bars. "We thought you were dead," he said, holding his husband's face in his hands. He pulled Gòrdan close and kissed him.

"Not to ruin the moment, but can we all try to get out of here so we're not actually dead?" Breccan quipped.

Ualan nodded, finding the correct key for Gòrdan's cell, and helping him out. He then returned to Breccan and Tagwen's cell.

"Where are the others?" Tagwen asked.

"Hopefully to the mainland by now. I told them I was going back for you — dead or alive. They worried I would find nothing until Ylerïan beckoned our aid — said she heard a cry for help deep in darkness."

Tagwen bowed her head in gratitude. "Thank you," she said. *Thank you, too*, she thought silently to the Lady.

Ualan smiled at her as he opened the door. "Don't thank me yet," he warned.

"Our swords — they took them. Any idea where they're being stowed?" Tagwen asked.

Ualan nodded. "The Hunter's taken them as a prize, it seems. They're planning on sailing back into the storm from the sounds of it," he reported. "You can get other swords, right?"

Tagwen instinctively objected, "No! No, we… must get them back, Ualan."

Breccan came forward. "Tagwen, it's okay, I'd rather we just get —"

Tagwen stopped her. "No. No, you don't understand," she argued. "Something Erul told me back in Thrindūl. He thinks my sword can be used against Ruèhnar. And from what you read of the page; I think… I think it's the final instrument."

Breccan cursed under her breath and shut her eyes, trying not to panic. Ualan also let out a weighty sigh.

"And you just let him have it?" Ualan asked.

Tagwen leaned against the bars in exasperation.

"We really didn't have much of a choice — you should've seen these things. They were like animals at his command. It was… creepy," Breccan shuddered.

"Well, they are at his command, and that occultist's, Goraidh. Can't bear to think what they did to turn Oswallt into that monstrosity," Gòrdan lamented.

"The Hunter is Oswallt Trahern? Roìbert's captain?" Tagwen asked in shock. It made sense now that she had not seen him in Middling, but it felt worse that this was the fate that found him.

Gòrdan nodded, then shook his head despairingly. "These creatures make no moves unless they've been told, but I've seen some — some get a strange look in their eyes, like a wild mare ready to break. Something's not right with all of them, and I'd hate to be on the other end of whatever that is," he explained.

"Truly. They seemed mindless to anything — the guardianship of this tower was remarkably unaware of anything that moved in the shadows," Ualan added.

"Please," Tagwen begged, "I have to get it back."

Ualan nodded. "Even if the sword isn't what we think, I'd rather not ignore the risk. Let's move."

Ualan cast off the foul disguise and Tagwen unpinned the elven emblem and removed her cloak. She wrapped the woolen cloth around Gòrdan, who attempted to refuse the kindness.

"My lady, I am honored, but I cannot take this from you," he protested.

Tagwen affixed the cloak in place with the emblem. "Nonsense, Sir MacCaibe. Besides, this token belongs to you. I was honored to have been its caretaker," she said. She could see the matting of his hair and beard, the slack in his skin, and the bruising upon his feet. His lips and the skin of his hands were cracked; the darkness under his eyes was heavy. Despite this pitiable appearance and the pain he was surely in, his smile was radiant.

Gòrdan bowed deeply in thanks, and she saluted him.

After latching the doors closed again, the three followed their savior silently as he listened for potential adversaries.

"I know there's two of them that make a round continually.

Every four hours," Gòrdan whispered.

Ualan paused near the metal door that was to be their exit and turned back to them. "There *were* two guards that patrolled the stairs leading outward to the back bridge — if one has noticed the other is missing, we'll need to run a bit faster, understood?" he instructed.

Nods confirmed their understanding, and Ualan guardedly clicked open the door. The hall sounded clear as he motioned them through. It opened to a spiral staircase leading both upward and down — they were on one of the many floors that existed within.

"One floor up," Ualan whispered, pointing.

Up they crept, noiseless were their steps as they tip-toed upon the frigid stone.

A door then creaked above them, and all froze. Armored footsteps began to walk out of the room, but sounded as if they were walking away from the escape party. Ualan motioned them to step backward to break the line of sight, but as they moved, Gòrdan slipped. Ualan caught him by the arm, but the shuffle and audible grunt caused the resounding footsteps to cease. They held silent and the steps turned again to depart. Sounds of a doorway echoed before they moved again.

Ualan pulled his husband close and signaled to begin the remainder of their ascent, climbing to the next floor.

"Through that door, we'll need to make a run for the bridge — we'll have limited cover, so stay close behind and nearest to the wall away from any light. Then, if we're to catch them before they depart, we'll need to move swiftly to the gorge Northeast from here. The Hunter has a designated charter there," he said.

"Have a chat with them all on the way up to find this out?" Breccan asked in jest.

"It is with fortune, dear captain, that these creatures are so preoccupied with their directives that I could find my way in here as easily as I did," Ualan responded.

Before they could make their leave, the door to their salvation opened again, and in walked a warden of the tower. Covered entirely in shrouding armaments, the sentinel appeared as a shade — lacking any humanizing features save for the form of its body. Instantly the soldier maneuvered into a combative stance, unsheathing their flail. Their carmine eyes focused on the perceived adversaries, but they did not yet move, as if they were waiting for a trigger.

Ualan slowly approached, and the guard seemed to twitch, caught between the modes of fighting and fleeing.

"Can you understand me?" Ualan asked, but the soldier remained unmoved.

"We don't have time for this — do something," Tagwen urged, instinctively keeping her arms in front of Breccan and Gòrdan.

Suddenly, the gaoler began writhing, dropping its flail. It moaned and wailed in what appeared to be pain as its body contorted and shook about itself. The figure crouched into a fetal position, wrapping its arms around its torso, shaking as if it was cold.

"What's wrong with it?" Breccan asked.

Ualan approached slowly, unsheathing his saber. He stepped

too close, and the warden's head snapped upward as it bared its teeth at him. Caught off guard, Ualan was thrown against a door as the nightmare lunged at him, and he dropped his dagger. Ualan and the monster twisted around the small alcove as he tried to contend with its strength.

"A little help!" he shouted.

Tagwen rushed to the floor, dodging their wild dance and grabbed the dirk before twisting around and stabbing it into the neck of the beast. It let out a gurgling breath as it slunk from Ualan's grasp and onto the floor.

"Thanks," he said breathlessly, brushing himself off.

"You alright?" Tagwen asked.

He nodded, glancing down at his left forearm.

"It bit you," Tagwen said, noticing the puncture wounds.

Ualan shrugged. "Not the first time I've been bitten by an animal. Hardly hurts," he said.

"Told you — there's something not right with these things," Gòrdan said as he and Breccan approached. "Are you sure you're okay?" he asked Ualan as he gingerly grasped his arm.

Ualan put a hand to Gòrdan's face, "More than you know."

"Well, let's not stay here to face more of them, eh?" Breccan urged.

Ualan nodded and retrieved his dagger and the flail from the guard and cracked open the outlet door. He signaled for the party to follow him, and they crept into the night. Clanking of metal and machinery dominated the atmosphere, concealing much of the sounds of their movement. Employing the cover of the wall, they snuck down the western steps, pausing as a march crossed ahead of them.

Their opposition moved far enough away and Ualan continued the advance to the viaduct. Blockades of crates and weaponry littered the span. The group dropped behind a stockpile to hide, as another line of guards marched through to the tower. The flames from below radiated around the whole area, causing everyone to sweat. Tagwen wiped the perspiration from her brow as she tried to catch a glimpse of the machinations below.

"What are they doing here?" she whispered to Gòrdan.

Gòrdan shook his head. "I've no idea, Your Majesty. Fashioning weaponry, I imagine, of a fearsome sort. Enough to take over the continent, I'd assume. But that seems less of a worry."

"Are ya sure about that?" Breccan interjected.

Gòrdan let out a sharp exhale as he cleaned the sweat from his eyes with a sleeve and nodded. "I heard a whisper once — seems crazy, and maybe it is, but I caught someone say, 'dragon fire'. They must be trying to emulate it or something, seeing as how dragons don't exist anymore."

Tagwen watched as the regiment moved on, their formation unwavering. It was unsettling to know they were not of their own mind, but given the recent display, she was convinced it was the lesser of evils.

Peering into one of the crates, Breccan pulled a flail and a hatchet. A strange collection of hand-sized, gourd-shaped jars, tucked within a bed of straw, also caught her eye, and she grabbed one.

"Here, this looks normal," she whispered, handing a flail to Gòrdan. "Better than nothing," she shrugged.

Tagwen followed Ualan's gaze but was distracted when she realized he was not perspiring as they were. No droplet clung to his skin. "Are you feeling alright?" she asked him.

Ualan regarded her. He looked… younger. The signs of age around his eyes were hardly present, and Tagwen thought it must just be the dark. He nodded and handed her the flail he'd taken from the warden.

"When they get closest to us, make for the bridge," Ualan instructed.

She noted the bridge away from the tower was close ahead, but its patrol was unceasing.

Awaiting the opening, the group crouched in preparation. The guardsmen reached the desired point in their route and Ualan sounded the order to run.

Immediately targeted, the group clashed with the two initial guards. Shrieks of the falcon above alerted the rest of the watch to their presence. Swinging wildly, Tagwen's flail contended with the warden maces until it was caught, and she was disarmed.

Ualan moved with sudden alacrity and pushed her behind himself as they continued to make their escape. Being the only one effectively armed, he managed to subdue their adversaries, sending them over the bridge's edge to the cavernous depths below.

Horns from the top of the tower were sounded, and a horde of the dark army was being compelled toward the escapees across the bridge in a perfectly squared military formation.

Tagwen's group reached the bridge's end, but the advancement of enemies was nearing.

"We won't outrun them!" Gòrdan yelled.

Breccan stopped to look back at the bridge and lobbed the peculiar jar from her hand toward the onslaught.

Upon impact, an eruption of flame accompanied by a deafening blast enveloped the swarm, causing many to become ignited and others to abandon the pursuit, squirming in the same manner as the first warden they had dealt with.

The group was dumbfounded by the occurrence, backing away in awe, confusion, and terror at what they had just witnessed.

"Dragon fire," Gòrdan remarked with his mouth agape.

Accepting the providential diversion, the four ran from the encounter in haste toward Remeirath Gorge.

12

THE ONUS OF TIME

Sĩne heard Lachlann's command from behind her, as if he was screaming in her ear. She saw the fallen Logroscan hero fading away in front of her. Her perceptions grew blurry in the fervor of her rebellion.

The mare she found was fast — brilliantly fast. Her thunderous strides raced over the grassland with ease. Though it was early afternoon, clouded skies hid much of the sunlight. Raindrops whipped across Sĩne's face as the horse ran, forcing her to squint, which made the journey even more difficult.

Her passenger kept her grounded. She had someone in her charge, and his frantic attempts to stay upon the mare kept her from spiraling about the choice she was making.

Their current speed would bring them into Marez near early evening, but Sĩne was not convinced that it would be enough time. She did not know what to expect of the city, of the enemy, or the state of the Braithes. Nonetheless, onward they rode, the mare restless in her ambitions and Sĩne grateful for her help.

The hours grew dark, and the cliffs of Marez began to come into view, as did the smoldering embers of the surrounding hamlet, Màdiz. She reared the horse to a halt and stared in panic at the destruction before her. "No, no, no, no..." she muttered.

Eachann tapped her forearm. "Let's see if we can find anyone," he suggested.

Urging the mare forward, they trotted upon the scorched earth. A cluster of roughly ten families lived in the area, all with generational ties since the middle of the Second Age. Sĭne knew they had neither defenses nor riches to plunder — this had been done purely in malice.

The snapping of still-burning wood and the sizzle of embers as the light rain evaporated upon them was all Sĭne could hear. Homes were completely ruined, their roofs caved in, and doors splintered open. Blackberry crop fields, which Màdiz was known for, had been reduced to ash.

No cry nor cough sounded as they rode through the small stretch. Sĭne approached a charred cart and dismounted. Cautiously lifting the remains of a canvas tarp, she was relieved that all she saw were the burnt remnants of food supplies and clothing.

Eachann guided the horse alongside Sĭne. "Some may have made it out in time," he tried to comfort.

"No bodies might mean you're right," she agreed.

Her eye caught something tucked underneath a box, and she reached for it and pulled out a small fabric doll. Its short flaxen hair and dark eyes reminded her of her brother, Emyr. She pondered the doll for a moment and placed it safely within her pocket.

Distant horns sounded far beyond the cliff. Sĭne ran to the

edge to peer below into the city. She recognized the alarm to be the watchman's tower — a separate army had broken through the gates. "We've wasted enough time here," she said with urgency.

She turned to Eachann and the mare, mounting again.

"Hyah!" she screamed to the beast.

With a flick of the reins, the mare rushed them out of the ruin. Around the crescent of the cliffside, Sĭne could now see the whole crag had been consumed in flame. Riding to the break in the cliffs, at the slope's peak, they could see into the Marezian gates. A horde much like the one they had just run from flushed into the city but were met with the city's forces.

"We need to find Jaelan and the monster he's with," Eachann said.

Sĭne nodded, and they ran headfirst into the fray. Trampling through some of the dark army, the Marezians backed out of the horse's way.

"Matharnach!" Sĭne heard her name called.

"Hold, hold!" she shouted at the mare as she pulled her around.

Sĭne scanned the crowd and caught sight of Lieutenant Briones hailing her.

"Lieutenant! I've come from Logrosca — they've attacked there as well!" she called.

Dodging elbows and a wild javelin, Captain Briones shouted at her, "Where is Queen Braithe and the rest of your company?!"

Sĭne took a shaky breath. "Captain, I must get to the castle; the royal family is in danger!" she yelled.

Captain Briones nodded, seeming confused by her lack of an

answer. "Hurry! Warn Tarragona to lock the keep and maintain a watch of the family and the Prince of Middling," he instructed.

Sĭne's entire body went cold. "The Prince of Middling is already here?" she asked with horror.

"Yes! Hurry! They all must be protected," he insisted. He turned and gave another order, "Langanes, get to the bell! Gerrig might be hurt up there!"

"Go! Now!" Sĭne yelled at the horse, who snapped into action once again.

The horse turned back to the main cobbled street but was promptly stopped by an ignited market awning that fell and blazed across the road.

Sĭne looked to the cliffs and saw more fiery arrows being launched into the city below. Structures in the market and lower town began to catch fire and civilians were scrambling to the central wells to put them out. The streets quickly became flooded with impediments, and the raining hellfire was unceasing.

Amidst the screaming and sounds of destruction, Sĭne realized the bell tower still had not yet rung. The coastal bells were the only method of hailing the outer towns of Torrerìn, Gilèdo, and Tarravedra to alert their soldiers. Hearing the clash of the Marezian force behind her, she knew they could not hold back the enemy alone.

The castle stood to her left down the main road and the bell to her right, through the outlet to Versard Bay. She pulled the mare away from the mounting inferno, through an alley not yet doused in flame.

"Where are you going?!" Eachann yelled from behind her.

"The city won't hold!" she shouted back.

"But the Braithes!" Eachann screamed.

"We need help, or everyone dies," she argued as they weaved through crowded alleyways.

Jumping over barriers and avoiding falling structures, Sïne tried to guide them through the city, but at every turn the pathway was blocked. Turning to what she thought would be the final corner, a flaming pile of lumber stood between them and the remaining pathway to the bay. The horse whinnied and backed away from the burning wood. Sïne struggled to get her to refocus.

"Æruv!" Eachann commanded.

The horse flicked her head around as she realigned to the street and began to gallop toward the flame.

"Ærusah!" Eachann directed, and as the mare approached the fire, she sprung up and over with ease.

Sïne smiled at the mare's magnificence, and they continued to the bay.

Compared to the chaos of the city, the bell tower stood serenely in the moonlight. Sïne could not see a watchman above as they approached. She pulled the mare up to the tower and jumped off. "Can you ride?" she asked Eachann.

He nodded.

"Get to the castle. The path up from the other side of the docks should lead straight to—"

"I can handle it," he cut her off. "Go."

Sïne nodded and Eachann took hold of the horse and ran off toward the keep. She entered the base door of the tower and looked upward. There was no sign anyone was there.

Clambering up the spiral staircase, she ran as fast as her legs would take her. The floor below the top deck was connected by a wooden ladder. The hatch was opened to the top, which indicated that a watchman should be there.

"Hello? Gerrig?" she shouted upward.

No answer.

Without wasting more time, Sīne hoisted herself up the rungs, and as she poked her head through the opening, she gasped. There, upon the floor, with an arrow piercing his forehead, was Gerrig, the watchman.

Sīne pulled herself completely through the hatch and looked behind. Marez was burning. The sight of her home falling to ruin made her cry. Mustering her strength, she turned back to ring the bell, but something in the distance caught her eye. She moved to the watchtower's half-wall. Upon the waters, beyond the bay, Sīne swore she saw a ship.

Then she saw another.

Two tall ships on the horizon blurred like shadows below the intermittent glow of the moon. The city was being surrounded.

In haste she moved directly below the bell, and with all her might, gripped the thick rope and pulled. Clanging heavily, the bell resounded, and she pulled thrice more. Four rings total to call all arms and warn them of the threat at sea. Wincing from the loudness of the brass, she moved to the ledge to listen for answering bells. She wondered if they would answer; a threat at sea had been unheard of for centuries.

A moment later, they rang.

First, in the South, Tarravedra, then Gilèdo up North. Finally, further in the distance, she could hear the chime of Torrerìn.

Sĭne took a deep, relieved breath, knowing that help would soon arrive. However, her celebration ended quickly, as she was struck down.

Dropping to the floor, screaming in pain, she looked to see an arrow stuck through her bicep. Its bone shaft and dark plumage were hauntingly familiar. The pain was searing. Breathing through gritted teeth she tried to overcome the agony. She stayed low, hearing more arrows whip past or clatter off the bell.

"You dimwit," she cursed, realizing they had marked this location.

Once the sounds of the shots ceased, she turned to her injury, removing her right gauntlet and glove to reach the end of her sleeve. Rolling the leather glove as best she could, she placed it between her teeth. Biting down, she gripped the shaft of the arrow. Tears streamed down her face as she looked away, counting down in her head. On the last count she snapped the shaft, shrieking at the stinging torment.

Removing her knife, she cut a piece of her tunic to tear a shred for a tourniquet. With the bandage ready, she then braced herself to remove the remainder of the arrow from her arm. Dropping her left gauntlet to get a better grip, she took a deep breath and grabbed the arrowhead. Pulling carefully, she fought through the anguish until the arrow was removed.

Vision blurred through tears; she wiped her face quickly before pushing up her sleeve. The wound was bleeding profusely as she worked the tourniquet around. Spitting out the leather bit, she utilized her teeth to pull the bandage tight. She then cut off her sleeve to create an outer wrap.

Satisfied with her efforts, she lay on the floor for a moment to collect herself. Pain still throbbed through her entire arm, but with the sounds of war echoing beyond, she pulled herself to a crouch with her good arm, sheathed her knife, and crawled backward through the hatch. Awkwardly, she shuffled down, nearly slipping off the ladder. Catching herself instinctively with her right arm she screeched and held still for a moment to recover from the pain.

She then cradled her arm near her chest and focused her left arm to descend the remainder of the rungs. Relieved to be at the bottom, she blinked through the pain and caught her breath. Her goal now was to reach the Braithes.

Moving down the staircase, she heard shuffling below. She reached her left arm down to unsheathe her sword that was positioned upon her left hip. Quietly she twisted and turned until it was loosed. It felt awkward in her non-dominant hand, as she held it ready to strike, but its weight began to prove too much.

She thought to reach for her dirk instead, but the footsteps quickened and began hiking up the steps, and a guttural growl let Sine know this was not a friend. She tried to hold her stance to meet the foe head-on. Her heartbeat pounded in her chest, the anxiety teasing the pain in her arm. Rounding the corner was another bone-veiled face with scarlet eyes and Sine panicked. Instead of attempting to strike, she kicked them down the steps. They tumbled down the entirety of the staircase and Sine listened to determine if they'd survived. No sound came after the fall and Sĭne descended, blade falling at her side.

In a heap on the floor lay the fallen adversary.

Lucky there was only one, she thought, cringing.

Moving over the body and out of the tower, she looked around, relieved the ships had not yet reached the bay, though they were unwelcomely closer. The havoc of the lower town spread; most of Marez was now under siege. Pressing up against the wall of the tower, she tried to avoid being sighted, in case more of the opposition was near. She saw citizens with small children running down from the city toward the bay, trying to escape the carnage. She stopped herself from running toward them to help.

You need to get to the keep, she reminded herself.

She was glad to see Marezian soldiers guiding a group of civilians out from the city in a coming wave. She ran to blend in with the crowd, avoiding the gaze of the soldiers. Every bump from a passerby yielded a wince as she attempted to ignore the pain. Breaking through the crowd, she reached the last sector of the lower town. Fire had not yet spread here, and she was grateful for the cover. Through an unkempt alleyway, she slipped through unnoticed, looking for the opening that led to the castle's steps. She wound through the streets and found her bearings, coming upon the entrance to the keep, when she saw it was being patrolled by masked guards. Ducking quickly behind a wall in hopes that they had not seen her, she realized she would need to find another way inside.

Back against the wall, she tried to picture the castle's map in her head. If she were able, she could climb the wall to the courtyard, but her injured arm now made that an impossibility. She kicked the wall behind her in frustration, then cursed her stupidity as she rushed through the alley. Turning a corner, she heard a series of hushing sounds coming from one of the doors. She noticed one slightly ajar and creaked the door open, trying to ready her sword.

Inside, crying in a corner, were a woman and a little boy.

"Please, please don't hurt us!" the woman cried.

Sīne wriggled to sheathe her blade. "I'm not here to hurt you," she assured them, holding up her good arm.

The woman breathed a sigh of relief as Sīne came out of the shadows.

"You should be headed to the shores. The city is burning, and civilians need to evacuate," Sīne said.

"The bells — four strikes. The threat is also at sea. Where is it we can go to be safe?" the woman lamented.

"Momma," the boy muttered. She turned to soothe him, holding him in her arms as she wept.

Sīne approached and knelt to the boy. "Hi there. My name's Sīne. What's your name?" she asked.

The boy looked at his mother, who nodded.

"Rayan," his little voice squeaked.

"Rayan, you, and your mum need to get somewhere safe. We're going to need everyone to be really brave," Sīne said.

Rayan shook his head and Sīne frowned. She then remembered the doll in her pocket and pulled it out. "This is Emyr. He's really scared too and needs a friend to help him. Do you think that could be you? I know he'd really appreciate it," she said with a small smile.

Rayan's eyes lit up and he gingerly reached for the doll, pulling it close to his chest. He looked to Sine and nodded. "I'll help," he said.

Sine looked to his mother, and she nodded, as well.

"Good," Sine said, looking back to Rayan. "You and your mum follow me, and I'll take you all to the shore."

Rayan nodded and he and his mother stood, preparing to leave.

The woman saw that Sine struggled as she stood and noticed the tourniquet on her right arm.

"You're hurt," she said with alarm.

"It's nothing. I'll be fine," Sine said.

"Hold on," said the woman. "Let me take a look." She directed Sine to a chair in the corner, turning it toward the window for light and saw the makeshift bandage soaked completely through. "This won't take but a minute," she determined.

Sine nodded and the woman undid the bandage, peeling it away from the congealing wound. Sine bit her lip and clenched her fist to avoid screaming in pain.

Rayan reached for her hand. "Be brave," he said.

Sine nodded and smiled at him as best she could as his mother brought a cloth to the wound, wiping away at the blood that kept trickling.

"Hold the cloth," she directed Sine.

Sine held the wet rag on her wound as the woman searched

through a cabinet of glass jars, procuring one, dumping its contents into a mortar on the table and grinding it into a paste.

"What's that?" Sine asked with a frown.

"Early milfoil," replied the woman. "You're still bleeding — this should help."

Taking the paste, she applied it liberally to the gash, then took a fresh bandage and rewrapped Sine's arm.

"Thank you," Sine said with a nod and a smile.

The woman bowed. "I'm Renlyn, by the way," she greeted.

Sine stopped. "Renlyn Bethel? Queen Braithe's handmaid?" she asked with shock.

Renlyn nodded just as a crash from outside caught their attention. A roof had caught fire on a building nearby and caused it to cave in. More people were flooding the bay.

"Let's go," Sine ordered.

Renlyn grabbed her son's hand and the two followed Sine to the door. She rushed them out and around the alley corner where their house sat. People ran past, nearly running over Rayan before Sine pulled him back.

"You're one of Queen Braithe's men, aren't you?" Renlyn asked. "I thought I remembered your face. Is she back? Is she safe?"

Sine turned to her and hung her head. "She was fine last I saw her, but I know not where she is now. All I know is that the rest of her family is in danger, and the castle is surrounded," she revealed.

Renlyn's face went pale. "Who is attacking us?" she asked.

"Jaelan Dùghlan has betrayed the peoples of this realm,"

Sïne revealed.

"This is Middling's doing?" Renlyn asked, shocked.

"No, something is wrong with the king's son. This is solely his crusade," Sïne explained.

When the path was clear, she ushered them onward, reaching the opening to the bay.

"Find a soldier, get on a boat, stay safe," Sïne urged.

Renlyn paused. "The family must be trapped in there with him. I knew there was something sinister about him and that companion of his," she said. She then reached inside her apron and provided Sïne a key.

"This is to the staff quarters. Behind the castle are the dorms, this will get you in there. From there, you'll come to the tunnels that lead into the kitchens. Go through the rightmost tunnel and up the stairwell — it'll get you to the tearoom behind the banquet hall. Hopefully, you'll find your way from there," she said, her eyes filled with worry.

Sïne breathed a huge sigh of relief. "Thank the seas I was brought to you," she said with a warm smile.

Renlyn hugged Sïne, careful of her injury, and her son did the same, hugging at Sïne's legs. Sïne returned the gesture, thanking the seas continuously in her mind for the fortune that had been bestowed upon her.

"Go," Renlyn nodded, "you may be their only hope."

Sïne saluted with her uninjured arm and urged them toward the shore, watching as they blended into the crowd looking for salvation. She turned back to the alley; thankful she knew where to head.

Down the longest street of the final quarter, fires littered her path. Jumping over smoldering cloths and crates, the blazing heat nipped at her legs. She looked up to get a view of the castle and turned down each alley accordingly. As she neared the main commotion, she saw shadows roaming through the streets. She dodged behind smoking debris of structures, covering her face as best she could to refrain from coughing.

A pair from the dark army patrolled past, unaware of her presence. She waited until they were far enough away to make a break for the next spot of cover. Erratically inhaling and exhaling in a pocket of open air she tried to quickly catch her breath. She noticed then that she was on the path that led straight to the servant's quarters.

Peeking around the corner to confirm her clearance, she saw no unwelcome company and rushed for the staff entrance. Fumbling the key from her pocket, she undid the lock and slipped inside, latching the door behind her. The quarters were silent; no staff were present. All the staff room doors were open, and she walked cautiously to peek inside. Beds unmade, meals left unfinished, the entirety of the dorm was mostly untidy. She searched a few of the servant's rooms, finding a pair of leather boots to replace her noisy sabatons, and nearly screamed in anguish as she worked her coat of mail off her body. She knew she would need the help of silence more than the protection of steel, as her ability to fight was greatly diminished. Walking down the corridor, she came upon a door, also opened. Sneaking along the wall, she listened closely for any life before turning the corner. Silence, save for her own ragged breathing, was now all she could hear.

The stone tunnel led, as Renlyn had described, directly to the staff commissary. There, makings for dinner were sprawled about the preparatory tables — vegetables, cheeses, and a few haddock. She noticed a pot of water holding still on the stove. A couple of rats had made their escape when she entered, taking with them the spoils they had acquired.

Sĭne noted her hunger but felt reluctant to waste more time. She walked through the kitchen, still listening carefully. The scuttle of rats now echoed about the floor, but thankfully they were her only company. At the other end of the kitchen was a swinging door. She gently pushed it open, cringing at the creaking of its hinges. Through the portal, she paused against the wall, the pain in her arm aggravated again. Taking a few labored breaths, she encouraged herself down the hallway, coming to a fork.

She was relieved to hear no sound still, until the thought of being too late elevated her anxiety. Shaking her head to retain focus, she tried to remember which tunnel she needed.

"Think, Sĭne, think," she whispered.

Distant clattering down the left hallway stopped her.

Let's hope it's this way, then, she thought, as she turned down the right-hand corridor.

A moderate passage then led to a stairwell, much to her relief, as she remembered the detail. Climbing yet another set of twisting steps, she listened apprehensively at every footstep for someone to be around the bend. No foe was found, and she continued up. She came to an alcove that opened into the castle's kitchen pantry. All manner of floral and spicy notes wafted through the air, and the sweet scent of dried dheldora caught her, too.

She was transported momentarily to her mother's small kitchen. Too small, she could barely see over the counter as her mother fixed an elixir, crushing different manner of leaves, herbs, and flowers, then delicately bathing them in a bowl of hot water. Sĭne remembered the patterns of steam and how they reminded her of the morning fog on the rolling hills of Torrerìn. She thought of her mother's apron — stains of the plants she used left streaky and spotted patterns of wild colors.

Sĭne opened her eyes to find herself back in the keep. Fighting the comforts of nostalgia, she looked for the banquet hall's door. Upon the back wall was a deep oak wood ornately decorated, its face carved into the crest of the royal family. A light turn of the knob let the door whisper open, and Sĭne checked first through its crack.

Facing away from the door was a short figure sitting at the head of the large banquet table. Sĭne backed through the door and held still to confirm they had not heard her. When no disturbance could be heard, she reached for a kitchen cleaver and peeked again.

They still sat unmoved in the seat, but an oddity caught Sĭne's eye. Their arms were strapped to the seat by some manner of twine. The figure rustled slightly, trying to free themselves, and Sĭne saw them drop their head in defeat. She scanned the remainder of the room that she could see, before sneaking behind the captive — knife held at their head.

She walked silently around until she was near their periphery, and they jumped as they caught sight of her. Bound and gagged was a dwarf. He realized she was not one of his captors and his eyes went wide, looking around frantically.

Sĭne painfully lifted her right hand to her lips to caution him to remain quiet. He nodded eagerly, and she carefully undid the tie around his mouth.

"Mountains bless yeh. There are monsters in the castle, girl. The staff, the family, they took them all down to the dungeons, they did. I was sent to warn this house of war, but I was much too late. Been tied in this bloody chair since I got here. That man-child thinks he's king. And the dark one he was with left just before the horns. A right evil git that one is," he prattled on in a whisper.

Sĭne worked on removing his bonds. "You need to get to the shores; the city is under siege. Go as fast as you can," she instructed.

The dwarf nodded, undoing the ties on his legs. "A soldier also, they took him. He tried to fight 'em but looked in a bad way — took him to the dungeons too, I think," he told her.

"Thank you for telling me all this," Sĭne said appreciatively.

"Yer surely not thinkin' of stayin'?" he asked, aghast.

Sĭne nodded. "I need to try to save them," she explained.

He hugged Sĭne around the torso and she tried to return gesture despite her injury.

The dwarf shuddered. "Be wary. Halls are crawlin' with demons. There may be no one left to save," he said ominously.

Sĭne bowed to him. "I understand. Go quickly through

the kitchen, down the stairs and the hall will take you straight through to the staff quarters and out. Warn more soldiers if you can," she requested.

The dwarf nodded and ran toward the swinging door, disappearing from the room.

Alone again, Sĭne wandered the darkened banquet hall. Candles and sconces were fortuitously still lit, providing enough light for her to see. The chamber was grand, enveloping a gorgeous dwarven fir table fit to seat twenty at a time. Sĭne remembered her knighting ceremony celebration being held in this hall. Knighted by King Arlon, her class of soldiers had been the penultimate group who would receive his blessing before he passed. She had dined with friends — newfound and old. She had made her father proud.

A large, steeled chandelier glistened above with twisting vines, rearing lions, and patterns of waves upon the sea. It provided much of the light in the room, allowing Sĭne to see the late King Arlon's portrait above the mantle. A bouquet of rhododendrons lay below the frame, and Sĭne recalled the king's passing near a year ago to the day.

"Help me rescue them," she whispered to Arlon's long-suffering face. The glow of his eyes in the candlelight felt like she was looking into Tagwen's.

Hearing movement from the main hall, she hastened toward her purpose. The banquet hall had a series of doors lining its eastern wall, a few of which were already opened to reveal the primary hallway. Sĭne moved to the southern end of the room, to catch a view outside one of the open doors. There she could see much of the carpeted length leading up to the large threshold in the north that would lead into the central courtyard.

Two dark guards emerged from that court and began a patrol of the main hall. Similar to those on the battlefield, they were obscured by masks of bone and blackened armor covering the entirety of their persons. They walked in step with one another, perfectly, and drew nearer to Sĭne. She quickly looked for a means of escape. Catching sight of the other side of the corridor, she saw an open door to the library. As the guards were closing in, Sĭne reached for a trinket on the mantle: a small, bronzed lion. She tossed it to the other side of the banquet room and watched their reaction.

To her satisfaction, they turned, almost mechanically, to find the source of the noise, moving toward the northern end of the banquet room as she slipped out the door to the library. Once inside, she pressed herself against the wall and held her breath. She heard their footfalls back in the hallway, pacing up and down a small portion of its length. She moved to hide behind bookshelves and peeked around their edges to watch them through the doorway. They turned about themselves, as if uncertain where to go, as if her distraction had disrupted their purpose. They moved out of her vision beyond the door, and she crept from her hiding place, searching for their whereabouts. She found them opening the castle doors to leave, presumably to continue their patrol. Knowing this was now her chance, she scrambled to the courtyard entrance opposite their departure, struggling to crack the massive double doors just enough for her to slip through.

The center courtyard was shadowed under the castle walls and towers behind. Bordering colonnades squared off the court, leading back into the maze of hallways Sĭne would need to navigate. Limited cover forced her to move swiftly. She had been to the dungeons only once in her career, during an introduction to the castle layout. Her duties never called her to keep watch at the prison because it was hardly ever used under the Braithe reign.

Hearing a guard approach, she ducked behind a pillar of the arcade, pressing herself uncomfortably to the ground. The darkness was enough to conceal her presence as she waited for a clearing.

Her head began to feel light, and she was forced to coax herself out of the need to heave. Feeling a trickle down her arm, she saw the wound had finally bled through the new bandage — she assumed then it would not heal, and that she needed to hurry.

She was free to move once again and hoisted herself up, using the nearest column for support. Peeking through the archways, she saw her chance and lurched forward into the central channel. She foggily recalled her need to find an antechamber that led to the dungeon's stairwell. A series of rooms lined the walls, each of which was as likely to be the antechamber as the last. She struggled to remember. Her feet carried her onward, though, as if propelled by an innate navigation. She began to trust herself, making a series of determined turns down halls she vaguely recalled.

She caught a second wind as she dodged behind a hallway to avoid another passing guard. Blinking intentionally seemed to clear her head as she slunk around a corner. At the end of the passageway, she recognized the final door: an iron construction unlike the rest of the wooden structures. Its bar was unlatched, but the real impediment was chained to its frame — a sleeping warg.

The beast's massive paws were equipped with steel claws and a spiked metal helm was affixed to its head. Sĭne could hear its breathing from where she stood, and its growled exhalation was bone-chilling.

Her heart was pounding. She squeezed the hilt of her sword with her left hand in contemplation. There was little hope that the creature would not stir as soon as she neared, but she had no other choice. She steadied herself and tip-toed closer when an opening caught her eye.

Turning toward the open door she snuck inside. It was a modest storage room that appeared mostly ransacked, save for a few woven rugs and empty barrels. Sĭne's head tilted at the idea of baffling the creature — that perhaps it would give her enough time to make her way through the door.

Giving it no more thought, she grabbed a rug and crept back into the hall. The animal was still asleep, and Sĭne managed to get within a foot of it. She swallowed shakily and tried to steady her breathing. Creeping around the hound, she held the rug in both hands, ready to spring, but it seemed to take no note of her, deep in its slumber. Keeping one eye on the monstrous creature, Sĭne gingerly reached her left hand to the door.

Instantly, as her hand grasped the metal handle, the demon's yellow eye opened and its blood-stained lips curled away to reveal a mouth of razor teeth. Before it could move,

Sīne launched the cover over its head and opened the door. It scrambled, snarling, and snapping its jaws at the hindrance, as she closed the entry behind her. She could hear it clawing its metaled hooks against the iron door and backed away, safely inside.

"I cannot believe that worked," she said to herself.

To her relief, no one was within the antechamber, but she knew the hound would give away her plan much too soon. She grabbled her sword and rallied quickly to the stairwell in the back of the room. Sword-first, she descended the stairs. Five turns down the spiraled staircase led into a darkened tunnel — the entryway to the dungeons.

Distressingly, she reached her right arm for the lit torch upon the wall. Navigating this section of the castle in the dark was nearly impossible. She listened for any sign of life, welcome or unwelcome. Puddles of dank water splashed as she stepped through them, and the occasional squeak of a rat could be heard throughout this catacomb-like abyss. All the cells glowed empty as she passed them, so she delved deeper.

She shook in a chill, as she felt a breeze on her sweated-through tunic. Her hands, too, were increasingly clammy. "Come on, where are they?" she said quietly to herself.

Murmurs then echoed from the deepest reaches of the dungeon. She tried to glimpse through the shadows to detect their origin. The closer she thought she got, the quieter the voices became.

"Hello?" she called.

"Here!" a few voices called back in unison.

Sīne hastily followed the sounds and came upon the final cul-de-sac of cells. She shone the light and saw what appeared to be nearly twenty staff members. They were crying, coughing, talking.

"Praise the seas!" a woman blessed.

"Matharnach?" asked a weak voice.

Sīne looked around and saw the captain of Oburim, bruised and beaten, laying upon the floor, being tended to by a woman. She rushed to his cell.

"I'm so sorry," she said.

"Eh, you didn't do this to me," Eachann chuckled, trying to sit up.

The woman who was tending to him looked up to her with bloodshot eyes — it was Rhona, the Princess of Yeacralas.

"Your highness!" Sīne exclaimed.

"Thank the seas," Rhona said gratefully as she helped Eachann to his feet.

Eachann moved to the cell door and his expression fell when he saw the state of their rescuer. "You're hurt," he frowned.

Noticing the bloodied bandage, he reached an arm through the bars and gently touched her injured limb.

"Was this an arrow?" he asked.

Sīne gingerly pulled her arm back. "We don't have time. We need to get you all out of here," she said, looking around.

Eachann nodded toward the opposing wall. "The buffoons left the keys."

Sīne took a big sigh of relief as she set down the torch to grab the ring. Working as quickly as she could, she went to each cell and set everyone free. They all gathered, and Sïne wondered how she was going to get them all out and past the cursed dog.

Princess Rhona said, "We need to hurry; my daughter is still up there. She and Elnan are trapped with that bastard!"

"Where are they?" Sïne asked, feeling faint again and fighting to stay upright.

Eachann caught her by her good shoulder and stabilized her. "You're going to die if we don't get you out of here," he warned.

Sïne shook off the dazed feeling once again. "No, I'm not leaving them," she declared.

"Sergeant —" Eachann started.

Sïne glared at him. "I will not abandon another!" she exclaimed angrily. She looked at the crowd of concerned faces before her. "There's a hound up there, a nasty one that's likely alerted them I came down here. There are patrols everywhere, but if we move as one, we might be enough to push through to get out of here," she explained, changing the subject.

Rhona spoke up. "Actually, there's another way out — as children, Tagwen and I got creative with hide and seek," she shared. "I can lead us to it." She looked at an older woman in the crowd. "Sorry, Mairead," she said sheepishly to her childhood teacher.

The delicate elderly woman managed a smile and shook her head. "Guess I should be glad for it now, dear," she said.

Sïne agreed to let the princess show them the way. Following back out of the cul-de-sac of cells, she turned a corner down another hallway of cages. At the very end was one large prison — with a hole in its back wall.

"Rovicus' tunnel," Rhona gestured. "It goes under the North watchtower that will let you out through the cellar hatch."

Sĭne handed a servant the torch she was carrying and undid the lock. "The city is under siege. Stay vigilant, and may the seas get you all out alive," she said.

The man who took the torch nodded and led the procession of staff members. Sĭne gestured for Princess Rhona to follow them.

"No. I am going to save my daughter," Rhona said firmly.

"Princess, you may well be the only Braithe alive," Eachann said.

Rhona whipped her head at him. "Do not dare say that!" she spat.

"Your highness —" Sĭne pleaded.

Rhona fought the tears welling in her own eyes. "I cannot leave them—" she stammered.

"I will find them," Sĭne promised.

"We — will find them," Eachann corrected, looking at Sĭne.

Rhona nodded as she wept. The sight of both soldiers was disconcerting. Sĭne and Eachann both were worse for wear — embattled and bruised, but miraculously still standing. "I think they are being held in Elnan's chamber," she told them. "You two are my only hope," she said. "May the guidance of the sea follow you where you tread." She choked on the last few words and wiped her eyes.

"You best be keeping your wits about you. Seas help you if I have to explain this madness to your mother," Mairead warned from beside the princess to Eachann, her nephew.

He smiled sadly as he embraced his aunt before stepping away. "You won't have to," he promised.

Sïne saluted the princess, and Rhona bowed to them, turning with Mairead, and left through the mouth of the tunnel.

"Is Matron Ghuinne a relative of yours?" Sïne asked.

Eachann nodded. "She's my aunt."

"Seems I'm learning quite a bit about you," Sïne muttered, almost to herself.

"How *did* you get past that dog?" Eachann asked, his smile was crooked at the swelling of his cheek.

"Doesn't matter, because I can't do it a second time," Sïne quipped. "We need to move," she prompted.

Snarling then echoed throughout the dungeon and Sïne's heart skipped a beat.

"Follow my lead," Eachann whispered.

Sïne nodded and Eachann gestured for her to hand him the keys. Once she did, he opened the lock of one of the cells lining the corridor.

"What are you doing?" Sïne muttered at him as she watched him slip into the open cell and hold the door barely closed.

"Brace yourself," he warned.

"Wha—" Sïne could hardly utter a word before Eachann held his hand to his mouth and produced a deafening whistle.

Sïne froze as the note rang out. The charge of steeled claws raking against the stone floor accompanied by the horrible barking sounds of the beast grew louder and louder. Sïne saw the monstrosity round the corner. Facing her head on, the warg sprinted to her with all its strength, but just as it reached

Eachann's cell, he sprang open the cell door and the animal charged into the iron bars instead. The hound's helm caught within the bars at an angle fortuitous enough to render it still.

Sīne let out a shaky breath she had been holding and turned to Eachann with a look of shock and horror.

"Well, that worked a lot better than I thought it would," he smirked, then winced at the pain from his bruised face.

Sīne was still catching her breath when a mœrdeth soldier showed itself, as it was running after the dog. They stood two meters tall and were differently clad than the others Sīne had encountered. Armored in steel from head to toe, the helm they wore covered the entirety of their face, save for a darkened slit in the center, but Sīne could see no countenance underneath.

Catching sight of the two, the barbarian ran toward them, spear in hand. As he neared, he launched the spear, and Sīne was still transfixed by the sight of him. Eachann moved quickly back into the cell, pulling Sīne with him in time to avoid the impaling blow. The giant cleared its defeated beast, but as it turned to strike at them, Sīne struck first. Thrusting upward from where she had stumbled, she wounded the creature in its voided face, and it fell upon her sword. Pulling the blade away, a black ichor dripped down the fuller, the assailant dropped in front of Sīne, and all went quiet again. She was breathing heavily now; adrenaline had found her once again, numbing the pain of her body enough to carry her onward.

Listening for a moment, Eachann helped Sīne balance once again. "Have a feeling there's no more hound at the door," he joked.

Missing Eachann's quip, Sĭne was vexed by the unguent and enormity of the mœrdeth soldier, and knelt by the body. She pulled at the helm to remove it from the corpse, but as she did, a hiss of grim smoke leeched its way out. The gloves and exposed undergarments deflated, the limbed parts of the suit of armor clattered to the ground. There was no body within. Sĭne gasped and stepped away, dropping the helm as she did.

"Certainly have no idea how to explain that," Eachann said, equally aghast. He ushered her out of the cell. "Let's keep going," he urged, and Sĭne nodded.

They pushed back to where the entrance to the dungeon began. Into the antechamber they found the iron door swung open. The chain that once held the menacing warg was broken. Upon the floor remained the rug, and Eachann smiled at Sĭne.

"Clever," he grinned.

Sĭne scoffed as she scanned the hall. She knew the royal chambers were across the courtyard on the eastern side of the castle. She guided Eachann to the central corridor and they rushed through to the other side.

The glow of the fires spreading about the lower town lit the clouds above them with the full moon gazing down upon the destruction. Sĭne wished for rain, for help, for the sea to swallow the *monsters* whole.

Despite the ongoing chaos, the castle's interior grounds were not yet bustling with activity. Sĭne thought that the dark army must have still considered the keep conquered.

They reached the eastern wing of the castle and crept into the keep. Entering the foyer, Sĭne tried to get her bearings. The pause made her dizzy again — Eachann held her up.

"We need to get you out of here," he insisted.

Sĭne shook her head with furrowed brows, wincing at the effect of moving her head too quickly. "No. No. I just need to remember," she said.

Eachann groaned.

Once she regained some clarity, Sĭne followed her feet's instincts again. The lefthand arch in the back of the foyer led to a short hall that opened into a larger section of the castle, where three chambers were housed. Creeping along the hall, the pair peered within, and standing at attention, above the bodies of fallen Marezian guards, were two more guardians of the same barbarity they had just met, only these were wielding tremendous, menacing, morning stars.

"Great," Sĭne sighed with exasperation.

Hearing the door creak open, the two backed into the shadows of the hall… watching. Out of the room stepped the Prince of Middling. His stature was dwarfed by the appointed guardians, but to Sĭne his presence felt even more monstrous than theirs. She watched as he spoke to them, and one of them began to follow him toward where they were hiding.

"Quick!" Eachann whispered.

They backed out of the hall and further down the other length of the corridor, rushing into a hall closet. Eachann peeked out of the cloakroom to see Jaelan and his guard walking out into the foyer. Once they passed, he opened the door, gesturing for Sĭne to follow him. His light movements made him appear to glide across the floor as he looked to confirm that they had left.

"I'll distract the other guard. Hide in the storage room until you hear us round the foyer. Then move in quickly to get Elnan and the princess' daughter out," he whispered.

Sĭne exhaled. "Let's hope we have enough time," she said.

Eachann shook his head. "We don't. I'll give you as much time as I can but… be swift."

Sĭne nodded. She went back to hide in the closet but first turned to Eachann. "Be safe," she told him as she offered her sword. "You're probably better equipped to wield this than I," she said.

Eachann bowed his head, taking the sword. "You be safe as well."

Once Sĭne was secured in the hiding place, she heard Eachann whistle again. "Hey! Brute!" he shouted.

Sure enough, it elicited the desired response — Eachann began luring the gladiator from his post into the foyer and out of the wing.

Sĭne rushed to the now unguarded door and pulled it open. Sitting at the head of the central table with his head down was the Prince of Yeacralas, and in the large, canopied bed behind him, Sĭne could see a young girl sleeping.

Moving toward Elnan, Sĭne bowed. "Your highness, we need to leave at once," she whispered in greeting.

Elnan's eyes were lidded, his hair unkempt and his face shadowed. He lifted his tired head to face Sĭne. "I know your face," he whispered, peering at Sĭne through exhausted eyes.

Sĭne saluted him. "Sergeant Sĭne Matharnach, your highness," she said.

His face lit for a moment. "Matharnach?" he echoed. "You were with Tagwen, then. Where is she?" he asked anxiously.

Sĭne swallowed as she searched for an answer. Elnan's shoulders lost their brawn as he looked at her. "Is she gone?" he asked.

"My heart tells me she is not, but where she is, I know not," Sĭne replied.

"How do you come by this way then? You seem either a deserter or a lone survivor, though in your present state I cannot tell which."

Sĭne straightened. "I am here for reasons unknown even to myself, your highness. I heard only the call of my home, and in her cry, she bid me here," she explained. A beat of silence hung in the air before Sĭne continued. "Your highness, I have little time to rescue you from this place. We need to depart," she insisted.

"They have Rhona in a cell. He is holding her as ransom so I will give him what he wants," Elnan reported.

"We have freed Rhona and the staff of your house," she told him.

Elnan stared at her for a moment. "You speak not in deception?" he asked sternly.

Sĭne shook her head. "No, your highness. I come from the heels of her freedom, now seeking yours and her daughter's," she assured him.

Elnan finally softened. His shapely face, though distressed, became kingly. He gestured his head toward Enania. "Wake her. Hurry," he instructed.

Sine shuffled to the bedside, and gently nudged the child's shoulder. Her golden curls lay sprawled over her face and pillow. Suckling her thumb in a deep slumber, she stirred and rubbed at her face. "Momma?" Enania mumbled.

"I'm going to take you to your mum, okay? I need you to come with me and your uncle, dear," Sine coaxed. She noticed the child's bright green eyes and felt their familiarity, somehow.

"Where Momma?" Enania wondered as she lifted her tired head.

"I'll take you to her. Come now, sweetie," Sine smiled, gathering the little girl to her.

Nodding wearily, the child sat up. Rubbing at her eyes with one hand and clutching a stuffed sorrel and blonde-maned horse in another, Enania made her best effort to wake.

Sine helped her out of bed with her one good arm and walked her over to Elnan. "Alright, your highness, let's go," she said as she began to reach for his cart positioned at the opposite end of the table. He held up a hand to stop her.

"Your highness—" Sine began.

Elnan then reached for Enania, and the child came forward to embrace him. "Go with her to find your mother, okay, Enania? Listen to what she tells you and remember that I love you. Promise?" Elnan asked gently.

Surely, he does not mean to stay.

Enania nodded sleepily in the embrace and then moved to take Sine's hand.

"Prince Elnan I can get us all out of here, but we must hurry," Sine insisted.

With tears in his eyes, Elnan looked up to Sĭne. "If I go, none of them are safe. You say Rhona and Tagwen are alive, yes?" he asked.

Sĭne nodded. "Yes, but I—"

"Jaelan will stop at nothing. He is bound by some darkness that will not seek to spare any. The man I once… knew, is gone," he interrupted.

Enania shuffled her feet. "Momma?" she asked again, sleepily, tears beginning to form in her eyes.

Sĭne dropped delicately to a knee and patted the child's back. "It's alright dear we're going to get your mum right now I promise." She looked back at Elnan whose soft blue eyes were glistening with tears.

"Protect them, please," he begged in a whisper, clutching his right fist to his heart.

"Your highness, I cannot let you—"

A clattering outside the doors and shouting voices stopped her.

"There is no time! Serve them well for me, please," Elnan pleaded.

Glancing between the prince and the door, Sĭne paused, fear and sadness gripping her face.

"The wardrobe, it connects to the next room. Go!" Elnan ordered.

Sĭne shakily nodded and saluted him, reaching for the child's delicate hand. "Let's go, dear," she urged Enania.

"Elno." The child reached out to her uncle, who grasped her little hand once more. "Go find mum, Nani. Don't worry, I'll be there soon," he comforted, looking to the ceiling to control his tears.

Nani? Sïne recalled the final words of the Horseman she and Eachann had tried to save and realized then the resemblance — he must have been the child's father. Her chest tightened at the thought.

Sïne guided the girl quickly to the wardrobe as the sounds neared the room. Crawling inside and shutting the door just as the source of the racket entered, Sïne did not have time to open the back latch to the connecting closet wall. Slinking down to the wardrobe's bottom, she cautioned Enania to keep quiet, and held the child close. She could hear the commotion within the room — Eachann had been caught.

"I thought I had put your meddling to rest, but it seems as though you insist on remaining a thorn in my side," hissed the Prince of Middling.

"Go rot, you clotpole," spat Eachann.

Sïne cringed as she heard a blow being dealt. The captain of Oburim coughed and tried to regain his breath.

"Let him be, Jaelan! All of this is nonsense. It is not him you want," Elnan cried.

Jaelan snorted. "He will be dealt with as we see fit. A favored pet of the elves will do well in our hand," he snickered. "You and —" Jaelan stopped. "Where is the child?!" he roared.

Sïne heard stomping move to the bed, then back to the center of the room. She held her breath and soothed Enania, as the child squirmed at the distressing sounds.

"I will not ask again!" Jaelan yelled.

Elnan cleared his throat. "I do not know — I cannot move, Jaelan," he replied.

"Find the girl!" Jaelan commanded.

Sĭne heard weighty footfalls leave the room, presuming them to belong to the same guards from earlier.

She heard Jaelan move over to Elnan. "First Tagwen — struck down upon the plains of the Greyrest, a fate so grim and unforgiving," he baited. "Now Rhona lies within my grasp, shackled within the depths of these halls, guarded by beasts and soldiers fiercer than your entire army, and who would sooner dole out a similar sentence to her, save for my benevolence," he grinned maliciously. "A kindness that is destined to be revoked if you do not cooperate, Elnan," he threatened.

"I cannot move, Jaelan. Enania must have slipped past me whilst I nodded off," Elnan theorized.

"Liar!" Jaelan howled, slamming his fist upon the table. A dagger was unsheathed and Sĭne heard shuffling. "Did he have something to do with it? Clever to slip out of chains and distract a guard — perhaps gutting this one will tell us where she is," Jaelan suggested.

"Jaelan, stop! This is not who you are," Elnan protested.

"You know nothing of who I am!" Jaelan screamed.

"I know the boy my father welcomed into these halls, the man who wished to find purpose and friendship, who wanted to learn and bring greatness to the halls of his own father," Elnan recalled.

Jaelan laughed a wicked, throaty laugh. "You fool. I will bring greatness to all Vostheloren — greater than our fathers or their fathers before them. To preserve the lands and the men who reside upon it and save them from the darkness that they will inflict upon themselves. I alone will bring the land a king it has so long desired. I will fulfill the duty you so utterly failed to serve. Leaving your pathetic sister to take the throne… so feeble and gullible to the pleas of lesser beings," Jaelan taunted.

"Do not dare speak of Tagwen or my father with that forked tongue," Elnan warned.

Sïne could feel her face warm at Jaelan's wicked words, but it soon faded to a clammy chill. Her arm was beginning to numb. She sat and flexed her hand to retain some mobility but found the endeavor to be increasingly difficult.

"She was weak. The world knew it. It's why she fell so easily in favor with the elves, and why she fell so easily upon our army's sword," Jaelan sneered.

"Now who fills his mouth with lies?" Elnan chuckled.

Jaelan cackled and Sïne could hear a muffled crack of lighting outside the bedroom window. "Marez is lost, Elnan. Your kingdom needs a king — since you are too weak to take its helm, I am destined to take your place," he proclaimed.

"No one will ever see you as king," Eachann choked, as he spat upon the ground.

Jaelan growled, "Silence! I'll hear none of it from you — a loathsome traitor to his own kind."

Sïne heard the doors open once more, but this time a chill entered within, a cold that was not of her own body's making. It was as if all the warmth of the world had been stolen away. She heard muffled whispers before an unknown voice spoke.

"Hubertus Tolmach — or should I say, Eachann Ghuinne, the bastard son of Muireall Ghuinne? Either way, you have been quite instrumental in the success of this whole operation. I must thank you for your naive efforts — sending Tagwen to the elves, rending this city's helm free — it was all a remarkable service. You will serve one more, however, before you are through. I have more elves for you to lure," said the fearsome and mysterious voice.

Sïne gasped at the revelation that the entirety of their journey had been part of some iniquitous ploy, and that this "captain" was more of a stranger to her than before.

"Snake," Eachann spat. "I'll not serve you or the like."

The voice let out a light laugh. "You already have," it said.

"Goraidh, the child is missing, we must expand efforts to—" Jaelan began.

"Relax, dear boy, the city is surrounded — even with that damnable alarm having been rung, no one will escape unseen. We will find her. I am, however, disappointed that he has not yet been dealt with," Goraidh complained.

Jaelan chortled for a moment. "There's nothing he can do. He cannot even walk, he is not an impediment to our plans," Jaelan insisted.

Goraidh clicked his tongue in disappointment. "They will not see you as king if he remains. Both sisters have already been dealt with, the child is a mere nuisance, but he — he is an heir whom they believe in. We cannot let that stand, even if he cannot," Goraidh said, pleased with his play on words.

Sïne's heart rushed in the moment of silence that followed.

Looking down at her debilitating wound, she cursed herself for not being strong enough to fight.

"Jaelan, you do not have to listen to him — he is poisoning you," Elnan tried.

"Come now, you know the truths I have spoken — you've seen them," Goraidh hissed.

Another moment of silence wracked Sïne's nerves — she wished vehemently to burst from the closet to cut down the evil where it stood. Instead, she felt fainter than before, desperately blinking to keep herself awake. Enania began to fuss and Sïne leaned close to shush her whilst patting her back. Her throat constricted at the silence that followed, worried she had been heard.

"He has chosen you, Jaelan, as king of the new world. You alone can save them," Goraidh reminded him.

Sïne breathed a small sigh of relief that they remained unnoticed, but heard footsteps move about, creeping across the floor.

"You spineless traitor!" Eachann shouted.

"Silence him," Goraidh instructed.

Sïne heard the heavy footsteps of the guards, and Eachann fought as he was struck and gagged. She winced at hearing the struggle, tears streamed freely down her face onto the curls of Enania's drooping head.

"You could surrender. You would lose nothing more than you already have. Just accept the defeat," Jaelan suggested almost pleadingly.

Sïne heard then an awkward shuffling, and a struggle as

a chair slid upon the tiled floor. Noticing a slight crack in the wardrobe's closure, she moved her head gingerly to see. Through the peephole, she saw Prince Elnan gathering all the strength of the working limbs of his body, pulling himself to the table. He hoisted himself up, maneuvering clumsily, his legs giving from underneath him.

Jaelan moved to help, realizing the man was trying to stand. Elnan brushed him off as he reached for the chair. Jaelan moved the high-back chair over so Elnan would have something to hold onto. The moment of kindness gave Sine hope.

Wrestling himself upright, with no feeling in his body from the waist-down, Elnan battled to speak. "Put me then… to death. Remember me not… in pity, brother. For I… give will-ingly… my life… in hopes that I — saved theirs," he uttered painfully.

Sine held her breath as she watched Jaelan twist the dagger in his hand.

"The midnight hour beckons. You know what you must do," the demon spoke again.

Sine's throat closed as she watched Jaelan's grip tighten around the hilt, her breathing ragged as she tried to calm herself. She heard Eachann's muffled and defeated protests through the tie around his mouth.

Jaelan put a hand on Elnan's shoulder and gazed into the prince's eyes. He brought the dagger upward, a hiss of breath escaped Elnan's lungs, and Jaelan caught the prince in his arms.

Sine turned away at the sight, pressing her head to the child's and holding Enania closer. She tried to stifle her cries as she heard the traitor set the body of the prince upon the floor.

The Lion had fallen.

13

TORN ASUNDER

Despite moonlight shining high above Tagwen and the others, she noted there were no visible stars, as if the guardians of the heavens had decided to turn their face from the darkness that was encroaching upon Vostheloren.

As they ran, Tagwen thought of home and of those who had pledged themselves to her home's protection. She found herself unsure whether delaying her return to retrieve a token was senseless or necessary, but reminded herself that A'elūdèr was more than a keepsake. Now Tagwen's inexplicable connection with the blade threatened to lure them all into another palm of danger.

The arid steppe brought them no comfort nor cover as they dashed across the flatland. Far enough away from the imposing tower, they began to slow, regaining their breath and strength after adrenaline had abandoned them. Not a sip of water pooled upon the dried earth to give them relief.

The four companions were exhausted and thirsty. Winter's chill did little to aid their progression. Gòrdan halted first, nearly falling upon his own feet, the malnourishment of his body was taxing his energy. Ualan slowed his gait and draped Gòrdan's arm around his shoulders to carry him onward. They moved as such until they reached the outskirts of the Brœkk Highlands that sat above the gorge. Gòrdan finally collapsed upon his knees.

Holding his hand to his chest, Gòrdan breathed raggedly. "Let me not be a further hindrance," he rasped.

Ualan knelt beside him. "Nonsense," he said, pausing to place a hand upon his husband's shoulder, "I am not losing you again."

Tagwen looked behind them; no sign of their enemy appeared to have followed close enough, but she knew they nevertheless had little time. Her bones ached, every muscle tightened in pain, her stomach sought to consume her from the inside out. Still, she worried more about the state of her accomplices in this harrowing task.

She regarded Ualan. "If you can get me near the Hunter's vessel, I can handle the rest. No sense endangering your lives more than has already been done."

"Should have grabbed a second jar," Breccan muttered to herself.

Ualan nodded at Tagwen, while attempting to soothe his long-lost love.

Tagwen wished for a moment that Ualan would fight back and insist on accompanying her. She trembled, pretending to combat the chill, as she pushed the selfish thought from her mind.

Few moments passed as they waited for Gòrdan to be fit to continue to the ridge. As they pushed further into the highlands, the crest of the gorge came clearer into view. Overlooking the ledge, Tagwen could see specks of torchlight near the river below. Upon the waterway was the sought-after vessel. She could see a few attributes in its construction. It was smaller than the other galleons that bordered the isle, which meant a smaller crew, as well.

Less to deal with, she thought, considering the bright side.

As she searched the high ground for the pathway down, she spotted a light in the East. She nudged Breccan and motioned for her to look.

Breccan narrowed her eyes at the target, watching its movements as Tagwen saw it disappear below the ledge. "That appears to be the way down," Breccan said.

Tagwen turned to Gòrdan and Ualan. "I bid you not come any further than you wish. If our road is to end here, so be it."

Gòrdan stood, having briefly recovered. "I wish to aid you in this effort, my lady," he bowed. "It would be the least I could do," he said weakly.

Ualan, too, stood, brushed the sand from his trousers, and nodded at Tagwen. He seemed slightly taller. "There is strength in having us all," he told her.

Tagwen breathed a sigh of relief, simply happy that she had him along at all.

They continued their pursuit, coming to a carved path upon the walls of the rocky valley where the light had vanished. The crag was unlike the mountains in the southern part of the Isle. The deep rusty, gray, and copper sediment was consistent throughout the striations along the cliff face. There was no scar of a volcanic past, but there were remnants of plant life that could no longer thrive. Roots jutting in and out of the rock yearned for vitality, the malevolent air choking any chance of survival.

Their approach along the path was unnoticed. The dhow that sat at the edge of the waterway finally came into view as their descent brought them near. The ship's hull and sails were black as the others, but its construction was unequal to anything Tagwen had known. The canvas was not squared, but rather sported sharp angular forms that represented bat wings. Its long-raked bow was strangely spear-like, as the tip of it reflected in the moonlight. A moderate dinghy hung off its stern below the top deck.

Along the shoreline, they could make out a few figures loading the vessel. Tagwen caught sight of Oswallt and his demonic hound — they appeared to be waiting for the others to complete readying the yacht.

He's not Captain Trahern anymore, she reminded herself.

"I've only counted four of them… minus the dog," Breccan whispered.

"Can you make out what they're loading?" Ualan asked.

Breccan shook her head. "Not really, but they look to be nearly done; our swords are probably already aboard," she said.

Tagwen searched for an opening, to somehow find themselves close enough to rescue their belongings and leave. The shadows were all gathered along one side of the vessel. The other was open, but it was facing the water. "I could swim," she thought aloud.

Breccan moaned at the thought, but soon recognized that there would be no better opportunity whilst they were ill-equipped. She began removing her cloak, handing it over to Ualan, but reaffixing the token from Ylerïan upon her shirt.

"What are you doing?" Tagwen asked.

Breccan rolled her eyes at her and continued fidgeting with her shoe. She then pulled out the folded page of the tome and handed that also to Ualan. "Keep that safe, would you?" she asked.

Ualan palmed the vellum as if it were an egg, holding it close so it would have no chance of being destroyed, and quickly secreted it within a pocket.

"We can maybe provide a diversion for the two of you — keep their eyes off the boat a moment," Gòrdan suggested.

Tagwen shook her head. "Do nothing that would endanger your lives. I mean that for you as well," she said to Breccan.

Breccan scoffed and began to creep along the rock. They were shadowed by the cliff but would need to cross under moonlight to reach the waters.

Tagwen looked at Ualan and Gòrdan. "We will be quick, but please do not hesitate to run should you need to," she directed.

Ualan saluted the queen in the manner of her people. "It would do you well to hurry — we will give you the best chance," he replied.

She nodded, and followed Breccan, who was now quite a distance around the gorge. Creeping along the rocky terrain, she kept her eye on the accompaniment that stood along the bank. They remained preoccupied by their preparations as Tagwen and

Breccan made it completely to the opposite side.

Ducking below a pile of large boulders, Breccan peeked over the top. "Thank the seas there's a ladder," she whispered.

Returning back down, she looked to Tagwen. "You ready?" she asked.

Having removed her boots and gambeson, Tagwen nodded, and they moved around the rock to slink into the moonlit waters. The icy river startled Tagwen awake. She swam faster with purpose and motivation from the cold. Gliding through to the port side of the vessel, they held for a moment in the chill, listening for anyone aboard.

The two friends nodded to each other, and Breccan made the first ascent. Once she was over, she motioned for Tagwen to climb. Grabbing the rungs of soaked rope, Tagwen pulled herself upward and out of the water. Sliding up and over the deck, they both stayed low, attempting to quell the sounds of their dripping clothes.

Watching through the taffrail, Tagwen could see their opposition still seemingly unaware of their presence.

"I don't see anything on the deck," Breccan whispered. "We need to get below."

Tagwen nodded as she carefully picked herself up from the floor. She squeezed the excess water from her clothes as best she could before dipping into the door to the hold.

Below deck, a lantern lit the cargo bay that had been constructed as a partial passenger vessel. A narrow hall between two quarter doors led to the open storage area. Stacks of boxes and sacks lined the wall — most were sealed, as Tagwen and

Breccan began rifling through their contents.

Tagwen jumped back as she opened one of the boxes, dropping the lid to the floor.

"What's wrong with you?" Breccan hissed, spooked by the sound. Seeing Tagwen's expression, with her hands covering her mouth, Breccan turned to survey the box. Inside were stacks of various bones and a collection of skulls.

Breccan picked up the lid and replaced it upon the box. She regarded Tagwen. "One thing at a time," she said.

Tagwen nodded and continued searching. No box or wrapping seemed to hold their belongings. She closed her eyes and took a sharp, deep breath.

"I don't think they're in here," Breccan whispered.

Tagwen shook her head. "They have to be," she insisted.

"Are you sure this sword's that import—" Breccan stopped when they heard shouting coming from above.

Footsteps jogged along the deck above them and began to walk toward the cargo stairs.

"Quick!" Tagwen whispered, and rushed Breccan into one of the passenger rooms, closing the door behind. They pressed against the door to listen, hoping they had chosen the right place to hide for a moment. The footsteps descended, walked past the doors, and delivered a box to the hold. They then quickly retreated up to the top of the deck, eliciting sighs of relief from the two women.

Tagwen leaned her back against the door as she thought of what to do next, when a wrapped cloth upon the bed caught her attention. Guardedly, she approached, preparing herself for disappointment. Taking a corner of the sinister cloth, she opened the fold, revealing her prize.

Unsheathing A'elūdèr from its wicked hiding place, Tagwen held the blade aloft. Breccan caught sight of the bounty and rushed to grab her own blade, Saìde. With reverence, she brought the token close, looking at Tagwen with a satisfied smile.

"Let's go," said Tagwen.

Turning to make their escape through the door, they felt the vessel rock. Bracing, they heard more shouting, and a pair of footsteps running throughout the boat. Tagwen's throat closed at the sound of clawed steps raking against the upper decks.

"This can't be happening," Breccan breathed.

Tagwen could not tell if she was trembling from cold or fear. She clutched her sword tightly as she moved to the door, listening for anyone coming below deck. She could feel the boat picking up speed. The masts creaked as the sails unfurled the entirety of their length, catching the full of the minor winds that pulled them out of the gorge. She clenched her teeth and took a breath.

"We're getting out of here," she growled. Opening the door, she stepped delicately outward. "Stay here. I'm going to try and lure them down here," she instructed.

Breccan nodded and stood ready, and Tagwen moved to the cargo. Grabbing at a box lid, she dropped it forcefully on the ground and waited. She could hear walking above her coming to the stairs. Sword at the ready, she didn't take her eyes off the end of the deck. A shadowy figure descended, nearly too tall for the space. It spotted Tagwen immediately and rushed toward her, but turned around the instant Breccan opened the door to surprise it.

Steel met, ringing throughout the hold. The combatant was adept, thwarting the efforts of both Breccan and Tagwen simultaneously, despite the disadvantage it held in space. When the being turned, Breccan tumbled to the floor, unexpectedly, striking its legs. With a howling, void-like screech, the creature dropped to its knees and Tagwen knocked it to the ground and punted away its rapier.

"Run!" she shouted at Breccan, who hightailed it to the stairs. Above deck, the rain had picked up, and Tagwen noticed they were much closer to the horizon's storm. Wide-eyed, she was caught by the sounds of a fight. She watched her captain's silhouette flash in the surrounding lighting in a tangle against the outline of another warden. Breccan moved swiftly around the guard, who was heaving a flail. The creature was a shade against the darkened sky, but Tagwen saw it swing wildly in mistake, giving Breccan the opening she needed to kick it overboard.

Tagwen breathed a sigh of relief until, in an instant, Breccan was tackled. A monstrous blur of fur lunged from the top deck, snarling as it pinned her to the floor.

"Breccan!" Tagwen screamed.

Tossing and dodging between snapping jaws, Breccan held at the beast's throat to keep it from clamping down. Tagwen ran over to assist when the boat careened violently, knocking her clear across the deck. The warg had dug its claws into the wood, stabilizing itself from the maneuver. Tagwen fell prone against the taffrail, A'elūdèr had been knocked from her hand. The impact bruised her back and shook her senses. She looked up through the downpour to see Breccan still fighting the fiend. On the top deck, she could now see the Hunter steering the ship. Noticing she had been disarmed, she panicked, searching the deck frantically, when the glinting steel caught her eye. Upward near the bow was where the sword had landed — too far for her to reach. She looked back to Breccan and scrambled to stand, catching her balance in the rough waves that threatened to throw her overboard. The sword beamed in her periphery as it teetered closer to the edge.

Quickly she ran and dove across the deck, knocking the beast from its prey. With Tagwen now entangled with the monster, Breccan rolled out to reach for her own blade. Just as she grabbed the sword, she heard Tagwen scream — her blocking arm had slipped, and the beast had sunk its teeth into her shoulder.

Breccan charged the creature, slicing through its side. Yelping in pain, it let go of Tagwen and stumbled backward, realigning itself to charge at Breccan. The beast reared itself to lunge, but Breccan anticipated its move. Evading the attack, she twisted around the creature as it fell, slipping flat upon the ground. Her sword pierced the animal's head as she rendered it lifeless. Its cry before the silence called to its master, who abandoned the post above to contend with the intruders.

Tagwen grimaced in pain as she watched the Hunter jump down from the top deck, his mace clashing with Breccan's sword. She rolled on her good side to try and stand, but the boat was heeling furiously now that it had no captain. Earsplitting cracks of lightning boomed more frequently now that they were enveloped within the storm. In her misty vision, she saw shimmers of bright silver light a few feet ahead of her and realized A'elūdèr had found its way within her grasp.

Crawling upon the deck in searing pain, as raging ocean waters splashed over her and onto the deck, she reached for the sword's hilt. Mere seconds before she could touch it, the boat was struck violently, throwing everyone across the deck. Tagwen was tossed against the mast, the wind knocked from her lungs. She tucked her arms to her chest as she coughed, breathing wildly to stabilize her airway. Fighting against the ache of her back and the agony of her shoulder, she wrestled herself up from the floor.

Struggling to see, she glanced around, finding Breccan scrambling to stand. The Hunter was contending with being caught in rope against the taffrail. Tagwen saw Breccan take the chance to climb to the top deck in an attempt to gain control of the vessel; with the rate at which the boat was heeling, they were at risk of capsizing. With the Hunter still momentarily preoccupied, Tagwen hugged the mast. The rocking of the boat hindered her stability, but she managed to remain upright. Gripping the lines, she scanned their surroundings. The entirety of their view was clouded, rain still bucketing from the skies, flickers still of the lightning revealing just how deep into the storm they were. A wall of dense clouds stood mere meters in front of them.

Glancing back to Breccan, Tagwen shouted, "We need to turn around!"

"I'm trying!" Breccan screamed back.

Tagwen held on as Breccan attempted to gain control of the wheel. Seeing then, glowing upon the bow, her sword, Tagwen desperately lunged forward, swaying with the turbulent swings of the dhow.

A mast's beam fell loose, rushing toward her. She instantly dropped to the deck as the threat of it knocking her off the boat blew past. Gritting her teeth through the pain, she reached for her blade.

"Tagwen!" she heard Breccan shout as she was struck in the side.

Tossed across the boat again, excruciating pain radiated from the impact. Every breath she attempted threatened to bring more anguish. Looking back to the other side of the vessel, Tagwen saw the Hunter bend down to pick up her sword.

Streams of tears mixed with frigid saltwater irritated her eyes. Almost effortlessly, the Hunter graced the deck. Sword in hand, he raised it, the radiance of the blade gleaming in the quivering light. He moved to Tagwen and pointed the blade toward her. "Pity," he rasped.

"Oswallt… it's me… Tagwen," she sputtered to try and break through the curse, but the Hunter remained unfazed.

He held the sword aloft so as to become Tagwen's executioner, bringing the blade down upon her neck.

Breccan screamed in protest from the wheel.

As the Hunter looked down upon his prey, he saw that she had not succumbed to the blow — that his strike had missed entirely.

"It… does not… serve you," she managed to utter.

His expressionless eyes widened in fear as he saw her stir.

Breccan let go of the wheel, not having seen what happened, allowing the vessel to hurtle as it wished. She rushed down to the main deck as she saw the Hunter drop the blade. Stampeding toward the demon against the rolling of the ship, she managed to tackle him away from Tagwen.

"Breccan!" Tagwen's voice grated as loud as she could muster. Watching her captain wailing against the monster, she could not get her attention. A'elūdèr finally slid within reach and Tagwen grabbed it, shifting with her little remaining strength to stand. Clutching at her side, she stumbled to the foredeck mast. The Hunter had managed to push Breccan off and the two tumbled past Tagwen.

Breccan saw her friend leaning upon the spar and laughed in relief as she scrambled to reorient herself. The Hunter moved to strike at her when all three became transfixed by the sound of a great bellowing beneath the sea. Undulating, deafening roars broke out from the sea as a great shadow flashed in the storm's clouds.

Breccan struck at the distracted Hunter with Saìde, catching him in the side. He writhed in pain as he swung wildly to catch her in the side with his mace. Breccan was tossed backward against the stairs to the top deck.

Tagwen could not move fast enough to reach her, when the boat was struck again, the force splintering the central mast and much of the port hull. Breaking apart like a felled tree, its sails and beams collapsed on top of the Hunter. Tagwen turned to see the source of the impact. Looming high above their craft was a serpent, its face snouted not unlike the beast in Aūraèlon, but this beast was adorned with massive twisting, curled horns. Scales of deep midnight blue glittered in the strikes. Tagwen knew then that the tales were true. Bludrynd thrashed its head back into the sea and disappeared, the waves and rain beating against the boat in its wake. Sounds of fracturing wood snapped as the boat began to succumb to the strain.

The monster's shriek shook the entirety of the sea. Tagwen saw Breccan pulling herself up. As she stood, Breccan shouted across the deck. "Get to the dory!"

Tagwen gathered all her dwindling strength and began to stumble toward their escape. Breccan feebly climbed up the stairs and pulled herself onto the top deck, dragging herself across the floor to the lifeboat that hung on the back. She reached the boat and looked back at Tagwen, who was contesting the rage of the vessel and waters.

"Come on!" Breccan shouted.

Suddenly, Tagwen stopped. A pain in her chest bloomed. She looked down at her person. No wound had shown, but the feeling was real. The sounds of rain, thunder, and the crashing of waves began to fade. Breccan's echoing cries became muffled. Tagwen held at her heart, its beat resounding in her head. Grave was the feeling — a part of her had perished. She could not discern its source; no voice spoke in her head. An eerie silence quieted her mind, and for a moment she was horribly alone. Breathing became labored, her heart began to race. Spots of darkness began to further cloud her vision as she stumbled backward. She fought to regain consciousness as faint shouts broke through her stupor. A vision of Breccan begging her to return brought her again to the present moment, but it was too late.

Reemerging from the depths, Bludrynd's colossal form dove out and back into the water. The tail of the monster whipped out from the sea and came crashing down upon the vessel.

The dhow split in two. Tagwen was thrown backward toward the bow. Breccan fell within the small craft as it was severed from its host. Managing to grasp the faltering mast, Tagwen held tightly, screaming in agony for Breccan, for salvation. She watched as the boat splintered apart; the deck shattered. She jumped to land on a portion that would seemingly serve her best as a raft, nearly collapsing at the pain that jolted through her torso. Squinting through tears and rain toward the sky, she saw she had reached the core of the storm's wall. Tagwen looked behind once more at the sinking ship. Bracing herself for whatever was to come, she wished again for home.

Storm and surf then swelled in a shroud, claiming the Lion of the Sea.

Characters in Order of Appearance/Mention

Tagwen Braithe: **TAG • WHEN - BRAY • TH**; Queen of Yeacralas, Daughter of Arlon Braithe and Netta Ròsach, Guardian of the Tear, Champion of the Sea, Soulbind of Eïluèl, Sister to Rhona and Elnan, Best Friend to Breccan Kenefick, Human, 28 years old

Breccan Kenefick: **BREK • CAN - KEN • EH • FICK**; Captain of the Yeacralan Guard, Personal Paladin to Tagwen Braithe, Best Friend of Tagwen Braithe, Daughter of Mæranedïl and Deìrdre (Saìde), Final heir of Ærèg Èlasïl, Half-elven, 29 years old

Mercher Preece: **MER • CHUR - PREE • S**; Chef and barman of The Siren's Whistle, Human, 50 years old

Morys Blàr: **MORE • ISS - BL • ARE**; Fisherman of Marez, gifts Tagwen Braithe the scale necklace of Bludrynd/Œdêrèg, Human, 68 years old

Arlon Braithe: **ARE • LON - BRAY • TH**; (deceased) Former King of Yeacralas, Father of Tagwen, Elnan, and Rhona, Husband to Netta Ròsach, Human, 55 years old

Eubha: **AY • VA**; (deceased) Morys Blàr's wife, Human, 59 years old.

Bludrynd: **BLEWD • RIN • D**; See Œdêrèg

Lucas Kenefick: **LOO • KAS - KEN • EH • FICK**; Monk in Yeacralas, Adopted father to Breccan Kenefick, Human, 79 years old

Olwenna Glas: **OLE • WHEN • UH - GLASS**; (deceased) Queen of Yeacralas by Marriage to Ynyr Bowen in the late Second Age, The Usurper, Mother to Reese Glas-Bowen, Human, 44 years old.

Renlyn Bethel: **REN • LIN - BETH • ELL**; Tagwen Braithe's handmaid, Mother to Rayan Bethel, Human, 25 years old

Gòrdan MacCaibe: **GORE • DAN - MACK • KAYB**; Messenger of Middling, Outrider of the Isle, one of the Hallows of Ylerïan, Husband to Ualan Ambarsan, Father to Mairi and Artur, Human, 53 years old

Mairi: **MY • REE**; Daughter to Gòrdan MacCaibe and Ualan Ambarsan, Human, 14 years old.

Artur: **ARE • TER**; Son to Gòrdan MacCaibe and Ualan Ambarsan, Human, 8 years old.

Roìbert Dùghlan: **ROH • EE • BERT - DUGH • LAN**; King of Middling, Father to Jaelan and Mòrrea Dùghlan, Human, 53 years old

Declan Tarragona: **DECK • LAN - TERRA • GO • NUH**; Castle Guard in Marez, Human, 33 years old

Rhona Braithe: **ROW • NUH - BRAY • TH**; Princess of Yeacralas, Mother to Enania Caimbeul, Lover to Seathan Caimbeul, Sister of Tagwen and Elnan, Human, 24 years old

Enania Caimbeul: **EH • NAN • EE • UH - CAME • BULL**; Daughter of Rhona Braithe and Seathan Caimbeul, Human, 3 years old

Seathan Caimbeul: **SHAY • THIN - CAME • BULL**; (deceased) Horseman of Logrosca, Scout, Father to Enania

Caimbeul, Lover to Rhona Braithe, 33 years old.

HORSEMEN OF LOGROSCA: **LO • GRAH • SKA**; The Men of the Yeacralan city of Logrosca who breed horses for strength and stability, Primary suppliers of steeds for the entire continent, Notable scouts for the Kingdom of Yeacralas, Humans

MAIREAD GHUINNE: **MAY • RE • ADD - GE • IN • UH**; Teacher for the Braithe household, Sister to Muireall Bivins, Human, 68 years old

ADRELGHARD TUGROM: **ADD • RELL • GUARD - TUG • RUM**; Dwarven liaison for the dwarves of the Dholdon'lièr Mountains, Personal friend of Tagwen Braithe, Dwarf, 49 years old

ELNAN BRAITHE: **ELL • NAAN - BRAY • TH**; (deceased) Prince of Yeacralas, Brother to Tagwen and Rhona, Human, 32 years old

LACHLANN CATACH: **LOCK • LEN - CAT • ACK**; son of Alenia and Colum Catach, Captain in the Yeacralan Guard, Human, 33 years old

SĪNE MATHARNACH: **SIN • UH - MAT • AR • NACK**; Sergeant in the Yeacralan Guard, Sister to Emyr Matharnach, Human, 31 years old

JAELAN DÙGHLAN: **JAY • LAN - DUGH • LAN**; Prince of Middling, Usurper of the Yeacralan Throne, Son of Roìbert Dùghlan, Human, 30 years old

MÒRREA DÙGHLAN: **MOW • RAY • UH - DUGH • LAN**; (deceased) Princess of Middling, Daughter of Brìgdhe Catrìona and Roìbert Dùghlan, Sister of Jaelan, Lover to Tasar Vanelis, Uniter of Vostheloren, Human, 18 years old

BRÌGHDE CATRÌONA: **BRIG • DEH - CAT • REH • OWN**

• **UH**; (deceased) Queen of Middling, Mother of Jaelan and Mòrrea Dùghlan, Wife of Roìbert Dùghlan, Steward of the Letter of Yacendïl, Human, 49 years old

Seasaìdh: **SEA • SIDE**; Mare to Tagwen Braithe, 6 years old

Arofel: **ARROW • FELL**; Steed to Breccan Kenefick, 8 years old

Tom Bivins: **TOM - BIV • INS**; Oülle Gate Master, Husband to Muireall Ghuinne, Stepfather of Eachann Ghuinne, Human, 71 years old

Reese Glas-Bowen: **REESS**; (deceased) Former King of Yeacralas, Attempted Usurper of Middling, Son of Olwenna Glas and Ynyr Bown, The Tyrant, Human, 28 years old.

Torcadall Pablan: **TORE • KA • DOLL - PAH • BLAN**; Owner and barman of The Breezy Thicket in Oülle, Human, 46 years old.

Enania Llewellyn: **EH • NAN • EE • UH - LOU • ELLEN**; (deceased) former Queen of Yeacralas, Grandmother of Tagwen, Rhona, and Elnan, Namesake of Enania Caimbeul (great granddaughter), Mother of Arlon Braithe, Human, 83 years old

Muireall Ghuinne: **ME • UR • REAL - GE • IN • UH**; Barmaid in The Breezy Thicket, Mother to Eachann Ghuinne, Second wife of Tom Bivins, Sister to Mairead Ghuinne, Human, 74 years old

Netta Ròsach-Braithe: **NET • UH - RAW • SAK - BRAY • TH**; (deceased) Former queen of Yeacralas, Wife of Arlon Braithe, Mother to Tagwen, Rhona, and Elnan, Human, 50 years old

Eachann Ghuinne: **EEK • EN - GE • IN • UH**; see also:

Hubertus Tolmach, Outrider of the Isle, One of the Hallows of Ylerïan, Captain of Oburim, Son of Muireall Ghuinne, 34 years old

DAÏDH ARASGAIN: **DAY • DTH - AIR • AS • GAIN**; King of Oburim, Human, 56 years old

HUBERTUS TOLMACH: **HUE • BEAR • TUSS - TOLL • MACK**; see also: Eachann Ghuinne, Outrider of the Isle, One of the Hallows of Ylerïan, Captain of Oburim, Son of Muireall Ghuinne, Human, 34 years old

GORAIDH: **GORE • AID • TH**; Elven name: Gegènlïf, Sage of Middling, Servitor of Ruèhnar, Brother of Erul, One of the cast-out Viethèl, Elven, 4000+ years old

TASAR VANELIS: **TUSS • ARE - VAN • ELL • ISS**; Scout of Thrindūl, Lover to Mòrrea Dùghlan, Elven, 23 years old

OSWALLT TRAHERN: **OZ • WALT - TRAY • HERN**; Former captain of Middling, Former personal paladin to Roìbert Dùghlan, The Hunter, Human/Undead, 46 years old

UALAN AMBARSAN: **WAL • EN - AM • BAR • SAN**; Outrider of the Isle, Son of Eoghann Ambarsan, One of the Hallows of Ylerïan, Husband to Gòrdan MacCaibe, Father to Mairi and Artur, Human, 45 years old

EOGHANN AMBARSAN: **YO • GAN - AM • BAR • SAN**; (deceased) Father of Ualan Ambarsan. Human, 76 years old

BARINGR: **BARE • IN • JIR**; Steed of Lachlann Catach, 4 years old

THESDEN ELDROPP: **THEZ • DEN - EL • DROP**; Queensman in the Marezian Army, Human, 21 years old

BEITRIS GRANND: **BAY • TRIS - GRAND**; Queensman in the

Marezian Army, Human, 20 years old

DANIEL MACLEÒIR: **DAN • YELL - MAC • LER**; Corporal in the Marezian Army, Human, 24 years old

BRIAN MACLEÒIR: **BRY • AN - MAC • LER**; Corporal in the Marezian Army, Human, 24 years old

AILBERT ROID: **AIL • BERT - ROYD**; Corporal in the Marezian Army, Human, 30 years old

SAMUEL MACCULLACH: **SAH • MULE - MAC • CULL • ACK**; Corporal in the Marezian Army, Human, 27 years old

CALLON HELLIG: **CAL • ON - HEL • IG**; Corporal in the Marezian Army, Human, 33 years old

IÒSAPH RUISEAL: **YO • SAPH - ROY • SAL**; Corporal in the Marezian Army, Human, 32 years old

AELIN: **AY • ELLEN**; Sïne Matarnach's mare, 9 years old

FALDÏR EILFAREN: **FALL • DEER - AIL • FAIR • EN**; "Steel Tide", Lord of Thrindūl and Protector of the Ebrïhèïlè, Son of Uhèrad Eilfaren, Husband to Ylerïan, Twelfth son of the Eilfaren House, Elven, ~230 years old

YLERÏAN EILFAREN: **EE • LER • EE • EN - AIL • FAIR • EN**; "Moonlight", Lady of the Ebrïhèïlè, The Matron of Moonlight, Half-sister of Mæranedïl, Aunt of Breccan Kenefick, Elven ~240 years old

KIRION ROVICUS: **KEER • EON - ROW • VICK • US**; (deceased) Captain of the Yeacralan Navy in the late Second Age, Human, 44 years old

BHAUDR THE SLAYER: **BOW • DER**; (deceased) Chief of the Rogues of the Black Isle, Human, 40 years old

Rogues of the Black Isle: Independent group who has settled within the Black Isle, known for their barbarity, it is unknown if any still remain

Ègúlet: **EGH • HUE • LET**; "Proof in Art", Song-keeper of Thrindūl, Elven, 120 years old

E'rulèïl "Erul": **ERR • OO • LIE • EEL / ERR • ULL**; "Earth 'After' Guide", Mærênar (Son of Stars), One of the Viethèl, Brother to Goraidh, Guardian of the Light of the Èlavïl, Keeper of the Tome of Collective Memory, Counsel for the House of Itelūnèl, Elven, 4000+ years old

Uhèrad Eilfaren: **OO • ERR • ADD - AIL • FAIR • EN**; (deceased) Father of Faldïr Eilfaren, Lord of Thrindūl and Protector of the Ebrïhèïlè, Eleventh son of the Eilfaren House, Elven, ~364 years old

Yacendïl: **YEA • KEN • DEEL**; (deceased) Father of Yeacralas, one of the First Men, Husband of Anabeh, Father of Ærèg Èlasïl, Orator, Human, 67 years old

Ærèg Èlasïl: **ARE • EGH - EH • LASS • EEL**; (deceased) "Sea Half-Elven", Son of Yacendïl and Anabeh, First Half-elf, Ancestor to Breccan Kenefick and Mæranedïl, Half-elven, ~300 years old

Avantèas: **UH • VAN • TAY • AHSS**; (deceased) "Long neck", Great Heron, Oracle, provider of Varucïel

Anabeh: **AH • NAH • BVEY**; "South", One of the five Èlavïl, Blessed Southern Star, Wife of Yacendïl, Mother of Ærèg Èlasïl, Elven, 4000+ years old

Ruèhnar: **RUE • EH • NAR**; "Death's Embrace", Êdūnar (Sun Star), Son of Lïflèn and one of the five Èlavïl, Death's Embrace, Demigod, 4000+ years old

Girean Nundulir: **GEAR • AYN - NONE • DO • LEER**; (deceased) Great Dwarven King of Dholdron'lièr Mountains in the early Second Age, Dwarven, 134 years old

Pàdair Barindroun: **PA • DAR - BAR • IN • DROWN**; King Under the Mountain, King of Dholdron'lièr Mountains, Dwarven, 188 years old

Durifrael Berunli: **DUR • IF • RAIL - BEAR • UN • LEE**; (deceased) renowned dwarven craftsman of the First Age, Husband to Aèdu, Dwarven, 250 years old

Eecrelêne: **EH • KREH • LEAN**; (preserved) artist, Partner of Guódnè, Elven, ~3000 years old

Guódnè: **GOO • OATH • NAY**; (preserved) poet, Partner of Eecrelêne, Elven, ~3000 years old

Ehlïf: **EH • LEAF**; "Life" The god of Life, Creator of Lïflèn, Unknown, Infinite

Eïluèl: **EH • EE • LOO • ELL**; "Earth's Smile" (deceased/ soulbound) Poet, Swordsman, Adventurer, Lover to Avourel, Wielder of A'elūdèr, Human, 33 years old

Naovïlrūn: **NOW • VEEL • ROON**; The "Guardians of Obedience", Unknown, ~4000 years old

Èhalūs Odægūl: **EH • HAY • LOOSE - OWE • DA • HOOL**; Captain of Thrindūl, Elven, 130 years old

Gelandric Kikdreth: **G(*gob*) • ELL • AND • RICK - KICK • DRETH**; Captain of Kâr Boldhir, Dwarven, 69 years old

Mæranedïl: **MER • AN • EHDTH • EEL**; "Angel Son" Heir of Ærèg Èlasïl, Lover to Deìrdre, Father of Breccan Kenefick, Steward of Yacendïl's letter, Elven, ~200 years old

Œdêrèg: **WED • THERE • EGG**; "Dark Sea", Sea Drake, Twin of the Beast of Aūraèlon, Serpent, 4000+ years old

Alenia Catach: **AH • LEAN • EE • UH - CAT • ACK**; Lachlann's mother, Human, 55 years old

Colum Catach: **CALL • UHM - CAT • ACK**; Lachlann's father, Human, 62 years old

Avourel: **AH • VOR • ELL**; (unknown) "Heaven's Iron", Daughter of Itelūnèl, Princess of Ardenïl, Lover to Eïluèl, Elven, ~2500 years old

Itelūnèl: **EE • TELL • LOON • ELL**; (unknown) "Forged in Iron", Father of Avourel, King of Ardenïl, Elven, ~3000 years old

Lïflèn: **LEAF • LEN**; "Water", Goddess of Water, Mother of Ruèhnar, Lover to one of the Èlavïl, Mother of the god of Fire: Vostheros, Mistress of the God of Death, Creator of the Èlavïl, Creator of the Earth, Unknown, Infinite

Viethèl: **VEE • ETH • ELL**; Light guardians, those tasked with guiding the Èlavïl with distributing their light across Vostheria in the First Age, Elven

Ūlagenol: **OO • LAGH • EN • OLE**; "Golden Fear", Dragon born of the Athèrèc, Dragon, ?? years old

Urèc: **OO • RECK**; (deceased) "Rock", One of the three First Dwarves, Keeper of an Athèrèc, Dwarven, ~400 years old

Værèc: **VAIR • ECK**; (deceased) "Stone", One of the three First Dwarves, Former keeper of an Athèrèc, Dwarven, ~370 years old

Ïorhèl: **EE • OR • ELL**; (deceased) "Iron", One of the three First Dwarves, Former keeper of an Athèrèc, Dwarven, ~370 years old

Deìrdre: **DARE • DRUH**; (deceased) Also known as Saìde, Mother to Breccan Kenefick, Lover to Mæranedïl, Human, 35 years old

Afesal: **AH • FESS • ALL**; Herald of Avantèas, Crow, Unknown

Okerfair: **OAK • ER • FAIR**; (deceased) Founder of the Outriders, Human, 58 years old

Peric Deyne: **PAIR • ICK - DAYN**; (deceased) Outrider, Human, 47 years old

Cillian Avelson: **KILL • IAN - AVE • ELL • SON**; Outrider, Human, 33 years old

Bevron Crag: **BEV • REN - CRAG**; Outrider, Human, 49 years old

Thorfin Quinne: **THOR • FIN - KWIN**; Outrider, Human, 45 years old

Ina Deyne: **EYE • NUH – DAYN**; Peric Deyne's daughter, Human, 15 years old.

Master Mæraca: **MER • AH • KA**; "Promise son", Quartermaster, Elven, 120 years old

Mïraglèn: **MEER • AGH • LEN**; (unknown) "Great mother", One of the Viethèl, Elven, ~ 4000 years old

Èlavïl: **AY • LA • VEEL**; "Light Guardians", The Five Maidens of Lïflèn, Bringers of the Light

Valœclènè: **VAL • OCK • LEN • AY**; "Forgotten ones", The beings that attack inside of Aurilon Peaks, Formerly Human/

Elven

Aèdu: **AID • TH • OO**; (deceased) "Maker", One of the First Elves, Known as "The Anvil", Husband to Durifrael Berunli, Elven, ~2000 years old

Emyr: **EM • EAR**; Sine Matarnach's brother, Human, 23 years old

Ä'bafat: **AH • BAH • FAHT**; (deceased) "Tear/rip", Warg to The Hunter

Darragh Briones: **DARE • AG - BRY • OWN • ESS**; Lieutenant of the Yeacralan Guard, Human, 42 years old

Berrat Gerrig: **BEAR • AT - GARE • IG**; (deceased) Watchman of the Yeacralan Guard, Human, 23 years old

Rayan Bethel: **RYE • AN - BETH • ELL**; Son of Renlyn Bethel, Human, 4 years old

Locations by Realm

Vostheloren: **VOSS • THEH • LORE • EN**; "Vostheria Lost", Continent of the West

Southlands:

Aurilon/Aūraèlon Peaks: **ARE • EH • LON / OW • RAY • ELL • ON**; "Far leader", Mountains below Haverlow Forest, Contain the Misty/Broken Pass

Clerlūn: **CLAIRE • LOON**; Ruins below the Marshlands,

Once a town of the Yeacralan Realm but has been deserted due to frequent flooding of the Terrishire river

ENBRON WOODS: **EN • BRON**; Small forest between Oülle and Clerlūn, hold the Oakbreak Stand Outrider stead.

GILÈDO: **GILL • AID • THO**; Major town of Yeacralas

HAVERLOW WOODS: **HAVE • ER • LOW**; Darkened Woods, An independent forest that was once part of the Ebrïhëïlè

LEONAN POINT: **LAY • OH • NEN**; Yeacralan military outpost where Elnan Braithe was paralyzed

MÀDIZ: **MAD • THESE**; Small hamlet of Yeacralas

MAREZ: **MAR • EZ**; Capitol city of Yeacralas

OÜLLE: **OWL**; Small town of Yeacralas

TARRAVEDRA: **TAR • AH • VAY • DRA**; Major town of Yeacralas

TORRERÌN: **TORE • ERR • IN**; Major town of Yeacralas

YEACRALAS: **YA • KRA • LAH • SS**; Name of the the Southern Realm

MIDLANDS:

DAWNSHIRE: **DAWN • SURE**; Small town of Middling

ELTAH: **ELL • TAH**; Small town of Middling

GREYREST: **GRAY • REST**; The heartland of the continent

LUNNENETTE BRIDGE: **LOON • EN • ETTE**; Bridge that crosses the Terrishire/Guódnè River

MARSHLANDS OF DRŸS: **(D)RICE**; Marshes that surround the Terrishire/Guódnè River

MIDDLING: **MID • LING**; Name of the Midland Realm

MISTVALE: **MIST • VALE**; Surrounding Mountain range in the West of Vostheloren

WESTVEIN: **WEST • VEIN**; Capitol of Middling

NORTHLANDS:

DHOLDRON'LIÈR MOUNTAINS: **DOLE • DRON • LIAR**; "King Dheldron's Mountains", Mountain of the Dwarves

KÂR BOLDHIR: **CARE - BOLD • EAR**; "Mark of Boldhir", Kingdom of the Dwarves

OBURIM: **OH • BURR • IM**; Northern Realm

STONEHEIM GROVE: **STON • HIGH • M**; Small forest in the North

ELVEN LANDS:

AVÏRIA: **AH • VEER • EE • AH**; "Renew", Ancient elven city now in ruins

BRIERHÏL: **BRY• ERR • HEEL**; Common name for the elven Forest, See: Ebrïhèïlè

EBRÏHÈÏLÈ: **EBB • VRE • ISLE**; "Elven keep/fortress", The Elven Forest

LERÏACŪL SEA: **LER • EE • AH • COOL**; "Light water", The

Sea to the East of the Vostheloren Continent

MÏRABASIA: **MEER • AB • VAS • EE • UH**; "Great library", Ancient elven library/temple/records chamber

THRINDŪL: **THRIN • DOOL**; "Garden gate", Elven Kingdom

THE BLACK ISLE:

REMEIRATH GORGE: **REM • AY • WRATH**; Canyon holding a small inlet bay in the Northeastern part of the Black Isle

DESOLATION STEPPES: Desert hills on the lowlands of the Black Isle

ATHŒVAB: **ATH • OH • VAB**; "Fire Cave", contained the pedestal of Yacendïl

BRŒKK HIGHLANDS: **BROKE**; Highlands that surround Remeirath Gorge

LOCATIONS MENTIONED NOT ON THE MAP

ARDENÏL: **ARE • DEN • EEL**; "The land of the Elves"

ATHŒVAB: **ATH • OH • VAB**; "Fire Cave" Tunnel that used to be part of the volcanic range of E'batheron

E'BATHERON: **EBV • ATH • ERR • ON**; "Fire Mountain", Volcano Lost in the First Age

OSÈCERO: **OH • SEK • ERR • OH**; "Tree Room", The

Arboretum in Thrindūl

UHODOR MOUNTAINS: **OOH • HUH • DOR**; Mountains in the Eastern part of the world

Items

A'ELŪDÈR: **AY • LOOD • THERE**; "forevermore", Sword, Instrument of Fate

ATHÈRÈC: **ATH • ERR • ECK**; "Fire Rock", Dragonhide Obsidian, Instrument of Fate

DHELDORA: **DELL • DORA**; Rare flower found on the continent of Vostheloren

ÈTŪGŪR ÚCÈSAH: **EH • TOO • HOOR - OO • KEH • SAH**; Healing purple flower found in the valley of Thrindūl

QUILL OF AVANTÈAS: Varucïel: **VAR • OO • KEY • ELL**; "True thought", Quill, Instrument of Fate

SAÌDE: **(S)AID**; Breccan's sword, Named after her mother's working girl name.

TENALOETOR LÏFLÈN: **TEN • AH • LOW • TORE - LEAF • LEN**; "Tears of Lïflèn", The flower gift from the goddess of Water that provides elves with immortality wherever its roots grow

TOME OF COLLECTIVE MEMORY (AFEGÈLŒF Ò ÆSELŪNELÈR): **AH • FEH • HEH • LOAF - OH - AH • SE • LOON • ELL • ERR**; Book of Power

Elven Phrases

Æruv: **AY • ROOV**; Run

Ærusah: **AY • ROO • SAH**; Jump

Æsūd èdūs üv'èterèf? **AY • SOOD - ED • THOOS - OOV • ET • ERR • EFF**; What do you need?

Adagèsè o'rüla: **AHD • THA • HEH • SAY - OH • ROO • LA**; Calming remedy

Alud èlal arulavè: **AH • LEWD - EH • LAHL - ARE • OO • LA • VAY**; May the light guide

Andarïè: **AHN • DAR • EE • AY**; Help

Æpèlad arog atès: **AH • PEL • AHD - AIR • OGH - AH TESS**; Welcome back, friend

Avœlèn: **AH • VOH • LEN**; Heaven's tongue; ancient elven language

Êadura üv: **EE • AHD • THOO • RA - OOV**; Thank you

Ètalæg u'atèro: **AY • TAL • EGH - OO • AH • TERR • OH**; Protect the Forest

Færūn èlasïl/?: **FAH • RUNE - ELL • AH • SEEL**; She is half-elven/Is she half-elven?

Lènagïlen: **LEN • AH • HE • LEN**; Earth's tongue; current elven language

Mærhïl: **MIRE • EEL**; Elf son

Mærênar: **MAR • EE • NAR**; Son of stars

Mœrdeth: **MORE • DEATH**; Evil guard, Warden of Ruèhnar

Nala'evanegtas: **NALA • EV • AHN • EGH • TUSS**; Many beautiful greetings

Naladhïl: **NAL • ADTH • EEL**; First elves

Œnè tèūlæhœv: **OH • NAY - TAY • OO • LAY • OVE**; I cannot tell

Ú'anelū: **OO • AN • EH • LOO**; My love/I love

Úel anelū, atèro, alè ebæl: **WELL - AHN • ELL • OO - AHH • TERR • OH - ALL • EH - EH • (B)VAIL**; For love, forest, and family

Ú ènū alœr æs üv egèïl: **OO - EH • NEW - AH • LORE - AHS - OOV - EGH • AY • EEL**; I will speak with you later

Üv'acūs: **OOV - AH • KOOSE**; You say…

Üv andarïè ov äh: **OOV - AHN • DAR • EE • AY - OHV - AHH**; Can you help with this?/Your help with this

Üv ean æpèlad: **OOV - AY • AHN - AH • PELL • AHD**; You are welcome

Vostheria: **VOSS • (TH)EE • REE • UH**; Land of Vostheros, name of the land mass before the rift

Yaceralan: **YEA • CARE • UH • LON**; Yacendïl's creation

Dwarven Phrases

Analek khradiin: **AHN • AHH • LEK - HRA • DEEN**; "Greet Dawn", Dwarvish greeting / wishing well in a new day

Fertrath Nundulonok: **FAIR • TRATH - NOON • DUE • LON • OHK**; "Forth the valor of Nundulir", Dwarven battle-cry paying homage to the first Dwarven King of Dholdron'lièr Mountains, Girean Nundulir.

Khradiin elne kel vâ urek venlahsk: **HRA • DEEN - ELL • NEH - KELL - VAH - OO • REK - VEN • LAH • SK**; No dawn/light will reveal upon the rock (Light not will the rock reveal)

Krarnolim: **KRAR • NO • LIM**; Runic language of the dwarves

Vefrak dhondri: **VEF • RACK - DON • DREE**; "Forever Mountain", Dwarven battle-cry invoking the strength of Dholdron'lièr Mountain.

Yukanskei drofiindahk: **• YOU • KHAN • SKAY - (D) ROW • FEEN • DOCK**; Dwarven curse – *is not very nice*.

Drawn Map of The Black Isle: Athœvab Entrance

Biddance of the Naovïlrūn

Ú'alerūn u'atèro

OO • AL • ERR • OON - OO • AHH • TERRO

Atèro ihlèn alœränlèn

AHH • TERRO - EE • LEN - AH • LOW • RAHN • LEN

Ú ènū arèf alè bèlïa u'tælah

**OO - EH • NEW - ARE • EFF - ALL • AY - BVAY • LEE • UH
- OO • TAH • LAH**

Úlufèlèn œt orèbän

OO • LOO • FELL • EN - WET - OR • EH • BVAN

I obey the Forest

Forest has spoken

I will listen and follow
the path

Leaving nothing broken

Song of the Èlavïl

Òu eïlèc Ardenïl

OO - EH • EE • LEK - ARE • DEN • EEL

aèdlen ecūlonè èlal

AH • EHD • LEN - EH • COO • LOW • NAY - EH • LAL

Mïraelerïa òu naênar

MEER • AH • EH • LER • EE • AH - OH - NAH • EE • NAR

Uceleòl en u abacús

OO • KEL • AY • OLE - EN - OO • AHB • VAH - COO(S)

Æten Èlavïl nalïfūr ebsa

EH • TEN - EH • LA • VEEL - NAL • EE • FOOR - EBV • SAH

Er alè arèf u'edavu

ERR - AL • EH - ARE • EFF - OO • EDTH • AH • VOO

Of the Land of Ardenïl

Created by Water's Light

Brightest of the Stars

Casting out the Night

Dear Èlavïl, maidens fair

Watch and hear my prayer